Marion Lennox has written over one hundred romance novels, and is published in over one hundred countries and thirty languages. Her international awards include the prestigious RITA® Award (twice!) and the *RT Book Reviews* Career Achievement Award for 'a body of work which makes us laugh and teaches us about love'. Marion adores her family, her kayak, her dog, and lying on the beach with a book someone else has written. Heaven!

Fiona McArthur is an Australian midwife who lives in the country and loves to dream. Writing Medical Romance gives Fiona the scope to write about all the wonderful aspects of romance, adventure, medicine and the midwifery she feels so passionate about. When she's not catching babies, Fiona and her husband Ian are off to meet new people, see new places and have wonderful adventures. Drop in and say hi at Fiona's website: Fionamcarthurauthor.com.

Discover more at millsandboon.co.uk.

RESCUED BY THE SINGLE DAD DOC

MARION LENNOX

THE MIDWIFE'S SECRET CHILD

FIONA McARTHUR

MILLS & BOON

First Published in Great Britain 2019
by Mills & Boon, an imprint of HarperCollins*Publishers*
1 London Bridge Street, London, SE1 9GF

Rescued by the Single Dad Doc © 2019 by Marion Lennox

The Midwife's Secret Child © 2019 by Fiona McArthur

ISBN: 978-0-263-27956-6

MIX
Paper from
responsible sources
FSC® C007454

This book is produced from independently certified FSC™ paper
to ensure responsible forest management.
For more information visit www.harpercollins.co.uk/green.

Printed and bound in Spain
by CPI, Barcelona

RESCUED BY THE SINGLE DAD DOC

MARION LENNOX

MILLS & BOON

With thanks to Mary Michele,
whose kindness made this book so much easier.

This book is for Denise, who, with her wobbly mate
Molly, helps make this place home.

CHAPTER ONE

DR RACHEL TILDING enjoyed treating kids. If they couldn't speak it was often up to Rachel to figure out what was wrong, but in general kids' needs were uncomplicated. They didn't intrude on her personal space. If all Rachel's patients were kids—without parents—she might well be looking at a different career path.

As it was, her aim was to be a radiologist, interpreting results from state-of-the-art equipment and having little to do with patients at all. But the terms of her scholarship specified she had to spend her first two years after internship as a family doctor in Shallow Bay. She'd geared herself to face it.

What she hadn't prepared herself for was living next to a house full of kids. Their noise was bad enough, plus the yips of excitement from their dog. Then, a mere two hours after she'd moved in, a ball smashed through her window, almost making her drop the carton of glassware she'd been unpacking. The ball landed in a spray of shattered glass in the kitchen sink.

Count to ten, she told herself. These are kids. Don't yell.

She'd been telling herself that since she'd arrived. These were her new neighbours. It wasn't their fault that she valued privacy above all else. Someone would call them in for dinner soon. They'd go to bed and she'd have the silence she craved.

But kids as such close neighbours…

Shallow Bay's nurse-manager had sent her pictures of this little house, a pretty-as-a-picture cottage surrounded by bushland. A five-minute walk took her up to the Shallow Bay Hospital, and five minutes in the other direction took her down to the beach.

What the pictures hadn't shown, however, was that it was one of three cottages, huddled together in the dip before the bay. Hers was the smallest. The largest was the middle one and that seemed to be filled with boys.

She wasn't sure how many yet. The noise they were making could have denoted a small army. She'd been trying to figure how she could intervene without turning Shallow Bay's new doctor into Dragon Lady.

Now she had no choice. A cricket ball was sitting in her kitchen sink, surrounded by a spray of glass.

But before she could react, a shock of curly red hair appeared at the shattered window. Underneath the hair were two huge green eyes, fear-filled. The window was high for a child, so he'd obviously hoisted himself up to see where his ball had landed.

The head disappeared and a hand appeared in its place. And groped into the sink. Through shattered glass.

'No!' She'd been standing behind packing boxes on the far side of the table. She launched herself across the kitchen, but the groping hand reached the ball before she did.

There was a yelp of pain and then hand and ball disappeared.

She hauled the back door open, raced down the steps

and cut the child off before he could back away. He'd lurched back from the window and was staggering.

'Don't move!' Her order contained all the authority of a doctor who'd spent her two years of internship working in emergency medicine. The child froze, staring down at his hand in horror.

Their little dog, a black and white terrier—a ball of pseudo-aggression—came tearing across the lawn and barked hysterically, as if it was Rachel who was the intruder on her own lawn.

It had…three legs?

'Tuffy! Tuffy, back. He won't bite. Please… Kit's just getting our ball.' The voice from the far side of the hedge sounded terrified. The oldest child?

They were all redheads. The two on the far side of the hedge looked about ten and six. The child under her window was maybe eight.

They all had huge green eyes. Pale skin with freckles. They all looked rigid with fear.

Maybe her voice had done that to them. Even the little dog was backing away.

Was she so scary?

Rachel had little to do with kids except as patients, but the middle child was now definitely a patient. He was still clutching the ball, but he was holding it out in front of him. A line of crimson was dripping onto the garden bed.

'Don't move,' she said again, because the child was looking in panic across to his brothers—they had to be brothers—and she knew his instinct was to run. 'I'm not angry.' Okay, maybe she was, but this wasn't the time to admit it. There'd be an adult somewhere, responsible for leaving this group unsupervised. They deserved a piece of her mind, not this child. One thing Rachel was very careful about—a lesson learned from the long years of an unjust childhood—was that fairness was everything.

'You've cut your hand on the glass,' she told the little boy as she reached him. She took his arm and raised it, applying pressure around the wrist. 'You need to stay still.'

The eyes that looked up at her were huge. He looked terrified. There'd be pain. With this much blood, it had to be deep. The blood wasn't pumping—the radial artery must surely be intact—but the gash from multiple glass shards tentacled out from wrist to palm. In a child, this amount of bleeding could well lead to collapse.

'I'm a doctor,' she told him, gentling her voice. 'The glass has cut your hand, but we can fix it. Right now, though, it's looking messy, so we need to stop it bleeding. You'll feel better if you don't look at it until we've cleaned it up. Look at your brothers, or look at the hole in my window. That's quite a hole.'

She was manoeuvring his hand upward, edging her body to block his gaze. The ball fell to the ground as she lifted his hand high, curling his palm in slightly so the hand created its own pressure on the pierced palm. There could well be shards of glass in there but now wasn't the time to remove them. She needed a surgery, equipment, help.

'Can you run inside and get your mum or dad?' she called to the two boys on the far side of the hedge. 'Ask them to bring out a towel. Run!'

'Tell me your name,' she asked the little boy.

She got a blank look in response. Fear.

'He's Christopher,' the elder of the pair behind the hedge called. 'But we call him Kit. Are you really a doctor?'

'I am. Could you fetch your parents please? Now! Kit needs your help.'

'We don't have parents. Just a stepfather.'

Just a stepfather.

Why did that make her freeze?

The wave of nausea that swept through her was as vicious as it was dumb. Her past was just that—past— and it had no place here, now. Somehow, she managed to fight back the bile rising in her throat, to haul herself together, to become the responsible person these boys needed.

She needed a plan.

She needed a responsible adult to help her.

Her phone was inside. Where had she put it? Somewhere in the muddle of unpacked goods?

She daren't let Kit's arm go to find it herself. He was too big for her to pick up and carry. He was also looking increasingly pale. Had these kids been left on their own?

'Where's your stepfather now?' she asked, and stupidly she heard the echoes of her dumb, visceral response to the word in her voice.

'At work,' the eldest boy told her.

'Is there anyone else here?'

'Christine's inside, watching telly.'

'Then fetch her,' she ordered. 'Fast. Tell her Kit's hurt his hand and he's bleeding. Tell her I need a towel and a phone. Run.'

'Can you just put a plaster on it?' the older boy asked. 'We don't want to tell Christine. She'll tell Tom.'

'What's your name?'

'Marcus. And this is Henry. Please don't tell. If we misbehave, Tom'll make us go back to our grandparents.'

'You haven't misbehaved. The ball broke my window, not you,' she told him. She'd tell him anything he liked to get help right now. 'Marcus, this cut is too big for a plaster. Kit needs Christine. I need Christine. Run.'

He shouldn't have left the boys with Christine. Normally Tom Lavery used his next-door neighbour, Rose, as childminder. Rose was in her seventies, huge-hearted, reliable. The boys loved her, but this morning she'd fallen and hurt her hip. It was only bruised, thank heaven, but she needed rest.

This weekend was also the annual field-day-cum-funfair at Ferndale, two hours' drive across the mountains. For the isolated town of Shallow Bay, the Ferndale Show was huge. Practically the entire population took part, with cattle parades and judging, baking competitions, kids' activities. As Shallow Bay emptied, Christine, Rose's niece, had become his childminder of last resort.

'Worrying?' Roscoe, Shallow Bay's hospital nurse administrator, was watching Tom from the far side of the nurses' station. Tom was supposed to be filling in patient histories. Instead he'd turned to the window, looking down towards the cottage.

'Go home and check,' Roscoe said. For a big man—make that huge—Roscoe was remarkably perceptive. 'You'll be writing Bob up for antacids instead of antibiotics if you're not careful.'

'I'm careful.' He hauled his attention back to his job. 'Christine can cope.'

'As long as there's no ad for hair curlers on telly. You know she's a dipstick,' Roscoe said bluntly.

Roscoe's smile was half hidden by his beard, but it didn't hide the sympathy. 'Go home, doc,' he told him again. 'I'll ring you if I need you, and I'll drop these charts off for you to fill in after the boys go to sleep tonight. I wish you could be taking the boys across to Ferndale, but hey, you have another doctor here on Monday. All problems solved, no?'

No, Tom thought as he snagged the next chart and started writing. It was all very well for Roscoe to say he could do these tonight, but if he fell behind in his paperwork he'd never catch up.

Another hour…

But he glanced at the window one last time. The boys were capable of anything.

For what was maybe the four thousandth time over the last two years he thought, What have I let myself in for?

How long's for ever?

And then his attention was diverted. There was a car speeding up the track from the bay. A scarlet roadster. A two-seater.

Tom's cottage was one of only three down that road. Few people used it except for Tom, Rose and Rose's occasional visitors.

And the new doctor? He'd been told she'd collected the key from Reception a couple of hours back. Poppy, the junior nurse who'd given her the key, had been frustratingly vague when asked for a description. 'Quite old, really,' she'd said, which in Poppy's twenty-two-year-old eyes meant anything over twenty-three. 'And ordinary. Just, you know, dullsville when it comes to clothes. Didn't say much, just took the key and said she'd be at work at nine on Monday. She drives a cool car, though.'

If this was it, it certainly was cool, a streamlined beauty, the kind of car Tom used to love to drive—in another life.

So this would be Rachel Tilding, the new doctor, the latest of the Lavery Scholarship recipients, here to pay her dues with two years' service. He imagined she'd be heading to the shops to buy supplies or a takeaway meal for dinner. He should drop over tonight to say hi.

But tonight he didn't have his normal backup of Rose, who was always ready to slip over and mind the kids whenever he needed to go out. He could scarcely go over bearing wine and casserole and say, Welcome to Shallow Bay. Plus, he was dead tired. If he had the energy to make a casserole there'd be no way it'd leave his house.

He sighed and started to turn back to the desk—but then he paused. The car had turned off the road and was heading down the hospital driveway.

He could make the driver out now. The woman seemed slight, fair-skinned, with brown curly hair tumbling to her shoulders. Leaning against her was a child.

A child with his arm raised, caught in some sort of sling. An arm which was bright crimson.

Kit!

Running in hospitals was forbidden. From training it was instilled into you. No matter the emergency, walking swiftly gets you there almost as fast, with far less likelihood of causing another emergency.

Stuff training. Dr Tom Lavery ran.

She'd collected this gorgeous little car three weeks ago and she still practically purred every time she looked at it. Two years of internship, living in hospital accommodation and being constantly tired, meant that she'd spent practically nothing of her two years' wages. The condition of the scholarship which had funded her training meant she was now facing two years of 'exile' in the country. This car would be a gift to herself, she'd decided, to celebrate being a fully qualified doctor with her internship behind her. It'd also be something to remind her of the life she'd have when she could finally return to the city.

She'd driven it to Shallow Bay with a beam on her face a mile wide, blocking out the thought that she'd had to hire a man with a van to bring her possessions, as nothing bigger than a designer suitcase would fit in with her.

But now she wasn't thinking of her car. She had a child in her passenger seat, a little boy so white she thought he was about to pass out. She'd put as much pressure as she dared on his arm, slinging it roughly upward before somehow managing to carry him to her car. Her cream leather was turning scarlet to match the paintwork. Any minute now Kit could throw up. Or, worse, lose consciousness.

Please, no. She loved this car but if she had the choice between vomit or coma…

'Hold on, Kit,' she muttered. The decision to get him to the hospital rather than calling for an ambulance had been instantaneous. He still had glass in his hand. The blood he'd lost was frightening and the hospital was so close…

'I want Tom,' he quavered.

Tom? His stepfather? That was the name the kids had used. And Christine? The overblown, overpainted woman had emerged from the house, taken one look and fled back inside, saying, 'I'll ring Tom.' So much for practical help. Rachel had hauled off her own windcheater and used that as a pressure bandage and sling.

'Tell Christine—and Tom—I've taken him to the hospital,' she'd told his terrified brothers, and then she'd left. There was time for nothing else.

'We'll find Tom,' she told Kit now, as he slumped against her. 'But first we need to stop your hand bleeding. We can do this, Kit. Be brave. Isn't it lucky I'm a doctor?'

The sight that met him as he emerged from the Emergency entrance was horrific. All he could see was blood. And one small boy.

For a moment he felt as if his legs might give way. Kit's face, his hair, his T-shirt, were soaked with blood. The T-shirt was a treasured one, covered with meerkat cartoons. Tom couldn't see a single meerkat now, though. All he could see was blood.

Kit.

'Mate, you're doctor first, stepdad second.' It was Roscoe, placing a huge palm on his shoulder as they both headed for the car. 'Right now, Kit needs a doctor.'

The words steadied him but only a little. He reached the car and hauled the door open.

Kit was leaning heavily against the driver. Had she hit him? A car accident? What…?

'Lacerated hand.' The woman's voice cut across his nightmare, her voice as incisive, as firm as Roscoe's. 'From a broken window. No other injury, but severe blood loss. I suspect there'll still be glass in there. His name's Kit and he's asking for Tom.'

'Kit.' His voice sounded as if it came from a long way away. Kit was struggling to look at him, struggling to focus. 'T-Tom…' he managed—and then his eyes rolled back and he lost consciousness.

Kit!

It was Roscoe who took over. For those first appalling seconds—and it must only have been seconds—Tom froze, but Roscoe's voice boomed across the entrance, calling back into the Emergency ward behind. 'Trolley,' he boomed. 'IV. Blood loss, people. Move.'

And then as Barry, their elderly hospital orderly, came scuttling out with the trolley, and Jenny, their second most senior nurse, appeared with the crash cart, Tom recovered enough to scoop Kit out of the car.

Somehow Tom's years of training kicked in. Triage. Look past the obvious. Get the facts and get them fast.

The woman had been wedged between Kit and the driver's door. She looked almost as gory as the child. Thirtyish. Jeans. Long shirt, bloodstained. A smear of blood on her face.

'Are you hurt yourself?' he managed.

'No,' she snapped, hauling herself out of the car. 'Just the child.'

Jenny had the crash cart beside him. With this amount of blood loss, cardiac arrest was a terrifying possibility.

'I'm a doctor,' the woman said. 'Rachel Tilding. Who's senior here?'

She was asking because he wasn't acting like a doctor. Roscoe, Barry, Jenny all looked in control. Not him.

He made a huge effort and hauled himself back into his professional self. Terror was still there but it was on the backburner, waiting to surface when there was time.

'IV,' he managed, laying Kit on the trolley. The little boy's hand had been roughly put in a sling to hold it high.

A doctor...

What had she done to Kit?

'It's only his hand.' She was out of the car now, moving swiftly around to the trolley. 'He smashed my window with a cricket ball, then reached in to try and get it.'

Only his hand…but this amount of blood?

'Straight to Theatre?' Roscoe demanded.

'Yes,' she snapped back at Roscoe. 'I'll help if there's no one else. I don't know about parents. I didn't have time to find out. Just this Tom…'

'I'm Tom,' he said heavily. 'I'm his stepfather. He's my responsibility.'

'Stepfather…' She glanced at him in stupefaction. 'What sort of a…?' And then she collected herself. 'No matter. Kit needs a doctor, now.'

'I'm a doctor. Tom Lavery.'

'What the…you're working as a doctor and employing that…that…'

She obviously couldn't find a word to describe Christine. Neither could he. Maybe there wasn't one, but he and Christine were obviously grouped together. Dr Tilding's look said Tom's position in the hierarchy of life on earth was somewhere below pond scum.

'Never mind,' she snapped. 'You can give me all the excuses in the world after we've seen to Kit's hand. Let's get him to Theatre. Now.'

CHAPTER TWO

AND THEN THINGS reassembled themselves. Sort of. This was a small country hospital but it was geared for emergencies, and many emergencies involved rapid blood loss.

Kit had lost so much that cardiac arrest was still a real possibility. Treatment of his hand—apart from stemming the bleeding—had to wait until that threat was past.

And in Rachel he had a godsend. She was an angry godsend, judgemental and furious, but she was a doctor.

Maybe he could have coped alone—maybe—but he was acting on autopilot. A part of his brain seemed to have frozen. The sight of one little boy, unconscious, a child he'd learned to love, had knocked him sideways.

It was an insidious thing, this love. It had crept up and caught him unawares, and loving came with strings. He couldn't care for these kids—and love them—without his heart being wrenched, over and over again.

It was lurching now, sickeningly, and after that one incredulous look, that one outburst of anger, Rachel had subtly taken control.

As he went to put in the IV line his hand shook, and she took the equipment from him. 'Get the monitors working,' she told him. 'I'll take over here.'

The cardiac monitors… He needed to set them up. He did, with speed. A shaking hand could manage pads and monitors.

'Pain relief and anaesthetic,' she said. 'Do you have an anaesthetist?'

'There's only me,' he told her.

'Two of us, then,' she said curtly. 'Or one and a half if you're emotionally involved. But I'm trusting you have a good nursing staff.'

'The best,' Roscoe growled, and she nodded acknowledgement. This was no time for false modesty and she obviously accepted it.

And then Kit's eyes flickered open again, fighting to focus. Falling on Rachel first. Terror came flooding back, and Rachel saw.

'Hey, we found your Tom,' she told him. 'And here he is.' Her anger and her judgement had obviously been set aside with the need for reassurance. She edged aside so the little boy could see him. 'Kit, we're going to fix your hand. The bleeding's made you feel funny, and I know it hurts, but we're giving you something that'll make you feel better really fast. Tom's just going to test your fingers. Will you do what he tells you?'

And she stepped back, turning to the instrument tray, setting the scene so Kit could only see Tom.

She was impelling him to steady. She was pushing him to do what he had to do.

He had to focus and somehow he did.

Appallingly, he was still seeing terror as well as pain in the little boy's eyes. Legacy of his ghastly grandparents?

'Hey, Kit, you're here now, with me,' he said as they rolled the trolley into Theatre. He touched the little boy's face, willing the fear to disappear. 'You've cut your hand but we'll fix it. I know it hurts, but we'll stop it hurting really soon.'

'I broke… You're not mad…?'

'Dr Rachel tells me you broke her window,' he managed. 'I broke four windows when I was your age. I used to tell my mum and dad the cat did it. They didn't believe me but they weren't mad and neither am I. Accidents happen. Kit, can you tell me what you feel when I touch your fingers? Can you press back when I press? Here? Here?'

He was now in professional mode—sort of—but the lurch in his stomach wasn't going away.

And the information he gained from Kit as they settled him into Theatre wasn't helping.

He was checking for damage to the tendons that ran through the palm and attached to the finger bones. Secondly, for nerve damage, which could result in permanent loss of function or sensation. Tom was applying gentle pressure to the tips of Kit's fingers, asking him to push back.

The responses weren't good.

And Rachel got it. She was focusing on the IV, on getting pain relief on board, but she was listening to Kit's quavering answers. Knowing what they meant.

'Okay, Dr Lavery, tell me the set-up,' she said as Tom's testing finished. 'Do you have anyone here who can cope with paediatric plastics? Or someone who can get here fast?'

'No,' he said shortly. Stemming the bleeding seemed straightforward. It looked as if the radial artery had been nicked—it must have been to cause this amount of bleeding. They could fix that. But what his examination had told them was that Kit needed a plastic surgeon or a vascular surgeon or both if he wasn't to lose part or all of the use of that hand.

That meant evacuation. It was eight hours by road to Melbourne, ten to Sydney or Canberra. Shallow Bay wasn't the most remote place in Australia but its position, nestled on the far south-east coast, surrounded by hundreds of miles of mountainous forests, meant that reaching skilled help could be a logistical nightmare.

'Where?' Rachel said, and he had to give her credit for incisiveness.

'Sydney.'

'You have air transfer?'

'It'll take medevac an hour to reach us in the chopper, but yes.'

'Can someone organise that?' she said to Roscoe. 'Now?' And then she turned back to the child she was treating and her voice gentled. 'Kit, we're going to get your hand bandaged now, and stop things hurting, but there's a bit of damage deep inside that might make your fingers not as strong as they should be. We need to take you to a big hospital to get your hand mended.'

'Tom can fix it.' Kit's voice quavered.

'He can,' she said, injecting her voice with confidence. 'I know that. And so can I, because Tom and I are both doctors. If Tom agrees, I'll do the first part now. But have you ever seen Tom sew something that's ripped? Like a pair of jeans?'

'He did once,' Kit managed, trying gamely to sound normal. 'Big stitches. It came apart again.'

'Hey, how did I guess?' she said, smiling down at him. 'So Tom's not very good at sewing and neither am I. Kit, there are things in your hand called tendons which make your fingers work. You've hurt them, so what you need is a doctor who's really good at tiny stitches. Don't worry, we'll give you something that stops you feeling what we need to do. We'll make sure nothing hurts, I promise. You'll end up with a neat scar you'll be able to show your friends, but a good needleworking doctor will make sure your fingers end up stronger than ever. So what that means is that we need to take you to Sydney.'

'I don't want to go.'

'I understand that,' Rachel said. 'I've just arrived at Shallow Bay and it looks a great place. But have you ever been in a helicopter?'

'I... No.'

'Then what an adventure. Your friends will be so jealous. Tom, will you be going with Kit, or is there someone he needs more?'

And she looked straight at him.

So did Kit.

Is there someone he needs more?

Her eyes were challenging. Angry? He didn't get the anger, but he couldn't afford to focus on it now.

Kit needs his mother, he thought, and it was the belief he'd had reinforced about a thousand times in the last two years. But Claire was dead.

Kit's father was who knew where? Steve had been Claire's folly. The responsibility was never going to be Steve's.

Kit's grandparents? Claire's parents? They'd glory in this drama. They'd use it against him and his fight for custody would start all over again.

So he had to go with Kit, but to leave Shallow Bay... To leave two more needy children...

'There's no one but me,' he said, and it nearly killed him to say it.

'We'll manage.' It was Roscoe, gruff, stern, decisive. 'You need to go, Doc. And hey, we have another doc here now.'

'But Marcus. Henry. I can't.'

'They can stay at home,' Roscoe told him. 'We'll find someone to stay with them.'

'Not that childminder.' When Rachel spoke to Kit she was gentleness itself but when she faced Tom he saw judgement that he'd left the kids with such a woman. 'She's unfit.'

'She's awful,' Kit quavered. 'I don't like her.'

'It's okay,' Tom said, feeling helpless. He took Kit's good hand and squeezed. 'I'll fix this.' But how?

'Their normal minder is Rose,' Roscoe told Rachel. 'She hurt her hip yesterday but she's great. The kids love her. She'll stay with them.'

'She can't,' Tom said, option after option being discarded with increasing desperation. 'Not by herself. Not with her hip, and I can't trust Christine to help her. And with the field day at Ferndale—how many people are free this weekend?' He sounded desperate—he knew he did—but he was torn in so many directions. Kit needed him, but so did Marcus and Henry. As a parent, he was failing on all counts.

'We'll find someone,' Roscoe said, but he was starting to sound unsure. He turned to Rachel, explaining Tom's dilemma for him. 'The annual show at Ferndale is a huge deal and almost all the locals go. There's an added problem, too. These kids have had a bit of a tough time in the past and they need to stay in their own beds. Farming them out's not an option. I'd offer but my wife's almost nine months pregnant. What if she goes into labour?'

'You can't do it,' she said bluntly. She was still looking at Tom as if he was something she'd found at the back of the fridge, something that had been mouldering for months. 'So who can these boys depend on?'

'Me,' Tom said bleakly.

'Which is why we have one child with a sliced hand and two children with no carer.'

'We'll find someone,' Roscoe said again, but Tom felt ill. Rachel's disdain was obvious and he deserved it. Who could he ask, given this amount of notice?

But the expression on Rachel's face had changed. She looked…as if she was about to step into a chasm? It was a momentary look and then her expression became one of resolution. As if a decision had been made, but the decision was scary.

'Okay, then,' she said briskly, as if what was about to be said needed to be said before she changed her mind. 'Decision. If there's no other option, I'll accept responsibility. The boys don't know me, but I'm dependable. I can't imagine you'll need to stay in Sydney for more than a couple of days.'

'I can't… They won't…'

'I'm not offering to do this on my own,' she said, still brisk. 'Nor should you agree if I did. There's no way you should trust me. But if Rose of the hurt hip is otherwise okay… Would she agree to stay with the boys to give them the security they need? If she's willing, then I'll stay too. I can do housework, anything physical, and I can care for Rose as well as the boys. I don't mind sleeping on the floor if I need to. I've had experience of living with kids. I can cope with anything they throw at me.'

'I can't ask that of you,' Tom said, but she skewered him with a look that said he needed to get his act together.

'So what are your options?'

There weren't any.

'Rachel, with Tom away, we'll be needing you as a doctor,' Roscoe said, sounding stunned. 'I know you're not supposed to start until Monday but there's no one else. You know our last doc left us in the lurch. She had one of those scholarships you're on, but bang, she got herself pregnant and her fiancée paid her way out. So there's only Tom. And now there's only you.'

Then his face cleared. 'But maybe it would work. Rose isn't disabled, just sore. She lives in the third cottage down on your bay and she's slept at Tom's before. There's a spare bedroom, and I imagine you could use Tom's bed. There's an intercom from Tom's living room to the nurses' station here, so someone can always listen in if you need to be at the hospital. That works if Tom has to fix a drip or something at three in the morning. Tom works around his family. I guess you can, too.'

'I guess I can,' Rachel said.

'I can't ask…' Tom managed, but he was cut off.

'You have no choice.' Once again he heard anger, but she was moving on. 'Okay, Kit, let's get your hand fixed up ready for your helicopter ride. Dr Lavery, I'll need your help to stabilise things, but then you need to go home and pack.'

'You've only just arrived,' Tom said. He was feeling as if the ground beneath him was no longer solid. Who was in charge here? Not him. 'You can't…'

'Dr Lavery, I have no idea yet of what *you* can and can't do,' she said with asperity. 'But *me*… Don't tell *me* what I can and can't do without seeing me in operation. Do you or do you not need a childminder to stay with Rose?'

'I… Yes.'

'And is Rose dependable?'

'Of course.'

'So if I turned out to be a terrible person…would she kick me out?'

'She would,' Roscoe said from behind them. He was starting to smile—problem solved? 'If she was worried I dare say she'd boss me and Lizzy to move, with or without our new baby. She's one strong lady.'

'And so am I,' Rachel retorted. 'So, Dr Lavery, if you don't want me to stay with your boys then say so, but don't tell me I'm not capable.'

'I guess… I'm starting to think you're very capable,' Tom told her and tried to smile.

'Thank you,' Rachel told him, but there was no hint of a smile in return. He was still hearing anger. 'Now, Kit, let's get this hand fixed and show your stepdad I'm capable there as well.'

What had she promised?

Argh!

If there was one thing Rachel Tilding had learned in her twenty-eight years it was not to get involved.

Eight years ago she'd applied for the Roger Lavery Scholarship because it was the only one which offered to pay her entire way through medical school. Her education was sketchy, to say the least. She'd officially left school at fifteen. Since then she'd worked where she could, odds and sods for years, before ending up on night shift in a metal fabrication factory. She'd couch-surfed with anyone who'd put up with her, all the time saving, doing whatever she could to get the marks and the money to enter medical school. The day she'd heard she'd won the scholarship she'd been so tired she'd wept over the assembly line all night.

But then, thanks to the scholarship, things had eased. She'd been able to find somewhere permanent to live. She'd had security and a future, which was more than she'd ever dreamed of. The only cost to her was a contract at the end of her internship to work for two years in this end-of-the-earth place.

'Two years?' She thought of one of the other students on her med course, of his appalled reaction when she'd told him her plans. 'Shallow Bay? A tin-pot hospital with no specialists, in the middle of the National Park, cut off by bushfires in summer, floods in winter? I'm guessing you'll be married with babies by the end of the two years because there'll be nothing else to do.'

'I'm not into families.' She'd snapped it before she could stop herself, almost a fear response.

'You will be if you go there,' her fellow student had said. 'My uncle's a county doctor, on call twenty-four-seven. His wife and kids hardly see him, but he says they're the only thing that keeps him sane.'

A family? Keeping her sane? As if.

And now she'd offered to be part of one.

But it was only for a couple of days. She could do this. After what she'd been through, she knew she could pretty much do anything she needed.

But this was what someone else needed. Tom.

A stepfather. A man who'd left his kids with someone totally irresponsible.

So why had she made the offer? It wasn't her fault the

kid had hurt his hand. She didn't get involved—she never had. And yet here she was, two minutes after arriving at Shallow Bay, putting her hand up to move in with a house full of kids. It was so unlike her it left her stunned.

Was it the thought of kids being left with a stepfather? After all this time, the word still made her feel sick to the stomach.

She was overreacting, she knew she was. Cinderella's stepmother... Her own stepfather... They'd given the roles such a bad name.

One was a fairy story, she told herself, but her own...

Get over it.

Luckily she had medicine to distract her. It was a relief to move back into treating doctor mode. She was using local anaesthetic. Kit was awake and terrified, so she needed Tom to be Kit's support person.

Roscoe had set up a screen so Kit couldn't see her work. Tom could see over the screen but she had to block both Tom and Kit out. It was only Kit's hand that mattered.

The anaesthetic block was cutting off sensation and Tom was keeping the little boy still. Conscious all the time of doing no more damage, she started removing slivers of glass. Left in situ, they could move during the flight and cause more damage.

There was enough damage already. He must have dragged his hand backward as he'd felt it cut. The glass had sliced from palm down to wrist and then across as he'd jerked back out of the shattered window.

She was focusing fiercely. Broken glass was appallingly difficult to clear from wounds, as its transparency made it notoriously hard to see. Roscoe was in the background, handing her what she needed, but Tom was right there. One of his hands was under Kit's head, cradling like a pillow. The other was on Kit's elbow, stopping it moving.

Despite her concentration on the wound, she couldn't quite block out his presence. He was holding the little boy still but hugging him at the same time.

'This is going to be an amazing scar,' he was telling Kit. 'You'll need to make up a great story to go with it. Maybe we could get Dr Tilding to make marks that look like crocodile teeth to go with it. Then we could tell everyone that instead of staying with your grandparents last year you went croc hunting. Maybe one attacked Henry and you fought it off with your bare hands. I think it was a whopper, twenty feet long with teeth the size of my hedge-cutters. But you fought and fought and finally it held up its hands—paws?—what do crocodiles have? Anyway, your crocodile surrendered. And you told him it'd be okay as long as he said sorry and let you have a ride on his back.'

And to Rachel's astonishment the little boy managed a weak chuckle. 'That's silly,' he quavered. 'Kids don't ride crocodiles.'

'I bet superheroes do,' Tom said. 'This scar looks like a superhero scar. Does it look like a superhero scar to you, Dr Tilding?'

She'd just fielded a sliver of glass. She held it still for a moment in her forceps, making sure her grip was secure before she tried to shift it, then transferred it to the kidney dish.

'It'll definitely be a superhero scar,' she agreed. 'You might need to buy a new T-shirt, Kit. One with Batman on the front?'

'Batman?' Kit said, with a brief return of spirit. With

scorn to match. 'Batman's old.' And then his face crumpled as he recalled another grief. 'My meerkat T-shirt… It's all bloody.'

'We'll try and fix it,' Tom told him, but even Rachel could hear the doubt. And Roscoe grimaced behind him. To get monitors on the little boy's chest they'd simply sliced the T-shirt away, not only to get fast access but also to check there were no other lacerations underneath. The T-shirt was now a mangled mess.

But she could fix this. Rachel's splinter skill was internet shopping. Or, to be truthful, internet window-shopping—years of dreaming of what other kids could buy.

There'd been a great library in her neighbourhood and the librarian had been kind. She hadn't seemed to notice just how much time Rachel spent there—or that when her books got too much for her she'd just sort of sidled to one of the computers. Patrons were supposed to pay for fifteen-minute slots, but when the library was quiet…well, Maureen was a librarian with a kind heart and she didn't seem to notice. Sometimes Rachel had been asleep in a cubicle. Sometimes she'd been at the computer, dreaming of stuff she could never buy.

But she could buy stuff now, and memories of a weird search came back to her at just the right moment.

'Hey, I have a solution,' she told Kit. She was almost done. There'd still be tiny slivers in the wound but it would be up to the plastic surgeon in Sydney to retrieve them. The shards that could have done more damage were gone, and if she foraged more she risked making that damage worse.

'A solution?' Tom said.

'A meerkat superhero.'

'There's no such thing.'

'Of course there is. Kit, you tell him.'

'I haven't seen…' Kit said doubtfully.

'You haven't? You're obviously looking in the wrong places.'

Meerkats had been a bit of a thing for her during her teens; they had fascinated her, taken her out of her bleak world for a while. She still had a sneaky affection for them, and even now her internet browser seemed to find them almost by itself.

'You must know there are online comics,' she said. 'I bet there are even online movies and I definitely know there are meerkat superhero T-shirts. I could order you one this very night, if you want. It'll need to come from overseas so you might need to wait for a few weeks, but something like that would be worth waiting for, don't you think?'

'A meerkat superhero…?'

'Marvel the Meerkat?' she mused. 'I'm thinking that's who I saw. Maybe I have the name wrong. We'll have to wait and see.'

'But I broke your window,' Kit quavered, sounding astounded.

'So you did. So you'll have to pay.' She was closing, with steristrips because stitching a hand that needed further surgery was pointless. She glanced at Tom and saw the look of strain on his face. More than strain. She'd seen this reaction before, during her internship in an emergency department in Sydney. It was the reaction of parents whose foundations had been shaken after injury to their kids.

The look set back her prejudices a little. He cared?

So what was with the neglect? If he was a stepdad, where was Mum?

It wasn't her business. Focus on Kit. She'd just told him he'd have to pay.

'Can you fish?' she asked the little boy, guessing what the answer would be. She'd already noticed fishing rods stacked outside the next-door garage.

'Tom showed us how,' Kit said, confused.

'There you are then,' she said decisively. 'I can't catch fish but I love eating them. When your hand's better I demand three fish for payment. What's your favourite fish to catch?'

'Whiting,' Kit said and then looked doubtfully at Tom. 'Tom would have to help me.'

'I don't mind who helps,' she said. 'But I'm charging three fresh fish for my damaged window. Not all at once because I can only eat one at a time and I like them fresh. Then I'll charge two more for the new meerkat T-shirt I'll order tonight. Is that a deal?'

'D-deal,' Kit said and even managed a watery smile.

'That's that, then,' she said matter-of-factly. 'Now, if you'll excuse me, I need to unpack a few more boxes before I'm needed again.'

And she smiled at Kit, at Roscoe, but not at Tom, and then she headed out of the door.

He caught her just as she reached her car.

Her car… He saw her stop in dismay as she saw the mess, as she realised just what damage had been done. He saw her face go blank, almost as if she'd been slapped.

Back in his office he had a file on this woman. The file was in his possession not because she was a future colleague; he had it because Rachel Tilding was the recipient of the scholarship his grandfather had endowed, and as Roger Lavery's grandson he was one of the trustees of that endowment. Every two years a scholarship was awarded to a student who wouldn't otherwise be able to attend medical school but had shown determination and rigour to get where they were.

Rachel had won the scholarship eight years ago, when Tom's father still headed the trustees, but his parents were now living overseas and the file was in Tom's possession. When it was time for Rachel to take up her appointment, Tom had hauled it out and read it.

It didn't make pretty reading. Poverty, foster homes, eventual homelessness but, throughout it all, a grinding determination to be a doctor. She hadn't had the highest marks of the applicants but her sheer grit had made the award a no-brainer.

Now she was looking at her car as if this was a catastrophe. He watched her face crumple, her hand go to her eyes.

'Rachel?'

She gasped and swivelled, swiping her face fiercely with the back of her hand. Her long-sleeved shirt was still blood-stained where Kit had leaned on her shoulder in the car. Her soft brown curls were tangled back behind her ears, there was a smudge of blood on her cheek and her brown eyes looked too big in her too-pale face. She looked younger than the twenty-eight years she was, he thought. Defenceless? It was a strange adjective to describe her but that was how he saw her.

'You shouldn't be here,' she said, struggling to find control. 'Go back to Kit.'

'We're not really at the end of the earth,' he said gently, because something told him what was before her was more important than a messy car. 'We might not have plastic surgeons but we do have a car dealership. Roy's talent—aside from selling people cars they haven't realised they need—is detailing. He can take a farm bomb that's been lived in by farmers, pigs, dogs, whatever, and turn it into a gleaming bargain of the century. And this...'

He looked at the gorgeous scarlet lacquer, the sheer beauty of the little roadster. 'This would be his absolute pleasure to clean. The only thing you need to fear is him putting it into his showroom window when he's done.'

'Really?' She sniffed and eyed him with distrust. 'But it's blood. Don't people have rules about contamination?'

'He might charge more,' Tom agreed. 'But this was an accident, Rachel, caused by my stepson. My insurance will more than cover it.' He wasn't actually sure that it would, but there was no way he was saying that now. The responsibility was his. He'd pay a king's ransom to get her a clean car if necessary. 'Meanwhile, I'm heading to Sydney, thanks to you, so you can use my car.' He motioned to the car park, to a large serviceable SUV. 'You might even think about buying such a car for here. It's much more sensible.'

She had herself under control again now. He saw her regroup, and then gaze at his battered SUV with dislike.

'I might need to be a country doctor for two years,' she said. 'But there is nothing on earth that'd persuade me to swap my Petal for that...that...'

'Don't say it,' he said urgently, and smiled. 'That's Moby Dick, christened by the boys, and Moby's sensitive.'

'Moby doesn't look like he has a sensitive nerve in his body.'

'Looks are deceptive.' He hesitated. 'But…you will drive it? Just until I get back? Rachel, I can't tell you…'

'I don't want you to tell me,' she said, the anger he'd sensed from the start resurfacing. 'We all do what we have to do, Dr Lavery, and if that involves me driving Moby Dick…'

'And taking responsibility for two small boys. And starting work three days early. It's a huge ask.'

'It's not an ask. It's just what is,' she said. 'Whatever *what is* needs to be faced, and there's no use arguing. And for you… *What is* includes doing what you need to do for your stepsons. You've failed in that department already today so it's time to do better.'

Her anger was right there, in his face. Her brown eyes were flashing. Challenging.

'You're judging me?' he demanded.

'Of course I am. You really think Christine is a reliable childminder?'

'I had no choice.'

'Isn't keeping kids safe the most important choice of all?' She closed her eyes for a moment and seemed to collect herself. 'That's your business, however. I don't know your circumstances. It's not serious enough to report to the authorities…'

'The authorities,' he said, gobsmacked. 'You'd go there?'

'If I think children are seriously neglected, of course,' she snapped. 'Stepfather or not.'

'Is this your background speaking?'

That silenced her. She stared at him blankly for a moment before responding. 'What…what do you know of my background?'

'I'm the grandson of Roger Lavery. I'm a trustee for his scholarship fund. I read your application.'

'Then forget it,' she snapped, the picture of outrage. 'As my colleague, it smacks of prying, and it has no bearing on what's happening now. Dr Lavery, I have to organise myself if I'm to stay with your boys and so do you. The evac chopper should be here soon. You have packing to do, plus explaining to Henry and Marcus what's happening. They're confused and upset and they're still with the appalling Christine. So that's your *what is*. They need to be reassured, Christine needs to be sacked and you need to get packed. Go do it, Dr Lavery. Ring Rose if you can, and tell her I'll be there with my toothbrush in an hour.'

'Rachel, I can't tell you…'

'Then don't tell me,' she said angrily. 'And don't you dare pry into my private business again. Just get things done.'

An hour later he was sitting in the rear of the evac chopper, wondering what on earth had happened.

How had it come to this?

Kit was asleep, courtesy of the strong painkillers he'd been given. The two paramedics on board were more than capable of taking care of Kit medically. Tom's role was that of parent.

Parent.

The word still hung heavy.

He remembered the night Claire had asked him. 'Please, Tom, will you marry me? I can't think what else to do.'

What followed had been one marriage, three adoptions and Claire's death, and his life had changed for ever. He sat in the helicopter looking down at one injured child, thinking he'd just dumped two others on a woman he hardly knew. This was a nightmare. And if Claire's parents found out...

He raked his fingers through his hair, struggling to get his head around the logistics of this mess, and the paramedic next to him glanced at him in sympathy.

'You've had a shock too, mate. We can set you up on the other stretcher if you like, give you a chance to close your eyes and regroup.'

It needed only this, to be treated as a patient.

But that was what he felt like at the moment, as if he'd been punched in the guts. He was so out of his depth.

Who was the woman in charge of his children? A fiery newcomer who'd judged him and found him wanting. A woman he'd met only hours before.

He had Roscoe in the background, he reminded himself, and he had Rose. They'd keep an eye on her.

But her anger stayed with him.

He looked down at Kit's white face, at his limp little body. These kids had been through so much. And his lack of care had caused more pain... She'd been right to look at him with fury.

'Lie down,' the paramedic said again, gently, and he thought maybe he needed to.

He looked sick because that was how he felt.

What had she done, offering to mind two boys for days?

She didn't get involved. Ever. What crazy impulse had led her to say she'd help out?

Medicine was what Rachel used to settle her and it was medicine she focused on now. She sat in Tom's office and read through histories of the patients in the hospital. Five were elderly, recuperating from falls or waiting for home care arrangements. Three were here for rehab, transferred back from city hospitals, preparing to go home. One was a thirty-seven-weeks-pregnant mum with five kids at home. Tom had written in heavy letters—*'Bed rest until her sister arrives from Canada!'*

The final history was that of a farmer with an infected leg after being kicked by a cow. According to the history, he was responding to antibiotics. There seemed nothing she couldn't handle.

She did a round and introduced herself. Without exception, the patients were full of questions but she backed away fast. That was something else she'd been warned of with country medicine. 'Everyone will know everything about you in two minutes.'

Tom Lavery already knew more about her than she was comfortable with. At least she could back away from patients before they got personal.

Roscoe found her as she saw the last one. 'Everything's arranged,' he told her. 'Christine's feeling bad about what's happened. Big of her, but she's decided to be helpful. She's moving her Aunt Rose in now. Rose will give everyone the hugs they need. The boys love her. If you can…your job is just to be there at the edges. Make sure Rose doesn't start washing or scrubbing. She has osteoarthritis and her hip's probably more painful than she's letting on, but she loves the boys.'

'That's great,' Rachel said, feeling relieved. 'I can do whatever else needs to be done but the hugging is her department.'

She didn't do hugging. Almost unconsciously, her fingers drifted to one of the bands of scar tissue she could still feel around her upper arms. After twenty-eight years she didn't know how to hug. She didn't know how to love, and she had no intention of trying.

So now what?

'Roy Matheson's outside, checking the damage to your car,' Roscoe told her. 'Tom must have phoned him. All he needs is your keys and he reckons he'll have her good as new in no time. Here are Doc's keys for Moby Dick. We'll call you back if we need you. Meanwhile, you go and do what you have to do.' He hesitated. 'You know how grateful we all are that you're doing this? It's really generous.'

'I hardly had a choice.' She couldn't help it; her voice sounded waspish.

'You could have refused. We'd have found a way. This is a tight community. If you hadn't offered we'd have muddled through somehow. No one's left in the lurch here. We care.'

And why did that make her feel weird?

Her childhood. The loneliness.

No one's left in the lurch here.

Enough. She gave herself a mental shake and took the proffered car keys. She needed to find…Moby Dick? She also needed to figure out the boundaries of the next few days.

For boundaries had to be set, she told herself. Boundaries were what she lived within.

She could do this.

But at the back of her mind a question was niggling. She'd wanted to ask Roscoe but her boundaries had stopped her.

These were Tom's stepsons—what on earth was a man doing with three kids who weren't his own?

Hadn't he heard of boundaries?

CHAPTER THREE

THREE DAYS LATER the medevac chopper deposited Tom and a recuperating Kit back home, on the landing pad three hundred metres from Shallow Bay Hospital.

They'd arrived earlier than Tom had expected. Air transfer was available only in emergencies. Transfer home to Shallow Bay wasn't classified as an emergency. That meant Tom had been trying to decide whether to hire a car or wait for road ambulance transfer. However, on Monday morning a scuba diver had come up too fast after a dive south of Shallow Bay. Worse, he'd gone diving alone. He was in extremis when his friends found him and he'd died before they'd found somewhere with enough mobile coverage to ring emergency services.

The coroner needed the body and the coroner was in Sydney. Thus the chopper was on its way, but there was no rush. The crew who'd taken Tom and Kit to Sydney had kept tabs on where Kit's treatment was up to. Kit's hand was stable, with no more need for specialist intervention. They'd been offered a ride back.

Thus they rode back in style, arriving at Shallow Bay mid-morning. Tom emerged from the chopper and lifted Kit down after him. A still shaky Kit stood by his side until Roscoe drove up to meet them.

'Hey!' he boomed in greeting, and Tom was aware of a wash of relief at the sight of his friend's broad smile, at the hug Roscoe was giving Kit. 'It's great to see you, mate,' he told Kit and then he straightened and grinned at Tom. 'And you too.' Tom's hand was enveloped; the hold was tantamount to a hug, and Tom felt better for it. 'It's great to have you back.'

'The place hasn't fallen apart without us?' Tom took Kit's good hand and held on because the little boy was still shaky. His arm was a swathe of white under his sling but it wasn't only the shock and the injury that was making him shaky, Tom thought. These kids had had their foundations shaken by their mother's death.

'All good,' Roscoe was saying. 'You've hardly been missed. Our Dr Rachel is a beauty.'

'Really?'

'Efficiency R Us,' Roscoe said. 'You have no idea how a ward round should be conducted until you see Our Rachel at work. She can get a full history in less than three minutes. The patients don't know what's hit them.'

'You're saying she cuts corners?'

'I didn't imply that at all,' Roscoe said, swinging Kit up into his arms, giving Tom the illusion—at least for a moment—that responsibility was shared. 'No corner dares to be cut on Dr Rachel's watch. Now, mate,' he said to Kit, 'where are you up to?'

'We'll be keeping Kit in hospital for the next few days,' Tom told him. 'Until his stitches are out.' The job the plastic surgeons had done on Kit's hand was stunning but broken stitches could see him being sent back to Sydney. There was no way he was letting Kit near his rough-and-tumble brothers until they were out.

He'd need to spend time with him, running through

the exercises the hand therapist had set. At least with Rachel here he'd have the time. To have an efficient colleague was a blessing.

But what Roscoe was saying had sown doubts. He thought of the frail, elderly patients in his hospital, their need for human contact, for reassurance, and he thought, Three minutes for a history?

'Where's Rachel now?' he asked.

'On a house call,' Roscoe said. 'Herbert Daly. District nurse asked if she'll check his legs. He has three ulcers now, but the old coot won't take care of them, nor will he come in. But Rachel's on to it. Expect to see him in Ward One by lunchtime.'

'She's bossy?'

'Just organised,' Roscoe said. 'You'll see for yourself soon enough. Now, Kit, I'm betting your dad would like to take your gear home and catch up with Rose. Your brothers are both at school. How lucky are you to get this time off? Let's get you settled into the kids' ward. We have the best video games, plus Xavier Trentham's in there with a broken leg. He fell out of a tree on Saturday. He's in your class, isn't he? Dr Rachel's fixed his leg but she's keeping him in hospital until the swelling goes down and she can put a proper cast on. Meanwhile, he's aching for company. Come in and help him fight it out with Battle-Axe Warriors or whatever you kids play when we leave you alone with those game consoles. Tom will be back to see you within an hour, right, Tom?'

'Why do I feel like *I'm* being organised?' Tom said faintly and Roscoe chuckled.

'It's rubbing off,' he said. 'The Rachel effect. She's here for two years—I can't begin to imagine how we'll be by the end of it.'

'Assembly line medicine?'

'She's not that bad,' Roscoe said. 'She's good.'

But underneath Tom thought he heard doubt.

'Go see Rose and she'll tell you the same,' Roscoe said and lifted Kit into the car.

'I'll walk,' Tom said, grabbing his gear. 'It's only five minutes. It'll give me space to get my head organised.'

'See, what did I tell you?' Roscoe said and chuckled again. 'Organisation. The Rachel effect already.'

The lovely, dependable Rose was settled on the living room window seat overlooking the bay when he arrived. He paused at the door, taking in the scene before she realised he'd returned.

This place had been his grandparents' home, where he'd come for holidays as a kid. He'd loved it. He'd had freedom to wander. He'd learned to surf here. The locals had always made him welcome, had always treated him as a local.

But then his career had taken off and life had become frenetic, fun, city-centric. With his grandparents dead, his parents overseas, there'd been little reason to come back to Shallow Bay. It was only when he'd been landed with three grieving kids that he'd thought the only place they could be happy was here.

There'd been no other way. Decision made, he'd moved them here and tried to be content with the messy, kid-filled space his life had become.

But it wasn't messy now. Rose was sitting with her feet up, placidly knitting. That part felt normal. The rest of it, though, wasn't normal in the least. His usually messy house looked as if some sort of whirling dervish had swept through, but instead of creating chaos it had transformed it into… Home Beautiful?

Occasionally, during his bachelor existence, after the cleaner had been in, his city apartment had looked this tidy, but this was different. Not only was his house tidy, it seemed to have been transformed.

The furniture was arranged differently, invitingly, not wherever the kids had hauled it to get it out of the way when they were playing. Rugs were neat, vacuumed, not a wrinkle in sight. The pictures on the walls, seascapes painted by his grandmother, pictures he hadn't even realised were out of line, were now in straight lines. A couple that had descended to be propped on the floor had been rehung.

There was more. The jumble of seashells—generations of family beachcombing left in dusty piles wherever—was now arranged on a side table, with a couple of pieces of driftwood supporting them. Instead of a jumble, the shells now looked like an eye-catching art installation. The kids' books and puzzles were tidy but, more than that, they'd been arranged in enticing stacks. There was a jar of native bottlebrush on the sideboard, crimson, gorgeous.

Tuffy, the kids' fox terrier, bought in desperation from a rescue shelter in those first appalling weeks after Claire's death, had been asleep on the mat. He'd sensed Tom's arrival now and was rising to greet him. Last week Tom had been dumb enough to give him a bone and the resulting mess had still been horrible when he'd had to leave. Now he looked brushed, washed, almost presentable.

'Rachel's an amazing lady.' Rose had now realised he was there and was smiling a welcome. 'Welcome home. She hasn't let me do anything.'

'So don't do anything now,' he said. 'I'll make you a cup of tea.'

'I'd like to go home if I can,' she said, rising and packing away her knitting. 'I'll come back before the boys get home from school. Rachel and I have it organised. Tell me, how's Kit?'

He told her and her face cleared. 'Well, that's wonderful. We can go back to our old arrangement then, me being on call as needed. But Rachel tells me she's here too, if I need her. She's very bossy about my hip. I haven't felt so fussed over for years.'

'She sounds…bossy.' Tom had stooped to pat Tuffy but he was still looking around the room, still trying to figure all the differences.

'She likes to be busy,' Rose said, and he heard the same doubt he'd heard in Roscoe's voice. 'She's kind, but she can't sit still. Last night there was a lovely movie on the telly but she was polishing every shell while she watched it.'

'That's…great.'

'And cooking. She has three casseroles and two pies in the freezer for you. I told her I usually cook for you and she said, "Not with your hip."'

'I'll thank her.'

'You do that,' she said and then she paused. 'Oh, here's your car now. She must be dropping by to check on me before she goes back to the hospital. She makes me feel like I'm a patient myself.' She paused. 'Not that I'm not grateful, but I'll slip out the back way and leave you two together.' And she gathered her knitting and disappeared.

Tom Lavery was on the rug in front of the fire. He was scratching behind the ears of the misbegotten little mutt the kids called Tuffy. Tuffy was practically turning inside out with pleasure.

And for some reason the sight of this man stopped Rachel in her tracks.

She had things to do. She'd dropped by to make sure Rose was okay, and then she was due at clinic. Tom's call to Roscoe had said he'd be back some time today. She hadn't expected him this early.

He was tall, six two or maybe more. His dark brown hair was a bit unruly, tousled, sun-bleached at the ends. He was wearing casual chinos and a short-sleeved khaki shirt. His deep green eyes were crinkled at the edges— from the sun? As he looked up at her she thought he looked weary.

He'd have been at Kit's bedside for most of the last few days, she thought, remembering legions of parents watching over their kids in the paediatric wards of her training days. Some hospitals provided beds for parents, but medical imperatives and the needs of scared, ill or hurting children meant sleep was hardly ever an option.

There'd be a reason this guy looked haggard.

And maybe tiredness was a constant state for him. Roscoe had filled her in on his background over the weekend, not because she'd asked—he'd just told her.

'Tom was a surgeon in Sydney until the boys' mother died,' he'd told her. 'Their dad disappeared. Tom's all they've got.'

The boys were his stepsons. He'd married their mother and then she'd died, Roscoe had told her.

But how could he care so much for kids who weren't his? It was beyond her but looking at him now she had no doubt that he did care, and he was exhausted because of it.

Roscoe's story had made her feel more than a little guilty that she'd let her prejudice show when she'd first met him. He might be a stepdad, but stepfathers shouldn't all be tarred by the same brush. It was just the word. *Stepfather*... After all these years it still made her feel ill.

'Welcome home,' she said now, trying for a smile. His obvious weariness seemed to be making something twist inside her. Normal sympathy for a tired and worried parent? For some reason it felt more than that, and the sensation made her unsettled.

'How's Kit?' she asked, pushing aside her niggle of unease, heading back to talk medicine. Work was always safest.

'Roscoe's putting him into a bed in the kids' ward,' he told her. 'The surgery's gone well. Flexor tendons were damaged as well as nerves but the surgeon's done a great job and he has every hope that there'll be no long-term damage. If he was an only child I'd bring him home, but he and his brothers play rough. He has a protective plaster so maybe I'm being ultra-cautious, but given how far we are from help I'd prefer him to stay where he is until the stitches are out. He knows I'll be in and out. Henry and Marcus can visit. It's good to have him home.'

Then he gazed around the room again, slowly, as if taking it in. 'It's good to be home too,' he said. 'Thank you for your care.'

She followed his gaze, noting with satisfaction that nothing had been disturbed after her clean. 'You're welcome. I'm not bad at dusting and polishing.'

'It's not actually the dusting and polishing I'm thanking you for,' he told her with a slightly crooked smile. 'That's great, but with three kids I've pretty much learned not to value them. It's for starting at the hospital three days early, but mostly it's for caring for Marcus and Henry—and for Rose too. I can't tell you how grateful I am.'

'It's just what needed to be done.' She shifted uncomfortably. He was thanking her for care rather than cooking and cleaning? She didn't care, at least not in the emotional sense. She did what she had to do to keep her world functioning as it should, to keep her patients safe, to keep herself safe. She accepted responsibility when she had to, but that was as far as it went.

Caring was something that had been driven out of her from a time so long ago she could scarcely remember.

So now…she looked at Tom's weary smile, seeing the telltale lines of strain around his eyes, and she thought it wasn't caring to accept a little more responsibility. It was simply doing what needed to be done.

'You look like you could do with a sleep,' she told him. 'Why don't you take a nap now? Roscoe and I have things covered. There's nothing urgent. We don't need you.'

'I'd like to see everyone, though,' he said diffidently. 'You've been out to see Herbert Daly?'

'His son's bringing him into hospital,' she told him. 'He should have been in days ago, but he's stubborn. I had to insist.'

'He likes his own space,' Tom said neutrally. 'But you're right—he could do with some bed rest. What about the rest of our patients?'

'Frances Ludeman's still in. Her blood pressure's still up but only mildly. It was only after her husband brought the other *five* kids in to visit that I saw why you wanted her to stay.'

'She needs all the rest she can get,' Tom said. 'And Roscoe says Xavier Trentham's in the kids' ward.'

'Fractured tibia. It's a clean break but he fell through a hedge and there's too much swelling to cast it yet. Like your Kit, there's too much chaos at home for him to be safe without the cast.'

'Chaos?'

'Other kids.'

'Right.' He gave her an odd, sideways it looked like she didn't understand. It felt strange, doing what seemed like a medical handover in his living room, but efficiency seemed to be called for. He moved on. 'Bob's infection from the cow kick?'

'There's still some necrosis. He wants to go home but I've said another three days.'

'He'll hate another three days. We can probably organise him to go home with visits from district nursing.'

'He'll need more than just nursing. He'll need to be checked, by you or by me.'

'I can do that.'

'Why? It's much easier to keep him in hospital.'

'Yes, but he has problems,' he told her. 'Have you met his wife?'

'I gave Lois an update yesterday. She's accepted that he won't be home until Thursday at soonest. He has no choice.'

'He does have a choice. I'll organise it.'

'Why?' she asked, startled. 'You can hardly do house calls. He lives fifteen minutes out of town.'

'I don't mind. Lois's stressed herself. She has high blood pressure, and she worries about a daughter living in New Zealand. I suspect they care for her financially and that's pushing the farm income. I don't want Lois ill.'

'But it's Bob who's your patient.'

'I need to care for them all,' he said simply. 'Like I need to go do a ward round now.'

She stilled. 'I've already done a round. You don't trust that I've looked after them?'

'I'm not saying that.' He was watching her as if he was trying to understand something that was puzzling him. 'Rachel, this is a country medical practice. We don't treat patients in isolation. Every person comes with a story around them, farms that need tending, debts, kid worries, elderly parent concerns. If you ignore them then they come back to bite you. This is your first shot at family medicine, right?'

'Yes.'

'And you're only doing it because of the scholarship?'

'I'm hugely grateful for the scholarship,' she said, a bit awkwardly.

'But family medicine isn't what you want long-term?'

'I'm pushing for radiology.'

'Where you don't need to look much past the image to the patient.'

'Is that a criticism?'

'Of course it's not.' He shrugged, and once again she had the impression of deep weariness. 'Heaven knows we need good radiologists—they helped save Kit's hand. But here it's purely country practice, and country practice means looking out for everyone. If we leave Bob in hospital for much longer, Lois's blood pressure will go through the roof. We send him home.'

His tone was final. Fair enough, she conceded. Tom was, after all, the senior doctor in this set-up. But to choose to do house calls when there was an alternative... She'd had to do a couple already and they made her un-

easy. It felt like stepping into an intimate space she had
no right to enter.

'I'll do the house calls,' he told her. 'If they worry you.'

How had he guessed? Was her face so transparent?

'We share the work,' she told him brusquely. 'My
contract says full-time family practice for two years. I
can do it.'

'You'll be a better radiologist for time spent in family medicine,' he said, still with that odd assessing look
on his face. 'Believe it or not, I believe I'm becoming a
better doctor because of it. And I can still do some surgery, which is my passion.'

'You're joking. How much surgery can you perform
here?'

'Not as much as I'd like,' he admitted. 'But I do the
small stuff. Ferndale has specialists, but it's a hard drive,
all curves and kangaroos. Cath Harrison's the anaesthetist there. She comes over to Shallow Bay once a week
or so, and we do a list together. Simple stuff that would
be a pain for the locals to have to go to Ferndale—or
Sydney—to get done. It keeps me happy.'

'But it's simple surgery.' How on earth could it make
him content? 'So how can you say you're a better doctor because of what you're doing here?'

'Because I'm learning to treat the whole patient,' he
told her. 'I hope you can get what that means. But now…
I'll head over to do a ward round and then get to clinic.'

'I'm running the clinic and there's no necessity to do
a ward round. I told you. Everyone's sorted.'

'So Roscoe said.' Once again she got that wash of
weariness. This man should be in bed, but he wasn't
going there. 'I need to see everyone…for me,' he admitted. 'I'm not doubting your medicine.'

'Then why aren't you being sensible?' She knew she was sounding stubborn, but so was he.

He took a deep breath, regrouping. 'Okay,' he conceded. 'You take clinic, as long as you ring me for any problems, but I will do a ward round.'

'You don't trust me.'

'I do trust you. Your credentials are impeccable.'

'Then what?'

'Rachel, it's just because I care for them as people,' he said, sounding a bit helpless. 'I need to see for myself how everyone's doing, and it's not just the medical side I'm interested in.'

'I don't know what you mean.'

'Which is why you're here for two years and I'm stuck here for life,' he said, and suddenly his voice was grim. 'As doctors...Rachel, you and I might have belonged to the same species once upon a time, but now... Well, somehow, I've evolved into a different breed. Darwin might have said I've evolved through necessity, for survival. Your survival's assured. You're just marking time before you can head back to your own world. But here, Dr Tilding, I need you to pretend to evolve, just for two years. You're useless here without caring.'

Then he shook his head. 'I'm sorry. That's probably too big a statement. You obviously do care. You're responsible and you're generous and I'm deeply grateful. Believe me, I'm grateful for what you've already done. Anything else has to be an extra.'

They walked back to the hospital together, but they walked in silence. He'd offended her, Tom thought. He knew what he'd said had been clumsy, but he was too tired to get the nuances right.

So now she walked beside him and he couldn't think where to take it. And it wasn't just tiredness that was throwing him. Would he have accused any other doctor of not caring? After she'd spent the last three days doing just that, it seemed unfair.

There was something about her that had him off balance.

She was gorgeous. Half a head smaller than he was, she was packaged just right. Bouncy brown curls—well, he'd seen them bouncy, though she had them tied up tight now. Brown eyes, nicely spaced. A wide, generous mouth and a smattering of freckles. She was dressed conservatively—too conservatively for such a warm day, in neat black trousers and a long-sleeved shirt—but her plain clothes didn't disguise the curves underneath.

It wasn't the fact that she was cute—well, more than cute—that had him off balance, but he didn't know why.

Was it the bleak notes in her scholarship application? Was it the way she'd said the word *stepfather*, as if the name itself conjured horror? Was it the anger he'd seen when she'd thought the boys were neglected?

Or was it the traces of fear that appeared and disappeared, as if there were things, emotions, Rachel Tilding was still hiding?

How did you get over a childhood of neglect?

Tom had had a blessed childhood. His father had left Shallow Bay early—*'I can't stand the sight of blood—there's no way I could have done medicine.'* He'd done law, been hugely successful, moved into politics and then into international diplomacy. His mother's career was equally impressive. Tom's arrival had been an accident—they'd been too busy to have children—but in the end they'd welcomed him. They were a power couple but their love for their only son had been unstinting.

As his grandparents' love had been. Tom had had the run of embassies, of political powerhouses, and of Shallow Bay. He'd learned languages, he'd studied, he'd surfed, he'd dated gorgeous women, he'd had fun.

He'd also rescued things. Anything. Beetles lying upside down on wet paths. Unwanted kittens. Bullied kids at school.

He couldn't bear to see hurt, even though sometimes caring caused chaos.

Like the time he'd brought a huntsman spider home, a female, laden with a huge egg sac. He'd found it at the back of the lockers at school, missing two legs, and decided to rehome it in the laundry. He'd forgotten to tell his mother—who'd found about a thousand baby spiders in her clean washing.

Like the first time he'd seen Claire, being yelled at by her father as she was dropped off at infant school.

Like the time Claire had phoned him after her diagnosis. 'Please, Tom, help me…'

Was the same drive to fix things attracting him to Rachel? He'd always been a sucker for the needy. He knew it.

'It's just the way you're made,' he told himself. 'It's in your DNA. So leave it. Rachel doesn't need you. She's tough and she's bright and she'll do what it takes to get on in life. You do the same.'

It made sound sense.

So why did a niggle of doubt tell him that life was about to get more complicated?

CHAPTER FOUR

THE WEEK THAT followed was busy but not frantic—thanks to Rachel. Her efficiency might set some patients' backs up, it might make Tom edgy, but there was no doubting that it lowered his workload.

Heather Lewis, breeder of Hereford cattle, president of the local Country Women's Association and stander of no nonsense, met him in the car park late on Friday. He'd just returned from a house call. Heather sauntered over to meet him, a big woman, bluff, kind, bossy. Ready to gossip.

'She's good, isn't she?' she said without preamble.

'You mean Rachel?'

'I've just been to see her for my foot. Fungal infection. She gave me a script, instructions and a lecture about wearing wet boots. In and out in five minutes. That's my kind of medicine.'

'Hmm,' he said doubtfully. It was the kind of medicine Heather liked, and mostly it was what people needed, but how many consultations were that easy?

'And she's here for two years. We need to get her involved. Does she play tennis? Ride a horse? Play mahjong? I tried asking but she brushed me off. Fair enough, it was a medical consult after all. But what's she interested in, Tom? How can we pull her into the community?'

'I have no idea,' he said faintly. 'She seems to like keeping herself to herself.'

'But she's there when you need her. It was trial by fire, landing her with your boys last week. She must be a good'un. Worth prodding below the surface.'

'I guess.'

'And she's single,' Heather went on relentlessly. 'There's a thought, Doc. You and her… You could surely use help with those boys. You still got Kit in hospital?'

'He'll be home tomorrow.'

'They're a handful. A partner would be good. You might want to think about it.' And Heather drove away and left him standing.

Think about what?

Rachel?

A love life?

Ha.

Even if he had the time for such things—which he didn't—even if there was a possibility of dating when he was solely responsible for the care of three troubled kids… *Rachel?* An uptight, self-contained woman who'd stepped in when needed but who'd stepped away fast.

As any woman would from his situation.

But the niggle he'd felt almost a week ago was growing, and as he walked back into the hospital he allowed himself a moment to think about it. Rachel Tilding was about as far from his type of woman as it was possible to get. BK—Before Kids—he'd had a definite kind of partner. Not serious—never serious. He liked feisty, fun women who didn't take life too seriously. Women who could give as much as they got, who demanded no promises, who didn't cling, who were happy to step into his world and then out again as life called them in a different direction.

There didn't seem a lot of joy in Rachel Tilding's world. Life seemed serious. Organised.

He put the idea firmly aside, heading in to walk through the wards and say hi to everyone who'd appreciate a visit. There wasn't much for him to do medically. Rachel had obviously done her rounds earlier. Charts had been filled in. Every need had been met.

Except talking. He talked his way round the hospital now, calming worries, explaining, listening. Just being there.

His final visit for the day was Kit. Tom had been in a few times during the day, as much as he could manage. Now he found him engrossed in a battleship conflict. His friend, Xavier, was still in the next bed. There'd been no pressure on the ward, so the decision had been made to keep them longer. They were both due to go home in the morning.

Tom got a short greeting between battles—plus a quick, one-armed hug which was a message on its own. Kit might be content for the moment, but he was still needy.

Finally he headed home. From the track he could see Rose in her favourite seat. She'd be knitting while the kids watched the telly show they always watched on Friday nights. He'd go in, say goodnight to Rose and then cook his standard Friday night fare of hamburgers.

And try not to miss Friday nights of the past. Socialising. Fun.

Suddenly he was hesitating. Rachel's arrival really had made a difference. It was only five-thirty, far earlier than he usually finished. The ingredients for hamburgers were in the fridge and Rose would enjoy putting them together. She liked eating with the boys. It was a warm night. The beach beckoned.

He could use some me time.

Ten minutes later he'd headed back to town and bought two low-alcohol beers—he was on call. A sunset, a beer, time to reflect—it wasn't up to the standard of Friday nights of his past, but it'd have to do.

He parked outside his cottage. Rose saw him from the window. He waved towards the beach, put his finger to his mouth in a signal for her not to tell the boys, and she waved back her acknowledgement.

Bless her, he thought. She'd guess he needed space. What would he do without her?

Life was okay, he told himself as he walked down the beach path. He had a great housekeeper. He had a colleague to share his work, to halve his call roster.

He had two low-alcohol stubbies to celebrate Friday night.

Alone.

'Morose R Us,' he muttered as he headed down the track. 'Get over it.' There wasn't a thing he could do about his situation and self-pity would get him nowhere. He needed to be grateful that Kit was okay, that Rose was giving him space, that he had two stubbies—and he had a new colleague.

He rounded the bend that blocked the view of the bay from the track—and his new colleague was sitting on the sand in front of him.

She'd obviously been swimming. Her hair, normally tied tightly back, had come loose and was coiling wetly down her bare back. She was wearing a simple one-piece bathing suit. She looked…

Gorgeous?

She swivelled and struggled to her feet, grabbing her towel to cover herself—and all he could see was fear.

She hauled the towel up in front of her.

Not fast enough.

Every time he'd seen this woman she'd been wearing long sleeves. At work she wore formal business-type blouses, tucked into trousers or skirts. At home she wore long-sleeved T-shirts with jeans or shorts.

He thought of the first time he'd seen her, with Kit. She'd been wearing a long-sleeved shirt then. It had been covered with blood and looked truly shocking.

What he saw now, in the moment before she hauled the towel around her, seemed just as shocking.

Blotches were etched deep into the skin of her upper arms. No, not blotches. Scars. Many scars. He hardly had time to see them though, before the towel was wrapped around her, shutting them from view.

She was standing now, fear fading as she realised who he was. But she took a step back, making a clear delineation between the two of them.

'Sorry,' she muttered, her voice shaky. 'I shouldn't have sat so close to the path.'

'And I should have whistled as I walked,' he told her, trying to drive away the panic he still sensed. 'I usually do. It scares the Joe Blakes.'

'Joe Blakes?'

'What the locals call snakes. The advice is to sing as you walk, but if you heard me sing you'd know that it'd scare more than Joe Blakes.'

'Are there snakes here?' Her voice was still shaky

but he knew it wasn't from fear of snakes. Why was she frightened?

'I doubt it,' he told her, gentling his voice. 'It pays to be careful, but we haven't seen any in the dunes for ages. They're more scared of us than we are of them. The boys' noise will be keeping them at bay.'

'Oh,' she said neutrally, and he could see her fight to get her face under control. Her towel was drawn tight, concealing all.

Or not quite. One of the scars was just above her breast. Until now he'd put her long sleeved tops and high necklines down to her general uptightness. Now…

He'd seen scars like this. A long time ago. In paediatric ward during his training.

Abuse.

Cigarette burns.

Hell.

'Rachel…'

'I was just going,' she stammered, reaching down for her bag. 'I came down for a swim after work, to get some peace. I imagine that's what you want, too. I'll leave you to it.'

She was ready to bolt.

Cigarette burns.

He knew nothing about this woman apart from the fact that she had an impeccable medical record—and she'd won his grandfather's scholarship. And there'd been foster homes.

Her scars were completely covered now, and he couldn't ask. Maybe she hoped he hadn't seen them.

He had to leave it like that, but he didn't want her to bolt. There were ghosts behind this woman's façade, and he was intrigued.

'You know, once upon a time when I finished work on Friday nights I'd head to the pub beside the hospital,' he told her, casually moving so he wasn't blocking her way. So she knew she could leave if she wanted to. 'Half the medics we worked with would be there. I can't remember a single moment of peace but I wouldn't have missed it for quids. Noise, laughter, a general debrief of the week's traumas. Friends.'

He looked down at the two stubbies he was carrying and made a decision, right there and then, that the supreme sacrifice was called for.

'So the drinks menu here might be limited,' he told her. 'But, in memory of all those Friday nights, I'm very happy to share. Do you drink beer?'

The fear and shock were subsiding. She had herself together. Almost. 'I need to go home,' she said.

'No, *I* need to go home,' he told her. 'But not yet.' Why did he get the feeling she wanted to run? He was sensing his way, the same way he'd approach a scared and wounded child. Or a startled kangaroo. 'The roster says *I'm* on call tonight, not you,' he said. 'The boys are at home, but Rose is with them and they're happy and settled. Kit's safely in hospital. My phone's in my pocket and I can be there in minutes if I'm called. I have a sliver of time to myself.'

'Which is why you need peace.'

'Which is why I need company,' he said bluntly. 'Of the adult variety. Of the colleague variety. Which is why I'm making the extraordinary gesture of offering you one of my precious stubbies.'

She stared at him for a long moment, as if trying to read his mind. Then she looked down at his stubbies.

'You brought two.'

'And I'm offering you one. You can't imagine how generous that makes me feel.'

Her lips twitched, just a little.

'Beer,' she said.

'I know, a piña colada with a sliver of lime and a wee umbrella would be more appropriate, but the ice would have melted while I walked down here. You want to slum it with me?' And before she could answer he plonked himself down on the sand.

She stood, looking down at him. Disconcerted? She was torn—he could sense it. Part of her wanted to leave, but it would have been a rebuff.

He set the stubbies in the sand and waited. Stay or go? He was aware, suddenly, that he was holding his breath. Hoping?

Why? She was simply a colleague, paying her dues for two years before she got on with her life.

Or…what? Was that a tiny sliver of hope? A resurrection of something he'd once taken for granted?

Like a love life.

Heather's words came back to him. Dumb. Ridiculous. He knew it.

Still, he kind of hoped she'd stay.

'I don't mind a beer,' she said tentatively, and he grimaced.

'Lady, you're going to have to do better than that. I carried two stubbies all the way down here. That's a fair commitment on my part. So now I'm offering to share, but not with someone who "doesn't mind a beer." It has to be "I'd love a beer" or nothing.'

And suddenly she smiled. He'd seen her smile before, greeting patients, being pleasant, but her smiles had been tight, smiles to put people at ease. This one, though, was something much more. It was a wide, white smile with a chuckle behind it.

Cute.

More than cute. Gorgeous.

'My lukewarm response was simply because you pre-empted your kind invitation with a vision of piña colada and umbrella,' she admitted and, splendidly, she sat herself down on the sand again. But where most women—most anybody—would set the towel down and sit on it, she kept it firmly wrapped around her arms, a cover for what lay beneath.

'Where in Shallow Bay would I get a piña colada?' she asked, and he had to stop thinking about scars on arms and focus on what was important. Piña coladas.

'Dougal's pub doesn't run to them, that's for sure,' he said. 'I had to twist his arm to stock low-alcohol beer. Apparently, it's for sissies.'

'Or doctors on call.'

'As you say. So…beer or no beer?'

And her smile flashed out again. 'I really would love a beer.'

That smile… He found himself grinning to match, though he wasn't actually sure what he was grinning about. She disconcerted him and he didn't understand that either.

So back to basics. He twisted the ring-pull and handed her a bottle, then did the same for himself. 'Here's to the end of your first week,' he told her, clinking bottles. 'May your next week be not so exciting.'

'Apart from the first couple of hours when your son tried to stab himself to death, it hasn't been very exciting at all,' she told him. She took a swig of her beer and seemed to enjoy it. 'I suspect it's been a lot more exciting for you, and I'm so glad it's turned out well.'

'You and me both. And I'm incredibly grateful. I wish it could have been piña colada.'

'I told you, I'd love a beer.' She held up her bottle and regarded it with affection. 'The fact that I've been on the beach for two hours and forgot my water bottle—and there's no piña colada in sight—has nothing to do with it. Beer's great.'

And there was the smile again. He liked it. A lot.

'But wouldn't you be more comfortable drinking your beer at home?' she queried, and he thought, She's made the decision to come down here—alone. It confirmed what he was learning of her. She was a woman who valued her own company, which made what she'd offered to do last weekend even more extraordinary.

'The kids are at home,' he said. 'Added to that, they have a video game which requires at least three players. It involves bombs and flames and dragon babies turning into things I don't want to think about.'

'So...' she said cautiously. 'They play it a lot?'

'Is that a judgement?'

'Hey, I'm no judge. I'm just happy to have intact windows.'

'Yeah,' he said morosely. 'You and me both. The game's okay. Fun, even. But, right now, they can't play because, stupidly, I bought a game that needs at least three players. I bought it so they'd be forced to include Henry, who often gets left out. Unfortunately, Kit's now away. Rose holds up her knitting like armour whenever they approach, so I'm their only available third man. It's a wonder they didn't have you playing last weekend.'

'They tried,' she said. 'I was busy.'

'Is that what you said?'

'Of course.'

'Then why doesn't that statement work for me?'

'You're obviously a softie,' she told him. 'But if you don't like playing with them…'

He knew what she was asking. It was the question that he asked himself more than a dozen times a day. 'You want to know why I took them on?'

'It's none of my business,' she said hastily, and he sighed and took another swig of beer and wished he'd had the forethought to buy a dozen.

'I do like playing with them,' he admitted. 'Mostly. But that's what got me into trouble in the first place.'

'I don't get it.'

'Their mother was my best friend,' he said simply. 'We were mates from pre-school, right through med. school and beyond. Never lovers, though. Claire had appalling taste in men, from the time she kissed Terry Hopkins behind the shelter sheds when she was ten. Hopkins used to squash snails down girls' dresses. Why did she not see that could only end in tears?'

'She married a snail-squasher?'

'She escaped Terry Hopkins but she did worse. She married a serial cheat and a bully. Claire's parents are loaded. Her father's something huge in the financial world. My parents are wealthy enough, but they're nothing compared to Claire's. Steve took one look at only-child Claire's inheritance prospects and moved right in. But as soon as they were married he reverted to the slimeball he was. He had affair after affair, treating Claire like dirt.'

'Which left you as a friend.'

'I'm godfather to each of them,' he said, trying to eke

out his beer to last through a bleak story. 'And they're great kids. Claire and I worked in the same hospital as interns. It was easy to help her out in emergencies. I didn't mind taking them to soccer on Saturdays, doing the occasional childminding. It was even fun.'

'Until…'

'Until.' He gave up on his stubby, planting it in the sand. It was still a quarter full but maybe he'd need it at the end.

He usually hated telling this story, but he glanced at Rachel and saw only casual interest—the sort of interest a doctor might show a patient describing symptoms. She wasn't emotionally involved. She was simply a colleague who was…asking.

Strangely, it made it easier to keep talking. Every one of his friends had reacted to his story with dismay, horror, sympathy. Rachel was asking—because she'd like to know? Or because she thought she ought to ask. The differentiation was hard to make but somehow he appreciated it.

Her detachment made the story easier to tell.

'Claire was diagnosed with hypertrophic cardiomyopathy when Henry was two,' he told her. 'She collapsed at work. Dramatic. Awful. If she hadn't been in a hospital when it happened she would have died but she pulled through. Just. By this time Creepy Steve was almost a thing of the past and her illness was the last straw. He never had time for the kids and when Claire fell ill, when her parents made it clear there'd be no money for him, ever, he signed over rights to access to his kids and was heard of no more.'

'Which left Claire alone.'

'Yeah.' He stared into the middle distance, remembering her terror. Remembering his own fear. 'She had irreversible pulmonary hypertension, a contraindication for a heart transplant, but a transplant did end up buying her enough time to think about the boys' future without her. While she was ill her parents took her and the boys back into their home. She had enough time to accept the boys could never be happy with her parents as sole carers.'

'Why not?' Weirdly, once again she seemed detached. The way she was, he wouldn't be surprised if she produced a clipboard from her beach bag and started taking notes.

But her detached manner helped. He found himself wanting to outline the events that had propelled him here.

'Her parents are…overpowering,' he told her. 'Because we'd been friends for so long I already knew that. Claire had been pushed as a child, really pushed. Ballet, piano, violin, gym—polo, for heaven's sake—and she was expected to be brilliant at everything. To be honest, I suspect that's why she fell for Creepy Steve and the other creeps before him—it was a dumb attempt to rebel. I gather, after she fell ill, the relationship with her parents grew more strained. Anyway, even before she had the transplant she knew the odds—she knew she wasn't going to be around long-term for the boys. In the end she was desperate for me to have some influence in the way they were raised—so she asked me to marry her and adopt them.'

What followed was silence. Normally friends or colleagues jumped in at that point in the story. Not Rachel. She seemed to be taking her time to think it through.

'That was some ask,' she said at last. 'I can't imagine how it made you feel.'

'We were good friends,' he said diffidently. 'And it wasn't as if marrying and settling down was my style.' He gave a rueful smile. 'I worked, I surfed, I had fun. Family wasn't on my radar. And we thought—Claire and I both thought—that it'd be simple enough. If by some miracle she survived long-term then we'd divorce. If she died, then her parents would do the hard yards of parenting—they saw the boys as their responsibility and had already made it clear that's what they wanted. I'd just be around on the edges, giving them another long-term person for security, but with enough legal authority to step in if her parents pushed too hard.'

'Still, it's a big deal.'

'You wouldn't have done it?'

'You said marrying wasn't your style. It's so far off my radar it's another world. That kind of involvement—any kind of personal involvement—isn't my scene.'

'Really?' He eyed her curiously and once again that sense of a clipboard between them came into his mind. 'Yet last weekend you were there for me.'

'There wasn't a choice. Not that I minded. It was a finite commitment with the end in view. What you're describing… Long-term involvement seems a given.'

'There was no way I thought it'd interfere with my Friday nights though,' he said with another rueful look down at his beer. 'But look at me now.'

'So what happened?'

'She died,' he said simply. 'She tried for another transplant, which went horribly wrong—she was never going to be strong enough to deal with it and she knew it, but her parents were fighting with every means they had. When it was over the boys stayed living with them and I tried to take up where we'd left off, seeing them occasionally, taking them to soccer. Only it didn't work. The kids got quiet. You know the rule in Emergency? Triage? A kid comes in screaming its lungs out and a kid comes in limp and silent. Which one needs attention? The limp one every time, and they were limp.'

'So…a problem.'

'Claire had given me custody in her will,' he said. 'She didn't think I'd need it. All she'd asked is that I accept the power to override her parents if they did anything I knew she'd hate. So I kept hanging out with them, being a mate rather than a dad. But the months wore on and they kept getting quieter. I knew things weren't right, but I couldn't nail it.

'And then one night I went around and they'd just brought their school reports home. School reports for kids. Henry was in infant class. You know the kind of report? *Henry: A+ for finger painting, A+ for tying shoelaces.* But Kit, who was two years older, had a slightly more precise report. *Kit is struggling a little. B- for reading.* The housekeeper let me in, and I could hear a row. I walked into the study and Claire's dad had them lined up, waving reports in his hand and blasting Kit. Almost spitting into his face. *"You let a five-year-old beat you. What are you? A pansy? You take after your no-good father. No grandchild of mine lets a five-year-old beat him, you good-for-nothing little…"'*

He fell silent, remembering the sick horror as he'd realised what had to be done. By him.

Friday nights were the least of it.

'They'd been authoritarian with Claire in her childhood,' he said, speaking almost to himself rather than Rachel. 'That's why she worried, but she knew they loved her, and she thought they loved her boys. But when she died... I think their grief has left them a little unhinged. It doesn't help that the boys all have Steve's red hair—they look like him. I'm no psychologist but it seems there's a part of them that can't bear the boys to be...not Claire? I looked at them that night and saw no softness, only determination that the boys fall into line. And the things the old man said when I tried to defend them... It was almost like he was blaming the boys for her death.'

'So you stepped in.'

'It couldn't continue,' he said heavily. 'They were determined to keep control, but I had the authority and I had them out of the house almost before they realised what I was doing. That night we sat up and watched dumb movies and ate junk food and didn't talk about report cards once. I had a one-bedroom hospital apartment. They slept on the floor and I didn't hear a complaint. I was then hit by a battalion of lawyers, plus Charles and Marjorie practically hounding the boys. Losing control was unthinkable. They were at the school gates, demanding the boys come home with them. They were calling me everything under the sun...'

He broke off. It was too much to recall—his struggle to explain that if they'd just back off, give the boys a bit of space, let them be kids, then things could work. His realisation that it wasn't going to happen. The acceptance that his life had to change.

'In the end I knew it'd never work,' he said. 'I started looking for another apartment, but when the old man hired a couple of thugs to collect the kids from school, thugs who were prepared to see me off with force, I just...' He stopped, closed his eyes, then forced himself to go on. 'I quit at the hospital. I knew this place was here. My grandparents built this house and it still belonged to me. I knew Shallow Bay could use any doctor they could get, so here we are.'

'Safe,' she said softly, almost a whisper.

'Not quite safe,' he told her. 'Charles and Marjorie have applied for custody. Claire's death might have left them a little unhinged, but as blood relatives they have a case and they're powerful. They say their daughter was mentally unfit when she signed the adoption papers. I'm single, I work long hours, I need to use childminders. Regardless, my lawyers tell me they have little chance unless they can prove I'm an unfit parent. Which is why it's important they don't find out about Kit's hand.'

'That was hardly your fault.'

'They won't see it like that.' He was confronting his worries now. There was something about this place, this woman…

No. It was simply that there'd been no one to talk to for so long. With Rachel… She seemed dispassionate, almost like a psychoanalyst, letting him go where he willed with no judgement. It was a weird sensation and he wasn't sure why he was reacting to it, but the need to talk was almost overpowering.

'Marcus is too serious,' he told her. 'He blames himself for Kit's hand. He blames himself for everything. When his grandfather looked like he was about to hit Kit, Marcus shoved himself in between. 'Hit me instead,' he was yelling. 'My report's worse.' Only of course it wasn't, and afterwards he even asked me if he should try and fail a few tests at school to make Kit feel better.

'Henry's littler, less complicated, but he has nightmares. I carry a radio in my pocket. If I'm called out at night Rose listens in and so do I. It's not great, not even totally safe, but it's the best I can do when I've been on call twenty-four-seven. So Rose and I hear the minute he wakes and it's a race to see who can get there first. Because of what I do, it's usually Rose but he holds himself rigid, sweating, until I get there.'

He paused. Was he waiting for her to comment? She didn't, just watched him, waiting for him to continue.

He wasn't even sure if she was interested but… What was it with this woman?

'And then Kit,' he said. 'Left alone… Well, his cut hand is the least of it. Sometimes he wants me to be there for him, but not often. Tonight he hugged me, but that's unusual. There's a part of him that actively tries to drive me away. It's like he's testing me, expecting me to leave like his parents, thinking the sooner it happens the sooner he'll get it over with. So how do I break through that?'

Once again she didn't answer. He finished his beer and stared at the empty bottle. Rachel gazed out over the ocean, watching the water turn a soft tangerine with the reflections of the setting sun. Somehow she seemed to be melting into herself, folding, tucking herself neatly away—to where no one could touch her? To where personal stories didn't hurt?

'Your parents?' she said, almost absently, and why should he answer that? But he did.

'Loving but absent,' he told her. 'Overseas. Caught up in their careers. These kids have nothing to do with them.' And for the life of him he couldn't keep his voice from sounding bleak.

He heard it and he flinched. He sounded needy. Him. He didn't need anyone.

Except he did need help for the boys, and he didn't know where to begin to ask.

The silence stretched. It seemed they were both staring into the future. Or the past?

What was her story? She wasn't saying.

'Kids are resilient,' she said at last, breaking the spell. She stood up and brushed the sand from her legs. 'You're doing the best you can. They'll survive.'

'Like you survived?'

She froze at that. 'I don't know what you mean.'

'Cigarette burns,' he said neutrally. 'Unmistakable once you've treated them.'

'And none of your business.'

'So I spill my all to you…'

'And I don't spill back.' She shrugged. 'You've been generous but one low-alcohol beer does not a contract make. I need to go home. I'm hungry.'

'We have hamburgers at my place.'

A glimmer of humour returned and her lips twitched. 'So you're asking…what? You'll give me a hamburger in return for me being third man in Dragon Doom or whatever?'

'Hey, I never said…'

'You didn't need to. I guessed. So, no, thank you.' The smile was still there. 'I have home-made lasagne, which will heat while I'm in the shower. Then I have a date with a movie. So while Dragons are tempting, sorry. Bye.'

Home-made lasagne. A movie. Maybe a bottle of wine. It was like a siren's song and it was so far out of his list of possibilities that he couldn't even think about it.

He rose as well, aware of emptiness. Of leaving without her.

And then his phone vibrated.

He closed his eyes for a second, but this was almost inevitable, a call on Friday night. Why not?

He snagged his phone from his pocket. Unknown number. Local.

Work.

'Dr Lavery.'

'Doc? It's Col Hunter here.'

His phone was set on loudspeaker—he set it every night as he left work because of the times he had to listen over the racket the kids were making. Col's voice was deep and booming, disturbing the silence of the beach, but Tom left it on loud. After all, Rachel was a colleague.

'How can I help you?' Already he knew there was trouble. Underlying Col's booming voice he could hear pain.

'I fell over the pig,' Col managed. 'Got her in, got her fed, thought she had her snout in the trough and then suddenly she's shoving her way between me and the gate, trying to get out again. It's me 'taters she wants, Doc. Spent all bloody summer trying to get a decent crop. She's been watching me water 'em, fertilise 'em and now she wants 'em. Dutch Creams—the best 'taters you can get—and Mavis isn't bloody having 'em.'

'You've hurt yourself.' Cut to the chase, Col.

'It's me hip,' Col said. 'Had to crawl inside. Managed to get the sty gate shut though, so I won. Bloody pig.'

Tom almost grinned but didn't. Col was in his eighties and had suffered osteoarthritis for years. A fall, a damaged hip…

'Is there anyone with you?' he asked.

'You know Pat left me years ago,' Col managed. '"The pigs or me", she said and off she went with some life insurance fella. Kids are both in Melbourne. Doc, I can't seem to pull meself up. Reckon I need you, mate.'

'I reckon you do, too,' Tom told him. 'Your place is right up the top of Bellbird Ridge, right?'

'You got it. I remember you coming here with your grandpa when you were a little fella.'

'I'm coming again now,' Tom told him. 'It's probably best if you don't move until I get there.'

'You don't need to tell me that, Doc,' Col said. 'Passed out twice getting to the phone. Not risking that again. But…could you make it fast?'

'I'll make it fast,' Tom said. 'Grit your teeth, mate. I'm on my way.'

'I'll come with you.'

Where had that come from? She wasn't on call. She and Tom had sat down last Monday and defined their call duties. Tonight she was off—unless for emergencies.

This was hardly an emergency—an old man falling, possibly breaking a hip. Shallow Bay had an ambulance service of sorts, a vehicle equipped with stretchers, manned by volunteers trained in first aid. Tom could easily assess the damage and call her in if he needed her.

So why was she offering?

She had no idea. Maybe it was the slump of Tom's shoulders as he disconnected, a slump that spoke of regret.

Why, though? If he was back in Sydney she'd understand it. He'd be leaving his friends, his good time. Here, this call would mean little more than being home late for children who weren't his, children who were already being adequately cared for.

Except he did care. That was the part she was struggling with. Taking children from their grandparents when they were being obviously mistreated—that was understandable. He'd had no choice. But she'd met Rose. She knew that lady was a carer in a million. The boys were safe.

Tom had already confessed he didn't want to play their video game. This was the perfect excuse. So why the shoulder slump?

She didn't understand—but neither did she understand the imperative urge to help.

'Rachel, thanks, but I need to go now.' Tom was gathering the empty bottles, turning towards the track.

But she'd already hauled her dress over her swimsuit. She grabbed her beach bag and headed after him.

'I can cope,' he said as she fell in beside him. 'There's no need for you to come as well.'

'You have trained paramedics?'

'You know we don't, but...'

'But you're sure I'd be useless? Tom, I can get you home to the boys faster. I'd go by myself but I don't know the way and risk getting lost. Plus you've already told him you're coming and it sounds as if he knows you.'

'Everyone in Shallow Bay knows me,' he said. He hadn't eased his stride to accommodate her but she was keeping up.

'Because you came here as a child?'

'The people here loved my grandparents,' he said, talking briskly as he walked. 'My grandpa cared for everyone. My grandmother wasn't a doctor but she cared even more. They only had the one child, my dad, but that didn't stop their house being stuffed to the plimsoll line with people in need, stray dogs, pot plants Grandma was looking after for people in hospital—whatever. I was

supposed to have my own bedroom in the school holidays, but in the end I carved out a niche in the attic and
called it mine. I told Grandma if ever I found a needy
anything in there, animal, mineral or vegetable, I was
heading straight back to Sydney.'

'Did you mean it?'

'Of course I didn't.'

'And now you're right back in the chaos.'

'As you say,' he said briefly.

They'd reached his car, parked outside his cottage. He
paused. 'I'll duck in and tell Rose what's happening. But
there *is* no need for you to come.'

'You don't want help?'

He gave her an odd look, as if considering. Then he
nodded. 'Of course. Two doctors are always better than
one.'

'Which is why I'm here,' Rachel said. 'Instead of
where we'd both be happier, back in Sydney.'

'Okay, then,' he told her and tossed her his phone. 'Accepted. Can you find "ambulance" in Favourites? Mag-
gie coordinates the ambulance volunteers. Tell her we
need a car up at Col Hunter's place. Probable fracture.
No lights and sirens, though, take it easy.'

'Why not lights and sirens?' Surely there was a need
for haste.

'Because our volunteers love lights and sirens,' he said
grimly. 'And it's getting dark and the roads are narrow.
Once upon a time I lived and breathed adrenaline but not
any more. Shallow Bay might have two doctors now, Dr
Tilding, but let's not go asking for trouble.'

CHAPTER FIVE

ONE ELDERLY FARMER. One injured hip.

As soon as she saw him, Rachel knew she'd made the right call to accompany Tom. The old man's breathing was shallow and rapid, shock and pain taking their toll. She did the busy work, setting up an IV, organising oxygen, finding cushions and blankets to keep the old man as warm as possible until the ambulance arrived. Tom did the assessment—and the reassurance.

Tom was senior to her. She'd have been happy to take a back seat anyway, but Tom was offering more than medicine.

The old man reacted to his presence with humbling gratitude. 'Thank God you're here, Doc. I'll be right now.' She saw the absolute trust and she thought, that can't have developed solely in the time Tom's been a doctor here.

And then she thought of his grandfather, here for forty or more years. She'd read of his work when she'd accepted the scholarship. He'd been an old-fashioned family doctor, he and Tom's grandmother devoted enough to their community to set up the foundation that had sent her here.

And it seemed Tom had inherited that trust. He was Doc Lavery. Shallow Bay's own.

His grandparents would be proud of him, she thought. She watched his gentleness, his skill, and she thought Shallow Bay was blessed to have him.

But he didn't want to have Shallow Bay. He'd been forced to be here.

As she had—but Tom was here for life. Because of emotional ties.

She didn't have them. She didn't believe in them. They let you down, over and over.

Claire had trusted them absolutely when she'd placed her boys in Tom's care, she thought. The ties had obviously been bone-deep and he'd had no choice but to accept responsibility.

All this she thought as she worked in the background, preparing what Tom needed to make the old man comfortable. The ambulance arrived, two youngish volunteers, farmers by the look of them. Women who knew Col well. Who accepted orders willingly, yet who didn't have the training to do more than lift and carry and keep safe.

How alone had Tom been before she'd arrived?

How alone would he be when she left?

There'd be another scholarship holder to take her place, she thought. Another itinerant. Tom was here, where he didn't want to be. For ever.

They were supervising Col into the ambulance. The plan was for Tom to accompany Col to hospital while Rachel drove Tom's truck. Yeah, well, she was used to Moby Dick now. Her own little Petal was gleaming again, but Tom's SUV was far more sensible for the roads around here. He handed her the keys but took her arm, keeping her back for a moment, out of earshot of Col and his fussing attendants.

'Rachel, how do you feel about operating tonight?'

'Me?' She stared at him in surprise. 'Operate?'

'Sorry.' He gave a rueful shrug. 'Wrong wording. The operator would be me. You know I trained as an orthopaedic surgeon before my life went pear-shaped? When I came here I brought all the equipment I need. I've hardly used it. We're not set up for major surgery, but in this case… How do you feel about giving the anaesthetic while I operate?'

'Tonight?'

'It depends on the X-rays, of course,' he told her. 'But every indication is that he's fractured his hip. He's eighty-seven and he's frail, but he's mentally fine. He loves his farm. He'll want to get back here as soon as possible. You know the odds on morbidity after hip fracture. It depends so much on getting him back on his feet fast. If he's not upright in days, he may well never get back up. I'd like him to wake up tomorrow to Day One of recovery instead of Day One in Sydney, waiting for specialist assessment that may not happen until Monday. Cath from Ferndale will come if I need her, but she's a couple of hours' drive away. So…are you up for surgery?'

An anaesthetic for a shocked, elderly and frail man? She'd signed up for family medicine. This wasn't in her contract. She had boundaries.

But it seemed her boundaries had been crossed almost the moment she'd arrived in Shallow Bay. Tom was looking at her expectantly. The ambulance ladies were watching them both, wondering what the problem was.

One old man was lying in the ambulance and Tom was asking for her help.

So get a grip, she told herself. This was peanuts compared to what Tom had committed to this place. Besides, she'd done an anaesthetic rotation in her internship. She could manage.

'I read your CV,' Tom said. 'I know you have the skills.'

'You don't know how confident I am.'

'And you don't know how skilled I am. So…are we prepared to trust each other?'

And how was a woman to respond to that?

No! The question should be, How would a *doctor* respond? she reminded herself. This situation had nothing to do with her being a woman. It also had nothing to do with the way Tom was looking at her, those dark eyes watchful. Waiting to see if she'd help.

But when she nodded and said, 'Let's do it,' Tom nodded his relief. Those gorgeous eyes smiled at her and she was forced to smile back…

No! This was crazy. She was in the middle of a medical crisis. She had no business to be even conscious that a colleague was smiling at her.

But she was only human.

No, she thought as she beat back totally irrelevant thoughts. She was only a woman. And that woman needed to get herself back under control, fast.

He'd said he was surgically trained. He was so much more. What Rachel saw in the next couple of hours was a masterclass in surgical repair.

Col Hunter was a big man with big bones but those bones had been eroded by osteoarthritis. It wouldn't have taken a huge knock to break his femur. It did take a huge amount of skill to repair it, but Tom was up to it.

Rachel focused on the anaesthetic, which took concentration, especially as she was working from a basic skill set. Col was frail and the shock of the fall, plus what seemed to be the tail end of a bronchial infection, had her hauling up everything she'd ever learned and more.

But they had a full theatre complement. Roscoe had come in, as had a couple of other senior nurses. They'd obviously operated with Tom before, anticipating his needs, leaving the way clear for Rachel to concentrate solely on the job at hand.

She had a little space at the edges to watch what Tom was doing.

This man could make a fortune as an orthopaedic surgeon, she thought. What a waste that he was stuck here, leaving those skills unused.

Except he was using them tonight. He worked swiftly, and Rachel thought Col couldn't have had better treatment if he'd been brought into a major city hospital.

As it was, he'd wake in a hospital he knew, surrounded by people he knew. With Tom's skill, he'd have a functional hip, far stronger than it'd been before the fall.

There was talk in the theatre, the banter that always went on between medical staff who knew each other well, but Rachel didn't contribute. Her silence was respected, though. Maybe the nurses as well as Tom knew how much she needed to focus on what she was doing.

Maybe they didn't notice that she was focusing just a little bit on Tom himself.

On his fierce concentration. On his skills. On the way he responded to the nurses around him.

Roscoe was anxious. He shouldn't be here—his wife's baby was overdue—but there was no way he'd have delegated tonight's surgery to someone junior. Tom chatted to Roscoe as he worked, including him, making him maybe even busier than he needed to be. It didn't deflect Tom's focus on the work at hand, but Rachel realised it was lessening the look of strain she'd been seeing on Roscoe's face for the last few days.

At last it was over. Col was being wheeled off to the ward next to the nurses' station. He'd be watched like a hawk all night, surrounded…by his own?

That was what it felt like, Rachel thought. These people…this community… It was almost family.

Left to herself, she headed into the scrub room, stripped off her gown and tossed it into the bin. And as she did she was aware of a sense of desolation.

A feeling she'd had often. A feeling of being on the outside looking in.

'Well done.' Tom had stayed behind in Theatre to write up orders. He entered the scrub room now and started stripping off himself. 'You're a real pro, Dr Tilding.'

'Not bad yourself, Dr Lavery. You really are an orthopod.'

'That's a past life,' he told her curtly and the way he propelled his gown into the bin had a bit more force than necessary. 'I'll operate in emergencies but not from choice. I'm now a family doctor.'

'I'm sorry.'

Rid of their theatre gear, they walked outside together. Rose had offered to stay and sleep with the boys for the night, but Tom would want to get home, Rachel thought. *She* wanted to get home. The image of community— family—was weirdly unsettling. She needed to be in her own cottage, with the door firmly shut, with the world safely at bay.

What was unsettling her wasn't just about medicine,

she thought. In fact it was hardly about medicine at all. It was Tom greeting her on the beach, sitting beside her, telling her how his life had changed. Exposing his past. It was Tom seeing her scars and knowing immediately what had caused them. There'd be questions in his mind that she wasn't prepared to answer, but he hadn't pushed and somehow that consideration had pushed her even further out of her comfort zone.

For it was Tom himself who disturbed her. Tom, who'd given up his life in Sydney, his career as a surgeon, everything he most valued, to bring three kids somewhere they could be safe.

It was Tom of the crinkly dark eyes, with the smile that reached…something that hadn't been touched for a very long time.

Had it ever been touched?

They were out on the veranda now. It was a five-minute walk down to the cottages but Moby Dick was in the car park. 'Well done us,' Tom said softly into the stillness of the night. 'Thank you, Rachel. You did great. You want a ride home?'

'You did great yourself, and I can walk.'

'Then beware drop bears.'

Drop bears. The imaginary animal used by Aussies to tease tourists, by mums and dads to make kids go 'ooh' and cling tight as they walked under tall trees. She managed a smile. Drop bears weren't real.

But this night didn't feel real. For some reason Tom had her so… What was the word for it? She didn't have a clue. And she had no idea why she was feeling…what she was feeling.

'I hear the antigowobblers are bad at this time of year too,' she managed.

'The jabberwockies are pretty scary as well,' he responded promptly. 'I haven't seen one for a while, but you can't be too careful.'

'Yeah, but I'll walk anyway.'

'Rachel, I won't hurt you.'

Why had he said that? She stilled while the ramifications of his words hit home.

'Why…why would I think you'd hurt me?'

'Because people have hurt you in the past. And it's still with you.'

'That was a long time ago,' she managed.

'But scars like that…'

'I don't want to talk about it.'

'There's no need to talk about it. Just know that I won't hurt you.'

'Th…thank you.'

'You were awesome tonight,' he said softly now, as if he knew that he'd scared her. 'You being here… The fact that we operated so fast… It may well make the difference as to whether Col walks again.'

'He should.'

'Thanks to both of us. We're a team.'

A team. She and Tom.

The concept was purely medical, she thought, but the way she felt… It was so much more.

But she said nothing.

Silence.

She should walk away, but her feet didn't seem to want to.

Nothing about her wanted to.

This was the back entrance to the hospital, dimly lit. The main entrance was on the town side. This veranda overlooked the ocean. Below them, they could see the shape of their cottages in the moonlight, with the lights on in Tom's living room. They could see the ribbons of moonlight beyond, rippling over the surface of the sea.

The silence seemed to be growing. There was nothing but the sound of the surf on the beach below.

There was nothing but each other.

A man and a woman.

And, looking at his face, she suddenly saw a side of Tom she'd never seen before. He was gazing down at the lights of his cottage and for a fleeting moment she saw something akin to panic. It was gone in an instant but she knew she'd seen it—and she knew what it was.

Behind him, in the hospital, was a small boy who was his responsibility, and waiting for him at home were two more.

As well as that, the hospital was full of the same responsibilities. Rachel was under no illusions as to why Tom's grandfather had set up her scholarship. It was to force doctors to come here. This place was so remote, so far from any services, so far from the friends, the life Tom knew...

And yet he'd taken it on and would continue to look after them all. Until the boys were grown, his promise to his friend was unbreakable.

The look was gone now, hidden under the veneer of strength and commitment. He'd head back to his cottage, say goodnight to Rose, check on the children, go to bed.

But the memory of that look stayed with her, somehow searing itself into her mind.

He was trapped.

And, almost unbidden, before she even knew what she intended, she reached out and touched Tom's face.

A feather touch. A touch of comfort? A touch to say she understood that look?

How could she have understood it—and what on earth possessed her to make her reach out? She'd never done such a thing. But she didn't pull back. Amazingly, the touch felt right.

She was a woman with boundaries, a woman who knew to keep herself to herself, and this was a man who seemingly had no boundaries. A man who collected strays and changed his life because of them. Who accepted that he was trapped for ever—because of a simple promise to a friend.

Was it wonder that made her reach out—as if touching a being from another world?

But it wasn't strangeness she was feeling. It was Tom's face. A face of strength. Of endurance.

Her fingers traced his cheekbones, feeling the stubble from a long day without a razor. Feeling his warmth. His familiarity? For it was as if she knew him. It was as if something inside her was responding to something she didn't understand. Something that maybe should have frightened her, and yet somehow didn't.

His hand raised and caught her fingers. And held. The fear should have been there—but wasn't.

'You did amazingly tonight,' Tom told her, and his voice was somehow an extension of the silence of the night. 'We both did well. Well done us.'

Medicine, she thought, and she knew why he'd brought it back to that. They both needed to focus on work. It was what they did.

And then his hand tugged a little, pulling her body closer.

And with that came panic.

What was she doing here? Why had she touched? She

never touched. She was suddenly hauling her hand back as if it burned, and he let her go instantly.

'Don't,' she said and she was stammering. 'Please. I should never… I'd never…' She was fighting to make her voice sound practical, acerbic, moving on. She'd watched love affairs spring up almost unbidden in the hothouse of medical workplaces, and when had any good come of them? And for her? It'd be a disaster.

'What are you frightened of?' His voice was gentle. He was watching her, quietly questioning. There was no pressure. She could turn and leave.

She should turn and leave, but it was she who'd instigated the contact. He deserved some explanation.

'I don't think… It's not me who's frightened,' she told him, struggling to make sense of what had happened. 'I just thought… For a moment it looked like you were afraid.'

'What would I be afraid of?'

'Of loving,' she said simply. 'Of being stuck with the boys because you think you love them.'

'I do love them.'

'But you're afraid of being trapped.'

'Well, the time for that's long over,' he told her, but he was watching her face and she had the sensation that he wasn't focused on the boys. He was focused solely on her. 'I'm committed and there's nothing I can do about it.'

'Then you shouldn't have let yourself care in the first place,' she blurted out. Almost instantly she regretted it. Who was she to say such a thing? It was none of her business. No one was her business.

'How can you stop caring?' He was watching her with eyes that seemed to see far more than she wanted them to see. 'How did you stop caring, Rachel Tilding?'

'I didn't. It's just… I don't get involved.'

'And yet you looked after my boys in an emergency. You couldn't walk away.'

'I accept responsibility when I must. That's not caring.'

'It seems like it to me.'

'It's not.' She sounded panicked, she knew she did, but there was nothing she could do about it.

'Is caring something to be frightened of?'

'Yes!' And how exposed did that make her feel?

'It shouldn't be.' His hand came out and took hers again, and his fingers slid up her wrist. She'd unbuttoned her cuffs and rolled up her sleeves before donning scrubs. She'd rolled them down again but her cuffs had stayed unfastened.

Now his hand slid up her arm, still gently. She could pull away but it was as if she was paralysed. She just… let him.

The scars were all above her elbows. Never below. Her stepfather had learned that early—if he hurt her where it could be seen then trouble followed.

Tom's fingers found them. Traced them.

His eyes asked questions she knew he wouldn't voice.

She could step away. She could keep her boundaries in place. But something seemed to be breaking and she didn't have a clue what to do about it.

'Who?' he asked gently and the question hung.

Walk away or tell him? Suddenly there was no choice.

'My stepfather,' she said at last, because the need to tell him was suddenly almost overwhelming. 'Stepfathers aren't always like you. Burning me was less effort than hitting me.'

'Rachel…' It was an appalled whisper, a whisper that made her flinch.

'They're old scars,' she told him, speaking too fast, wanting to get it over with. 'And it stopped. When I was eleven the school sports uniform changed, to capped sleeves instead of longer ones. I stuck to the old uniform until my gym teacher felt sorry for me and gave me one out of lost property. She insisted I put it straight on. I can still remember her face. I remember being terrified because of all the things my stepfather told me would happen if anyone found out, but in the end it was my escape. The school called the police and I didn't have to see him any more. Then there were foster homes. Decent food and clothes. Space to study. All the things I craved.'

'Your mother?'

That was the hard bit, but somehow she made herself continue. 'She…she stayed loyal to him,' she told him and even now it felt appalling to say. 'Even when he went to prison. But it was fine. I was looked after. I'd escaped. Not like you.'

'You can't compare my situation to yours,' he told her, still horrified. 'Not in a million years.'

'I wouldn't,' she said. 'But I'd never be in your situation. I never let myself care. I do what I have to do.'

'Out of duty? Why don't I believe that?'

'It's true. I accept responsibility but I never take it further.'

'So when you touched me then?'

'I felt sorry for you.'

'Really? Was that all it was?'

'Yes!' Emotion was threatening to overwhelm her. She wrenched her arm back, snatching it against her chest as if it hurt.

'I won't hurt you,' he said.

'You keep saying that. I don't for a minute think you're capable of hurting me.'

'Do you equate the two?' he said almost casually. 'Caring and hurting?'

'You're not my shrink.'

'I wouldn't want to be your shrink. I'm a surgeon. I see what's inside people's bodies, not their heads. But hell, Rachel, what you've lived through…'

'Leave it,' she said roughly.

'And leave you? You've just spilled your secret to me. Will you go home and sleep tonight?'

'I've slept after far worse,' she snapped and then bit her lip. What was she doing, exposing herself like this?

'It's not bad, telling people what happened,' he said, his eyes still watchful. Still caring? 'What happened to you was bad. Talking to someone who could be a friend should surely be the opposite.'

'I don't…do friends.'

'Then maybe you should.'

His hands caught hers again. Two strong hands holding hers. Warmth holding cold. Steady holding shaking.

Man holding woman.

'You're a strong, vibrant woman,' he said firmly now, as if he needed to convince her. 'You've come through a war and out the other side, and you need to get on with life. But life involves sharing. Caring. It involves warmth, passion, all the things you're most scared of.'

'I'm not scared.'

'Really?'

And then there was silence. A long silence. It stretched into the night, not peaceful but somehow not threatening either. It was a moment where the world seemed as if it could shift either way—it couldn't decide.

And then Tom said, 'I'd like to kiss you.'

Well, there was the signal to run. There was the signal to get off the veranda fast, to retreat to her cottage and bolt the door behind her.

But his hands still held. Gently, though. She could pull away if she wanted.

But his eyes held her too, and that was a link she couldn't break. She was gazing up at him in the moonlight, at this charismatic man, at warmth, compassion, strength, empathy.

Caring.

Everything she'd been afraid of for ever was right here and she couldn't break away.

She simply stood while his statement hung.

I'd like to kiss you.

She had to say no, but the word wouldn't come. His eyes held and held and held. The stillness of the night. The peace. The feel of this man's hands.

'Yes, please,' she heard herself whisper and then he kissed her, and the night melted into oblivion.

What was he doing?

This was a colleague, a woman he'd met only one week before. More, she was damaged, scarred, not only physically but mentally. That meant she was needy and heaven keep him from more need. He should be quietly sympathetic, empathetic even. He should talk to her about counselling alternatives—and then he should step away.

Instead he was drawing her close. Her breasts were

moulding against his chest. He was tilting her chin—
and he was kissing her.

And the moment his mouth met hers…

Something.

Some indefinable something. Some connection he
hadn't felt in all the years he'd dated.

Maybe it was the night, the stillness, the calm, the
beauty of the scene around them. Maybe it was the way
he felt about her, the sense that she'd been so badly hurt.
Maybe it was that he felt appalled, horrified for her.

But maybe it was none of those things. Maybe it was
the way her mouth seemed to melt against his. Maybe it
was the curve of her body. Maybe it was the tiny murmur she gave as his mouth touched hers.

Maybe it was because he felt her surrender.

And it was surrender. He'd been watching her, talking
to her, feeling his way, and he'd sensed fear. He'd seen
boundaries she'd never crossed. But like a wild kitten
enticed by food, by whispers, by warmth, he'd seen the
temptation to trust. He'd seen her let slip boundary after
boundary as she'd spoken to him.

And then she'd whispered acquiescence to this kiss
and the last of the boundaries had fallen away and she
was in his arms.

Not needy though. No longer needy. She was kissing him right back. Her hands went to the small of his
back, holding him, claiming him as much as her mouth
was claiming his.

And the kiss…

It was as if a spark had ignited a force he'd never expected, a force that held and held and held.

This woman. This night.

There were no barriers now. There was no room for

backgrounds, for discussion of past wounds, of current responsibilities. Everything had fallen away in the face of this wonder.

For that was it—wonder. This kiss was almost one of primeval desire. They were two people who'd forgotten what they needed most but had suddenly found it. Two people who weren't letting go.

Neither could break away. Why should they? This was time out of frame, a wondrous moment snatched almost from life. The feel of her…the taste of her…

How could someone he'd known so briefly feel so right in his arms? How could her surrender feel so right?

It was as if his world was changing yet again, a seismic shift, a shift where his heart felt it could stretch again.

And with that thought…

'Doc? You still out there?'

It was a voice from behind the screen door. Roscoe.

'I have Col's daughter on the phone from Sydney,' Roscoe was calling. Heaven knew whether he'd seen what they were doing, but his voice sounded prosaic. Matter-of-fact. 'We left a message earlier when we couldn't raise her, but she's called back now. She wants to speak to you. If you aren't busy.'

And in those last four words Tom heard a trace of humour. So they'd been sprung. Great; it'd be all over the hospital—all over the town—by the morning.

'Roscoe…' He pulled reluctantly back from Rachel. His hands still held hers. He was still half in wonder.

'Shall I tell her you're busy?' Roscoe boomed, laughter surfacing.

'Go,' Rachel said, and finally she tugged her hands

from his. 'I… I need to go myself. Goodnight, Tom and…thank you.'

And before he could stop her she'd turned and headed down the steps, onto the track to the cottages. He let her go—there was no choice—but he stood and watched as she made her way into the dark.

'She'll be all right by herself,' Roscoe said as finally he turned to go back inside. 'She's a woman who's used to coping alone.'

How much had Roscoe seen?

'You need to get home yourself,' he said abruptly. 'If that baby of yours doesn't arrive in the next couple of days…'

'Yeah, change the subject, why don't you?' Roscoe said, smiling. 'But you're right. Moving on. It's what we all have to do.'

What had she done?

Kissed Tom Lavery, that was what she'd done. Started an affair with a man who was technically her boss? Who was lumbered with three children he didn't want? Which was total anathema to her, after everything she'd taught herself.

She walked steadily down the track to her cottage, achingly aware of the man she'd left behind. It was all she could do not to run.

One kiss does not make an affair. She told herself that, and then, when she was sure she was out of earshot, she said it out loud. 'It was a kiss, nothing more. Heaven knows how many women he's kissed.'

But her…

She'd kissed—or been kissed—before this. Of course she had, but every time she'd pulled away. She didn't want the complications that went with any type of relationship.

But tonight she'd almost invited the kiss. He hadn't pushed himself on her. He'd asked and she'd agreed.

Because she'd wanted.

And that was what scared her most. She, Rachel Tilding, had suddenly wanted more than anything in the world to be kissed by Tom Lavery. And when that kiss had happened...

Her fingers crept to her lips. They felt full, swollen, the taste of the kiss still with her.

She wanted more?

'No!' she said out loud too, as the ramifications of what she'd done hit home. She was stuck in this place, as was Tom. She had no doubt that if he'd been back in Sydney he wouldn't have looked twice at the likes of her.

Had he kissed her because he felt sorry for her?

She reached her cottage, stepped inside, locked the door behind her and then leaned against it.

She was suddenly shaking.

'Get over it,' she told herself. Who needed a shrink when she had her own inner voice telling her what was sensible, telling her what she had to do to cope? 'It was just a kiss. Don't make a big deal of it. If you don't make a fuss, neither will he. Move on. Stay separate. To act like it was anything else would be...needy.'

And she wasn't needy. She was never needy.

But still she leaned on the door until the shakes subsided. Until she had herself back together.

Until she knew quite definitely that such a thing would—could—never be repeated. Her boundaries were up again, and they needed reinforcement.

So...

She made herself a mug of tea and headed to the internet, downloading a pdf of the latest research into post-polio syndrome. One of the elderly farmers she'd seen in clinic today showed every sign and she needed to research.

Work. Study. Medicine. It was her escape, her salvation—the only thing that mattered.

Tonight had changed nothing.

CHAPTER SIX

TOM HADN'T EVEN made it to bed before the phone rang again. This time it was Roscoe, and his voice was about an octave higher than his normal gruffness.

'It's Lizzy.' Tom could hear his voice shaking. 'I've just come home and she's in full labour. She didn't want to worry us when she knew we were concerned about Col, but contractions are five minutes apart. Hell, Doc… We're coming in.'

He didn't bother to wake the sleeping Rose or the boys, just headed back to the hospital, praying things would go okay.

He hated delivering babies here. Without specialist backup, with so far to travel to the nearest paediatric services, he felt incredibly alone. Shallow Bay mums were advised to stay in Ferndale or go to Melbourne or Sydney a few weeks before their due date, but they hardly ever did. The impossibility of leaving families, of paying for accommodation… They preferred to put their faith in Tom.

Which made him feel sick with responsibility. Births meant two patients, not one, and if things went pear-shaped one doctor wasn't enough. At least he had Rachel now, and he headed back to the hospital praying he wouldn't need her.

Roscoe Junior, however, gave no cause for grief. He arrived just before dawn, informing the entire hospital of his displeasure at his eviction. Exhausted, aching for sleep, Tom walked back outside to face the morning.

Rachel was walking up the track towards him.

He saw her hesitate for a moment, pausing as if regrouping. And then she deliberately start walking again. A new day, a new attitude?

It didn't feel like a new day, and the memory of that kiss was still with him.

'Good morning,' she said formally, and he answered her in kind.

'Good morning to you too.' Their greetings somehow seemed like the set-up between fencers as they prepared to duel. *En garde*.

'Trouble?' she asked as she reached the veranda. She'd be taking in the fact that he looked like a train wreck. He needed a shower, clean clothes, sleep. But Rachel's tone was professionally interested, nothing more. The emotion of the night before was obviously in the past.

'Roscoe has a son,' he told her. 'Born an hour ago. Still protesting. All's well.'

'That's great. I'll check on them both at ward round.' She smiled but it wasn't the smile he remembered.

She was back to distant.

'They're okay. No stitches. A straightforward birth, thank God. Lizzy's tired but happy. Roscoe's dazed and proud fit to burst. Bub's great. There's not a lot for us to do.'

'Sleep for you,' she said. 'I'll take over.'

'If you would. I need to relieve Rose and let her go

home. I've promised Kit he can come home today. I'll bring the boys up with me to collect him later.'

'And then spend the rest of the day supervising?' Her brow creased. 'It's Saturday. No school. No childminder. No sleep?'

'I can cope without it.'

'We do what we have to do,' she said enigmatically. And then she took a step back and looked him over, making no pretence that she wasn't doing a full assessment. 'You look like something the cat dragged in.'

'Thanks,' he said dryly. 'Is that a medical diagnosis for free?'

'Yes and you're welcome. You need to do something about it.'

'So what should I take, Dr Tilding? Any free advice while you're at it?'

'Rest.'

'Like that's going to happen.'

She chewed her lip in the way he was starting to recognise. As if she was weighing up options. 'If you fall over you're no use to anyone.'

'I've had these boys for a year and I haven't fallen over yet.'

'That's like jumping from a high-rise and shouting "I'm okay so far" on the way down.'

He sighed. 'Rachel, there's not a thing I can do about it. At least you're here now. The weeks since your predecessor left have been hell, but knowing you can share the medical stuff is wonderful.'

'That's what I'm paid for,' she said bluntly, but she was still looking at him with doctor's eyes. Eyes that were seeking information. Eyes that fronted a medical mind, used to diagnosing and making decisions based on facts.

'Right,' she said. 'Here's your treatment regime.'

'You're giving me a treatment regime?'

'I am, and I'm not even charging you for it. And before you get any ideas that this is a personal favour—or even anything to do with last night, which it assuredly isn't…' She hesitated and bit her lip. 'Tom…you know last night was an aberration.'

'An aberration?'

'That's right. Not to be repeated. I'm treating it as a warning and so should you. This morning I've woken up perky and ready to move on.'

'Perky?' he said faintly. He looked at her, in her black trousers and long-sleeved shirt, her curls tugged tightly back with a simple band, her businesslike pumps—and he thought *perky* wasn't the word he'd use for her. And then he thought…*Perky's under there somewhere.*

Maybe that was the Rachel he'd kissed last night.

But that Rachel wasn't here now. This Rachel was all business.

'You know darned well that if you're exhausted you make mistakes,' she told him. 'And as your colleague I'd be sharing them. So, because of that, and only because of that, I'm offering to take the boys this afternoon. Only if I'm not caught up here, though,' she added hastily. 'We both know there are no guarantees in this business. But it's Saturday so there's no clinic. I'll do a ward round and there are two house calls outstanding but after that I should be free. So the plan is that as soon as I'm available I'll take the boys to the beach while you sleep. Kit should be right for that, no?'

'He should,' he agreed faintly. 'The stitches are out.
Salt water might even help.'

'There you go then. Sorted. You do the kids' morning shift and I'll be there as soon as I can.'

'Rachel…'

'Yes?'

He had to say it. 'The boys… They think you're a bit
severe. They might not want to come with you.'

That set her back a bit. For a moment he saw a trace
of grimness in the set of her mouth, but she moved on
briskly. 'Are you giving them a choice? I can handle kids.
Tell them to expect sausage rolls and chocolate cakes.'

'Sausage rolls and chocolate cakes…' he said faintly,
thinking about timelines. 'How…?'

'I'll make mini microwave chocolate cakes while I
have lunch,' she told him. 'I have pastry in the freezer.
I can buy meat on the way home from house calls and
sausage rolls are a snap. My splinter skill, Dr Lavery, is
cooking. And, severe or not, I'm not into scaring small
boys. Yes, I was forceful while I stayed with them, but
the house was a muddle and they had Rose to do the
warm and cuddly. I was there to work. So you can tell
them that it's me and the beach or me glaring them into
silence in your living room while you sleep. So, Dr Lavery…agreed?'

To say he was disconcerted would be an understatement. Here, when he'd least expected it, was another of
her extraordinary offers.

She'd said she wasn't cuddly and she wasn't. She
was prickly, defensive, damaged. And yet it wasn't exhaustion that had impelled her to touch him last night.
It wasn't exhaustion that had made her want to melt
into him.

She'd stepped in today for purely practical purposes. He accepted that. He was so weary he was at the point where any medical decisions he made would be suspect and, as his colleague, Rachel's offer could be seen as purely practical.

And yet... He looked at her, a neat, compact, efficient, self-contained—and cute—package, and he thought of all the effort that had gone into putting that package together. He'd read her scholarship application. She'd left school at fifteen with no support, working while studying online. How she'd made the grades for medical school was a miracle all on its own. And suddenly there were questions all over the place.

And, before he knew what he was about, he asked, 'Rachel, why did you decide to be a doctor? It must have been so hard. What made you want it so much?'

The question was totally divergent from what they'd been talking about. He'd taken them both aback. 'What's that got to do with anything?' she demanded, and he struggled to find an answer.

'Nothing,' he told her at last. 'I just... Well, I want to know.'

For a moment he thought she'd brush him off, push the question aside, head into the hospital to the relative sanctuary of work. He was starting to know this woman now. Medicine was her haven. Would she retreat to that now?

But, strangely, her chin was tilting upward and her eyes met his in challenge. There was a moment's silence while she thought about it and then she answered. With a challenge.

'You first.'

What the...? How had that happened? One moment

they were saying good morning, the next moving to the intensely personal? And he'd started it.

So, how to answer?

That he'd been bright academically. That it had pleased the grandpa he'd loved. That he knew medicine would challenge him—and he also knew it made money? That he liked rescuing things, fixing things.

He could say all those things and they'd be true. But Rachel was watching, and he was suddenly aware that there was a deeper truth—and maybe she deserved it.

It was a truth that he'd hardly acknowledged to himself, but it was tucked away in the recesses of his memory and under Rachel's challenging gaze it suddenly resurfaced.

'When I was eight years old I was staying here with my grandparents for the school holidays,' he told her. 'Grandpa took me with him to do a house call, up on the ridge. The dad had had a tractor accident and was recuperating, so it was a simple house call for Grandpa and I was sent out to play with the kids. Then one of the littlies ran into the bush and met a brown snake. He stood on it and froze—and he was bitten. Not once. Several times. He collapsed almost straight away and by the time Grandpa got antivenom on board it was too late. He died within half an hour.'

'Oh, Tom…' Her eyes were still on his face. She didn't look horrified, though. She was a trained doctor. She'd have seen enough tragedies to stay calm in the face of such a story.

He was trying to match her calmness as he told her.

For some reason he'd never talked of it before. Why should he? After all this time he should hardly recall it himself. So why?

'It was the type of tragedy you and I have both seen and Grandpa was a doctor with years of experience,' he told her. 'And I scarcely knew what death was. Us kids were hustled out of the way by a neighbour who'd heard the screams and come over to help. I was aware that something big had happened, but I had no concept of its enormity. But I remember Grandpa's face as we drove home. Tight. Hard. He used to chat to me all the time but there was no chatting that day. And then, halfway home, he suddenly pulled over, cut the engine, put his head on the wheel and sobbed like a child. I remember him sitting there, his whole body shaking, and for me it was like the world was imploding. This was Grandpa. A rock. Grandpa, who could fix everything.'

'The best of us crack sometimes,' Rachel said neutrally, but softly, and he thought…hadn't her own adults let her down? And how much worse was the way they'd done it?

He wanted to make this about her—but he'd started the story and he had to finish.

'I don't know how long he cried,' he told her. 'It seemed an age but it was probably only minutes. Finally he pulled back and mopped up and turned to me. I have no idea how I remember it so well, but I can still hear him.

'"Tom, there are always tragedies in life. There are snakes and accidents and illnesses with no cure. We have to accept them. But Tom, if you can make a difference… If I'd had antivenom with me today instead of having to get someone to bring it up… If I'd had the skills… Tom, I don't know what you'll do with your life but today you saw what happens when the resources aren't there. No matter what you do—baker, banker, artist, whatever you decide to be—just think about what difference you can make. If you're a banker give loans to people who need them. Make bread that'll make people feel like they've had a feast. Paint paintings that'll make people smile. Because you never know. Make a difference, Tom, and that's all I'm going to say." And then we drove on and we never talked about it again.'

Silence. She was studying him, her face impassive. Still assessing? 'So medicine…'

'That day stayed with me,' he said simply. 'All the other reasons—knowledge, money, interest—they were the obvious reasons but there was always that day.'

Enough. What was he doing, talking like this, exposing himself? It must be weariness, he thought.

'Anyway, that's me. Now you.'

'Money?' she said quickly—too quickly. 'Security. All the things I never had as a child.'

'So why not law or commerce?'

Her chin tilted again, as if in defiance, and he thought, She's not going to tell me. The armour's back in place.

But she didn't look away. They stood facing each other in the weak morning sunlight, and it was as if there was some sort of invisible line between them. Or two lines.

He'd crossed his already, he thought. Would she?

'Safety was one thing,' she said. 'Plus…accepting responsibility.'

'Sorry?'

'That's what medicine means to me. Safety.'

'You mean you'll never be without a job? Never without an income?'

She shook her head, closing her eyes for a moment, and he thought, She's going to pull back.

'Fair's fair,' he told her. 'If you really don't want to tell me…'

And he watched her hesitate and then decide to let it out.

'Medicine did mean safety,' she said in a voice that was little more than a whisper. 'But not economic. Mine's a childhood memory too. My mother…she wasn't the best. Social welfare was called often when I was little. They came once after… Well, it'd been a bad time for Mum and I was obviously in a bit of a state. So they picked me up and took me to the hospital. I stayed there for a week. I remember doctors and nurses, staff who stayed when Mum came, who told her they'd be watching us, that if I came to them in that condition again, I'd be taken away and she could even go to jail. They were people who accepted responsibility for my welfare. And after that things got better.

'Then my stepfather arrived on the scene and it was awful again. The doctor who examined me when the teachers called the police… She did it again—she accepted responsibility for my safety. She moved heaven and earth to get my stepfather jailed. Me into foster care.

'It still wasn't over, though. There was always trouble. I told you Mum supported my stepfather when he went to jail? Well, she blamed me for that. She'd find me, yell invectives, make a scene. I was trouble for any foster parent who'd take me on. It messed with the other kids they had responsibility for, and I always had to move. In the end I fended for myself. But once… I cut my foot and it was infected. In the end I was scared enough to go to a medical clinic and the doctor there… She didn't just treat my foot. She gave me the number for crisis accommodation, the address of food vans. She let me use her phone. Then she said whenever I was in trouble to come to her, and she meant it. She accepted responsibility for me, and you can't begin to understand how that feels.' Her voice trailed off. 'And I thought then… To be like her… I couldn't, of course, but I'd get as close as I could.'

He was cringing inside. What she'd gone through… Yet there were still questions. 'Rachel, what she did… what all those people did…that's personal,' he said gently. 'You want to do radiology? Surely that's one of the most impersonal of medical careers.'

'So I'm not asking for miracles,' she said bluntly. 'I want to *be* a doctor. I want to accept responsibility for outcomes. But I can't *feel* like…well, like you seem to do. Accepting responsibility is one thing. Caring, though… Gut caring… That's something that's been wrung out of me long ago, if it ever existed in the first place.'

'So when you touched me last night…'

'An aberration,' she said briskly. 'A primeval urge, probably inherited from some dumb ancestor who owned a dog with all four legs and the ability to look cute. Anyway, that's that. Time to get on with the morning.'

Confidence ended. She gave a decisive nod and walked up the steps and past him. The steps were narrow and he felt the faint brush of her body as she passed.

He wanted to reach out.

No! This woman was complicated, needy, wounded. Surely the last thing he needed in his life was anything or anyone else who was complicated, needy or wounded.

And she didn't want or need to be rescued. She'd rescued herself.

Rose would be waiting to go home. Henry and Marcus would be waiting. He had to collect Kit. Hell, even

Tuffy would be needing a walk. Why had he ever agreed to take on a rescue dog? He had enough problems.

So back off, he told himself. Rachel Tilding had scars that must be bone-deep, but she had them in hand. He needed to take a lesson from her attitude to life. Rachel had accepted some of his responsibility and he was grateful. That didn't mean he needed to feel anything else.

Feeling…anything else…might make life very complicated indeed.

Her ward round was brisk, businesslike, professional, because that was how she needed to be. But she didn't feel like that inside. The time on the veranda had left her totally discombobulated.

How had they got so personal? Why had she told him so much about her past? It surely would have been enough to tell him she wanted the most secure profession she could find.

Except Tom had told her his story, and somehow she knew those feelings were usually protected as tightly as her own. Somehow his level of honesty had demanded the same of her.

And now she'd promised to take on three kids for the afternoon. When she'd planned to paint her bedroom.

She'd always planned her time off meticulously, knowing from past experience that idleness left room for depression. This weekend was for painting. Her little cottage was only her home for two years, but someone had once hung paintings in her bedroom, the marks were still there and it was annoying her.

Kids and beach instead?

It was okay. She needed to do ward rounds now and

then house calls and shopping and preparation. Then she needed to collect the boys and supervise.

Which was okay because, for some reason, she didn't want time to think, to remember Tom's face as he'd told her his story. And also…she didn't want to think of his face as she'd told hers.

The man cared.

She didn't want his care. She didn't want anyone's care and she didn't want to care back. Hadn't she learned the hard way where care led? She accepted responsibility when she needed to, because that was what good people did, but that was as far as it went.

So. Work. Now. She could hear Roscoe Junior starting a lusty protest. Maybe there was a problem. Had Tom had time for a full examination?

A baby crying as lustily as this could scarcely have problems, but Roscoe and Lizzy might be worried. A full medical examination could reassure them, and she would hardly have time to think about Tom when she was focused on a newborn and his anxious parents.

And that was what she needed. No time to remember the look of compassion on Tom's face. No time to think about the way his hand had reached out to her as she'd finished her story. And the way he'd looked down at his hand and then carefully pulled it back.

He'd made a decision, and she concurred.

There'd been enough emotion in both their pasts to last a lifetime. The last thing either of them needed was…to care.

CHAPTER SEVEN

WORK WAS NEVER a problem for Rachel. Work was Rachel Tilding's safe place, her time for blocking out the problems of the world.

She moved swiftly through the ward rounds and then made two house calls just as efficiently. Yes, Edith Carey wanted to show Rachel her entire collection of woolly caps she'd knitted for next winter's charity drive but admiring three—and agreeing on a cash donation for more wool—was enough.

Entertaining small boys and thus ensuring Tom had some sleep was a medical priority. She had no use for a colleague who was asleep on his feet. So she swept through the morning's work with speed. She did a fast shop, an even faster cook and then went to collect the boys.

Tom greeted her when she arrived, but his greeting was wary. As was her response. She backed away fast, and he seemed relieved to see her go.

'Enjoy yourselves,' he told the boys and his smile encompassed her, but briefly. 'Thank you.'

'Think nothing of it,' she told him, turning away as the boys zoomed out of the door and made a fast track to the beach. They might be wary of her but the beach was like a siren song, not to be resisted, even if it meant a childminder they were unsure of.

'I appreciate this,' Tom told her, but she didn't respond. She'd moved on to childminding mode and Tom was no longer on her radar.

Or he shouldn't be. He needed sleep. That was the only reason she was doing this. Medical need. Once the boys—and Tuffy—were heading down the track with her towards the beach, she closed her mental door firmly behind him.

She was here to do a job.

And, as far as jobs went, what followed was satisfactory, her planning more than paying off.

She sat on the beach and supervised while the boys and Tuffy whooped in the shallows, explored the rock pools, acted as if they hadn't seen the beach for years. They devoured her cupcakes and sausage rolls in two swoops on the picnic basket. They had little need of her, which was just the way she liked it.

And then, when things started to lag a little, when they started playing nearer to her, when she sensed they were starting to feel a bit needy, she produced her pièce de résistance.

During the time she'd been here, Shallow Bay's General Store had had a beach display in the window, buckets and spades, things kids could mess around with on the beach. Included were plastic figures seemingly welded onto miniature surf boards, characters about a hand-span high. The figures were labelled with names like Surfer Sue or Hang-Ten Ted or Rip-Tide Roger. She'd seen a family using these on the beach a few days back and this morning, on impulse, she'd bought three.

As backup. Which she now produced.

Their function was to be thrown out into the shallows. Internal weights righted them as soon as an incoming wave hit. The little figures then rode gamely in, standing tall. The boys pounced on them with glee as they hit the beach, then threw them out again, searching for waves that'd provide a longer ride. Great. She could retreat to caretaker mode again.

Tom could have a little more sleep.

Except he couldn't, because suddenly he was standing right behind her. She hadn't seen him approach. The boys were in the water and all her attention was on them.

'How's it going?' Tom asked and the unexpectedness of his voice made her jump. It was simply a startle reflex, she told herself. Her heart rate should settle again.

Except it didn't.

'F-fine,' she managed. 'You should be asleep.'

'I've had three hours. Luxury,' he told her. He was watching the boys, who hadn't noticed him. 'What are they doing?'

'Competing. Plastic surfers. Wipe-Out Wally. Tip-Off Tony. Grommet Georgie. They're trying to see whose goes furthest. Sadly, Henry's too little and Kit is one-handed. Marcus can throw further so he's winning by a country mile. They don't mind, though. They seem to be having fun.'

'You bought them plastic surfers?' he asked in a strange voice, still watching them.

'It gives me space to read.' She motioned to the medical journal beside her, which she'd been glancing at when the boys were out of the water. 'I know hardly anything about diseases animals can give you, and I'm thinking if I'm in the country for two years I should find out more. Did you know bats carry lyssavirus? They can give it to livestock, horses in particular, and it can be passed on. Symptoms…'

'I know the symptoms,' he told her. 'I read up on it when I got here. No case so far, touch wood.'

'When do you get time for reading?'

'When the boys are asleep. Or when my very kind neighbour takes them to the beach. Thank you for buying…what did you say?'

'Wipe-Out Wally. Tip-Off Tony. Grommet Georgie. They were the last on the shelf,' she admitted. 'Hang-Ten Ted and Surfer Sue must have been sold as soon as they arrived. These guys are the losers.'

'They're not losing now,' Tom said, watching the little figures wobbling in on the waves and the boys whooping encouragement as they neared the shore. 'You want to come down and see if we can beat Marcus?'

'They're busy,' she said shortly. 'They don't need us.'

'They might like us.'

'If you're taking over childminding, I'll read this.'

'Let's assume that one Shallow Bay doctor has a good grip on lyssavirus and the other now knows the basics. Surely that's enough?' He stooped and snagged a cupcake from her picnic basket. 'Wow, these are excellent. Well done, Dr Tilding. But work's done. Surely now it's time to have fun yourself. Let's see if we can outdo Marcus.'

'Why, when they're happy?' she asked. 'You should be sleeping some more, or reading, or taking the time to catch up on what needs doing.'

'But what needs doing most?' he asked gently. 'Sleeping, reading, working—or forging a relationship with kids who need it?'

She looked up at him curiously. His eyes were challenging. Why?

'Surely these kids don't need more relationships,' she said, feeling puzzled. What was he on about? Making the kids dependent on him? 'Haven't they already learned that? A father who's deserted them? A mother who's dead? Why try and build more bonds that'll eventually break and cause heartache?'

'Because I want to?' He turned to watch the boys again, talking almost to himself. 'Yeah, weird, but the thing is… I've learned to love these guys. Without love, this whole set-up would be a disaster but, as it is, I get home and they greet me with what's starting to be just normal kid acceptance of a parent. Like I'm their foundation. Isn't that the most important thing I can give them?'

'There's no such thing as foundations,' she said shortly. 'Soon enough they'll have to launch themselves out into a world that doesn't give a toss. They need to be resilient, not reliant on pseudo-foundations that can crumble at any moment.'

'Hey!' Tom said, sounding startled. He turned back and looked down at her. 'That sounds like Life for Beginners, when right now you should be immersed in Beach for Beginners. You're overthinking. Bottom line is that I might enjoy whipping Marcus in the surfing game. So… I'm inviting you to watch. Take off those sandals, Dr Tilding, and come paddle.'

'I don't need…'

'This isn't about need. This is about fun. No strings attached.'

'I don't want…'

'How do you know what you want unless you try?'

'Tom…'

'Just come,' he said gently and then, even more gently, 'I dare you.'

His eyes met hers, a challenge, a hint of laughter. A hint of understanding.

Oh, those eyes. She should run. She should…

'Fine,' she snapped before she could stop herself. She tugged off her sandals, almost angrily. 'But just for a few minutes. Now you're here to take over, I'll go home.'

'Back to work.'

'I need to finish this journal.'

'Lyssavirus waits for no man,' he said solemnly. 'But Rachel, I haven't seen a single bat in the entire time I've spent in Shallow Bay so I'm assuming we might be safe this afternoon. Come and play.'

Play. The idea was so foreign to her that it scared her.

'You might even want to take that shirt off,' he said and that was more than enough. She'd worn her swimsuit to the beach, with a shirt over the top. After all, she was here in care capacity. Beach lifesaver.

She could still be a beach lifesaver with this shirt on, though, and she could also stand in the shallows and watch the kids throwing plastic surfboards. Tom had seen her scars once. She had no intention of exposing them again.

'The boys probably won't even notice,' he told her, still watching her face. 'Or if they do then it's a ten-second explanation that they're old scars, the same as Kit will have on his hand, and it's done and dusted. Rachel, once they see them once, you won't have to hide any more.'

'But I need to hide.' It was out before she even thought about it. A sweeping statement. A statement that covered her whole life? The words hung in the stillness like an upraised sword, threatening. Stupid, stupid, stupid. What was it with this man that made her feel so exposed?

And his eyes were still on hers, holding. Understanding? How could he understand?

'Rachel, you don't need to do any such thing,' he said. 'You're far too beautiful to hide for the rest of your life. It's time to have fun.' And, before she knew what he was about, he reached down and took her hands, tugging her to her feet.

And once she stood, he didn't let go.

What was happening? She stood facing him, her hands in his, and the wash of vulnerability that hit her was so overwhelming she almost needed his hands to hold her up.

But she didn't need his hands. She didn't need anything. She had to leave.

'I need to go home,' she stammered.

'Liar,' he said. 'You weren't exactly packing up when I arrived.'

'That was because I thought you still needed to sleep. I thought you needed me to be here.'

'I still need you.'

'No!' It was almost panic. 'You don't.'

'I do,' he said placatingly. 'But not in a way that threatens you. I need you to see me whup Marcus in the…what did you say?…the Wipe-Out Wally, Tip-Off Tony and Grommet Georgie competition. I need an audience for my prowess and you're elected. You can keep your shirt on, Dr Tilding. This isn't scary. You might even enjoy yourself.'

'I don't…'

'Enjoy yourself. I can see that and that's why I'm asking. You prescribed me rest this afternoon because

I needed it so now I'm returning the favour. Fun, Dr Tilding. You might even have a go, too. Let's see if the boys will share.'

Share... For some reason the word sounded terrifying.

But he was tugging her down to the water and she didn't have a choice.

Tom was intent on having fun, and it seemed Rachel Tilding had to follow.

How seldom was it that Tom Lavery enjoyed himself nowadays? Really enjoyed himself, without the constant niggles of worry that continued to surface?

Answer—hardly ever.

He used to, he conceded. When Claire was well, he'd immersed himself in the role of best buddy to these kids. But when he'd collected the boys for an afternoon's soccer, she'd been waiting at home, ready to take over the moment he was called back to the hospital, or when the demands of his social life took over. He'd enjoyed his time with the boys with no strings. He'd been a joyful pseudo uncle, immersing himself in their fun and laughter, indulging as he liked and then handing them back at will.

He'd lost that, almost the moment Claire had collapsed at work. Sure, he still messed around with them, played with them, but there was always the overriding knowledge that the buck ended with him. If there was a problem, he couldn't mention it to Claire as he was handing them back. He had to fix it himself.

So now...he couldn't play until Claire rang— 'Tom, it's school tomorrow. Are you feeding them junk food? They'll be hyped and it'll be impossible to get them to sleep. Get them home.' Now, he had to judge for himself. Now, he had to face the consequences.

But not this afternoon.

Not with Rachel.

He was rested. He'd organised spaghetti for dinner. Who knew that deciding on what meal came next was such a drag? But, with the afternoon free, he'd sorted it before he'd gone to sleep. Now there was no pressure. The boys were delighted to see him. The competition to see which surfer dude would ride the longest was intense—and Rachel was right there to help.

She was a noticer. He'd had to practically haul her to the water's edge but, once she'd committed, once Henry had handed over Wipe-Out Wally and asked her—tentatively—if she could throw it for him—she'd waded right in. Tom's role turned out to be helping Kit throw Tip-Off Tony. Rachel's first toss went further than his. The boys whooped with excitement and the challenge was on.

But, no matter how much she was immersed in their fun, he saw Rachel constantly monitoring the kids, watching their expressions, seeing that no one was feeling left out. When Henry started to droop, she put Wipe-Out Wally into his hands, lifted him up and carted him waist-deep so he could throw it even further. Tom, who'd worn trousers to the beach—how dumb was that?—was stuck in the shallows. Kit and Marcus headed out too, so it was game on between the four of them, with Tom watching from the sidelines.

Rachel might be whooping with the kids, but still he saw that watchfulness. The care to shield Kit's hand, to edge around Kit so Marcus's wild swings didn't make contact.

He thought of her as she wanted to be, a radiologist

isolated in her technical world, not needing to interact, and he thought, What a waste.

She was lit up, vivacious, laughing, her reserve set aside, and she fascinated him. Her shirt was clinging to her body, hiding the scars. They were still there, but hidden.

Surface scars. He was watching her now, fascinated by the woman underneath.

She was gorgeous. Strong, feisty, caring…

Not caring. She wouldn't define it as such, he thought. She'd define it as accepting responsibility but as he watched her watching the boys, making sure each was safe and having fun, he thought she had the definition wrong. She just had to see it.

Could he show her what caring really was? Could he find the Rachel underneath the prickles? Underneath the wounds?

The memory of last night's kiss was suddenly all around him. He watched her hold Henry and jump a wave and he thought, She truly is beautiful.

But what was he thinking? A wave splashed up, foam spraying high, and the dose of cold water was what he needed.

He was standing behind three needy kids whose care was in his hands. Back on the shore was Tuffy, a rescue dog who'd been on death row when he and the boys had gone to the shelter to find a cute pup and brought home a three-legged, undernourished mutt instead.

Four rescued souls. But they helped each other, he thought. The boys had each other, and that made them far more independent than if he'd been landed with only one.

And Tuffy? Yes, he'd been rescued, but Tom had watched each of the boys form their own attachment to the little dog. Especially Henry, who had had nightmares ever since Claire's death. Tom's method of dealing with them was to wake him, hug him and then pop a very willing Tuffy into bed with him, and there were many times when each boy was comforted with individual Tuffy-cuddles.

There were still times when the combined needs of three small boys were too much for Tom, with or without Tuffy. But Tuffy had helped. Adding another 'rescue' had eased the situation, not added to it.

All this was floating as an uneasy, nebulous idea while he watched Rachel turn her back to a wave so Henry wouldn't get splashed, and then check immediately that the wave hadn't knocked either Marcus or Kit over.

If he could get through that shell…

He had to be kidding.

The reality of what his stupid, overtired mind was suggesting slammed home. Dad and three kids and dog, with mum to close the circle? Happy families?

This was nuts.

'Where's a wet fish when I need a good slap across the face?' he said out loud. No one heard him. They were having too much fun. All of them.

Family. Rachel?

He definitely needed a wet fish. A big one. He'd known her for a week. She was here out of necessity, not desire. She was scarred, in more ways than one. Her career path was set in stone and it surely didn't include Shallow Bay and a guy lumbered with three kids and a dog. And as for him…he had enough on his plate without being saddled with her baggage.

But the way she'd felt last night…

Then a wave, bigger than the rest, crested and broke straight over them. Marcus yelped and jumped and managed to avoid going under. Rachel jumped too, with Henry scooped up in front of her, but Kit wasn't so lucky. He was slapped hard and disappeared under the foam.

Tom was surging into the surf before he knew it, heading for where he'd last seen Kit, but Rachel was quicker than him. She still held Henry but with her other arm she scooped up Kit and tucked him firmly against her.

She was soaked. Her curls were clinging every which way. Her arms were full of kids. Marcus edged towards her and somehow she made contact with him too.

'Wipe-out,' she said matter-of-factly as Tom reached her and relieved her of Kit. 'I got us, even if we're all soggy. But look, guys, our little surfers are almost reaching the picnic basket. Look at them go!'

And she had their attention. The three little surfer figures, caught by the bigger than usual wave, were still cruising in, doing just what they were designed to do.

'They'll reach our picnic,' Henry breathed, forgetting about the wave. 'But mine'll get there first.'

'No, it's Kit's who's winning,' Rachel decreed as the wave surged over the dry sand. The tide was coming in fast and the picnic basket was definitely at risk. 'Tip-Off Tony's reached the furthest. In the interest of saving what's left of the cupcakes, I declare the competition officially closed. So Kit gets the pick of the medals I made specially. You want to see them?'

Of course they did. Of course Tom did.

'They're in a bag in the bottom of the picnic basket,' Rachel told them.

Trauma forgotten, Kit wriggled from Rachel's arms

and headed for shore. Tom watched with something akin to disbelief.

Was this the same woman who'd spent her first weekend here tidying to the point of compulsion? She was sodden. She'd lifted kids he could hardly believe she could carry. The water had helped, of course, but even so, the combined weight of Kit and Henry had probably been that of a decent adult. She was now watching them run up the beach, seemingly oblivious to the fact that water was still dripping down her face. That other waves were rolling in. That she was being buffeted by the sea.

Another wave hit and she rocked with it. He reached out to steady her but suddenly reality seemed to sink home. She'd been watching the kids and smiling but as his arm touched her she backed off, even as it meant she copped the full force of the wave.

'I'm okay,' she told him brusquely. 'But look at you. You're soaked.'

'You and me both.'

'Yeah, but I'm dressed for it.' She turned and looked out to sea at a boat chugging past, but he was aware that she was doing it to break contact between them. 'The fishing boat out there,' she said, and he heard a note of guilt. 'I saw it come past. I should have known it'd cause a surge.'

'It was hardly dangerous when you were so close.'

'I should have been closer. They were only out this deep because I was with them. I shouldn't have let them…'

'You were having fun,' he said gently. 'And so were they. They're safe and they're happy. That's all that matters.'

The boys were back at the basket now. Tom saw them raise three huge medallion-type circles on scarlet ribbon.

'They say "Super Surfer One", "Ace Surfer Two" and "Surfer Spectacular Three",' Kit shouted. 'I'm Super Surfer One!' He put the medallion round his neck and whooped off along the beach, his brothers whooping after.

'Where did you get those?' Tom asked faintly, watching three little boys, each with a medal thumping across his chest.

'A cornflake packet, Texta pen and gift wrap ribbon,' she said. 'I thought I might need something to finish the afternoon with. Organised R Us.'

'Where did you learn…?'

'I had a great foster mother,' she told him. 'Once. Briefly.'

'You're amazing.'

'No, I'm just organised. I think of all eventualities.'

'Because you've had to.'

'Let's not go there,' she told him brusquely, and then she shivered. 'I'm getting cold. Time to go home.'

Home.

Two homes.

One, Rachel's little cottage.

Two, his, where chaos reigned.

'We have spaghetti at our place,' he told her. 'Feel like sharing?'

'Why would I want to?'

It was a strange answer, harsh, an instinctive response rather than a thought-out one. She heard it and corrected herself almost instantly. 'Sorry. That wasn't very gracious. Thank you for the offer but no, I have work to do.'

'More lyssavirus study?'

'You never know when those bats will strike,' she

said, and he heard the effort she made to keep her voice light. 'So, moving on, Dr Lavery…' She shivered again.

Once again he had an almost irresistible urge to reach out to her, but he knew what her response would be. He could see it.

He could see fear.

This afternoon he'd needed her and she'd responded with generosity and thoughtfulness. Now, though, the need was over and she was withdrawing.

But he… He still needed?

That was a crazy thought.

She was moving on. He could only watch as she headed up the beach, grabbed a towel and started rubbing the water from her curls.

He wanted to help.

No, he didn't. If he started feeling like that, it'd make matters very messy.

Except he was feeling like that.

And suddenly Dr Tom Lavery was starting to see a plan. Right now it was no more than a thought bubble, but it wasn't to be rejected out of hand. There was time to see if it was feasible. Two years of time.

It did seem nuts, but the idea had lodged and wouldn't go away.

He'd need patience. He'd need luck and he'd need to be a lot surer than he was now. But the more he thought about it… He'd rescued three kids and a dog already. Was it even vaguely possible that one gorgeous, feisty, defensive woman could complete the picture for them all?

She headed back to her cottage, feeling weird.

She shouldn't. She'd acted according to need, which was her mantra. Do what was needed in order to survive.

In order to get on. In order to make the people around her be nice to her.

Hadn't she learned that the hard way? Placate and placate and placate, in the hope that conflict could be avoided.

There hadn't been the threat of conflict this afternoon, but there'd been concern about an exhausted colleague. She'd accepted responsibility. She'd sorted it. She should feel okay.

So why was she feeling weird? Why was she feeling as if she'd rather have stayed on the beach for a while, maybe headed back to have dinner with them? Be part of what they were?

That was the age-old yearning, she told herself. Rachel Tilding, on the outside looking in. Tom was somehow creating his version of happy families, and hadn't she learned the hard way what happened when you did that? Foster families had folded under the strain of having her associated baggage. Events had just…happened… leaving her more desolate than when she'd started.

Like her, Tom had acted according to need, she conceded, but he'd had no choice. He had to be where fate had placed him, but she had a choice. She'd made it years ago when she'd walked out of her last foster home and closed the door behind her.

She walked back into her little cottage and once again the door closed behind her.

Leaving Tom and his scary version of happy families firmly on the other side.

CHAPTER EIGHT

LIFE SETTLED DOWN to how it ought to be. How she'd expected it to be. She was working to the best of her ability before she returned to the nice anonymous city where she could get on with her future career.

There'd been a period after her afternoon with the boys where she'd felt unsettled. As if life was teetering towards something she couldn't control. The next time she'd seen Tom he'd smiled at her in a way she'd found disturbing, his eyes full of warmth and laughter. He'd told her the boys were looking forward to a repeat.

'Only in an emergency,' she'd said, more harshly than she'd intended.

'Why? Didn't you have fun?'

'They enjoyed themselves. That's all that matters.'

And that was that. She had no intention of taking anything further.

With one month down—only one year and eleven months to go!—she had reason to feel satisfied. She hadn't seen her first case of lyssavirus, but she was learning more about family medicine every day. Even the medical needs of the valley seemed to have settled. Col was back on his farm, on his beautifully repaired hip. Roscoe's son was thriving. Frances Ludeman had successfully delivered her sixth baby and declared that was the end of it.

'I need to feel like I have some control over my life,' she'd told Rachel. Rachel wondered how on earth having six children equated with control, but she could agree with the sentiment.

Control was what Rachel valued at all costs, and if she had to ignore the weird way Tom Lavery's smile made her feel...well, that was a small cost for keeping her world safe.

'You want to come to a birthday party?'

It was Monday morning. Rachel had just completed a ward round. Tom was due to run the clinic while Rachel was scheduled for vaccinations at the local library.

'We don't bring the babies into the clinic for vaccinations,' Tom had told her. 'There's an increased risk of catching bugs brought in by sickies, and besides, we don't want kids' first experience of clinic to be a needle. The library puts on morning tea. It has a toy section. Apart from a tiny prick, the parents enjoy it, and so do the kids.'

It wasn't as efficient, Rachel had thought as he'd told her, but then there was a lot that wasn't efficient in family medicine.

One year, eleven months...

'A birthday?' she said now, cautiously, and he smiled. Drat it, she wished he wouldn't. He was a colleague and why that smile twisted something that had no right to be twisted...

'Kit's birthday,' he told her. 'Saturday afternoon. Mostly in the garden if it's good weather, or in my living room—heaven help me—if it's not. Anybody who's anybody will be there—twelve kids at least—and Kit says he'd love you to come.'

'Kit scarcely knows me.'

'That's not true. He thinks of you as a friend.'

'How can I be a friend? I'm not.'

'Really?' He eyed her cautiously. 'So what makes a friend, Rachel Tilding?'

'I...'

'Is it someone who helps out in times of trouble?' He answered himself. 'That's a decent definition and you're a fine fit.'

'I do what I have to do,' she said a bit crossly, trying to avoid his gaze. Those eyes. 'I'll cover you medically, make sure Kit's party isn't interrupted.'

'Saturday afternoon's normally quiet. Can I tell Kit you'll come?'

He raised his brows in question, and his eyes still held hers. Smiling. There was understanding behind that smile, and it got to her.

He thought she was afraid?

She wasn't. Okay. A birthday party. Lots of people. She could pop in and out, get it out of the way.

'Fine,' she snapped, and then caught herself. There was no need to snap. This was a child's birthday party, nothing to be angry about. 'I'll make cupcakes.'

He grinned at that. 'That would be excellent, though actually I have a favour to ask. You did say you liked cooking?'

'I do.'

'Then how about a birthday cake? I was going to order one from the bakery, but the choice is pink or blue butter cakes and even I think they're a bit ordinary.'

She relaxed. This was something easy, even enjoyable.

It was also a reason she could tell herself she was going. She could put it in her 'accept responsibility' basket.

'I'd enjoy making a birthday cake,' she told him and was rewarded by a smile that seemed almost blinding. That had her taking an instinctive step back.

'Thank you,' he told her. 'Two p.m. on Saturday.'

'Tom…' She was fighting against that smile. Fighting to get herself back in control. Back to medicine, fast. 'Lois Manning… You know her? Her husband, Bob, was here with a cow kick when I first arrived. I admitted her yesterday with a chest infection. Her blood pressure's up, but not to worrying levels. X-ray shows a couple of minor suspect areas—still not enough to worry about, but I thought a night on IV antibiotics and a bit of enforced bed rest might clear things faster. But she's not settling. The next step seems to be an ambulance trip over to Ferndale for a CT scan, but the idea seems to be distressing her even more. Maybe you could pop in and reassure her?'

Which was sensible.

One of the things she'd learned in the last month was the power of Tom Lavery. It wasn't just the almost irresistible combination of his smile, his gentle bedside manner and his skill, though they carried weight with the locals—and with Rachel. It was the fact that Tom was the grandson of the old doctor. The community gave him a level of trust that she doubted she'd ever achieve. If this was to be her lifetime career maybe she'd try, but she was here as a temporary doctor. If the patients required trust, then she was sensible enough to call on Tom.

'Let's see her together,' Tom told her. 'You're her treating doctor. Let's put me where I belong, simply a second opinion before we go to the expense and trouble of a transfer.'

'Thank you,' she said, steadying as she retreated to work mode. Back to practicalities. 'Now?'

'Why not?' he said and glanced at his watch. 'Clinic for me and vaccinations for you. Both starting at nine, which is in ten minutes. Which means we're both already running late.'

'Then there's no need for me to come with you.'

'There is a need. We do this together,' Tom told her. 'If I'm seen as overriding you, then my workload will increase tenfold. I have to be seen as trusting you. Which I do. Absolutely. After you, Dr Tilding.'

And what was there in that to make her colour rise? She felt her cheeks flush with the compliment—with the warmth in his words—and then with the way he put his palm fleetingly against the small of her back as she entered Lois's room.

It was just as well he was behind her. There was no reason for her to blush, and no way she wanted him to see he had that power.

But then she was in Lois's room. Lois was turned away from her in the bed and Rachel's dumb reactions were put aside. Even from the door she could see Lois was sobbing.

Why was she so frightened? She thought of what she'd said to her. On the basis of pain and trouble with breathing she'd suspected there might be a pneumonia which would need immediate treatment, but she'd suspected nothing worse.

'Lois, there's no need to be frightened,' she told her, speaking quickly. 'The trip across to Ferndale is merely a precaution. I'm almost certain they'll send you straight back.'

'I know that.' Lois was a tall, gaunt woman in her late sixties, her face weathered from a life spent on the farm. She'd come across as sensible, but as well as an obvious chest infection Rachel had noticed trembling hands and a slight fever. She'd thought maybe fatigue was playing a part, which was the real reason she'd kept her in overnight. She'd been disappointed and mildly surprised when the symptoms had escalated.

'Lois, would you mind if I listen to your chest before you go?' Tom perched on the end of the bed and smiled reassuringly at her. 'Dr Rachel's already listened and she's not too worried. Can I listen in as well?' He hauled his stethoscope out of his pocket and leaned forward. It was an informal way of conducting an examination—doctor sitting on bed. Any old-fashioned head nurse would have a stroke at the sight of all those neat hospital corners messed up, Rachel thought, but Tom was nothing if not informal.

He listened and Rachel found a wad of tissues and Lois mopped her eyes and tried to look more cheerful. And failed.

'Your chest doesn't sound too bad,' Tom said when he'd had a decent listen and made Lois cough. 'A bit raspy but nothing a simple infection can't explain. How long have you been crook?'

'Three days. Maybe less. But yesterday… Bob was worrying. And maybe I got scared.' It was a tremulous whisper.

'So what's scaring you?' Tom asked bluntly. 'Are you thinking you have lung cancer?'

That took Rachel aback, but she watched Lois's face

and she knew it had been the elephant in the room, an unspoken fear.

'Yes,' Lois whispered.

'But the cough only started three days ago.'

'Y-yes.'

'Lung cancer doesn't usually move so fast,' Tom told her. 'It's likely that you've copped a simple infection which will respond well to what we're doing. A CT scan will check more thoroughly. Patterns of shadowing can identify areas of infection and suggest which bug's causing the problem. If it's anything out of left field a CT will let us nip that in the bud early. And yes, it'll also show a cancer if there is one, but Lois, I'd eat my fishing hat if we found cancer, and I'm very fond of my fishing hat.'

Lois gave a watery chuckle, sniffed and blew her nose. 'I…thank you. I know. It's sensible.'

'So how's Bob doing?' Tom asked, settling back on the bed as if he was here for the long haul. Rachel frowned and glanced at her watch. There was no need to make themselves even later by stopping for a chat.

'He's good.'

'His leg's cleared up? That was some kick he got.'

'Jerseys,' Lois said with disdain. 'We run organic now. It's the only way to make money from such a small farm, and Jersey milk is the best seller, but they're bast—hard cows to manage.'

'I've met one or two Jerseys in my time,' Tom told her. 'Grandpa ran them as house cows before Gran got fed up and made him swap to Friesians.' Then he added, almost casually, 'And your daughter? Sandra, isn't it? How's she doing?'

And Lois's face crumpled again. She sobbed into her

tissues and Tom sat and waited as if he had all the time in the world.

This was nothing to do with her, Rachel thought. It was nothing to do with medicine. She should edge out and head off for her vaccinations. But there was something about this tableau that had captured her. Tom looked totally relaxed. Casual. Somehow, he'd turned this into what seemed almost a fireside chat with a friend, instead of a consultation with a patient.

How did he do that? And what was the point?

He was acting as if he had all the time in the world. All the patience.

She felt as if she was in some sort of masterclass, seeing something she had no hope of replicating.

'Sandra's in a refuge,' Lois said at last, gulping, trying hard not to cry. 'One of those women's refuges. With the kids. The police… Stuart broke her arm, trashed the place. Her oldest—Will—he's got a really deep cut over his eye and bruises where his dad kicked him. The neighbours came. They got her and the kids away. Stuart got arrested but she thinks he's out on bail. He busted her phone, but she rang from the refuge—they let her use their phone. She says…she says she's okay, but we know she's not. Bob's trying to send her money but she's not game to even go out of the refuge to buy anything. And we want her to come here but there's something to do with the kids' passports and Stuart's permission, and she doesn't even know where the passports are because of the mess the house is in. She'd never be game to go back and search. And Bob and I need to go to her but there's the cows and we need the money to bring her and the kids over. And…'

And she subsided into her tissues again.

Leaving Rachel aghast. Shortness of breath and high blood pressure were symptoms of an infection, but how could they possibly improve with this behind them?

She should have asked. Why hadn't she asked?

She hadn't even known Lois had a daughter.

She did, though, she realised. Tom had told her when Bob was ill. And even if she hadn't realised, maybe she should have probed before heading straight to expensive scans.

She felt very junior, and very small.

'Right,' Tom said, sounding now very much like a consultant who'd figured the diagnosis and was prescribing treatment he was sure of. 'How long since you've talked to Sandra?'

'Yesterday.' Lois's voice quavered. 'She doesn't like to use their phone.'

'Then we can fix that. As a doctor, I can access links that'll let us contact the refuge. Not directly. There'll be all sorts of precautions in place to keep Sandra safe, but indirectly... If we go through the proper channels I'm thinking we could get her a computer-type notepad—a tablet— with internet hooked up. Do you use the internet?'

'Bob does.' Lois sounded confused. 'We have a computer at home he uses for bills and such. But it's old.'

'Let's get you a tablet, too,' Tom said. 'You know my grandpa set up an endowment for the hospital? This is just the sort of thing he wanted it used for.'

'I can't...' Lois breathed.

'You don't have to. Grandpa already did. So what's next? I'm going to ask Jenny's lad, Lachlan, to give you a lesson on how to use it. You know Lachie? He broke his hip rock-climbing a couple of weeks ago. He's wheelchair-bound, home from uni and bored stupid. I'll ring the techie store over at Ferndale and get them to put your notebook on the bus this morning and we'll see if we can get one to Sandra just as fast. Because it's a police case, I reckon I can use their Social Welfare unit to help Sandra. With Lachie's help and a bit of luck you'll be video-calling by dinner time.'

'Video-calling?'

'It's like telly,' he said, smiling confidently at her stunned expression. 'Looking at each other's face on the screen while you're talking. It's the next best thing to being with her. You can almost give her a virtual hug, and you'll be able to talk to each other all day if you want.'

He paused, thinking it through, but then forged ahead with the next thing. 'Next is the kids' passports and exit permissions. New Zealand and Australia are so close and there's good communication at high level. Have there been problems with Stuart before?'

'Lots,' Lois told him.

'Anything documented?'

'He hurt her badly last year.' Lois still sounded stunned. 'He ended up hitting one of the neighbours and the police were called. Sandra wouldn't press charges— she never does—but the neighbour did. Stuart got off with a suspended sentence or something. Sandra went back to him, of course. She says it's her fault, she annoys him. Over and over she says it; he has her too subdued to think about fighting. But this time he hit William and he's only seven. Will tried to stop him hitting Sandra and he turned on him. Surely she can't go back to him now.' She broke off and hiccupped another sob.

But Tom was nodding as if all was going to plan.

'Lois, this is excellent,' he said. 'Let's not think about the past. Let's focus on the future. So Stuart has a previous conviction for domestic violence. I'm sure we can use that. I have an old uni friend who's now a lawyer in Canberra, something high up in immigration. I lent him my dinner suit when I was nineteen—for his first date with a girl he was keen on. But apparently my suit was left on the bedroom floor, and before he could give it back his girlfriend's Labrador had puppies on it. He couldn't afford to buy me a new one. Over time I suspect he's forgotten, and I haven't called in the debt. I believe this is the time to remind him.'

He smiled, cheerfulness and optimism personified. 'So who knew puppies could be useful? For such a favour—I reckon he even owes me his marriage!—we might have Sandra and the kids helping milk your cows by Monday.'

Lois was looking even more stupefied than Rachel felt. 'You're serious?'

'Never more so. You know what? If Dr Rachel concurs, we might leave the trip across to Ferndale in favour of video-calling lessons instead. But for now...' He checked his watch. 'I really need to get things moving if I'm to get that tablet on the Ferndale bus. Let's get some details and then I want you to snuggle down and sleep until we have something concrete to tell you. Is that okay with you?'

'That's...that's fine,' Lois murmured, sounding totally bewildered.

Tom rose—and then, to Rachel's astonishment, he leaned over the gaunt woman in the bed and gave her a solid, reassuring hug. Then, still holding her, he forced her to meet his gaze.

'Lois, we'll do our best to fix this,' he told her. 'This is not all on your shoulders. We're calling in the big guns while you sleep. But sleep you will and that's an order. Do you concur, Dr Tilding?'

'I concur,' she said faintly.

'Excellent,' he said and beamed. 'There is still the matter of a mucky chest but the antibiotics might take advantage of sleep to get on with their work. I do like a definitive course of action.'

'Lovely,' Lois murmured and grasped his hand. 'You're lovely.'

'I need to go,' Rachel said shakily. 'I have vaccinations waiting. Excuse me.'

And she fled.

He'd seen her face as she'd left, and even though they were both late he suspected she wouldn't head straight to her vaccination appointments. He'd seen her before on the back veranda, taking a quick breather between patients, and that was where he found her.

It was the same place they'd kissed the night of Col's operation. Then, though, there'd been mutual relief at a great outcome. Now Rachel's hands were pressed to her cheeks. She looked a picture of mortification.

'Rachel?'

'How did I do that?' she whispered. 'Missed diagnosis. Argh! If you hadn't intervened she'd be in the ambulance, getting more stressed over tests she doesn't need.'

'Hey, you weren't to know.'

'I should have asked.'

'About a daughter you hadn't heard of?'

'I had heard of her. You told me when Bob was sick.'

'I tell you heaps of things about the locals. So does

Roscoe, and so does Jenny, and probably half the population of Shallow Bay. You can't be expected to remember all of it. Besides, she may still be sitting on pneumonia.'

'We both know it's unlikely. Shallow breathing, chest pain, fear… The only symptom not explained by anxiety is the fever, and even that was slight.'

'And there were shadows on her X-ray.'

'Marginal.'

'So you're beating yourself up why?'

'Because I didn't get it.' The sun was glinting on the sea below them but she wasn't noticing the view. 'It's not just that I didn't get it. It's that I *don't* get it. I don't read the signs. That's why I should be starting radiology right now instead of pretending to be a family doctor. You read Lois right off. Me, I floundered. I'm a medical technician. I join the dots I can see, but when the dots are emotional they're invisible. It's like I'm colour blind.'

'But you're learning,' he said gently. 'I've watched you. You care.'

'I don't care,' she said, almost wildly. 'I don't know how to. I've just learned to follow the rules.'

'You're saying you don't feel emotion?'

'I *can't* feel emotion. It scares me.'

'There's nothing to be scared of.'

'Of course there is. How can you doubt it? It gets you into all sorts of trouble. Like hugging a patient with an infection. Cross contamination? Why would you do that? And ethics? Hugging? That's the biggie. You must have attended the lectures on medical defence. You know the boundaries.'

'Well, contamination's hardly a problem,' he said dryly. 'Or I can't let it be. Do you know how many people sneeze at me every day? One hug is hardly likely to make a difference. And I didn't cross any ethical boundaries with Lois.'

'That's not what Medical Defence would say.'

'What, hugging a patient to comfort her, to say she's not in this alone? How is that ethically wrong? I even had a female colleague there as chaperone—you—but it wouldn't have mattered if I hadn't. Do you think she could possibly take it the wrong way?'

'I'd never risk it. I don't touch. Ever.'

'Really?' He looked at her with concern, seeing her internal struggle. He was starting to figure her out by now. So much had been hammered out of her by her awful childhood, by adults who'd betrayed her in the worst way—but there was so much still in there. He wanted to reach out and hug her, and it was an almost physical struggle not to.

But the more he saw of Rachel Tilding, the more he knew he had to try. And it wasn't just sympathy, he acknowledged. She made him feel...

Yeah, well, he couldn't go there. It was enough for the moment to accept that he had to get through those barriers.

'So...the night of Col's operation,' he said slowly. 'You touched me then. Was that comfort, or was that something else?'

And, rightly or wrongly, things suddenly moved to a whole new level. He watched Rachel's face and saw confusion. And panic.

She was remembering that kiss.

'You know that wasn't comfort,' she managed. 'You're right—it was something else. It was stupid.'

'It didn't feel stupid,' he said, and he could resist the confusion, the fear, on her face no longer. He reached out and took her hands. Gently though. She could pull away if she wished. 'But no, it wasn't comfort. Maybe it started that way but that kiss, Rachel, was something else entirely.'

'It wasn't. I mean…' She seemed to be struggling with words, struggling with the feel of her hands in his. Struggling with the urge to pull away?

She could if she wanted to, he thought, but her body didn't seem to be cooperating.

'Do you get the difference between comfort and what's happening between us?' Tom asked. The link between them felt warm. Strong. Right. 'Rachel, you need to forget the fear. Leave it in the past, where it belongs. Here are people you can trust.'

He hesitated for a moment, fighting to gather his thoughts, but then he forged on. 'Rachel, you're with a community now, with people you could learn to love and who could learn to love you. A lot of people. And, to be honest, I want to be included in that mix. I know this sounds dumb, but for the last month every time I turn a corner and see you I feel myself breaking into a smile. There's this thing between us. I think…'

'Then don't think,' she snapped, panic-stricken. 'And don't say it.' But still she didn't pull away.

'Don't say what?'

'That you care.'

'Why not?'

'Because there's no way I can care back.'

But the link of her hands sent a different message. The panic on her face… She was so torn.

'You can learn to care,' he said, steadily now. 'Like I've learned to care—deeply—for three kids. Like I've learned to care for one three-legged dog. Like I'm learning to care for this whole damned valley. I didn't ask to come here, Rachel. Left to my own devices, I'd be a practising orthopaedic surgeon, dating who I liked and surfing on the side. But here I am, in Shallow Bay doing what I can. Caring. And as for you... Rachel, you're beautiful, talented and you care as well. You wouldn't be distressed now if you didn't care.'

'I accept responsibility when I need to. That's not caring.'

'So the kiss between us was...responsible?'

'No!'

'So what was it?' His voice became even more gentle. 'Why the fear?'

'I'm not afraid.'

'I think you are.'

'Well, I'm not,' she said, struggling to sound cross rather than panicked. 'You have tickets on yourself if you think one kiss from you and I'm thrown for a hoop.'

'Tickets on myself?'

'Tom, this whole situation is inappropriate. We have work to do. We should not be standing on the hospital veranda holding hands, analysing a kiss that should never have happened. If you think that it was so important...yes, you have tickets on yourself. The conceit of the male race knows no bounds, you definitely included. Now, can I get on with my work?'

'If you can prove that one kiss means nothing.'

'It doesn't!'

'So...'

'Tom...'

'Okay.' He released her hands and held up his—surrender. 'I'm conceited enough to think that kiss *was* something more. But I'm excused because I'm admitting that one kiss…as you say…threw *me* for a hoop. Me, not you. Or was it both of us? Was it indeed an aberration? Okay, Dr Tilding, let's take this as a clinical trial. One more kiss to find out?'

'You can't be serious. How unprofessional is this?'

'A clinical trial's professional,' he protested. 'Compared to hugging patients… According to your rules I should be struck off every medical register in the country. So…one kiss, Rachel Tilding. Prove to me it meant nothing.'

'It did. I can't.'

'Why not?'

'Vaccinations,' she said wildly. 'Clinic. I'm late…'

'Rachel…' He grinned, putting his finger on her lips to shush her. 'One thing Shallow Bay knows is that our medical service works on a triage system. Priorities are allocated according to need. So right now you're looking at me with something maybe neither of us understand but it's something we need to diagnose. That need for diagnosis puts you—and me—right up the top of the list.'

'No! Tom, I don't want it.'

'Really?' He cupped her chin with his fingers, looking down into her confused eyes. Her panicked eyes. Maybe he should walk away, but he couldn't leave her like this.

He couldn't leave her.

'You really don't want me to kiss you?' he said gently. 'Really?'

'I…'

'Say it, Rachel. Say you don't want me to kiss you.'

'No…yes…no…'

'Decide, Rachel,' he said almost sternly. 'Say it.'

She looked so confused. Well, so was he, he admitted. He had no idea where this was going.

And this place was hardly private. A hospital veranda, mid-morning. Any minute now, nursing staff, patients, visitors could walk by. This was crazy.

So why did this feel like the most important moment of his life?

'Yes or no, Rachel?' he said, and he looked down into her gorgeous eyes and saw her panic and he saw her confusion, but he also saw…something else.

His hands were cupping her face, tilting her mouth. She was so close. So lovely.

This was crazy. He shouldn't…

'Yes,' she whispered—and then there was no need for words for a very long time.

She was mad. Utterly, incomprehensibly mad.

She'd let Tom kiss her and she'd kissed him back. Again!

She had no idea why she'd done it. Hormones, she told herself as she headed to the library to her waiting babies. It was the same hormones that saw fifteen-year-olds get pregnant when pregnancy was the last thing they wanted. Total, idiotic madness.

She wasn't fifteen years old now. The fact that Tom's understanding, his gorgeous smile, his crazy reasoning about clinical trials had broken her defences…

It was definitely hormones and she needed to pull herself together fast.

Once at the library she coped with vaccinations with professional competence. She smiled when she needed to smile. She comforted, she complimented, she gave injections to protect the babies of Shallow Bay from danger.

But why did it seem as if she'd just walked over a cliff herself?

* * *

'So...'

Clinic was finished. Tom was sitting in the hospital kitchen wolfing down a sandwich before he headed out on house calls. He was also waiting on phone calls from Canberra and New Zealand, which was the reason he was eating fast, aware that slabs of time would be taken up as soon as these calls came through.

Roscoe had come to find him. The big nurse had taken two weeks' paternity leave after the birth of his son and he was now back at work, looking a little sleep-deprived but also absurdly happy. And wanting to share his happiness with everyone.

'So?' Tom said cautiously between mouthfuls.

'What's happening?'

'With Lois?' He'd given Roscoe a fast explanation before clinic. 'The tablet should be here by now.'

'Yeah, Lachie's in there now, explaining video calls. Bob's there, too. Sandra hasn't received hers yet but it's happening. Meanwhile, they're practising calling my Lizzy. Lizzy's a huge fan of video calls—she uses them all the time to talk to her mum and dad in Sydney. When I left the room, Lois and Bob were being coerced into sharing nappy changing by video link.'

Tom grinned. Great. This was a terrific little community, he thought, and once they had Sandra here the community would protect its own.

'But that's not what my "So" was about,' Roscoe said, and plonked himself down and snagged one of Tom's sandwiches. 'You and Our Rachel.'

'Our Rachel?'

'She's been here over a month. She's therefore one of ours. And Our Poppy swore she saw you snogging out on the veranda this morning. And we both know it's not the first time, don't we, Doc? Anyway, Poppy said it's none of her business and she hates being a gossip, so she managed not to tell anyone for a whole three minutes. Which is huge for Our Poppy.'

And, despite the dismay he felt at being sprung, he had to smile at that. Poppy was Shallow Bay's most junior nurse. She lived and breathed romance, and now she'd seen a real live kiss…

'She has you married and living happily ever after, and she's already predicting three more kids,' Roscoe said. 'Two girls and another boy. She hasn't named them yet but she's close.' He munched his—Tom's—sandwich and Tom gave up trying.

'A bit premature,' he managed.

'You think?' Roscoe's grin was huge but then it faded. 'Seriously, Doc… You and Rachel…?'

'She feels good to hold,' he said simply, and his friend stared at him.

'You're serious.'

'Hell, Roscoe…'

'She's hardly warm and cuddly,' Roscoe said, obviously thinking it through. He frowned. 'I know, it's none of my business. But who knows what's under that cool surface?'

Tom shrugged, abandoned his sandwiches and gave up any pretence of keeping how he was feeling to himself. 'That's what I intend to find out.'

'You're kidding.' Roscoe even forgot his sandwich. 'Wow, Doc…'

'I know.' He shrugged. 'I'm playing with fire.'

'Yeah, if this goes belly up, we either lose a doctor

or we have doctors who won't speak to each other for two years.'

'And if it doesn't go belly up?'

'Doc, she's damaged. Even I can see that.'

'Then we fix it,' he said simply. 'This community…'

'You really are playing with fire.'

'Something has to warm her up,' he said. And then, more seriously, 'And something has to warm me up. Roscoe, I think I need this.'

'Wow,' Roscoe said again and whistled. 'And double and triple wow. Right, then. I have faith. I'll get straight back to Poppy and tell her to start sorting baby names. Two girls and a boy? Let's get this show on the road.'

One semi-public kiss and everyone in Shallow Bay was looking at her sideways. Sometimes not even that. Broad smiles greeted her, and she knew she was being looked at differently. It seemed the population of Shallow Bay was no longer seeing her as a temporary doctor but a long-term solution to what they saw as the gaping hole in Tom's inherited family.

'This isn't fair.'

'What's not fair?' Tom asked. It was Friday afternoon and they were passing in the corridor between patients. She'd been avoiding him all week. Now she had two more patients to see and then Tom was off duty for the weekend. Unless there was an emergency she wouldn't see him. She had promised to attend Kit's birthday party but that could be a quick drop in and run.

Run was the operative word, she decided. This community was driving her nuts. Her last patient had practically offered to do the flowers for her wedding—'I'll give you a great rate'—and everywhere she went there were conspiratorial grins.

She'd had it—and when she turned a corner in the corridor and practically bumped into the cause of the trouble she was ready to vent some spleen.

'How many women have you kissed in the past?' she demanded before he could say a word, and Tom looked taken aback.

'I couldn't say,' he said cautiously. 'Does it matter?'

'It does,' she said crossly. 'You've dated, right?'

'I…yes.'

'Teenage romance? Med school? All those parties as an intern?'

'I had spots in adolescence,' he admitted. 'I was a bit handicapped.'

'I don't care,' she snapped. 'Guesstimate, Tom Lavery. A hundred?'

'Surely not.'

'I bet I'm right, but I'll give you the benefit of the doubt. Let's say eighty-seven. You can adjust it up or down after you've thought about it.'

'Adjust it…where?'

'On the community noticeboard outside the library,' she told him. 'In big, bold lettering. And in the nurses' station. And anywhere else you can think of that might have all the sticky-nosed people of Shallow Bay saying, "Ooh, he kissed Dr Tilding, this means happy-ever-after." I want huge signs saying *Dr Tilding was Kiss Number Eighty-Eight and she doesn't intend to be Eighty-Nine.*'

He grinned, folded his arms and leaned back against the wall. 'What if I'd like you to be Eighty-Nine?'

'Get over it. It's complicating my life.'

'Maybe life's meant to be complicated.'

'Not mine. Tom, back off.'

'I don't want to back off,' he told her. Hospital corridors were definitely not the place for this kind of conversation, but it seemed there was no choice.

'Tom…'

'Rachel, I think I'm falling for you,' he said bluntly. 'And please don't ask me why. Maybe it's your warm and cuddly persona. Maybe it's the way you embrace life…'

'Cut it with the sarcasm.'

'Okay,' he said gently. 'I'll be serious. Maybe it's because I can see underneath that armour you protect yourself with, to the warm, vibrant woman you want to be. All you need is the courage to admit that you can care.'

'No one can give me courage.'

'I expect you're right,' he said, still serious. 'To be honest, I suspect it's already there, used now to keep yourself distant but ready to be used…for life.'

'Tom, you're scaring me.' She had no idea where this was going.

'I don't want to scare you. I want to get to know you.'

'Because you see me as a rescue pet,' she snapped, and watched his brows hike.

'What?'

'You've seen my arms. The moment you saw them things changed. I saw your reaction—so here comes Dr Lavery to the rescue. You helped your friend, Claire, and you rescued her three needy children. You even rescued a dog with three legs. And here I am, damaged as well, a good fit for your houseful of welfare cases.'

'My boys are not welfare cases,' he said, suddenly angry. 'And neither is Tuffy. They just need…'

'They need you. I agree. But I don't.'

'What if I say I need them? And more. What if I need you?'

'Don't be ridiculous. You're the hero. Sadly, I have no taste to be Rapunzel, waiting for rescue.'

'Your hair's too short,' he said, and he tried a smile. She had a sudden, stupid urge to smile back.

He copped a glower instead. 'Tom, please…'

'Could we just relax and enjoy this?' he asked her. 'Could we admit we're attracted to each other and see where it goes?'

'With the whole town watching? We have a quick romantic fling and then I'd be…'

'Left again?' He was watching her face and his eyes told her he was understanding. 'Rachel, there are decent people in the world. People who won't hurt you. People who won't walk away.'

'They won't have the chance,' she told him, totally discombobulated. 'I don't need anyone, including you. Tom, I don't need rescuing. Please, leave me alone. This is scaring me.'

'You like kissing me.'

'Okay, I do, but I don't like what goes with it.'

'What goes with it?' He unfolded his arms and held up his hands, as if in surrender. 'So…Rachel, I know this isn't fair, but will you give me a sop to my pride? Tell me if it wasn't for the boys you'd be all over me like a rash?'

All over him like a rash? What sort of romantic question was that? Weirdly, it broke the tension.

'You're comparing me to measles?'

'In the nicest way.'

'I can see that,' she said. 'But no, the boys have nothing to do with my reaction to you. If you were still a playboy doctor in Sydney I wouldn't be interested, but I bet you wouldn't be interested in me, either.'

'You'd be wrong there.'

She shook her head—and then looked around in relief as Jenny appeared along the corridor, bearing a covered bedpan.

'Clear the path, people,' Jenny said warningly. 'You guys look intense, but old Joe Crazer's enema has finally taken impressive effect.'

Which brought that interlude to a fast end.

Medicine had its uses, Rachel thought as she fled. But Tom's words followed her. Tom's question.

If it wasn't for the boys, would she be all over him like a rash?

No, she thought. In fact, the boys seemed almost a safety net, though they'd got her into trouble in the first place. They'd made her let down her guard. If Tom needed her rather than wanted her then maybe... Maybe.

She wasn't making sense, even to herself. Why would anyone want her? And how could she let herself want Tom? It was all too hard.

What she wanted was to pack her car and head back to the city, away from the prying eyes of a small community, away from a house with a makeshift family next door. Away from the threat Tom posed to her carefully built armour.

How to rebuild her armour?

She'd promised a birthday cake. Tomorrow.

She'd make it, drop it off and run, she decided. But after that...

She was stuck here for two years. How could she cope with that when running seemed the only safe option?

CHAPTER NINE

THE PARTY WAS scheduled from two to four. The kids had slipped an invitation under her door while she was hunkered down on Friday night, avoiding the world, avoiding even her own thoughts.

There'd be lots of people there. She could do this.

On Saturday morning she rang Tom. 'Do you need the cake before three? I might be late,' she told him. 'Jill Salter won't come in for check-ups and I'm darned if I'll give her another month's insulin without looking at what her sugars are doing. She won't be home until two.'

'That smacks of avoidance.'

'Who? Me? Plan to be late to a party, with noise, sugar, mess? How could you accuse me of such a thing? The cake will be there at three and that's a promise.'

He laughed and let her off the hook, but she disconnected feeling guilty. She could have been there earlier to help. She could have…been with him.

The cake's enough, she told herself savagely, and at three o'clock even carrying her cake across to the house next door felt too much.

The party was in full swing. Twelve children, Tom had told her, though from the noise it could have been a hundred.

Tom was in the centre of the back yard, holding a donkey—a huge stuffed toy she recognised as Henry's preferred pillow. They were playing what was obviously a version of pin-the-tail. Every child was blindfolded and armed with strips of fabric. She looked more closely and saw Velcro glued at the end of each 'tail'.

This was obviously pin-the-tail with a difference. The kids were a tribe with a common goal, to reach Tom and his donkey and get a tail—any tail—where it should be.

Working alone, they had no hope. As each child groped and stumbled and managed to touch the donkey, Tom chuckled and lifted the donkey higher, then slipped away.

There were shouts and laughter and tumbles across the lawn. Tuffy was barking hysterically. Tom was laughing and scooting and lowering the donkey so the next kid could just touch—and then whooping and raising it before scooting again.

Over the heads of the kids Tom's gaze met hers. His grin was wide and welcoming and the next kid grabbing for his donkey almost had it. Tom ducked this time, dropping to all fours with the donkey tucked under his chest. The kids disintegrated into confusion and Rachel found herself grinning.

He was an idiot, she thought. A laughing, loving kid himself.

Tom.

'Hey, guys, this isn't working.' It was Marcus, ever the thoughtful one, yelling from the centre of the melee. 'We need a trap.'

And while Rachel watched, bemused, Marcus organised all the kids to one side, their hands linked. A sweep started across the yard.

Tom had nowhere to go. The line moved inexorably. Henry reached him first, grabbed and yelled. Tom was almost instantly enclosed by seven small boys and five small girls. The donkey was stuck with random tails and an exhausted, laughing Tom declared the game over.

Blindfolds were removed. The multi-tailed donkey was paraded around the yard with more whoops but somehow Tom was still looking at Rachel. And she was looking at him.

A great, goofy kid.

A skilled surgeon.

A stepfather.

It was a word she hated but somehow Tom had changed the word for her.

Tom.

'Here's the birthday cake, people,' Tom called, still smiling, and the mob descended on her.

'It's a meerkat,' Kit yelled, skidding to a halt in front and staring in stupefaction at his cake.

It was indeed a meerkat. She'd wanted, quite badly, to make it stand tall, gazing in the inquisitive way that made meerkats attract kids the world over. Making an upright meerkat out of chocolate cake, however, had proved beyond her. Instead she'd made him squat, so his back curved in an arch. She'd got his face as she wanted though, peering upward, as if he'd just been disturbed as he foraged in the chocolate/dust at his feet.

'You'll need to beware bones,' she warned. 'Meerkats have bones.'

'Bones,' Tom said faintly, sounding puffed. Being pursued as 'donkey' by twelve kids must be something akin to running a marathon.

'Otherwise known as satay sticks,' she told him.
'Every meerkat needs a skeleton.'

'He's awesome,' Kit breathed, and Rachel smiled. It
felt okay. More, it felt great to have her splinter skill
appreciated. She'd put her all into this meerkat, struggling with satay sticks and chocolate cake and piping
bags until the small hours. She reckoned she'd made him
pretty realistic—apart from the line of candles along his
curved back.

'Too good to eat,' Tom said but the kids looked at him
as if he were dumb.

But Kit was looking at the package she had tucked
under her arm. A gift. Priorities.

It had arrived two days ago from the States. A T-shirt.
A grinning meerkat in Lycra and cape. Personalised.

Across the meerkat's muscled superhero chest was
blazoned *Kit Meerkat—Superhero*.

'Kit Meerkat,' Kit stammered and gazed at Tom in
awe. 'Can I put it on now?'

'Sure,' Tom said and grinned at Rachel as Kit did the
world's fastest quick change.

'There's another gift at the front door,' she told Tom.
'Maybe after cake?'

'You'll stay?'

She hadn't meant to. She'd thought she'd just drop
things off and make an excuse.

But Tom was smiling at her and Kit was beaming as
if all his Christmases had come at once and two little
girls were inspecting her meerkat cake, trying to figure
why the head didn't fall off...and suddenly the scene
was like a siren song.

It was all the things she avoided. Noise. Chaos. Family?

'Just until after we cut the cake,' she heard herself say. 'Just…to make sure there's no drama with the bones.'

And with that it was decreed it was time to stop for food. Tom hadn't needed her to help him, she realised as they headed into the kitchen. This was a guy's version of a party—piles of bought 'party pies', bowls of cocktail frankfurters, mounds of popcorn and crisps, soda and a huge bowl of watermelon as a nod to being healthy.

Within minutes the table looked as if wolves had descended. Candles were lit. 'Happy Birthday' was sung. Her meerkat was dismembered and devoured—and then Tom reminded them there was something else outside and the pack whooped out into the front garden, leaving chaos behind.

'Go out and I'll clear,' Rachel told Tom, looking at the mess in dismay, but Tom grasped her hand and tugged her out with him.

'Not on your life. We're in this together, Rachel Tilding. If this gift is water pistols, you're in the front line.'

'I'd never do water pistols,' she told him and swallowed a sudden memory of a children's home between foster placements and someone arriving with water pistols and the bullying that followed…

'Rachel?' He was watching her face.

'N-nothing,' she managed. 'Just…ghosts, maybe.'

'Then let's face them together,' he told her. 'Twelve kids hyped on too much excitement and too much sugar, and Rachel Tilding's ghosts. We need to be a team to face this.'

And before she could object he'd tugged her outside.

To where she'd left her birthday gift.

Kit's T-shirt would have been enough of a gift, she conceded, but she hadn't been sure it would arrive in time. She'd ordered this online as well, but from an Australian source. She'd spent an hour wrangling the dodgy pump which came with it. She'd then had to kick it in front of her as she came from next door while carrying the cake, but now the kids were circling what must be the world's biggest beach ball. Almost as high as Henry, all the colours of the rainbow, it bounced and flew whenever it was touched.

And she had plans for it. Once upon a time a foster dad, coping with a tribe of disparate kids, had fashioned this game, and she'd remembered. Now she headed over to the hedge where she'd parked four poles she'd painted the night before. She'd found them in the back shed—tomato stakes. She'd painted two green and two red and attached matching flags. Okay, they were dishcloths, but close enough.

Tom watched, bemused, as she planted green poles at one end of the garden and red poles at the other. 'Right,' she called. 'Two teams. Everyone on this side is on Marcus's team and everyone else is on Kit's. This is Maxi Soccer. Go for it.'

And two minutes later the ball was flying. Kids were flying. The ball was too big and too slippery to grasp. It bounced against kids, against the house, against Rachel and Tom—sometimes even between the posts. Rachel stood on the sidelines and grinned.

'Hey, Dr Smug,' Tom said, his voice full of laughter, and suddenly his hand was holding hers again. 'This is amazing. Well done, you. It's even too light to smash your windows.' He smiled down at her. 'So…no ghosts?'

'They've taken a step back for the duration,' she admitted.

'Kids and family can make that happen,' he told her.

They stood side by side, watching the game. Rachel was enjoying the kids' fun. She was also, she conceded, enjoying the sensation of Tom standing right next to her.

She just had to ignore the hormones.

'In a different life I'd ask you out on a date,' he said. They were still watching the game. A bystander would say they were engrossed in what the kids were doing.

They weren't.

'I guess I'd refuse,' she managed.

'Why?'

'Because I don't do relationships.' Flat. Definite. She had the hormones where they needed to be.

'Which is a crazy waste. Rachel, right now you're lonely and isolated and your ghosts are holding sway, but underneath you're a vibrant, loving woman who doesn't deserve to be stuck in a cottage on the other side of the hedge from…life.'

'So you're planning on rescuing me? Like you've rescued three kids and a dog already? Thanks, but I stopped needing rescuing a long time ago.'

'I don't think that's true. But as for rescuing…' He hesitated. 'Okay, I haven't figured it out yet and I always was one for leaping and then looking afterwards. But what I see in you… It makes me realise that rescuing could work both ways.'

'You want me to help rescue you from the kids?'

'I don't need rescuing from the kids,' he told her. 'I love the kids.'

And as if on cue the ball sailed towards him and hit him on the chest with a massive whump. The kids launched themselves after it, and it was all Tom could do to keep standing.

He managed. The ball sailed off to the other side of the garden and they were left alone again.

'Okay, I might need rescuing a bit,' he conceded.

She smiled but she couldn't get the smile to reach her eyes. 'Tom, don't,' she told him. 'Rescue or not… You and me…it's never going to happen. You're missing your career, your life in Sydney, your freedom, the whole life you had before you were lumbered with three kids. I can't help you there.'

'I wasn't lumbered,' he told her. 'I was blessed.'

'I don't believe you. And me… How is rescuing someone else going to help?'

'I won't be rescuing.' His smile deepened. 'Rachel, I'd be loving.'

'Stop! No. What have I ever said to make you think…?'

'You've kissed me,' he said, his smile still lurking. 'Twice so far.'

'Kissing is a huge way from…anything serious.'

'It is, isn't it,' he said, suddenly rueful. 'Rachel, I'm scaring you and that's the last thing I want. Okay. Maybe we should go on a little longer. Maybe not dating because that's hard. Shallow Bay has a limited number of dating options, to say the least. The Shallow Bay Chippy is hardly dating heaven. But maybe we could add to our occasional kissing total? Seven's a lucky number. When we get to seven…'

'We won't get to seven.'

And then the ball bounced back at them and she saw her chance. Instead of kicking it away, she grabbed it and ran. A muddle of kids surged towards her as she dived towards the goalposts. And scored.

And landed flat on her face.

She lay, winded and stunned. The team she'd scored

for roared its approval and the game took off again. Tuffy, though, sat down beside her and licked her face.

The grass was soft. There was no need for Tom to come to her aid. He didn't, for which she was grateful. He stayed watchful, but his smile had gone.

'He looks as stunned as I am,' she told Tuffy, and then she thought, Why wouldn't he be?

'Because propositioning me is ridiculous,' she told Tuffy. 'He's been drinking too much red lemonade.'

The ball was heading her way again. She had to move. Fast. But not towards Tom.

She got up, shook herself off and headed inside. Someone had to clear the mess. Someone had to be practical.

Someone had to keep her armour intact, and that person had to be her.

He'd stuffed it. She'd retreated and he'd had to let her go. He was pushing too hard, for something he hardly understood himself.

At least she'd retreated to his house and not hers, he decided, as parents started arriving to collect their offspring. He handed out party bags and watched the boys wave farewell to their guests and he thought maybe the boys might crash early tonight. Maybe he could take a bottle of wine...

Or not. She had to feel safe in her own house, and heading over after dark with wine...

Back off, he told himself and put a lolly bag into Sophia Lombridge's sticky hand and got a gap-toothed grin in return. Sophia departed, and that was the last of the guests.

Except someone else was coming. A sedan—large, gleaming, black. A model he recognised as being way out of his price range, even when he'd been a surgeon. And as it got closer...

That's all we need, he thought bleakly, for here were Claire's parents. The kids' grandparents. Charles and Marjorie.

He might have known this would happen. He'd endured months of phone calls, increasingly threatening. He'd said they could call the kids whenever they wanted—even though he'd have had to coerce the kids into accepting such calls. He'd suggested he could bring them to Sydney to visit. They were the kids' grandparents and the last thing he wanted was to cut them off completely. But the only thing that would satisfy this pair was custody, and the calls had become threatening.

And then there'd been calls from lawyers. 'It's going to cost you a mint, going down this path, Dr Lavery, and you won't win. Back off now and we can talk about access. If you don't back off you'll end up broke and with no rights at all.'

He'd consulted his own lawyers. He'd dug in. Claire's will had been unequivocal, but the sight of the approaching car made his stomach clench.

The kids saw it too. They left their ball game and came and stood behind him, silent. Scared?

Rachel appeared at the doorway, tea towel in hand. 'Tom, are these glasses yours or do they go back in the boxes?'

But then she saw the approaching car and she froze. Maybe it was the stillness of the kids. Maybe it was his own stillness.

Rachel had been tossed about as a kid as well. She'd have a nose for threats, he thought, and what was coming was definitely a threat.

Marjorie and Charles were a power couple, a pairing of financial giants. In their sixties, they were lean, gym-fit, immaculately groomed. They exuded power. Tom had lost count of the number of boards they were on, of the financial projects they controlled. Together, this couple seemed to run half of corporate Australia.

And here they were, emerging from their crazy-expensive limousine, every inch of them saying, We're here on business.

'Marjorie. Charles.' He made his voice deliberately light as he opened the gate to greet them. 'You've come for Kit's party? I'm sorry but everyone's just left. You've missed the cake.'

'You can still have little red sausages.' Henry spoke up from behind Tom, sounding worried but prepared to be hospitable. 'They're not hot any more but they're yummy.'

'We didn't come for the party,' Charles said, eyeing his grandsons with dislike. 'Although, of course, we knew about it.' That was down to Tom. Every week he insisted the boys write to their grandparents. 'Our lawyers tell us there's been an accident. Weeks ago, and we weren't informed. Christopher's hand. Why did we have to gain access to medical records to find that out?'

'It's better,' Kit whispered.

'It's good as new now,' Henry agreed. 'He cut it while Christine was watching the telly, but Rachel took him to hospital.'

'You weren't with them when it happened?' Marjorie snapped at Tom.

'I was at the hospital. I employed a childminder.'

'Not a satisfactory one,' she threw back at him. 'We've made enquiries. The childminders you're using are unqualified. They've not even undergone the working-with-children security checks. They're totally unsuitable.'

'Rose isn't unsuitable,' Kit said defiantly. 'She's cuddly.'

'According to our sources, she's in her seventies.'

'Could we go inside and discuss this?' Tom broke in. The boys were looking more and more distressed. He needed to get this out of their hearing. 'The boys are playing ball. We'll be better discussing this in private.'

'There's no discussion. We're here to take the boys home,' Charles decreed. 'According to legal advice, our challenge will be successful. Learning of Christopher's cut hand was the last straw. Your care is marginal, to say the least. We're the boys' grandparents. We're in a position to give them professional after-school care, as well as sending them to the best educational institutions. The idea of them attending a hick elementary school here, with heaven knows what sort of teaching, is unthinkable. You're not married. You employ unqualified childminders. You obviously can't keep them safe. You need to allow us to take them now, and if you deny us we'll make sure you have no access. Plus,' he added, almost as an afterthought, 'we'll ruin you.'

'But we don't want to go with you,' Marcus muttered, brave words but with a tremble beneath them. 'You're mean. Mum said Tom would always look after us.'

'She didn't mean live with him,' Marjorie snapped. 'You'll have your own bedrooms in our wonderful home. You'll have a nanny to take care of you. You will need to keep up with your studies but that's no problem. You know we hired a suitable tutor for Christopher...'

'He didn't like his tutor,' Marcus quavered. 'He hit him on the fingers with his pen when he got his spelling wrong. And once when he got them wrong twice he hit him really hard.'

'Then Christopher needs not to get them wrong,' Marjorie said. 'Don't be a baby, Marcus. You know you belong in our world. It's where your mother was raised.'

'Mum hated it there.' Marcus was starting to cry, his voice becoming choked. 'She said you were always away. She said her violin teacher used to hit her fingers, too.'

'For heaven's sake. Your mother didn't make the most of the advantages we offered her but I didn't think she was stupid enough to talk of such foolishness to her children.' Marjorie's voice was turning shrill but Charles laid a placating hand on her shoulder.

'Keep it calm, Marjorie. Heaven knows what these children have been told, by their mother and by this man, but we know where our responsibility lies. Our role is simply to get them back on track as fast as possible. So what's it to be, Dr Lavery? You put them in the car with us, or you face a court order and legal costs that'll make your head swim. Decide now.'

'We're not going with you.' Kit had started crying as well. 'We won't!'

'Don't be foolish, boy,' Charles said. He took a step towards his grandson and put a hand on his shoulder, tugging him towards the car. Kit pulled away but the grip tightened.

'Let me go!'

And then Tuffy decided it was time to step in. The little dog had been partying all afternoon and had retired to the back steps for a nap in a sunbeam. Now, though, with the boys' voices raised, he'd stumped down to see what was going on. Now he started barking, high, hysterical yips, clearly confused, clearly worried.

And then Charles grabbed Kit and Kit cried out and pulled away—and Tuffy saw his duty. Normally the most docile of dogs, he darted forward and sank his teeth into Charles's shoe.

It wasn't a bite. The shiny brogues were solid and, as a rescue dog, Tuffy was missing enough teeth to make any bite pretty much a token affair, but he managed to grip and hold. Charles gave his foot an angry shake but the dog's hold firmed.

'Get the damn thing off me,' he snapped.

Tom lunged forward but, before he could reach dog or child, Charles tried another tack. He set his foot down, then pulled back his other foot and kicked. Hard.

The little dog flew six feet away and landed with a sickening thud on the gravel in front of the car. For one appalling moment he lay totally motionless. Then, as Charles stepped towards him—to kick him again?—he struggled to his feet and headed out of the gate. He was around the fence and into the bushland at the back of the house, and he was gone.

With three boys running after him.

'Get back here!' Charles roared and made to go after them, but Tom gripped him and held.

'Leave them be. Don't you dare…'

And then Rachel was beside him, her tea towel flung aside.

'I'll go,' she said. 'You get rid of these people.'

It made sense. Every instinct told him to follow the kids, but the way Tuffy had run signified he hadn't been badly hurt. The boys were best out of the way while he said what he had to say to this pair. And Rachel was already following them.

'Let me know how Tuffy is, but take your time bringing them back,' he called after her. 'Though probably five minutes is all I need to say what needs to be said here. Charles, Marjorie, into the house. Now.'

CHAPTER TEN

IT WAS ALL very well to say she'd follow them, but she wasn't sure where they'd gone.

The track around the house led to a path winding down to the beach. She assumed that was where they were, but a fork a little way from the house veered upward. Rachel had investigated once and decided against exploring further. It was pretty much overgrown above waist height—or kangaroo head height—so she suspected it was used by wildlife rather than people.

But now she hesitated. It'd make sense for the boys to have taken the fork to the beach, but they'd been following Tuffy, and Tuffy could have gone either way.

She called and got no answer.

Okay, beach first. She ran, but three minutes later she was staring at a deserted beach. No footprints in the sand. Nothing.

Back to the fork.

She headed up the path, kicking herself mentally for wasting time. It did look as if they'd been this way. The leaf litter had been disturbed, leaving damp ground exposed. The boys were significantly shorter than she was. They'd have got through this easier than she could. Still, she moved fast.

Ten minutes later she was where the path ended, at an obviously little-used lookout giving broken views over the bay. She could see a muddle of fresh footprints but they weren't here now, and all around her was dense bush.

No dog.

No boys.

She stood and called.

Nothing.

There were smaller tracks leading into the bush, but they were surely animal tracks. It was drier up here. There were no tell-tale signs of disturbed foliage.

Had they backtracked? Had she missed them when she'd run to the beach?

Her phone was in her jeans pocket. Crossing every finger and toe, she phoned Tom.

'They've gone,' he said before she could speak. 'I told them they could sue me for every cent I own before I let them have the boys. Heaven knows what'll happen now, but you can tell them it's safe to come home. How's Tuffy? Is he hurt?'

'I can't find him. Tom, I can't find the boys.'

There was a moment's pause. The beginnings of alarm.

'They're not on the beach?'

'Nor up the mountain path. I'm at the lookout. I think they've come this way, but I've called and called and nothing.'

'They'll be hiding.'

'I guess.'

'I'll join you,' he said. 'Give me a couple of moments to ask Rose to come over. I don't want them coming back to an empty house.'

So she stood and waited, staring at the myriad of tiny tracks, agonising over what to do.

If they were indeed hiding it'd be okay. Surely.

But the tracks led into bushland, and the bush was dense. Shallow Bay National Park ran for miles in every direction. These were city kids. If they lost their bearings…

'I'm catastrophizing,' she told herself and forced herself to wait.

Tom was with her in minutes, looking anxious.

'I wasn't sure where to go from here,' she told him. 'There's lots of little tracks but I can't see any sign of which one they took. I thought…if I tried then I might cover up signs…things someone more experienced can see.'

'They must be hiding,' he said, sounding worried. 'But if Tuffy's hurt… I need to find them.'

He raised his voice and called—the 'Cooee!' that was used as an almost universal cry in the Australian bush. Apart from in movies, Rachel had never heard it—she was a city girl—but it was truly impressive. It echoed out to the bay, and back to the mountains behind them. Surely the boys could hear.

They listened. Silence.

'They must be close,' she told Tom nervously. 'I wasted time heading to the beach first, but I can't have been any more than fifteen minutes behind them.'

'They *must* be hiding,' he said again, but her fears were reflected on his face. 'They'll be terrified. Charles is a bully. I've talked enough to Marcus now to know he can use his fists as well as his words to hurt them. Claire told me he never physically hurt her, but she was a girl. Charles is older now, probably less patient, and to be honest I think Claire's death—something he couldn't control—has left them a little crazy. He sees the boys as a duty, to be licked into shape, no matter what it takes. They're not going back there.'

'They don't know that for sure.'

'I don't know that for sure,' he admitted. 'With the legal team that pair has at their disposal…and the fact that I'm single and only their stepdad…'

'The hitting…'

'They'll say I prompted the boys to say it. There's no physical proof.' He closed his eyes to disguise a wash of pain that looked bone-deep—but when he opened them the pain had been replaced by determination.

'Rachel, will you head home? I explored this area as a kid. Many of these paths meander down to the creek. If they reach the creek, they'll see a path that leads one way to the beach, the other into the town. I'll go down now and see if I can head them off. Meanwhile, if you could act as base, backing up Rose… If they get home… I don't know how badly Tuffy's hurt and they'll all need…' He broke off and closed his eyes again but then resumed.

'They'll all need cuddles. Rose will do her best but they'll need multitudes. Can I depend on you?'

'I… Sure.' Cuddles weren't her forte, but in this case…

Actually, in this case she was tempted to go for it right now. So why not?

Because she'd just backed off from Tom's warmth? Because she'd reacted this afternoon with almost as much fear as the boys running from their grandparents?

That's cowardice, she told herself, and Tom was looking grey.

She did it. For the first time in her life Rachel Tilding stepped forward and wrapped her arms around someone.

Not someone. Tom.

'You'll find them, and we'll work it out,' she told him, holding him close.

He put his face in her hair, taking deep breaths. Taking strength? That was fanciful, she thought, but the idea stayed.

'We?' he asked.

'We,' she said, more definitely. 'We'll get this sorted, Tom Lavery. You go find your kids and I'll go home and be ready with cuddles.'

It was a good plan—except he didn't find them.

What followed was a long, long wait, where Rachel and Rose sat and worried, and Tom's calls back home were increasingly desperate.

'Nothing,' she told him over and over, and as the sun sank he returned. His phone battery was dying. He was exhausted. He needed help.

'I assumed they'd come home by dusk,' he said heavily. 'It's time to call in the big guns.'

Five minutes later a police car pulled into the drive. That was followed by the local fire truck and a State Emergency Services vehicle. Men and women piled out, wearing serious faces and high visibility clothing. Kids lost in this bush meant trouble. No one was wasting time.

Locals were arriving too. Word was out. Shallow Bay was preparing to search.

Tom wasn't allowed to join in.

'No,' the local police sergeant told him. 'And no argument. You have scratches all over you already. You're exhausted and emotional. We're the professionals. You stay here and let us bring the kids to you.'

It nearly killed him, and it nearly killed Rachel to watch him. Like Tom, she'd prefer to be searching herself rather than going nuts with the waiting. But she wasn't even a local. Any volunteer with no experience of night-hiking and bushcraft was being sent home and she knew she'd be useless.

'Come back at dawn if we haven't found them by then,' the local volunteers were being told, and the words sent a chill right through her.

And watching Tom… Watching his fear…

He loved these kids. She saw it on his face and it left her feeling awed.

How could a man take three children into his heart, leaving himself exposed to such pain?

But how could he help it? She was starting to get it, she decided as the night wore on, because the thought of the kids out there was doing her head in. And every time she looked at Tom her own heart twisted.

She didn't do love. She didn't do commitment. It hurt. It was hurting so much now she couldn't bear it, but she had no choice.

Maybe this love thing was something that didn't get decided in any sort of rational manner, she decided. It was a scary thought, but she hardly had headspace to examine it now.

She should go home, get some sleep, Tom told her. There'd still be medical needs tomorrow. It'd be sensible to keep herself grounded, to stay rested and ready for whatever might be required.

She could no sooner go home than she could fly. It

was as if her heart had been ensnared, caught in a fine web of…loving?

She was so confused, so fearful, and as the night wore on it grew worse.

It was dark, late, and it had started to rain.

By midnight the police were treating it as deadly serious, and they'd called in the heavies. A helicopter arrived and started doing sweeps, using the house as the epicentre and moving out.

'It has heat-seeking cameras,' the sergeant told them. He'd set up base in Tom's living room. Rose had reluctantly gone home but they could still see her light on. She'd be pacing too.

Half of Shallow Bay seemed to be awake.

People cared.

'The chopper's thermal cameras are our best bet in these conditions,' the policeman was saying. 'Kangaroos make it hard, though. They're about the same mass as a child, so every warm body has to be checked. If we knew the kids were together we could cut out a lot of false sightings, but we can't assume it.'

'They'd never leave each other,' Tom said, his face bleaching even whiter than it had been before.

'If one of the kiddies hurt himself and another tried to go for help…' The sergeant's voice trailed off. 'Well, we don't need to tell you that.'

He headed back to his radio.

Rachel made tea and bullied Tom to drink it. She found some leftover party pies and made him eat them too. She even ate a couple herself, finding some sort of weird comfort in their warmth and ordinariness. It didn't last though. They seemed to sit in her stomach, making her feel ill.

Maybe it was other things making her feel ill.

Every time the radio crackled into life, Tom's whole body seemed to clench. He was sitting on the settee, leaning forward, as if he was willing the radio to give him good news.

Nothing.

Finally Rachel could stand it no longer. She moved across, sat beside him and took his hand in hers.

His fingers tightened on hers, almost convulsively. 'I can't bear it,' he managed. 'I have to do something. I'm going crazy. Sergeant…'

'You're going nowhere,' the policeman told him, not without sympathy. 'Sorry, Doc, but I've read the hand-book. First rule of thumb when you're looking for lost kids—or lost anyone, for that matter—is keep their family safe. I let you out there and you'd try and search the whole National Park on your own. You'd end up lost or injured or dead with fatigue. I know it's killing you, but you stay where you are.'

'He's making sense,' Rachel said softly. 'But I want to be out there, too.'

'You'd get loster,' Tom said, with a valiant attempt at humour. It didn't work. His voice broke and that was the end of any last thought of holding him at a distance.

He turned and held her. He just held. Hard. It was as if he needed every skerrick of warmth, of contact, he could get and there was no way she would deny him. She simply held, while the radio spat its stupid static into the room and the policeman toyed with his mug of tea and tried not to look at them. How did cops cope with see-ing this level of pain?

'You know what else?' Tom said into her hair. 'They'll use it. If…*when* we find them… Marjorie and Charles…

With this level of search, they'll know about it by yesterday. And they'll add it to the list. Cut hand through negligence. Now lost kids. They'll say it's my negligence and they're right, it is.'

'It's not,' she told him. 'It was them. They scared the boys.'

'Do you think I can prove that? I haven't a hope of keeping them.'

'I might be able to help there,' she said diffidently, and tugged back a little to retrieve her phone from her pocket. 'When Charles and Marjorie arrived… I guess you don't remember, but I came out to find you. And I stopped, thinking I was interrupting something personal, but then you and the kids looked so threatened…'

'We were threatened.'

'Backstory,' she said, still diffident. 'One of the kids I was in care with… Between placements. We were in a home with some pretty rough kids and one of the younger girls was hurt by a couple of bullies. Badly. And I saw it happen but even then there was this code of silence, and the bullies were protected. My word wasn't enough to hold weight. The social workers knew I was telling the truth but there wasn't anything they could do about it.

'But afterwards one of them said, half-jokingly, "You should have had a camera, Rachel. If all the world had cameras it'd make our job so much easier." Somehow, her words stuck. I guess…because of how I react to fear, because there's been…a few other times when I've been scared…if I can't do anything about it, my instinct is to document. It's paranoia, I know, but…'

'It's not paranoia,' he said gently, and he took her hand again. 'It makes sense. So…?'

'So I held up my phone and recorded it,' she told him. 'It was almost a gut reaction. I know it's an infringement of privacy and normally I'd delete it straight away but maybe… I just thought…it might help.'

She held up her phone and clicked on the video she'd taken. She'd been standing back and it was grainy, but there they were, the tableau of people she'd seen as she'd emerged from the back door. The sounds had been caught, too. She'd started recording as Charles had raised his voice, as she'd sensed the children's fear. As voices had grown more threatening she'd started moving closer, in an instinctive move to protect.

The camera zoomed in with her. Charles, large, loud, imperious. Marjorie, shrill and threatening. The two of them speaking harshly, without a word of greeting to their grandchildren.

The children's fear was appallingly obvious. As the tension escalated, the screen showed Charles hauling Kit towards the car. Kit was sobbing in terror, pulling back. Henry and Marcus were looking stunned, terrified. Henry was flinging himself at Tom. Tom was lifting Henry aside to try and reach Kit.

And then came Tuffy. The little dog gripped Charles's shoe, but even on the small screen it was obvious that Charles's foot was uninjured. All Charles had to do was shake him off, but he did no such thing.

The kick was vicious, ruthless, sickening, and the scruffy little dog went flying. There was a moment of appalling stillness while the dog lay on the gravel. Then he staggered to his feet and lurched away, tail tucked under his legs.

The boys ran after him. Charles yelled.

The video stopped.

They were left with silence.

'If anyone dares to say the boys are lost through negligence, I'll personally post this to any online forum I can think of,' Rachel said in a shaky voice. 'Tom, I'd go into debt to hire banners over Sydney Harbour if that's what it takes. You're not to blame.'

But he was past listening. He was still staring at the blank screen, as if he could make himself see what was happening to the boys now.

'They'll twist it,' he said savagely. 'Even with this… The lawyers they employ… The bottom line is that I'm single, I'm not related to them. I can't give them the care they can.'

'If you call what they're offering care…' she said and she closed her eyes. 'Okay.'

'Okay, what?' His voice was defeated. Hopeless.

'Okay, you don't need to be single any more,' she told him. 'If it's what you want, if it'd make a difference… You took responsibility for the boys so maybe…' She took a deep breath. 'Maybe I can, too.'

He stared at her incredulously. 'What are you saying?'

'That I might help. That I might even share. If you and the boys need it so much. Maybe…even if we were to be married…'

And where had that come from? The words hung like some sort of threatening sword.

Married? Was she nuts?

And he hardly reacted. Maybe he was beyond it. Maybe all he saw at the moment was defeat.

'Tom…' Had he even heard what she'd said?

'You're going to be a radiologist,' he said dully.

Help.

She was so confused she scarcely knew what she was

putting on the table, but at some level something in her brain was saying it made sense. She was heading down an emotional rabbit hole here, deep and dark, and she had no idea what lay at the end, but the compulsion to help this man, this family, was almost overwhelming.

'I don't need to be a radiologist,' she managed. 'I need to keep your boys safe.'

'Is that a reason for marriage?'

'Hey, it is.' The police sergeant was ostensibly focused on the radio, but he must have been listening in on their conversation as well. He'd visibly brightened. 'This is the first piece of decent listening I've done all night. Take her at her word, Doc. The boys'll have a mum and dad and we'll have two permanent docs for the town. More with that scholarship thing. Shallow Bay won't know itself.'

But Tom was shaking his head, looking bewildered. As if he was trying to clear enough room in his mind to answer.

'Rachel, no,' he said at last. 'It's an extraordinary offer and I don't have the headspace to figure it out, but I do know… You've said you didn't want to be yet another of my "rescues" and you were right. I might care for you—a lot. I also know—even if you don't—that you making this video, focusing on the boys, wasn't you accepting responsibility, it was you caring. As was what you said right now. But you don't know it, Rachel. You don't know what love is and without it…' He raked his hair with his fingers, grim and desperate. 'You can't not let me close because it reeks of rescue and then offer the same thing yourself. You just…can't.'

'But you married Claire without love,' she said, struggling to figure it out herself. 'Surely that was a decision made for convenience? Wouldn't marrying me be the same?'

And that broke through the desolation. He turned and stared at her as if she was something from another planet.

'You think I married Claire without love?'

'You said…'

'I said she was my friend. No, I didn't want her in the way that I want you, Rachel—and don't look like that. You must know how much I'm starting to want you— your body, your warmth, your love. But there it is again. The love word. Claire was my friend from childhood and I loved her. I also loved her boys from the moment they were born. I was their playmate, their big brother, their pseudo uncle, and if you think not being their dad means I don't love them…'

'But you married Claire for sensible reasons.'

'I did,' he agreed. 'But love was behind it. Yes, need was there. Claire needed me, the boys needed me, but if I hadn't loved them I'd be little better than Charles and Marjorie.' He groaned. 'I'm sorry. I'm not making sense even to myself.'

'I don't think either of us are making sense,' she managed. 'Maybe…maybe we could talk about it later. When we've found them.'

'Let's not,' he said heavily. 'Right now, loving's killing me. Loving someone who doesn't love back…' He closed his eyes again. 'Enough. I'm sorry.'

And then the radio crackled into life again and one form of tension was replaced with another. They strained to hear, but it was only someone reporting in.

They went back to waiting. Her stupid offer disappeared into the ether. It was just that, she thought. Stupid. All that mattered was that the boys were found.

Outside, the rain fell as steady drizzle. Somewhere in the hills were three small boys. And creeks that would be turning to rivers. And cliffs, and cold, and fear...

And Rachel sat and watched Tom without touching, and waited, and let responsibility and care and love churn into a chaotic, frightening morass in her mind.

And then, at three minutes past two—not that she was watching the clock or anything—the radio crackled again. 'Sergeant?'

'Here.' The policeman was suddenly sitting upright. There was something about the word, the voice, the tone.

'We think we've got 'em,' the voice said. 'Check the screen.'

The cop swivelled to a computer beside the radio. It'd been showing thermal images of the mountainside all night, taken from the helicopter. Almost before the cop turned, Rachel and Tom were on their feet, staring as well.

They saw search coordinates. Weird, grainy images of bushland.

'Coming around now,' the voice said above the sound of the chopper. And they watched as the coordinates changed, as the chopper flew lower.

And then they saw... Three blurred figures, tiny, beneath the canopy. White, almost ghostlike. Moving while the rest of the scene was still. Jumping?

'Not roos,' the voice said. 'Never seen a roo jump up and down in the one spot. Bit of a clearing a couple of hundred yards ahead. Not big enough to land but we'll send Michelle down on a rope and direct the rest of the searchers in. No promises, but the way the three of them are moving… I reckon we'll have three soggy, tired but well kids coming home in no time.'

The chopper hovered a little longer and they could see the tiny figures waving, trying to attract attention.

And then the chopper moved away, to reach the clearing. The scene was once again thick bush.

'Oh, Tom…' Rachel managed but Tom was no longer with her.

He'd headed for the bathroom and closed the door.

CHAPTER ELEVEN

THE BOYS WERE brought home in a patrol car just before three. Rachel stayed only long enough to see them sandwich-hugged in Tom's arms. Rose appeared from next door and started fussing about baths and blankets. Rachel watched tears, hugs—love?—and then edged herself out of the picture.

She was an outsider looking in. Wasn't that the way it always was?

'Tuffy?' she said to one of the policemen who'd brought the boys home, and he looked at her blankly.

'Sorry?'

'The little dog the boys were chasing.'

'Oh, yeah,' he said. He, too, was looking at the hugging tableau through eyes that were suspiciously moist. Every person here—and there were many, crowded inside or around the front yard—was soaking up this happy ending. 'There was a dog. The kids had it, but when the chopper flew low it took off into the bush again. The kids were upset about it, but it didn't come when they called and we weren't about to hang around. A couple of the locals said they'd head up there tomorrow to do a search if he doesn't come home himself. I guess he'll come home when he's hungry.'

So Tuffy wasn't messing with this happy ending, but as Rachel made her way back to her cottage he was still very much on her radar.

Along with everything else that had been said this night.

Loving someone who doesn't love back...

That one line kept reverberating, somehow intensifying what she'd just seen. Tom, crouching before the fire, holding as much of his boys as he could. The boys, hugging back. Rose, standing beside them, weeping with relief and joy. The searchers, mud-stained, weary, battered from a night of bashing through undergrowth but staying around, soaking in this happy ending. Even the cops with tears in their eyes.

Loving someone who doesn't love back...

And Tom...loved her?

How could he possibly? He'd known her for little more than a month. She'd hardly let him near. Had he so little control of his emotions that he'd let himself fall for someone like her?

Someone who so carefully never loved back?

Emotions were threatening to overwhelm her. She was fighting them back with every tool at her disposal, tools carefully built and squirreled away during a lifetime of emotional emptiness.

They weren't working. Tom. The boys.

And there was a gap.

Tuffy.

Back home, she showered—somehow she still seemed to be covered in stickiness from the birthday party—and headed for bed. She shoved her head under the pillow, trying to blot out the emotions of the day. They wouldn't be blotted. Where was the Rachel she'd fought so hard to become? Where was her armour? It was nowhere, and neither was sleep.

At five she was sitting at her kitchen table, staring into a mug of cold tea. At the first hint of dawn, she turned to stare out at the mountains behind the town.

Tom. The boys.

Tuffy.

A ragged little rescue dog. Hurt. Missing a leg. Would he be able to find his way home?

She checked her phone photos and saw the video again, Tuffy flying in to defend his boys against Charles. Boys he loved.

'That's anthropomorphism,' she told herself. 'Giving dogs feelings that humans have.'

Would she have bitten Charles?

'That's anthropomorphism backward,' she said out loud. And then there was another question slamming at her. 'So what am I asking? Can't I love as much as Tuffy?'

There was that word again. Love.

Tom. The boys.

Tuffy.

She glanced out of the window. The house next door was in darkness. She guessed Tom and his boys would all be in his big bed, huddled close. He couldn't leave them.

Her mind went back to the screen shot they'd watched as the helicopter had hovered over the boys. She could still see it. Three white shadows in a sea of unlit bushland. Three spots of heat.

She couldn't remember another heat spot, but then Tuffy was much, much smaller. What she could recall, though, were the numbers at the edge of the screen.

A photographic memory had always been her blessing, one of her few advantages in her struggle to gain a medical degree. She called on it now. She could still see those numbers. Coordinates.

She wrote them down and then flicked onto her phone. An internet search found a mapping app. She inserted the numbers and there it was, the exact place the boys had been found.

And the app showed her as well. She could see where she was as a little blue blob, with a blue line showing the distance of the blue blob to the coordinates.

Two kilometres. Not so far, but through thick bush…

What was she thinking?

Do nothing foolish, she told herself. There was a mantra given to every trainee doctor, written in stone.

Do not put yourself in danger when rendering assistance.

It wasn't just self-preservation, their first-year lecturer had thundered—and he'd been a pretty impressive thunderer. A doctor who put herself in danger escalated the situation to a whole new level, meaning those who came after could be facing a far bigger threat.

But Tuffy was up there somewhere.

She didn't know the bush.

She picked up her cold cup of tea and drank it while she forced her mind towards logic rather than emotion. Be sensible. Think it through.

She had the coordinates. The boys had reached this place, therefore it had to be somewhere she could reach if she was prepared to bush-bash. She had her phone with her app. All she had to do was keep herself—her dot—on the blue line. If it got too hard she could turn back. Her blue line would bring her home.

How could there be danger?

And could she be any use?

Dawn was breaking—just. Tom was stuck where he was. The searchers from the night before would still be solidly asleep. Meanwhile, Tuffy was alone.

Would he stay close to where the boys had been? Maybe he would, she thought, but surely not for long. By the time anyone else came to help, Tuffy could be anywhere.

He still could be anywhere.

She wouldn't think that.

Decision made, she hauled on jeans, windcheater, trainers, plus a rain jacket because it was still drizzling.

She tucked her phone safely in her pocket. Her portable charger was also zipped in. She grabbed a bottle of water and, thinking of a fearful little dog, she added a packet of bacon. What else did she need to rescue one scared, kicked dog?

Luck, she decided. Hope that he'd stayed where he'd last seen the boys.

And if she didn't find him?

Others will come up later, she told herself. I'm not the only one who cares.

Cares?

Loves?

'Quit it with the questions,' she said out loud. 'Just go find a dog.'

Tom stirred within a tangle of arms and legs. Every one of the sleeping kids needed at least some contact. He couldn't move.

The night had wrecked him. He felt drained, empty, devoid of anything except relief that he had them here.

They'd arrived home distraught, still frantic about Tuffy, but so exhausted they'd simply slept.

He had to let them sleep now. He was wide awake, but the moment he moved he felt them cling again. He was their security, their rock, their home.

Tuffy was still out there, a heartache that was yet to be faced. According to a weeping Marcus, the boys had eventually found him before becoming lost themselves. Apparently he'd been bleeding, his back leg damaged, and he'd panicked at the sound of the helicopter.

'We wanted to stay and catch him,' Marcus had sobbed. 'But he wouldn't come and the lady said we had to come home.'

Home. There was that word again.

'We'll find him in the morning,' he'd promised but it was already morning and there was no way he could move. Before they'd left, a few of the locals had agreed to meet at ten and set off to search. It was more than he could expect but ten... That was five hours away.

Then, through his window, he saw the light flicker on in Rachel's cottage. He'd tried to put away the emotions she'd shown the night before, the desolation and confusion he'd seen on her face. He had no time for it, he told himself, but it stayed with him still.

The light he could see was her kitchen window. Curtained. He could see no shape.

Was she thinking over the events of the night before? Calling herself a fool for having offered to marry him? Accepting his explanation that sensible didn't come into it?

They were so different. How could he possibly expect love from someone who'd never had it?

If it was just him, maybe he could take a chance, he

thought bleakly. The way he felt about Rachel had taken him by surprise. There was no sense to it. He wanted her, simple as that.

But the boys… A practical stepmother? A woman who operated by rules instead of heart?

Like Charles and Marjorie?

She wasn't like that, he told himself. She could never be like that. But still…

And then Rachel's porch light came on and a shadowy figure slipped out.

Rachel.

The weak dawn light was filtering through the grey. He couldn't see her clearly, but she had a torch and she was heading away from the house. Towards the bush.

What the…?

His phone was on his bedside table. He manoeuvred Henry's head a little so he could reach it, finding Rachel on his contact list. Her voice, when she answered, was a little breathless, as if she'd been rushing.

'Tom?'

'What do you think you're doing?' He was whispering, keeping still, knowing he couldn't wake the boys.

'You can see me?'

She'd just reached the edge of the clearing. 'Through the bedroom window. Yes.'

Astonishingly, the figure out there turned and waved. 'Wish me luck, then. I'm off on a Tuffy hunt.'

'Rachel!' He couldn't hide the urgency. The boys stirred. He lowered his voice again, but it was an effort. 'Are you…? Don't even think about it. We'll be searching for you.'

'I have a plan,' she said briskly. 'I remembered the coordinates from last night's rescue. I have an interactive map, showing me exactly where I am. I have my fully charged phone and I have my portable charger for backup. Oh, and I have bacon and a water bottle. Anything else you can think of?'

'No!' he practically groaned. 'You can't.'

'I know,' she said softly. 'You want to be here. To be honest, I'd like you here too. But the boys need you.'

'I can't let you go.'

'I need to go.'

'Why?'

'You know why.'

'Rachel, he's just a dog.' He hated saying it but it had to be said. 'You can't put yourself at risk.'

'I'm not risking. Hey, I know... Tom, my phone has this neat location sharing thing on its map app. On my map I'm a little blue dot and I'm following a blue line to where the boys were found. If I hit "Share" I think you can follow my little blue dot on your phone. You'll be able to watch me all the way.'

'Like that'll make a difference.'

'It'll make me feel less alone. I'll feel like you're with me.'

'Rachel...' Deep breath. The urge to toss back the bedcovers and head out there to stop her was almost overwhelming. 'Why are you doing this? It makes sense to wait until someone can join you.'

'And risk Tuffy getting further away? No. Tom, I will be safe. I have my blue line, my dot, my phone, my gear. I have you watching me. But I need to do this.'

'Why?' He felt as if he could hardly breathe.

'Because I love what Tuffy did for the boys,' she said softly. 'And I can't bear that he's out there. I think...I love Tuffy. Love... How scary's that for a confession? Tom,

I need to go. I'm sending my location now. You should hear the ping any minute.'

And she turned and headed away, walking steadily until her shadowy figure disappeared from the clearing. She was already on the track leading into dense bush.

He was staring sightlessly at the window. Henry's hand was clutching his arm; he was stirring from sleep. 'T-Tom?'

Had she disconnected?

'Oh, and this love thing…' he heard her say, and it was almost an afterthought.

'Rachel…' Henry's hand tightened in his. He couldn't move. He'd never felt more helpless.

'I can't talk any more,' she told him. 'I need to watch my feet. I just thought I should say… Last night we talked about love. This morning… Tom, I'm not sure what it is but I think I'm learning.'

CHAPTER TWELVE

THE RAIN KEPT right on raining. For the next two hours Rachel fought her way through the bush. Tom watched her little blue dot and held his boys, and he'd never felt so torn in his life. She was safe, he told himself. Rachel was sensible. She was in communication.

She was alone and he hated it.

It was okay—almost—when she was moving, when he could see the dot progressing. When the dot stopped, his head went straight to disaster scenarios—Rachel falling, broken ankle, head hit on overhead branches, drop bears, antigowobblers... He was going out of his mind!

She knew he'd be worried, though. Often when she paused, she texted.

Bit of a tough uphill. Taking a breather. Still good.

And...

Undergrowth's heavy. Taking a recce to see if there's another way around.

By the time the kids stirred the dot was pretty much where she'd set her destination. Which was good because almost as soon as the boys woke they were fretting about Tuffy.

He showed them the map and the blue dot.

'That's Rachel,' he told them. 'She's gone up to fetch him.'

'Rachel's bringing him home?' He watched their faces sag into relief.

'She hasn't found him yet but she will. She's just reached the spot.'

'But she's by herself.' Marcus was perusing the map with the eye of a scientist, expanding it so he could see details. Trying to see the unseeable.

'She shouldn't be there by herself,' Henry said, frowning. 'We were all together and we were scared.'

'It's light now, though.'

'But it'll still be scary,' Henry insisted. 'We should help her.'

'We could all go,' Kit said. 'We could rescue Rachel and Tuffy.'

He looked at them, his three kids. They were scratched, bruised, battle-weary. They'd been truly terrified last night. He'd tucked them straight into bed without bothering about baths. They looked like refugees from a battle zone.

They could rescue Rachel?

He looked again at her little blue dot and he thought, She knows where she is. She said she was fine. She was being sensible. She was on her blue line and she didn't need rescuing.

And then he felt the kids around him, the warmth of the big bed, the feeling of the kids depending on him—and, being honest, the way he depended on the kids—and he thought, did she need rescuing?

She might know where she was on the map, but where was she in the world? Did she have a place to come home to?

And then he thought—rescuing Rachel…the word was suddenly topsy-turvy. Why did it feel as if it'd be rescuing himself?

And as if on cue there was a knock on the door. The boys cringed—they were expecting Charles and Marjorie? But it was Rose. Of course it was Rose, bearing a pile of steaming pancakes and a jug of maple syrup.

In two minutes the boys had her up to speed. She stared at the dot Marcus was showing her and she set her pancakes on the kitchen table and glared at Tom. 'I don't understand dots,' she told him. 'But she's up on the ridge?'

'Yes.'

'There's only one dot.' It was an accusation.

'I couldn't leave the boys.'

'I understand that, but you can leave now,' she told him. 'I'll put some pancakes in foil and make you a Thermos while you pull your boots on.'

'Rose…'

'She's saving Tuffy,' she said. 'She shouldn't be alone, should she?' And then she fixed Tom with a look. 'Especially when you love her.'

'Rose…'

'Blind Freddy can see that you do,' she told him. 'You want to deny it?'

'I… No.'

'Then go,' she told him, and he paused only long enough to give her a big hug that somehow ended up embracing the boys as well.

'I'll ring Roscoe on the way,' he told the boys. 'I doubt

Marjorie and Charles would dare to come near us, but if they do… Roscoe will keep an eye on you all. You'll have half of Shallow Bay here to keep you safe in seconds.'

'Then all you need to do is keep Rachel safe,' Rose retorted. 'And find Tuffy and bring them both home.'

But she didn't need to say it. He was already gone.

It took quite a while but she found him.

She'd spent a miserable couple of hours bush-bashing through almost impenetrable undergrowth. She'd found the X-marks-the-spot where the coordinates on her phone matched the coordinates she'd seen on the screen the night before. She'd found irrefutable evidence that technology hadn't let her down. The clearing she was in was flattened from many boots, churned to mud in some places. There was even a wrapper from a chocolate muesli bar to prove this was where the rescuers had embraced the boys.

No Tuffy.

She'd called and called. She'd gone a little way in either direction, still calling. Nothing.

And then she'd come back to her X-spot, and as she'd sat on a wet log to think, a tiny movement caught her eye.

A mound of grevillea lay in front of her, an Australian native plant with crimson bottlebrush-type flowers and a scratchy, twiggy centre.

She lay down in the mud to try and see under. She shone the torch.

Two terrified eyes peered out at her.

'Tuffy?'

He didn't move.

She tried to wriggle under.

He growled and whined and shrank deeper.

He sounded terrified, she thought. She edged out, trying to figure what to do. If she pushed further under he might bolt. Having him run away was the last thing she wanted.

She unwrapped her bacon and set it under the bush, pushing it until he started backing away. Then she retreated to her log. And phoned.

'Tom? I've found him.'

There was a moment's silence, as though he'd caught his breath and wasn't sure what to say.

'He's under a really big bush,' she told him. 'I can't get him out.'

'Don't do a thing,' he told her. 'Stay right where you are, love. I'm on my way.'

'The boys…?'

'Are with Rose, with Roscoe standing guard. Everyone's safe. Stay still. I'm coming.'

This was a far cry from the neat, controlled Rachel Tilding he was accustomed to. This woman… Well, to put it bluntly, she was a mess. She was filthy and sodden. Her hair, hauled out of its knot from contact with undergrowth, was full of twigs. Mud smeared her cheeks. Rain was dripping steadily down her face.

Tom broke through the last section of undergrowth and he thought he'd never seen a more beautiful woman in his life.

She was seated on a moss-covered log. She looked huddled and shaky and alone.

She looked up at him as he emerged from the foliage, she smiled and approximately two seconds later, give or take a millisecond, she was in his arms. Gathered to his heart. Held and held and held, as if he could never let her go.

As he never intended to.

She was melting into his body, curving against him, hugging him as fiercely as he was hugging her. The rain dripped on regardless. It didn't matter. There was no need for words. In those first few moments promises were being made, vows formed, ties created that would last for the rest of their lives.

He could feel her heartbeat and it seemed to be in sync with his. That was how it was. That was how it would be.

'I've changed my mind about last night's offer,' he managed, and it was a struggle to get his voice to work. 'I accept. You will marry me. I don't care what we have to do to make it work but it will happen.'

She gave something between a sob and a laugh. 'Oh, Tom…' But somehow she remembered priorities. 'Tuffy…'

Their hold had lasted less than a minute, a hold which meant so much. It felt as if the world had changed. Or settled? It had righted itself on its axis and it was time to move on.

Tuffy.

'He's over there,' Rachel said, somehow pulling back. 'Under the bush. I put the bacon out but he hasn't gone near it. I can't see if he's hurt.'

She was freezing—what the hell was she wearing?—surely not bushwalking gear. Cotton trainers. Some sort of city rain jacket, designed for the odd light shower, not this deluge. Jeans.

He could feel her shaking.

'Tuffy,' she said again, and he thought of priorities and hypothermia but she was standing, pointing at the bush.

Tuffy was obviously right up the top in her triage assessment. A dog who'd saved his kids.

She was the woman who'd saved his dog.

First things first. He hauled off his oilskin and draped it round her shoulders. 'Get that wet top off and get into this,' he told her. 'Now.'

Something in the tone of his voice stopped her protests. She complied while he grabbed the torch and peered under the grevillea.

And there he was. The source of all the trouble.

No. He wasn't trouble, Tom thought. He was simply a little dog who'd brought joy, who'd done what he could.

'Tuffy,' he said.

Rachel's bacon was within reach. He pushed it a little way forward.

Tuffy was a rescue dog. He'd been mistreated in the past. Teaching him to trust had been huge.

It was a big ask now. Rachel hadn't been able to manage it, but then Tuffy didn't know Rachel all that well.

Could he trust now?

'Tuffy,' he said again, and the dog stirred and whined.

'Come on out,' he said gently. 'Come on, mate. We have bacon and we have warmth and we have Rachel. We'll keep you safe. Come on home.'

And, as if he understood, the little dog stirred and wriggled forward, slowly, tentatively. He reached the bacon and sniffed and Tom thought he might grab it and retreat.

But then he wriggled forward a little further. And sniffed Tom's fingers. And made a decision.

He was suddenly out from under the bush, on Tom's knees, every fibre of his small scruffy body wriggling in relief and doggy joy.

And Tom picked him up—and the bacon—and carried him back to Rachel on her log.

And hugged them both for a very long time.

Promises had already been made, deep and abiding. On the trek back to the house they were made again.

Tom had Tuffy tucked under his sweater. The little dog had a nasty gash on his hind leg but he seemed otherwise okay. Full of bacon and one of Rose's pancakes, nestled against Tom's chest, he was where he wanted to be.

As was Rachel. Tom had her hand. He wasn't letting her go for a moment. He was leading her down the mountain, treating her as the most precious thing in the world, and it was okay by her.

Life was okay. Her teeth were still chattering. Tom's coat was keeping the worst of the cold at bay, but the damage had already been done. She was soaked, shivering, but Tom was holding her and she'd never felt so happy in her life.

'We'll get married soon,' Tom said. They'd hardly spoken—Tom was focusing on his feet, on the path ahead, on his job to get them all safe and warm as soon as possible. But he said those four words and Rachel let them sit for a while, savouring them.

Knowing she should think about it. She should be sensible.

'Yes please,' she said, and he tugged her closer and kissed her fiercely on the mouth.

And that was her fate sealed, she thought as he led her on. Just like that, her armour had disappeared.

Just like that, Rachel Tilding decided that she'd fallen in love. And she'd fallen in love for ever.

* * *

An hour later she was dressed in a pair of Tom's jogging pants and an oversized singlet. Tom was towelling her hair while the boys fussed over Tuffy and Rose heated soup. It was almost a dream setting, Rachel thought—Tom's towelling, the way his hands touched her neck with each downward stroke, the warmth of the room, Rose's fussiness…the care…

And suddenly Marcus looked up, focusing on what Tom was doing. Focusing on Rachel.

'What are those things on your arms?' he asked, frowning in sudden concern.

'They're scars,' she told him but then as he kept frowning—Marcus knew by now what scars meant—she struggled through her mist of fuzziness, of peace, of home, to find an explanation.

'When I was little I had to face a dragon,' she told him. 'It wasn't a real dragon but that's what it felt like. So these scars are little dragon teeth burns—see, they're all the same? But you know what I did? I fought my dragon. Back then I fought by myself but now I realise I don't have to. Because people who love you always come to your rescue. Like you went to rescue Tuffy last night, and Tom came to rescue me. People who love you chase away your dragons and you don't have to worry any more.'

'Wow.' Henry rose to inspect the scars and was impressed. 'Dragon teeth!'

'That's better even than crocodile teeth,' Kit decreed. 'Cool!'

'I wish I had dragon teeth on my arms,' Henry said. 'You're really lucky.' But then he hesitated. 'I expect they hurt when you got them.'

'They did a bit,' Rachel said, drifting back under the

warmth of the towel, the gentleness of Tom's hands. 'But I'm lucky. I guess… I seem to have found so many people who'll scare away any imaginary dragon who comes near. I've seen your video game. You guys seem to be experts.'.'

'I'll chase away your dragons,' Henry said stoutly.

'And me,' Kit said. 'And Tuffy will help.'

'Me too,' Marcus said, though she could see, at ten, he was a little more dubious about the dragon teeth explanation. 'I guess…whatever it is we'll chase it away together.'

'I'm in, too,' Rose declared from the kitchen. 'Let any dragon come near us and I'll tell them what's what.' The boys giggled. The vision of plump, aproned Rose fending off dragons had them all chuckling.

'What about you, Tom?' Marcus said, figuring there had to be a full set. 'Will you fight for Rachel?'

'Most definitely,' Tom said, settling a kiss on her hair. 'Any dragon comes near this lady and he'll meet a fiery end. All of us will make sure of that. We're your family, Rachel Tilding.' And then, maybe because he thought there'd never be a better time to say it, he tilted her chin and stooped to kiss her.

'So what about it, Our Rachel,' he said softly, lovingly, with all the tenderness in the world. 'Now you're warm and dry, now we're back in the real world. Let's make it formal. I know it's crazy. I know it's way too soon. But what the heck… Will you marry us?'

'What? All of you?' She could hardly speak. She had every set of eyes in the room on her, including Tuffy!

'Yes!' Marcus yelled and whooped. And then he paused. 'But I won't be a pageboy. One of the boys at school says pageboys have to wear velvet suits. Yuck.'

'I don't like velvet suits,' Henry said worriedly, and Rachel couldn't help herself. This was supposedly the most romantic moment of her life and she found herself giggling.

But Tom was face to face with her, and his eyes were still questioning. This was a serious moment. It needed a serious answer.

Would she marry…all of them? Would she cast the last of her armour off and step into this strange, wonderful world of loving?

'Meerkats,' she said, and Tom blinked.

'Pardon?'

'If we can have all you boys wearing meerkat T-shirts at our wedding, then the deal's done,' she told him. 'And maybe I can sew a little meerkat coat for Tuffy.'

'Hooray!' the boys yelled, and Tom kissed her.

And then Rose bustled in with soup, and Tuffy yipped his excitement—and the rest of their lives started right there.

* * * * *

THE MIDWIFE'S
SECRET CHILD

FIONA McARTHUR

MILLS & BOON

To Dianne Latham, who won the name
in the book competition, and the Lilli Pilli Ladies
of the Macleay Valley, who raise money for those
being treated for cancer, towards their comfort,
and all the wonderful people who support
LPL's fab fundraising days. You rock.

CHAPTER ONE

Friday

FAITH FETHERSTONE TAPPED her watch as she stood under the meeting point for the Binimirr Underground Complex. Outside in the car park gravel scattered with a late arrival and the vehicle's throaty rumble deepened then silenced as the newcomer pulled in and stopped. The butcher birds, previously revelling in the bush sunshine, ceased their song as a lone cloud passed over the sun and Faith shivered.

The caves kiosk, which held all the caving equipment as well as promoting the cave-themed mementos of the area, straddled the entrance to the labyrinth which stood tucked into the hill ten kilometres south of Lighthouse Bay.

Faith, today's cave guide, tugged down her 'Ultimate Caving Adventure' T-shirt, which clung too tightly, and thought that perhaps her decision to tumble-dry it on hot when she was running late this morning had been less than wise.

She shrugged. It might stretch later and everyone would be looking at the caves not at her. She tucked away the hair that had escaped her ponytail to surrepti-

tiously study the varied group of adults assembled inside
the tourist shop, ready for her tour.

Dianne behind the cash register held up one finger.
So, one still to arrive; hopefully that had been his car outside. So far her only concern seemed the quiet man in his
twenties who chewed his nails and glanced towards the
entrance to the caves with an intense frown. She'd watch
for symptoms of claustrophobia down in the labyrinth.

The most striking group member at the moment had
to be the thin, twinkling-eyed older gentleman in an iridescent orange buttoned shirt and matching shoes, an
outfit that Faith thought just might glow in the dark once
they turned out the lights.

Barney Burrows, proudly seventy years young, had
caved in his youth, and chatted to the short, solid woman
in her forties, while her two taller teenage sons conversed
with a young backpacker couple.

The backpackers had smiling, animated faces and
Eastern European accents but their excellent grasp of
English reassured Faith they would understand her if
she needed to give instructions fast.

Sudden movement at the door made Faith's head turn,
her welcome extinguished like a billy of water dumped
on a campfire.

A dark-haired, well-muscled man with his haughty
Roman nose angled her way loomed in the doorway. A
full-lipped sensuous mouth, a mouth she'd never quite
been able to forget, unfortunately, held a definite hint of
hardness she'd not noticed the last time.

But that had been a long time ago. Those halcyon
days had ended after that cryptic phone call from his
family back across the world and had removed him from
her side.

This man had sworn he could never, ever come back to Lighthouse Bay. Yet here he was. Returned? The prickle on her skin as his glance captured hers was a heated reminder of a limited infatuation of a few intense days, but mammoth proportions. Lordy, she'd been naive, about twenty, and he a worldly twenty-eight.

Almost six years ago.

Raimondo Salvanelli, here?

The man who'd orchestrated her personal Shakespearean tragedy and the guilty party who'd exited stage left to return to Italy and instantly marry another woman.

She might regret her infatuation but never, ever the consequences of the ribbon of time that had changed her life.

She'd even fairly rapidly come to terms with Raimondo's inevitable absence, accepting they'd not been destined for happily ever after. Just an Italian doctor who didn't practise as a doctor and an Australian midwife, passing in the night.

Actually, several nights.

He'd said he wasn't coming back.

Um. So why was he here?

Worse, had he brought his Italian wife for the cave tour and she'd be right in behind him? No. She couldn't see that happening. Besides, her boss had only held up one finger.

The slight hysteria in the last thought resolved and Faith lifted her chin.

She looked again—and accepted that her daughter's father really had arrived and was going to be crawling around behind her in the dark for the next hour or so. Without any premonition on her part or warning on his. Excellent. Not.

To her disgust, she'd never found a man who could

hold her attention quite so effortlessly. Apparently, that inevitable fascination was still the same.

An immense man, and harshly handsome, with that mouth she only remembered for its humorous and sexy slant. Now there was grimness—which, unfairly, didn't detract from the picture as much as it should—hence the reason to watch him with the wary fascination she'd have if he were a magnificently coloured red-bellied black snake on a bush path.

Apart from his dark, dark eyes and his way too sexy lips she could see her daughter in him, something she'd always wondered about and a fact that perusal of the newspaper photographs had hidden.

Chloe's dad was here. Holy freakin' cow. And why now?

What did this mean for Chloe? Or Faith?

What made Raimondo present today when he hadn't responded when she'd written of her pregnancy?

He had been equally silent to her brief note after Chloe's birth. No reply by mail or any form of correspondence. Not even to enquire if they were both well, which had shown a coldness she hadn't predicted.

Well, the silence had been unexpected but understood. Sort of. After that phone call from his brother that had ended everything, Raimondo had announced he'd been going home to marry another woman. Hence the never coming back. Or responding to mail either, apparently.

Yet she'd planned to send another note when Chloe started school next year. And perhaps another when her daughter began her senior years.

She'd fought against allowing his disregard to inflame her because she should still pave the way if Chloe wished to pursue meeting her father in the future.

This had never been about Faith—it was about Chloe. All about Chloe.

But now he was here. Raimondo's dark eyes travelled slowly over her and, surprisingly, they narrowed, as did his mouth. Even as the eternal optimist, Faith could see something was wrong.

Well, whatever it was, she knew it wasn't her fault. She lifted her chin higher.

The possible implications of Raimondo revisiting her life opened like an unexpectedly dark flower in front of her and sent a flutter of maternal panic to quicken her breath.

He had rights.

She'd confirmed his claim in letters.

His name on the birth certificate, something she'd considered long and hard, saw to that as well.

She frowned and looked away in out-of-character confusion until accidentally glimpsing Dianne, her caving mentor, her caring friend and also her silver-haired boss, at the counter gesturing to Raimondo and the clock. The tour owner's hands were making exuberant waving motions as she encouraged Faith to commence the tour.

Faith glanced guiltily at the time. Five past ten already. The group peered her way expectantly.

All who had paid, including the man at the door, had arrived and it was time to leave. Good grief. It felt like too much to switch brains to tour guide after the shockwave of Raimondo's arrival.

Compartments.

Faith could do compartments.

Faith would have to do emergency situation compartments. Navigating herself and other people through life challenges was her bread and butter in her real profession as a midwife and she'd just have to drag that skill across to caving tours with the man she'd thought she'd never see again.

She could do that.

Mentally she clanked shut doors and boxes in her brain like a theme park gate keeper—clang, bolt, lock until all darting terrors were mostly inside… But Raimondo still loomed across the room. The man who was never coming back. And with a scowl as if he'd been the one left holding the baby.

Faith moistened her suddenly dry lips and cleared her throat.

Later. It would have to be later. 'Good morning. My name is Faith.' She remembered the way his soft vowels had caressed her name and, darn it, she could feel the heat on her cheeks but she pushed on and smiled more determinedly. 'I hope you're all as excited as I am to enjoy the glories of Binimirr Cave this morning.'

Her gaze swept over the others, avoiding the tall, overwhelming presence of the Italian man who'd positioned himself to the back of the group. With a tinge of tour guide unease she hoped his shoulders would fit through one particular narrow opening she could think of in the labyrinth ahead, but reassured herself he'd managed last time. When she'd given him the private tour all those years ago.

Her gaze refocused on the other participants, realised belatedly that the backpackers were in shorts and shook her head. She should have seen that earlier. Every time she crawled through the labyrinth she came home with scratches on her knees and she always wore jeans.

She said gently to everyone, 'This isn't your normal ramble through the paths and steps of a tourist cave. This adventure tour you've signed up for is off the level track and through rough confines. Which means you have to crawl over rough gravel on your knees, squeezing your shoulders and balancing on uneven rocks.'

Faith smiled, admittedly a little blindly, as her brain batted at her like a bat outside a window trying to comprehend why Raimondo would come back when he'd explained very gently five years ago why he never could or would.

Stop it. Clang. Stay locked.

She rubbed her own elbows and knees. 'Unless you're okay with losing your skin I'm very happy to give you a few minutes to pull some jeans on or buy some knee and elbow guards.'

Most of the participants had arrived on the dusty bus parked outside the shop and the scantily clad young couple peeled off from the group and headed for the tour bus at a fast jog. They were very sweet to be so eager. The quiet, nervous man crossed to the inexpensive knee supports and selected a set to purchase.

From the corner of her eyes she could see Raimondo standing to the back like a dark predator, motionless, an ability she suddenly remembered and had admired then, as others shifted and chatted, and against her will she slowly turned her face his way. Their eyes locked, his cocoa irises merging with the pupils, eyes so dark and turbulent with unexpected questions. And hers too, seeking answers and maybe reassurance as well.

Until the flare of connecting heat that she remembered from their first ever shared glance, all that time ago, hit her like a blast from a furnace. The flush of warmth low in her belly jumped into life and warned that despite her attempts at blocking out the past she 'knew' this man. In the biblical sense. Knew him too many passionate, mind-blowing times in that brief window of craziness.

A hot cascade of visceral memories flashed over her skin the way it had when he'd explored her with his hands. So long ago.

Heat scorched suddenly sensitive skin and molten memories surged with a thrust of explicit detail in her mind until she tore her eyes away, her breathing fast and her mouth dry. Like falling into a hot spring. Good grief.

How was she going to stay sane for the next ninety minutes, having him there, behind her, the whole way around the tour?

She glanced at Dianne but her boss was taking money at the till. Dianne couldn't help. Shouldn't help. It was Faith's problem. No. She'd do it. And when this cave trip was over she'd find out what this was all about because she'd done nothing wrong.

As usual, it only took a couple of brief wardrobe adjustments until the adventurers were ready—shame it had felt like hours—and she was glad Raimondo hadn't chosen this moment of waiting to approach. She told herself she was relieved. Very relieved.

Because she would do this on her terms.

Finally, the party reassembled and she directed everyone to the wall hung with helmets and headlamps, where she picked up a large and small helmet from the wall and two headlamps on elastic headbands. 'Grab a light and find a helmet your size—they're grouped small, medium and large—and I'll check your straps and talk about using your lights before we leave here.'

Then she lifted her head and walked steadily over to

Raimondo. Practising the words in her head. *This is unexpected. How unexpected. What a surprise.*

'Raimondo.' She handed him the helmet.

'Faith.' Just his smooth utterance of her name with his delicious Italian accent made the gooseflesh lift on her arms—unfortunately her hands were too full to rub the irritation.

'This is unexpected.' That had sounded too breathless and she reined in her control. 'As you can see—' she gestured with the helmet at the group just out of earshot '—it's my responsibility to return all these people safely to the surface.' That came out much more firmly. 'I can't have distractions so we can talk later, if that's why you are here.'

She waited.

'Certainly.'

She nodded. Get away now. 'I hope you enjoy the tour.'

He inclined his dark head. 'I enjoyed it last time.' The 'with you' remained unsaid. She spun away from him and began to check every other person's chin strap except his—she couldn't quite come at that—until everyone was helmeted, including herself.

After the usual jokes and selfie photos, and some fast Snapchat posting by the teens, they left the tourist shop to cross the dry grass in an enthusiastic crocodile of intrepid cavers.

She chewed her lip, a habit she'd tried to break when she was nervous, though it certainly wasn't the cave Faith was worried about. It was Raimondo and her own lack of concentration caused by the tall brooding man at the rear of the line.

She needed to remain focused on the safety of some-

times unwittingly careless people, and of course the
safety of the delicate structures and ecosystem of the
caverns, and she prided herself on her safety record.
Over two hundred successful tours. Which was why she
wanted to stay attentive while doing her job.

One tour nearly every week for the last six years. Except for the months of her pregnancy. She glanced back
and wished she could have asked Raimondo *not* to join
the tour but it was too late for that now.

They gathered at the entrance to the cave. She plastered her game face on. 'You might enjoy knowing a
little of the history as you crawl through so you can
imagine the past. We'll stop here just for a minute so I
can set the scene for you. And don't forget to ask any
questions as we go.'

Raimondo smiled grimly and her gut clenched. She
had to concentrate.

'Binimirr Caves. Binimirr is an Aboriginal word, in
one particular Indigenous dialect, for long hole, and those
clans knew of this cave for perhaps thousands of years.'
She smiled blindly at the assembled group and launched
into her spiel. 'As far as European settlers' history goes,
a lone horseman first discovered this limestone ridge and
then the caves in 1899. He thought them so spectacular
that he told others and they came to see them, despite
the lack of roads to Lighthouse Bay at the time. They
became very popular.'

There were some nods.

'These intrepid people climbed down with ropes and
candles and discovered a cathedral of stalactites and stalagmites and even though it was before roads came here
they still felt they could market the caverns for tourism.'
She pointed back towards the bus. 'That's what it's like

now so you can imagine how rough it was more than a hundred years ago.'

One of the teenage boys murmured a 'Wow' and Faith smiled at him.

'Thirty years after the caves were discovered, these early day entrepreneurs built a stately manor with huge picture windows overlooking the sea, to use as accommodation and enticement for visitors. You can see the ornate gates and driveway to the left when you first enter the car park. Maybe that was why it was honeymooners of the early nineteen-hundreds who were attracted by the mysterious caves, though others still came to celebrate the majestic setting. Later, that lovely old building closed to the public and became a private residence. We have a few old photos of what it used to be like in the kiosk if you are interested.'

She had a sudden forlorn thought of how she would have liked a honeymoon in that old mansion and, despite herself, her glance slid to Raimondo.

If it hadn't been for him making the standard so high she might have been married by now!

Faith shook her thoughts away and looked at the eager faces. Best only to look at them. 'Getting inside the cavern and caves is much easier today than it was then.' She gestured to the railed path. 'For them, after days of jolting rides they finally arrived and lowered each other down on ropes tied to the pepper trees, dressed in suits and hats, women in hoops and skirts.'

She waited for the oohs and ahhs to subside as the group imagined the potential wardrobe malfunctions. 'It took those plucky cavers ten hours of clambering, and no doubt countless torn flounces, to crawl through the caves that now take you an hour to circumnavigate when you use the stairs and boardwalks of twentieth century safety.'

She smiled again and it was getting easier to ignore the man at the back. This was her spiel, her forte, sharing this passion. 'In those days there were no pretty electric lights to backdrop the most magnificent of these natural wonders so far below the surface. Just lamps and candles.' She straightened her helmet. 'Okay. We'll enjoy the views you get today when we return to the gentle paths. But first we'll do some rough terrain ourselves and go deeper than the average tourist gets to see.

'Ready?' At their nods she moved forward to the entrance. 'I'll go first and point to where we're exiting the boardwalk. We slip under the rail to seek out the more remote and unusual areas of the cave. When we return you can take your time once you're back on the boardwalk and really savour the lighted areas of the larger caves.'

She looked around for the most nervous faces. 'Anyone who's feeling a little unsure—you should come up here next to me, with the most confident of you at the back.' The quiet man moved diffidently forward and Faith smiled at him. 'It's worth the effort,' she reassured him.

She noted Raimondo had stayed back and she felt the muscles in her shoulders relax a notch. Okay then. He wouldn't be breathing down her neck. Just watching her the whole time. Not great but better.

She went on. 'When you're traversing the cave please remember to use three points of contact to give you balance. Safety is the most important part of stepping off the boardwalk. As you know, we're heading for the dry riverbed which is more than forty metres below the surface and there's no lights down there.'

A few murmurs greeted that. 'If your heart does start to pound—' she slowed so everyone could hear '—if you can feel yourself becoming anxious, take a couple of deep breaths and remember...' They were all listening. She grinned. 'This is fun and there are more of these tours every week and we haven't lost one person yet.'

A ripple of relieved laughter eased the tension. 'Let's go.' Faith ducked her head and stepped down onto the sloping boardwalk. The air temperature cooled as she moved ahead, not too fast, because she could still remember the first time she'd entered the cavern and her open-mouthed awe of the ceilings and floors, but fast enough to encourage people not to stop until she made the point where they left the wooden planks.

A few minutes later she counted eight adults. 'Right then.' She crouched down, slid under the rail and put her weight on the uneven rocks off the main path, the stones like familiar friends under her feet. Then she slid sideways through a crevice, down an incline, and stopped to point out a particularly wobbly rock and let everyone catch up. 'Try to plant your weight on the big rocks— not into the holes.' She heard the crack of a helmet behind her as someone bumped their forehead. Bless the helmets.

'Now sit down on your bottom to slide off this small drop into the darkness below.' A stifled gasp from right behind her suggested someone had sat down too quickly and hit the wet spot on the cavern floor.

She raised her voice a little. 'It might be time to turn that headlamp on. Shine it on your feet, not into the eyes of the person in front, or into their faces behind you when you turn your head.'

This was all the fun stuff but she knew that most of

the tourists behind her would be stamping down the claustrophobia of being in a small tunnel space underground with someone in front and someone following them.

It was lucky Raimondo was at the back because the others might forget how much space he took up. Not something Faith could forget, though for a different reason.

She paused at a fork in the path and waited for everyone to catch up, then pointed at a magnificent curtain of rock.

'That veil of rock is where hundreds of years of dripping water have formed a bacon-rind-shaped rim of curved ice that divides the ceiling.' She remembered enthusing about that to Raimondo all those years ago.

She shook the thought off. The beauty truly did make her astonished every time. Lifting her chin, she pulled her imaginary cloak of confidence tightly around her again. 'Ahead are more joined stalactites to reach towards stalagmites and if you look over here there's a magnificent column that stretches from floor to ceiling. What a gift of nature—that took thousands of years.'

The reverence was back in her own voice because, despite the man at the end of the line of tourists, every time she came down here she shook her head in wonder. Which was why she still marvelled that Dianne actually paid her to savour this subterranean cathedral she loved so much.

They'd come to one of the tricky spots. 'This opening's narrow—be careful not to scrape yourself here.' This was the point she had wondered if Raimondo would have difficulty with sliding through.

He seemed even bigger than when she'd met him before. Hard to imagine but true. More wedge-shaped. Toughened and toned. Muscled and honed. Hopefully not so broad that he'd jam in the crevice like a cork in a bottle—but she had a contingency plan for the others if he did. Not so much for him. She stifled an evil grin. Tsk, Faith, she admonished herself.

Still, there was another, less accessible exit for emergencies, and nobody had ever really been stuck.

Yet.

She waited.

Tried not to hold her breath.

Her heart rate picked up as she heard the subtle crunch of rock fragments in a long agonising squeeze, then he pushed through into the small cavern they were all standing in with a slight rush. Close fit.

Her breath puffed out.

He was fine. Bet that made the sweat stand out on his manly brow though. She smiled.

Then frowned at herself.

Another tsk. Not nice, Faith.

This was unlike her and a measure of how much that grim visage of his had affected her equilibrium.

Stop thinking about him.

'We'll edge down this rock face now. The path narrows so please don't touch that glistening rock there,' She shone her headlamp at the shimmering silver wall. 'It has beautiful fragile crystals so you can take photos and admire it, but it will become disfigured if you accidentally touch it.' She watched them and saw with satisfaction how they all leaned the other way to protect the wall.

'Thank you,' she murmured. 'Almost there.' There were a few Hail Marys behind her and she stifled a laugh. The shy quiet man had turned out to be a Catholic comedian. You had to love him.

Finally, after another ten minutes of winding and uneven descent, she stepped into an opening with a sloping floor. It spread out into a wide cavern and she heard the sighs of relief to be able to spread out a little. The distance narrowed between roof and floor and she resisted the urge to duck her head. Enough of that soon enough.

'If you shine your lights down towards your shoes you'll see you're standing on red sandy soil.'

All lights tilted downwards and there were some comments of, 'All the way down here. Wow.'

'So, we're here. You're standing on the bed of a river from thousands of years ago, stretching away in two directions.'

She let that statement sit in the silence as the others thought about that and shone their headlamps around. 'As you can see with your lights…' and that was all they could see with, as no other light could penetrate this far into the cave '…there's a line of white rocks marking off a section of the cave. Also, in front of us, a circle of the same stones to protect an area of new stalactite formation.'

She crouched down and even now she could feel the excitement as her heart rate sped up with the wonder of all this subterranean world so far below the surface. 'See this—' She pointed out the new holes burrowing into the dirt in the centre of the circle.

'Every drop is making the hole larger and eventually it will form a pencil of creation.'

She breathed out and those standing next to her murmured their own awe. This was why she loved these tours. When she felt the connection from others at the opportunity to see something so few people had.

'If you look across from us—' she angled her head and the light shone on the roof '—hanging from the low roof like eyelashes, those are thin tendrils of tree roots that are searching for the water that left eons ago, but the moisture remains and even though the roots don't touch any water the filaments absorb moisture from the air.'

Someone said, 'Amazing.' She smiled in their direction.

'There's no natural light—the creatures who live here are small, without eyes, their bodies are see-through, almost like albino slaters.' She crouched down and drew an example the size of a cat in the red dirt with her finger.

Her comedian said in the darkness, 'That looks too big for comfort,' and laughed nervously. Several other voices murmured.

Faith grinned. 'Not drawn to scale.' She pointed out a tiny white beetle-like creature on a tree root. 'But if you see one of them in front of you when you're crawling, please scoop up a handful of dirt and shift him aside.'

The young woman next to Faith who'd changed into jeans said in a small voice, 'You say we are crawling?'

'Yep, we're sliding under that overhang on our stomachs, using our elbows, for about thirty metres, but it opens into a small cavern after that.'

'Perhaps,' she said in her lilting accent, 'I can stay here and mind the bags?'

Faith looked at her and noted her pinched nostrils and darting eyes. 'Perfectly fine. We'll only be about ten minutes' crawl away, though you mightn't hear us because the riverbed bends a little. Then it opens into another cavern where we can sit up. We'll be gone for about thirty minutes by the time we spend ten minutes there as well as crawling there and back. Will you be fine with that?'

She laughed nervously. 'I find it very peaceful here.'

'I'll stay with her,' one of the teenage boys offered with pretended resignation. It was so obviously what he wanted to do that everyone laughed.

Faith nodded. 'The rest of us can drop all our extra stuff, like cameras and jumpers, here. Too hard to crawl on your belly dragging a drink bottle or camera.'

There was a small wave of tense laughter as people dropped surplus bits and crouched down. The black semi-circular opening above the red sandy floor looked about three feet high and maybe ten feet wide, based with the red sand of the ancient river. A little too much like a mouth that would eat them, Faith had thought the first time, and she guessed a few of the others now thought the same.

'I'll go belly down into the damp dirt first so you know I'm ahead, but I need a volunteer to go last. Someone needs to make sure we all keep going.'

'I will go last.' Raimondo spoke quietly, his thick accent rolling calmly around the tiny space. When the others expelled breaths of relief he said, 'I have been on this tour before and have no concerns.'

Faith knew this last stretch tested the first timers' resolve as they slithered forward in the dark, seeing the backside and feet of the person in front, the circle of light from the person behind washing over them, the roof closing in over their helmeted head. She'd had the occasional talk down of a panicked group member at this part but in the end they all agreed the challenge was worth it.

Faith knelt down until she was lying on the damp sand

and glanced at Raimondo, looming above her. He nod-ded calmly and with a last flashing grin at the rest of the group she propelled herself forward along the riverbed, the circle of her headlamp piercing the darkness ahead with its warm glow.

She heard them behind her and the flicker of the oth-ers' lights occasionally shone past until she'd crawled all the way to the cavern.

She sat up and waited, watching the circles of light approach one by one as each crawled out of the hole and into the circle of the cavern.

'You can sit up now. There's a good foot over your head.'

'Gee, thanks,' the first arrival, the other of the solid woman's sons, muttered mock complainingly, and she grinned in his direction.

'Just shimmy around so the next person can sit up and move next to you until we have a circle.' It didn't take long for all of them to arrive and she wasn't sure how Raimondo ended up sitting next to her, but she doubted it was by accident.

Faith cleared her throat. She couldn't change the next bit and he probably knew it. 'We're going to turn out all our lights and just sit here, in the belly of Mother Earth, in the dark, and soak in the wonder of what we are ex-periencing.'

The same smart alec said, 'Why not?' But everyone laughed. Except Raimondo.

There was a murmur of further surprise and then slowly, as they all began to feel the magic of the space, she could feel the agreement.

She pushed on. 'And we'll sit in silence for a minute or two just to soak it in—where we are, how long this cavern has been here, and how amazing you all are to do this and still be having fun.'

A few murmurs of pride.

'After the silence I'll share an Aboriginal legend I was told about a good spirit from the ocean and a bad spirit from the cave, and how these caves were formed.'

Like good children, one by one they turned out the lights until the darkness fell like a blindfold over them.

Faith closed her eyes. She always found this moment, this silence, incredibly peaceful. The air she breathed felt moist on her nose and throat as she inhaled and she dug her fingers into the damp earth and collected two handfuls of the sleeping riverbed and held them with her eyes shut tight—not that it made any difference, open or shut, in the total dark.

She always felt blessed to have been given this moment in time to embrace the idea of being a part of this river under the earth. Breathing in and out quietly as the silence stretched for several minutes. Nobody fidgeted or spoke until she judged enough time had passed. Then she began to tell the story of the battle of the ancients.

CHAPTER TWO

RAIMONDO BRUNO SALVANELLI closed his eyes as Faith's lilting voice rose from the darkness beside him. He allowed her words to flow over and through him because he'd heard the cave story before, privately, and he wanted to find the peace she'd once told him she found here— for himself.

So, instead of listening to the story, he savoured the cadence of her voice and the reality that she had still been exactly where he'd left her so long ago. Again, he inhaled the oh, so subtle scent of her herbal shampoo and welcomed the warmth in the air from her body so close to his.

The sudden rush of possessiveness he'd felt when he'd first seen her from the tourist shop door had shocked him. An emotion he had no right to, a stranger very briefly in her life almost six years ago, a stranger still, and one who had told her he would never return after he had broken her heart.

That first time had been Sydney Airport where he'd caught her eye, she'd smiled, and he'd instantly invited her to join him when he'd seen her flight had been postponed along with his.

Then, hours later, because still he wasn't ready to

lose his new companion, they'd shared dinner in an airport bar, jostled by other stranded passengers yet alone in their own world of discovery, and she had captivated him. He'd watched her mobile face as she'd described her beautiful Lighthouse Bay. Her work as a midwife, her hobby of cave tours and her love of life.

Their flights had been rescheduled again and they'd spent the night stranded, and then, imprudently, tangled together making love in an airport hotel, lost to the wild weather outside that had grounded their aircraft.

The crazy urgency had grown until he'd done something so out of character, so reckless and impulsive, even years later he was still surprised. He'd changed his flight to match her re-booked one, delayed his return to Italy for two days, followed her home to the house on the cliff for the one night and two days he hadn't scheduled and found himself lost in unsophisticated and trusting arms.

This was a world of tenderness he hadn't known since he'd been a child and his parents had been alive.

When she'd taken him the next morning for a personal cave tour before he'd left he'd been captivated again by her passion for the natural wonders she'd shared. Had silently begun to plan to return and see where this craziness between them might lead.

Then the return to sanity from the craziness that had come upon him with Faith. He could have vanished into it for ever if not for that call from his brother—his grandfather lay dying, the man who had raised them since he was seven. The news had been a deluge of cold water that had dashed his dreams and dragged him home to filial duty and deathbed requests. His brother had warned him what lay in store so he had said goodbye to Faith with finality.

Never to return because they were from different worlds. Because of the commitment he'd made to his dying grandfather—one he would never have broken until it had self-destructed—his fault, his ex-wife's fault and also partly this woman's fault because his heart had not been available. His new wife had seen that and hardened her own heart even more. Then his twin brother's tragedy and the need for Raimondo to shoulder the leader's role until Dominico could recover.

At the time, returning to Australia had seemed impossible. His brother had agreed that the woman he'd had so brief a liaison with would have married by now, then the years had slipped by so fast after his marriage had dissolved—his new direction into a general practice for the needy, and the occasional international aid work, placating his feelings of failure and he didn't have the time to fly across the world on a whim.

There had never seemed a future, with Faith settled here and him a son of Italy for ever. Had he been wrong?

He would never have come back except for the news he'd heard.

News he hadn't believed.

News he hadn't been able to risk not investigating.

It had been the mention of a place called Lighthouse Bay in Australia, in a discussion of a wedding one of his colleagues had attended before she'd returned to Florence.

Raimondo had been drawn like a moth to the flame of that conversation.

'So, you have seen Lighthouse Bay?' he'd asked, unable to stop himself.

'Yes, I have been to two weddings there, now. This wedding in the church and one on the beach. Both very beautiful.'

His colleague had appeared mildly curious that he too had seen the place. Again unable to help himself, he had asked about Faith and the answer had stunned him.

'Yes, I met many people. And yes!' There had been an amused glance. 'In fact, I remember Faith, the brides-maid, and her little girl—so cute.'

He had not known she had a daughter. 'So, she's mar-ried then?'

'No, Mr Puritan. She has a daughter without a hus-band. The child looked about four or five.'

So he'd come.

And on his first sight of Faith, the woman he'd never forgotten but whose charisma had endured as if she were a distant enchanted dream, he'd felt the swell of an emotion he shouldn't have. Here he was, sitting on the sandy bed of an ancient river, forty-five metres below the earth's surface, listening to her so-charming voice as it caressed his ears and wishing he had never left.

That voice was still as restful and as calming. She was as beautiful as he remembered, with her slim but curved body poured into that ridiculous T-shirt and so tight jeans. It proved difficult to resist the urge to slide his fingers through the damp earth and find her hand to take in his, as he had when she'd brought him on a pri-vate tour of this place.

His empty hand could even remember the warmth and softness of her small fingers interlaced with his from all that time ago. How could that be? He didn't know. What he did know was that he had not planned well.

A week would not be long enough.

He knew that now from his first sight of her, the way his whole being had come alive from what felt like a deep sleep. And that was without the added possibility that they shared a child.

Faith. He'd lost her and her conviction in the goodness of others and perhaps he would find both again in this place of dark caves and far oceans. He'd forgotten so much about her and he wanted to learn it all over again.

Which would require some negotiation with the life he'd left behind. And his need to encourage his twin brother away from his obsessive focus on the business after losing his family. Raimondo's busy life suddenly seemed far less important than it should, compared to what was happening at Lighthouse Bay.

But that was for later.

He realised the story had finished, the cave silent for those few seconds after a well-told tale, and then soft questions broke out.

Faith answered them quietly then concluded, 'Okay then. Lights on. Those nearest the entrance can start to crawl back and congregate in the next cavern. I'm sure those waiting will be glad to see us. When we make our way back to the main paths and under the rail again, I'll do one more head count then you're free to wander. Just drop your helmets and headlamps back at the shop when you're finished.'

'What if we get lost?' The comedian.

'You'll be on the main path. And they'll switch the spotlights on and off in the cave when it's shutting, so you'll know when we are about to close. In about four hours.' There was a smile in her voice, one he remembered too clearly, and the group laughed.

'I'm used to the dark now,' someone said and the person next to them snorted.

He waited. He knew she would be the last to leave this cavern deep in the earth in case someone became lost or panicked. So he waited with her. As he should have waited before.

Six years! She'd been so young, beautiful, excited and as attracted to him as he'd been to her—the two of them like two silly moths mesmerised by the moment—grounded in an airport cocoon of wild weather and overwhelming fascination increased by the improbability of any future. Once he'd finished his business in Sydney he'd be flying home to Italy, her back to her seaside town and her beloved midwifery. She'd been barely twenty and he eight years senior and should have known better.

But they'd talked until their mouths were dry. Been amazed by the rapport that had sprung between them as if reunited friends from childhood. How could that be? From opposite sides of the world?

From a past life, Faith had said, and he'd hugged her to him for the endearing ridiculousness of that statement.

Though, once she'd laid her head against his chest, it was then that everything had spun out of control. For two full days until his brother had grounded him with familial duty, then he knew their love castles were built on dreams he couldn't follow. Could never follow. A truth he'd left her with. But was that all he'd left her with?

CHAPTER THREE

FAITH WATCHED THE headlamp lights disappear one by one. Damn, she'd missed her chance to send him first.

She tried telepathy.

Go!

She urged the man beside her to move off with the others but he obviously wasn't picking up the vibe. She couldn't go until he had, it was her way, and she broke the silence between them as the last lamp disappeared under the curtain of rock.

'I need you to go now, please.'

He didn't say anything, just moved forward and crawled away from her.

Faith took a moment to breathe deeply and centre herself, and here in the arms of the earth on the soft sand of millennia was a good place to do it.

Okay. She'd get them all back to the safety of the walking path and then they could talk. She didn't have to pick up Chloe until two p.m., just before work, when preschool finished. So she had a couple of hours to discover why Raimondo had returned to rattle her composure and her world.

She wondered what her aunt would say when she told her Chloe's father had arrived, far too many years too late.

* * *

Twenty minutes later she left the group at the boardwalk and her job was done.

Except one of the participants didn't stay behind and she could feel the heat from Raimondo's body as he walked beside her to the exit of the cave. His arm swung beside her arm and she tucked her fingers in close to her body so she didn't accidentally knock his hand.

Out in the bright sunshine Faith stopped on the path and the man beside her stopped too. She lifted her head and met his gaze steadily. 'So why are you here?' She'd done nothing wrong.

His eyes were that deep espresso brown of unfiltered coffee, dark and difficult to see to the bottom of the cup or, more to the point, to the bottom of his heart.

'I have come because I heard you had a child.' His cadence was old-fashioned, she remembered that, formally stiff, but it was a way of speaking she'd found incredibly sexy when she'd been young and silly, in its translated whimsy of sentence structure.

Then his words settled over her like the damp leaves had settled over the forest floor. Thick and stealing the light. He had heard?

She blinked. Pushed back his heaviness. 'I wrote you that. At the beginning and at the end of my pregnancy. Five years ago.'

'No. I did not see this.' He shook his head emphatically, but his face stilled and suddenly expression fled to leave an inscrutable mask of blank shock. 'Madonna.' A quiet explosive hiss.

'Chloe, not Madonna,' she offered with just a little tartness in her voice. She frowned at him. Trying to understand. 'I wrote twice.'

Again he said, 'No.'

He shook his head but he must have seen the truth in her eyes because his face softened slightly as he looked at her. The silence stretched between them until he said softly, 'Then it is as I suspected? You had a child that is mine?'

Unfortunate words if he wanted her to continue this conversation. 'No.' She watched him blink. Good.

He'd relinquished that role by his disinterest. 'You fathered a child who is mine.' She amazed herself with the steadiness and calmness of the answer while her heart bounced in agitation in her chest. 'Her name is Chloe and she is almost five. Chloe Fetherstone.' She needed time to think and her feet moved her forward. He reached out and caught her hand, not tight but with an implacable hold she couldn't shake off without an undignified tug.

She stopped and glanced pointedly at his big fingers on her wrist. 'Let go. I need a minute.' She wasn't the timid junior midwife who'd fallen for him years ago. She was a single mother, a senior midwife, a responsible niece to a woman she admired and who had been the rock this man should have been.

She held his gaze with her eyebrows raised.

His fingers released her.

Faith began to walk again and he fell into step beside her.

He hadn't known?

Had she addressed the envelope correctly?

She'd addressed it so many times until at last she hadn't torn up the letter. He'd told her his home town and she had based her identity search assuming he hadn't lied about that or his true name.

'Where did you send these letters?' His mind must be running along the same lines as hers.

'I looked you up. In the town you'd mentioned. Sent it to your house.' She recited the address. Funny how she could still remember it. She glanced at him. 'Two letters eight months apart. Don't get the wrong idea. I knew where I stood. I wasn't asking for anything. Just giving you information I felt you should have.'

His face had gone back to inscrutable. 'Did you not think it strange when no answer returned?'

'Of course. Though "strange" was not the word I would have chosen. Thoughtless. Uncaring. Bitterly dis-appointing.' She shrugged.

It was a long time ago now and she was over it. Over him. 'You said you would never return. I expected little. I did my part and it was not my fault if you defaulted on yours.'

'I did not…' His voice had grown harsher, risen just a little. 'Default.' Then the last word more quietly. He looked at her. 'My apologies. This is…difficult.'

She laughed with little amusement. So was meeting a transient lover from years ago when she'd been young and silly enough to fall pregnant. 'Take your time.'

Faith looked ahead to the tourist shop they'd almost reached. 'Give me your helmet and headlamp. I'll get my things and we can go for a coffee somewhere.'

She surprised herself with the stability in her voice when inside she was panicking and fretting. She wished her heart would settle into a cold calm. What did this mean for the world she had created for Chloe and her-self? She hated not being in control—even if it didn't show.

No. He would not cast her into turmoil again. She

had this. She had to have it. She was comfortable in her shoes as the one who had done the right thing and as a single mother who loved her child more than life itself. He was the one who had had the shock and would have to change the way he thought.

By the time she returned from the shop the tracks he'd made with his pacing showed dirt underneath the mounds of blue metal road gravel. Worn away with his exasperation. She almost smiled at that but if he hadn't known about Chloe at all then she could feel sympathy for his shock. She could still remember that cold horror from the unforgettable day her pregnancy test had shown a positive reading.

Yes, she had sympathy, but no, she wasn't relaxing. She didn't have the luxury of softness or at least she didn't have the headspace for it just yet. Would Isabel think her mad or prudent to let him into their lives? Then again, her aunt was a sensible woman with few prejudices.

'Which is your car?' Hers was way across the car park under a tree and they'd have to drive to Lighthouse Bay for coffee. She didn't want him following her straight to Chloe. They'd go somewhere first. Talk. She wasn't taking him home. Yet.

He indicated the black Mustang Shelby not far from her vehicle, well splattered with dirt and mud from the road into the caves, and even from a distance it seemed to glower at the assortment of vehicles in the cleared space. Like Raimondo had glowered when he'd first arrived. She wasn't taking attitude from either of them, gave the car a disdainful look then caught herself.

Silly, she chided. It was just a rental car and she was getting fanciful, but the model was unusual for these parts. Still, to him she raised her brows. Why was she not surprised he'd hire the most expensive and flamboyant one possible?

Years ago, when she'd searched on the web for him, she'd seen the terrifying extent of his family's influence and power, their pharmaceutical company, backed by a photo of Raimondo and his brother and an elderly, strong-jawed, massive-shouldered man who had to be his late grandfather—long Roman noses making it clear they were all related—and was almost glad she didn't have to meet that old man, that family, and parade her naïveté.

Though she'd decided when Chloe was older she could make the decision for herself as to whether she would contact her father or not and Faith would support her daughter's decision.

Well, that was moot now. He was here to talk about Chloe. 'That car looks like you.'

'How so?' His brow quirked.

'Expensive. Black. Muscly.' She had to smile. 'Low to the ground doesn't fit though.'

He was looking at her as if he couldn't quite work her out. She guessed she had changed from the agreeable, star-struck twit she'd been when she'd met him all those years ago into a seemingly confident woman. No. Not seemingly. She was confident. She wondered if he was having a problem understanding why she had hadn't fallen into hysterics when he'd appeared.

Time to show that maturity she had spent years acquiring. 'We can have coffee at the little café down on the beach at Lighthouse Bay.'

If he'd found her here he could find the town beach. 'I'll meet you there.'

'I will follow you.' He touched her hand and she looked back at him. 'When will I meet our daughter?'

She let the 'our' go. At least he'd shifted from 'my'. 'Soon. After we talk I'll let you know.'

The hard stare that followed her response made her pulse jump a little. She hadn't seen this side of him and she realised they'd both grown up. She reminded herself how he might be feeling and tempered her response. 'It will happen.' *As long as you're good*, but she didn't say that out loud. Might not be polite.

'Faith!' Dianne's voice called out and Faith spun to answer the urgency she could hear in her boss's call.

She jogged back to the shop and could hear Raimondo behind her, which was a good thing when she saw the lovely older gentleman from the cave tour, his iridescent shoes shining up at them as he lay face up on the floor of the shop with his wrinkled face quickly turning blue. Dianne knelt beside the man, shaking him. She had the box with the bag and resuscitation mask beside her but hadn't had a chance to open it. She was fumbling with the catch.

Her eyes were huge. 'He staggered in and then just sagged to the floor. I rolled him over but he's gone blue.'

'Dianne, you ring the ambulance then come back. We'll start here.' Faith knelt down to tilt the man's head and check his airway. She placed her cheek near his nose and mouth but couldn't feel any movement. 'He's not breathing.'

Raimondo nodded and shifted forward to lean over the man and begin efficient cardiac massage. Thank goodness she and Dianne weren't alone to manage until the ambulance came. As quickly as she could, Faith assembled the bag and mask Dianne had left and positioned them over the elderly man's face. She squeezed a breath into his lungs after every thirty compressions that Raimondo made.

After four cycles and no visible improvement they swapped places as Dianne came back. She was puffing from the run. 'Ambulance is on the way.'

'Do you have a defibrillator? An AED?' Raimondo's question made Faith's head lift. She felt like slapping her forehead. Why hadn't she thought to ask for that before Dianne went to the phone? She knew they had one. For every minute the patient didn't respond their survival rate dropped by ten per cent. The sooner the defibrillator was attached the better.

Dianne stared at Raimondo for a second as her brain caught up. 'Yes. On the wall.' She spun around and disappeared then reappeared almost instantly, holding the yellow box with the small Automated Emergency Defibrillator.

'Well done.' Raimondo shot her a smile. 'Can you take over the bagging from me after the next two breaths and I'll take over the cardiac massage from Faith? Count to thirty compressions and then two breaths. Faith can position the defibrillator while we continue on.'

Faith looked at him. Nice. It was exhausting work even though she'd made sure she had her shoulders straight over her locked hands. She was slowing already and Raimondo could make a much more efficient compression of the chest walls than she could when tiring.

She heard the two breaths go in, Raimondo put down the bag and mask and slid in beside her to take over with very little interruption to the rhythm.

Very slick, she thought gratefully as she moved quickly to the man's shirt and pulled it open. Luckily his chest had scarce hair so the connection would be good without the shaving they didn't have time to do. Peeling off the backing paper, she slapped the adhesive pads onto his chest wall above the right nipple and the left pad below the heart.

Switching on the machine, the automated voice intoned 'Stop CPR, do not touch patient, analysing.'

'Clear the patient.' Raimondo's firm voice reminded them not to touch the man in case a rescuer's pulse was counted accidentally by the sensors. Everyone sat back. Raimondo's eyes met Faith's. This was the man's best chance but they also knew that a shock would only be useful if the rhythm was one that could be corrected by an electric surge.

'VT or VF,' Faith hoped out loud as she crossed her fingers.

Raimondo said to Dianne, 'If it says shock, stay back and don't touch him. After the shock we will begin CPR again for two minutes. Then the machine will reassess so we will stop again. If it says "no shock required" we will recommence cardiac massage.'

'I never thought I'd see this thing used,' Dianne said shakily.

'Shock advised.' Said the machine.

'Stand clear,' Raimondo said again and it felt surreal to Faith that a man she hadn't seen for so long sat beside her. Not only that, he'd joined her in a resuscitation in a tourist shop near Lighthouse Bay. Not how she'd seen today pan out, but at this moment she couldn't be happier he was here.

The machine began the warning noises until the patient's body jerked with the surge of electricity and, with an odd gurgling noise, the man's chest heaved as he dragged in a shuddering breath. His eyelids flickered but didn't open.

Faith looked at Raimondo. 'Thank God,' she said at the same time as Dianne murmured the same.

Raimondo's lips twitched. *'Sì.'* He lifted his head and listened. 'The ambulance is nearly here as well.' They all listened to the faint wail in the distance.

Faith narrowed her eyes as she thought about the road in. 'It's a few minutes away. Will we roll him onto his side?'

'Yes.' They did so, the man mumbling something, causing Faith to bend down near his ear.

'It's okay. You've been unwell but you're looking better now. The ambulance is coming and they'll take you to hospital.'

He struggled to open his eyes and when he saw her he sagged back and relaxed, though his hand crept up to his chest. Whether from cardiac pain or bruising to his ribs from Raimondo, she couldn't tell. 'Faith. You. Thank you.'

'We all helped. Lie quietly. The ambulance will bring oxygen and pain relief.'

'Okay,' on an outward sigh as he closed his eyes. She had no doubt he would have some significant pain.

Five minutes later the ambulance arrived and everything moved quickly after that.

Faith left Raimondo to assist and explain to the paramedics and took Dianne into the shop for a cup of tea as the older lady looked shaky after the excitement.

Faith was feeling a little shaky herself. Cardiac arrest was not something she'd seen in the maternity ward, thank goodness, though, because it was possible, they all did their yearly competencies in resuscitation. It was reassuring she'd remembered what to do.

'So lucky we had the doctor here.' Dianne was still coming down from the good outcome.

'Yes. Very lucky.' She'd known Raimondo had finished medicine, but had thought he worked at the drug company, but he'd been as slick as an ED doctor. She guessed she'd find out. Six years was time for many things to change.

'And that you know him,' Dianne enthused. 'He was so calm. And you were too, dear. I'm very glad you were both here.' That last was said a little tearfully and Faith gave Dianne's hand a squeeze.

'You were brilliant too, Dianne. Barney is very lucky. Getting the equipment. Ringing the ambulance and then taking over perfectly while I put the chest stickers on. You were a marvel.'

'We were a good team.' Dianne nodded and lifted her chin.

Raimondo had made the difference out of all of them though, Chloe thought. Cardiac massage was hard work and without his arms beside her she would have been scrambling to get it all done and keep the perfusion up for Barney to give him that second chance.

Raimondo's big hands and strong arms. His presence. So many facets that had captured her so long ago, and she could appreciate them now. But she wouldn't be swayed into softening. She couldn't.

They heard the ambulance leave and Raimondo appeared at the door. Faith kissed Dianne's cheek. 'You did really well. I'll go now if you're okay.'

'I'm fine.' Dianne took a deep breath and plastered

a smile on her face. 'A day with a difference, that's for sure.'

Faith glanced at the man at the door. 'Absolutely.'

'You were excellent,' Raimondo said to Dianne. 'As was Faith.' He gestured to the AED, which was in Faith's hand.

'I'll replace the sticky pads from the hospital stores and bring it back.'

He nodded. 'All things we needed done were done.' He inclined his head. 'Thank you.' Smiled his killer smile at Dianne, who blinked and smiled back, half-besotted.

'Thank you, Doctor.'

Faith rolled her eyes. She was getting over the benefit side of Raimondo being there now and moving to the worry.

'Raimondo and I have to go,' she said and led the way from the shop to head across the car park.

CHAPTER FOUR

RAIMONDO'S GAZE REMAINED on her as Faith walked across the gravel of the car park, her tall, willowy body weaving between the parked vehicles with a natural grace that held his eye and made his heart pound. He'd been a fool not to return. And doubly so because of Chloe. If only he'd known.

But Faith? Faith made his heart pound even more than working on a cardiac arrest. *Dios.* What a day. Faith had been magnificent. Of course. He had known the young woman he had left behind all those years ago had strength and today he had seen the growth of that inner steel for himself.

With the resuscitation, the elderly man had been fortunate, and he wished him well. In fact, he would telephone the regional hospital he would be taken to. The paramedics had said they would bypass Lighthouse Bay Hospital for the more cardiac-focused regional centre. He knew instinctively Faith would want to know as well. Funny how already he was back to considering what Faith would want and including her in his plans.

But this moment, this second in the deserted car park, he could see her dark hair, halfway down her back now that it was loose from the ponytail she'd worn for the tour. Hair that glistened as it captured the sun in subtle red highlights, cascading in a riot of soft waves. He could almost feel the texture of those thick strands between his fingers and frowned at himself.

This was not why he'd come.

For these feelings to reappear was not reasonable. He'd come here because he'd suspected this woman had purposely excluded him from his daughter's life. And why had that been so incredibly painful that he'd boarded the first plane he could?

Probably because in his heart he could not believe that was like the Faith of his treasured memories. And yes, if letters had been sent, and intercepted, twice, with malice or agenda, then it would be like Maria to have done that. His bitter, conceited, forever dissatisfied ex-wife. It would have amused Maria to have caused that loss.

Yes, he believed it of Maria but not of Faith. The last damaging laugh to Maria. With Faith and her daughter the most injured parties.

Faith turned her head as if she'd caught his thoughts and he saw her brows crease. He waved and forced a smile. He needed to reassure her that he had no plans to do anything she didn't want. She did not trust him. Why should she? He had left her with a child and never answered her letters.

Dios.

As if encouraged by his smile, she waved back and climbed into her car and had him fumbling at the remote to open his own car in his haste to follow before she drove out of his sight.

He mused that this too was like the first moment he'd seen her walk by and felt this same sense of urgency to obey his instinct. What was it about Faith that grabbed him by the throat, shoved him by the shoulder, so he had to follow when he was in her orbit?

He slid into the car and turned on the guttural engine. Yes, he'd been self-indulgent with this hire, and not sensible really when he knew he'd be driving out along this dirt road to the caves, he thought as he shadowed her car down the dusty forest road towards Lighthouse Bay. But it was deeply, primitively satisfying to know she would not be able to speed away if she tried to lose him. He had it bad. But she hadn't tried to run.

Faith was as he'd remembered. With the passing of years she'd grown even more beautiful, more poised and personable, which sat well with her good heart. A heart he hoped he could still believe in because he was afraid he'd been fooling himself that he'd forgotten the woman who had captured his attention so easily.

See what he had done with his recklessness.

She had been left with a child.

He had carelessly altered both their futures and hurt the child he didn't know was his by his irresponsible actions. He shook his head as he drove, shadowing her car, unconsciously ready at any moment to pursue if needed.

Yet, despite his unexpected arrival today, she had not criticised him. Faith had spoken to him with kindness and sense; no rancour or revenge came his way when it should. He knew no other woman who would be so generous and honest. He'd met many who had nowhere near her decency.

Again, here was a growing need to understand what it was about Faith Fetherstone that touched him so much, as well as finding out about the daughter he had yet to meet.

When he'd first suspected about the child he'd done his homework. He'd looked Miss Fetherstone up and seen her address remained the same. Had decided on reintroducing himself at the caves because she couldn't avoid him in a group. Had even booked the tour online after confirming with the owner that the guide—*Faith, who had taken him before*—worked that day. Seemed the best way of making sure she'd be there before he'd booked his flights from Florence.

It had all turned out as he'd planned. And now he was to meet his daughter. Children had been his dream for so long but Maria had turned him from any thought of another arranged marriage.

But a child. Almost five? The thought suddenly filled him with trepidation that he was not worthy.

What if Chloe was afraid of him? He, a big dark-haired Italian man with no skill for children because only one nephew had bounced on his knee—a nephew gone. Coming from a family with everything except the richest prize. The next generation.

He remembered well when his parents had died how it had felt to face the stern grandfather who was to be his and his brother's future. No softness. Just duty. Sadly, he worried his brother was turning into their grandfather.

Imagine if his own daughter saw his grandfather in him.

He shuddered and his hands clenched on the steering wheel until he forced them to relax. He had faith. And Faith. She would help, but first he needed to convince her he meant no harm. He could appreciate the care she took of her daughter and understand the need to confirm his motives before she gave him access.

The problem was—how much access did he really want and how much would be good for his new family?

CHAPTER FIVE

FAITH DROVE STEADILY, trying not to glance too often in the rear-view mirror as she traversed the winding roads to the turn onto Lighthouse Bay Road. The big black car stayed reasonably back but she was constantly aware of the leashed power of the vehicle.

The charismatic power of the stern-visaged driver.

The relentless momentum of being manoeuvred into this meeting by a man she could see expected his own way.

How had he known she was at the caves? How much planning had he done before he'd arrived and how did she make sure she wasn't on the back foot trying to catch up to him?

All thoughts that continued to swirl fifteen minutes later when Raimondo solicitously ushered her into her seat at the beachside café as if she were a flower of extreme fragility.

A tiny pang pierced her composure. She remembered this feeling. This subtle olde-worlde charm of Raimondo. Being the focus of his dark eyes.

Nobody had pulled her chair out for her since, well, since Raimondo, and it did make her feel more feminine than she had for a long time. But then again, maybe someone else might have been equally caring if she'd been interested in looking for an escort. She'd been too busy being a mum and a midwife and ensuring the protection of her family life to risk a relationship.

Or she hadn't found anyone who made her feel as this man did and it wasn't worth the bother.

The reality of how she reacted to Raimondo made her grip the edges of her seat. He looked calm. Calm like she wanted to be, but she'd been working herself up on the drive, she realised.

His ease, and his ability to even glance around approvingly before he sat, suddenly agitated her. With a rising, and possibly irrational, irritation words spilled out as soon as his backside hit the chair. 'So what does your wife think of you coming all the way to Australia on the chance of paternity?' Shut her mouth. At least she'd said it quietly.

Grimaced at herself. Impatience had made her too blunt. To her relief the oblivious waitress arrived and took their coffee orders and when she'd left it wasn't surprising the silence hung between them.

He studied the table a moment longer before looking across at her and she watched his big fingers smooth the pressed shell and sand placemat in front of him without thought. 'My wife and I annulled our marriage after one year.' His tone remained matter-of-fact though there was an emotion which she couldn't identify lacing the dry words. 'Our legal commitments were met with regard to my grandfather's wishes and it was not required to continue.'

'Annulled?' Legal commitments? But the first part remained her focus. She couldn't help the disbelief in her voice. Her memories did not include a celibate Raimondo. Or a cold-blooded legal brain.

The whirlwind that had been their relationship had exploded into mutual, foolish abandon. Embarrassing in retrospect; though she could never regret her beautiful Chloe, she did regret her trust in this man. And he hadn't even made the woman he'd left her for happy?

Maybe she, Faith, had had a lucky escape.

'So does annulled mean something different in Italy?' How could they be married for a year and not sleep together?

He shrugged. 'I have little knowledge of your Australian laws. My grandfather in Italy was set on our marriage to combine the two great houses through our offspring. A pact of long standing. Without children the company would move from Florentine control to a Roman cousin. As this was his dying wish, and my brother and his wife had not yet conceived, I met his demands with little choice and speed before he passed—as I explained when I left.'

He'd left like a shot from a gun. 'At the time you said your life was in Italy and you were marrying because of a previous arrangement.' Might have been nice to know that before she'd invited him home.

Her shiny Italian hero had left without looking back. Her turn to wave away the past. 'That's all in the past. Now you're saying you never slept with your wife?' Really? Not the Raimondo she'd known.

'No.' He raised one brow and she decided he did it with a hint of satirical amusement at her expense. She narrowed her eyes. 'The marriage was annulled for infertility not disclosed—not celibacy. My ex-wife is barren. She did not tell me she had been forced by her father to wed or that she had known with certainty of her infertility. As my late grandfather's wish for our marriage relied on children, that made for reasonable grounds for annulment.'

And boy, did that sound horrible and cold. She rubbed her suddenly chilled arms. And this was her daughter's father? So she'd been lucky he'd been called away then. His unemotional recital made her wonder if his wife had been so dispassionate at being deemed unworthy. She shuddered. Like her mother and the small child Faith had been were deemed unworthy when her own father had left.

Her revulsion must have shown on her face because he said, 'Do not judge me for this. Maria never wanted me. She left with more wealth and has found a new husband. I wish her well.'

'Big of you.'

'Especially as she was unfaithful during our marriage.' Then he waved in the air. 'Pah!' He waved again, obviously annoyed with himself. 'This is not your concern. I find myself baring my soul to a woman I barely knew six years ago and again today. Forgive me.'

He was cross with himself all right. If he hadn't looked so sinfully sexy during his sudden almost-tantrum she would have laughed. But his honesty shone through the big hand that pulled regretfully over his face. Maybe she hadn't been as ridiculously blind as she had thought all that time ago. No, don't go there. Things were very different now.

She lifted her chin. 'My fault for asking. But at least I know a little more of you.' Though she didn't really. Except... 'You really didn't get my letters?'

'No. I am sorry.' His brow furrowed. 'Though I can guess who did.'

She supposed so. 'Your wife?'

He shook his head with more regret. Not helpful to Chloe, though. 'Hard to understand Maria could be so cruel, but she felt the lack of children greatly and re-sented our marriage even more.' He looked at her. 'I'm sorry I wasn't there when you needed me.'

No, you weren't there, she thought, but she could see why he hadn't been. 'My aunt Isabel was there for me. She's still my rock. Though younger than my mum, she stood as my mother's rock as well. We manage very well together.'

'No need for others?' He asked the question with a bitterness she didn't deserve.

'We manage very well. Thank you,' she agreed with composure that was slipping a little. Sadness for her daughter had tightened her throat.

A comedy of errors, five years of her daughter's life, and he was the loser if he'd wanted to be involved. And maybe it hadn't been all his fault. She'd lost as well be-cause even if they'd not ended up together she suspected this man would have been an attentive dad to her little girl as much as he could, considering the physical dis-tance between their two countries.

As in the past, their thoughts seemed to mesh. 'Tell me about your pregnancy. Her birth. Her infancy.' His eyes softened. 'About Chloe. Your daughter.'

Her daughter. Not his. He was trying to see her side too. But she couldn't soften too much. Couldn't trust that much yet.

Where did she start? 'Chloe was born here at Light-house Bay Hospital. A beautiful water birth. It was the most amazing day of my life.' Her eyes misted with the memory. The recollection of those first moments with the weight of her new daughter, pink and wet, heavy between her bare breasts. The scent of her, the downy head and snuffly noises against her skin and the glory that was the wonder of birth.

Her own pride in her achievement. She would never forget that. But that was all too private. Instead she said, 'It will be her birthday soon. She'll be five in two days.'

He leaned forward, his face lighting. 'Two days?'

'Seventeenth of November.'

'May I be there for her birthday?' Nice of him to ask, but she wasn't a fool.

She had no right to bar him, despite her misgivings. She didn't believe he'd cause trouble but to be wrong would be bad. 'That's up to you.' She met his eyes. 'And up to Chloe. And how long you plan on staying might be nice to know as well.' She lifted a hand, palm up, in question.

'A week. I have given myself a week. I fly out next Friday.'

She could do a week. If his family didn't call him back. Ha!

Could protect herself for a week as well.

Protect herself against the chemistry between them that she could still faintly feel, even through the thickest wall she could erect and had become very good at maintaining ever since Chloe's birth.

Then he would be gone and her life would, hopefully could, return to normal. She wasn't moving to Italy and he wasn't moving to Lighthouse Bay so all would sort in the end.

He sat back. Studied her with that intense expression

on his face. 'What is she like? This daughter of ours?' Avoiding discussion on what happened after he flew away again, but she guessed nobody knew the answer to that yet.

Knowing the extent of his stay was solid ground, as was the topic of Chloe. She could talk of her daughter until the sun set. 'She's dark-haired and strong...' *Like you*, the thought flashed through her brain, but a wholly feminine version of Raimondo's darkness.

She went on, '... With green eyes and long lashes.'

'Like you.' She lifted her head at the echo of her thoughts and she heard the smile in his voice as he said it.

Maybe. 'She's a minx who gives us pleasure in her company every single day.' She shook her head at the memories that swirled like bright confetti when she thought of her daughter. 'To hear her funny little cackle of a witch's laugh is to know the joy of being a parent.' She stopped. Could have snatched back the thought-less cliché. 'I'm sorry. Poor word choice in the circum-stances.'

He waved that away, still watching her face with an intensity she found discomfiting. 'You love her dearly.'

'More than life itself.' Twice today she'd had that thought and a cold foreboding washed over her. She shivered and his hand came across the table to touch hers.

'I would never do anything to hurt you or Chloe,' he said softly. Sincerely. His eyes held her gaze like his fingers held her wrist and warmth flooded over her. 'Never.'

She nodded. 'I hope I can believe you.' But still the feeling of foreboding didn't go away.

She changed the subject and eased her hand free. 'Where are you staying?'

He gestured to the hill with the same hand. 'In the guest house down from the hospital.'

She knew it well. 'Our locum doctors stay there.'

'Do they?' He smiled at her. 'And how is your little hospital that you loved so much?' As if again sensing her need to regroup.

A safe topic she could also talk about for hours. 'Grown. We birth over a hundred babies a year here now.'

'Then you must have found more doctors to carry on. There were staffing hardships before.'

'A lot has changed since you were here.' And wasn't that an understatement. Her. Their daughter. She thought about the new families in Lighthouse Bay. Her wonderful circle of friends that grew with each new relationship.

'We are a midwife-led unit now, so doctors come only for the general patients and obstetric emergencies.'

He smiled. 'I would be redundant already.'

'You never planned to work here.' Wouldn't that be a hard thing for her to come to terms with if he was here all the time? Crikey.

He inclined his head. 'As you say. I never planned this. Though I have been doing locum work since my wife and I parted. In poorer suburbs in Italy. A little aid work in Third World countries. My brother has occasionally forgone the pens of the pharmaceutical business and has sometimes joined me in aid work.'

She remembered he had mentioned his work doubts even when they'd met. His new focus helped her to relax a little more when he added, 'The work is much more satisfying and demanding to fill my life. I regret that even your Lighthouse Bay receded into a moment in time.'

Then he could have come back after his divorce, she mused. Come back at least to see if what they'd experienced really had been as special as she'd thought. He'd decided not to, obviously. But things worked out, or didn't, as the case might be, for reasons no one knew, she told herself. Out of sight, out of mind, she supposed a little drearily.

'Tell me what else has changed in this place you love so much over the years.'

She wasn't sure what he was thinking now but she ploughed on, relieved to have a lighter topic to discuss. 'My boss, Ellie, has married, and my friend, Catrina, as well.'

He lifted his head. 'Ah, Catrina.' He smiled and she tilted her head to understand why Trina's name had brought amusement.

He went on, 'It was this Catrina's wedding that brought me here. One of my colleagues at the hospital came to this wedding. She is a friend of Sam's sister and was back visiting—apparently she was at Sam and Ellie's wedding too, and mentioned to me about you and your Chloe.'

Faith stared at him. Trina's wedding? A guest from his town in Italy? 'Mentioned my daughter and me?' There had been some Italian doctors, friends of Sam's sister, but she'd thought them from the city. Surely not. 'Who was your colleague?'

'Francesca Moran. I heard her mention your Lighthouse Bay and I asked after you.' He spread his hands depreciatingly. 'It had been so long since I'd heard of this place so of course the name called to me.' He shrugged and there was a decidedly amused glint in his eyes. 'And, of course, my...' he paused as if searching '...ears prickled?'

'Ears pricked up. Yes.' With a little impatience. 'Why?'

She tried to remember if he'd met Trina before. But their intense relationship/liaison had been so short and all-encompassing she didn't think they'd left her cottage except to go to the cave.

As some of those very intimate recollections intruded her face warmed and she looked away. She'd had these memories locked up so long she'd almost forgotten the details. If she let herself relive how it was she might not sleep for a week.

Thankfully, Raimondo seemed to have missed her embarrassment and tutted as if impatient with the subject. 'I asked if she'd seen you and she remembered yes, because your daughter Chloe had been very pretty and had been chasing the tiny flower girl of Trina's husband.'

Faith remembered, though it was more than a year ago. Chloe had been adorable, as had Trina's stepdaughter Piper, and some of her embarrassed confusion seeped away and was replaced with maternal pride. 'She was charged with looking after Piper. And yes, Piper was only two and the flower girl. Chloe can be very responsible for her age.'

He smiled at her obvious pride. 'Of course she is. She will be composed like her mother.'

She didn't know about that—she was feeling anything but composed at this moment and she needed to get this conversation back on steady ground.

'And because of this you came?'

'Because of this I came.'

Nope. She didn't understand. 'I could have been married with many children.' But she wasn't, mostly because of the impact he'd had on her life, not something she'd dwelt on but she thought of it now. And narrowed her eyes at him.

A shadow crossed his face. 'As you say. Though I was told otherwise. My friend knew you had no husband and Chloe's age made me wonder.'

Obviously, it had made him wonder. 'Wonder enough to cross the world and see?'

'Yes.'

She watched his face. 'And did you investigate further?'

'As you say.' His expression remained unreadable. She decided he was being deliberately vague. 'I owe you many apologies,' he added.

Like that would help, she thought, but she'd decided against stewing in bitterness a long time ago. It changed nothing and she refused to colour her own and Chloe's lives with negative thoughts. That philosophy had stood her in good stead and she wasn't being driven by someone else to change now.

He asked quietly, 'Is there a special man in your life?'

She blinked. Guessed she could understand why he would ask as he'd just exploded into their world. She could say yes. As protection against the tendrils of attraction this man was already curling around her like wisps of smoke. She was fighting it but she had past experience that his illusion of smoke could lead to a sudden flame.

But she wasn't into lying either... 'No.' She lifted her head. 'Not at this time.' Apart from him, there hadn't been a man in her life, really. A few brief ones in uni. Before that, as a child, the father she could barely remember, who had left her mother and her. But she wasn't telling him that. 'Just male friends. And husbands of my friends.'

Her eyes met his and she explained lest he think it was

all about him. 'It's better for Chloe that I don't expose her to the whims of a passing relationship.'

She still didn't know what it had been about Raimondo that had penetrated her barriers years ago—why had she, as a young naïve woman, brought this stranger from another land into her home, to all the places that were dear to her and allowed him access to her heart? To her body?

Because of the magic. And that was the torment of it. Spending time with Raimondo had been like sprinkling fairy dust over her world until she'd felt alive and aware, hypersensitive to the beauty all around her. She'd been caught in the bubble of his admiration and returned it to him tenfold. She wouldn't do that this time.

She looked across at the beach in front of her, frowning at it. Even now, the ocean seemed bluer than it had been this morning, the flowers in pots brighter, the sounds of the waves more clear. It was fainter, but she could feel that magic now. Again. Looked back at him as he sat back in his chair and studied her too.

In the past this man had soared into her life like a comet, searing away her reserves, and she knew what had happened the last time with the heat of their collision at the airport. But then he'd rocketed straight out again.

Oh, she was over her feeling of abandonment but she didn't want that for Chloe. No way.

Not really surprising she hadn't rushed into making herself vulnerable to a man again. Not bitter. Just not open to trusting closeness again.

She expanded on her answer, letting him know where her priorities lay. 'I will give Chloe all my time until she starts school before I see if I want to cultivate a man's company on a more permanent basis.'

He raised his brows as if she'd said something vaguely unsettling but he closed his mouth and silence fell between them.

To fill it she said, 'My need for male company has been easily satisfied by social outings with my friends and their husbands or the families of the babies I've welcomed.'

He nodded. 'Then this is good as it is not confusing for Chloe during my visit.'

He was concerned about her daughter's feelings and, against her better judgement, she softened towards him again. A tiny voice whispered plaintively that it was only because of Chloe he was glad there was no another man.

Then she pulled herself up. No. Now she could feel the heat in her cheeks again, damn him. This was how he had managed to get under her guard last time, with solicitude and care and treating her as if she were a princess he needed to guard from the world. Something she'd had no experience of from a man.

And hadn't that changed when his brother had called? Oh, yes.

She knew where she really stood. Just a phone call and he'd be gone. Not his fault. Oh, no. But family calls...

Her aunt had always said that for the Italian men their family was everything. Well, she had a family, Chloe and Izzy, and she needed to make sure her daughter was safe from the disappointments an unreliable father could bring to her life, so she wasn't falling for his transient solicitude again until he'd proven himself. She would be calm. Careful. Consistent in her barriers.

Who knew what crisis would make him leave next time? She would protect Chloe from the devastation she could suffer when his larger-than-life presence disappeared in a moment. She knew how it felt and Chloe would too in seven days' time. Faith needed to be clear on expectations with Chloe ASAP.

But it was so strange talking like this with a man she'd thought she would never see again.

He'd been watching her silently and she wondered if he could read her thoughts and if they'd crossed her face for him to see. 'What of your friends in your life? Will they be worried that I have come back?'

Did he think it odd she had no man in her life? It could have been tricky if she'd had a boyfriend.

'All my male friends are married to women I care about. Though my aunt has been hinting that when Chloe starts school I should look to building more… adult friendships outside my work.' She looked at him. 'I might look at that then.'

Raimondo glanced around pointedly. 'And no single men have been clamouring at your door? Are they blind not to want to capture you for themselves?' He looked so pleased with her lack of suitors her irritation rose.

She gave him a level stare. 'I've been a fool once. So, of course, I'm reluctant to go there again.'

He winced. 'Of course.'

They'd finished their coffee and she glanced at her watch. It was lunch time. 'I have to go. I need to be at work by two-thirty for the afternoon shift.'

He glanced at his own watch but his face remained difficult to read.

There was a tense pause and finally she said, 'I'm off duty tomorrow.' For Sunday and Monday as well, but she didn't add that. 'If you'd like to come and meet Chloe and my aunt, Isabel, then you could come for breakfast at eight. We could go down to the beach after, as Chloe likes to have a play in the water when she can.'

'Thank you. I would like that. Your aunt cares for Chloe while you work?'

'Yes.' She raised her chin. 'It would have been very difficult without her help.' Again, she noted his grimace of distress, but she'd said it more to show appreciation of her aunt than to make him feel bad. 'Izzy moved in with me just before Chloe was born. She was my mother's youngest sister and only fifteen years older than me and we are our only family. She's put her life on hold for Chloe and me.'

'I imagine there is much closeness between you.'

'There is. Very much. Next year, when Chloe goes to school five days a week, Izzy will be less tied and I'm going to shift to night duty again, which I did in the beginning. There's a young woman from the preschool who has agreed to sleep over with Chloe when I'm at work if Izzy is away. I'll be home to send her off to school and there when she comes back.'

He shook his head. 'I do not like to hear of these hardships inflicted unknowingly on you by my lack of responsibility. I owe you and your aunt a great debt.'

'No. You don't.' No way was he finding a foothold there. 'I love Chloe and there are lots of mothers juggling similar schedules and worse. I get help and wonderful support from my friends as well as Izzy.'

His brow furrowed at being thwarted. A bit too used to getting his own way, she mused, as he said, 'I hope to have some input. But we have time to see.'

She said steadily, 'I've been extremely fortunate and need nothing from you.'

Now his face appeared bland. 'Perhaps this is for another discussion.'

She met his eyes. *Oh, yeah? Let it go, Faith*, she told herself. When she didn't reply he half smiled as if he knew it was her restraint not her change of mind that kept her quiet.

He inclined his head. 'Thank you for your invitation and I will see you at eight tomorrow.'

She did need to get away to think. 'Do you remember where I live?'

He laughed with little amusement. 'Before the cliff. To the left of the crofts. The siren's house above the sea. I remember.'

She laughed. 'I've never been a siren in my life. I'm afraid your memory tricks you.'

One dark brow rose. 'Does it?'

CHAPTER SIX

FAITH DROVE TO the preschool and picked Chloe up way too early. Her daughter didn't see her enter the brightly festooned, noisy room because she sat with her tongue pushed against her teeth as she glued a black felt eye onto a cotton wool ball with fierce concentration.

Her two dark pigtails bounced as she nodded her head to something the little girl beside her said but her attention remained fixed on her task. Chloe was always surrounded by little friends and Faith wondered who she'd inherited her outgoing personality from.

Perhaps Raimondo.

'Chloe, I've come to pick you up.'

'Mummy?' Chloe looked up from her work and her face shone her delight at seeing her mum. She put down the cotton wool ball and jumped up. Threw out her arms. 'My mummy is here. I have to go.' She glanced around the room as if to be sure everyone could see how special the occasion was. Her daughter bounced up and down at the exciting change in routine and happily gathered her new paintings and crafts.

Faith met the amused eyes of the preschool teacher and they both smiled. Chloe ran to the teacher, hugged her, and then back to her mother and caught her hand. 'Let's get my bag.'

Faith savoured the warmth of the little hand in hers, the chatter floating up and the skipping of her daughter's feet as they walked to the car. Her Chloe sunshine.

At least Faith would get home with extra time before work to get her head together. Dashing out to preschool pick-up just before starting shift would have jumbled her thoughts again and she was jumbled enough.

As soon as Faith walked into the little house on the cliff her aunt's dark brows rose and her green eyes widened. Isabel or Aunty Izzy as Chloe called her, didn't miss much. Yup. She knew something had happened.

Izzy took the preschool bag from Faith's slack hand and received her kiss from Chloe. 'Your sliced pear and milk is in the fridge, darling,' she said, pointing the little girl towards the sink and towel waiting for her small hands without taking her eyes off Faith.

As Chloe happily followed routine, Izzy touched Faith's shoulder and concerned eyes searched her face. 'You okay?'

Was she okay? She'd been solid as a rock while she'd been with Raimondo but at this moment she felt weak at the knees.

'Raimondo Salvanelli turned up at the caves this morning.' The words sounded strange even coming from her own mouth. Spreading her hands helplessly, Izzy didn't appear enlightened.

She'd get it. 'He didn't know about Chloe and someone at Trina's wedding mentioned us and he flew in from Florence.'

Izzy's eyes widened. 'The Italian from the airport?' Then she mouthed silently, 'Chloe's father?'

Faith sank onto the sofa, her eyes drawn to her daughter happily setting her own table, playing house with her milk and fruit on her child-size table setting.

'How could he not know? You wrote. Twice.' Izzy manfully tried to catch up.

Faith turned back to her aunt. 'He said he never received the letters, though the address I sent the letters proved correct. And his marriage has been annulled.' She waved her hand impatiently. 'Long story.' She looked at Chloe again. 'He's coming tomorrow morning at eight.' Lowered her voice. 'To meet Chloe.'

'Who's coming to meet me?' a bright voice piped up. Chloe proved she might be quietly doing her thing but she wasn't oblivious to the tension at the other side of the room.

Faith and Izzy exchanged looks. 'One of mummy's friends from a long time ago is coming to visit tomorrow for breakfast. Of course he'd like to meet you too.'

Chloe's bright eyes studied them both. 'Does your friend have a little girl?'

'Not yet.' Another frazzled look at Izzy from Faith. 'But I think he'd like one.'

Izzy made an inarticulate sound and turned away so Chloe couldn't see her expression. She turned back to Faith, her face composed. 'Well, then. Much excitement.' She glanced at the clock on the wall. 'Why don't you go have a nice freshening shower? Chloe and I will make lunch while you get ready for work.' Her aunt looked at her. 'Unless you don't feel up to going?'

That was more of a joke than a question because Faith would have to be dying to not turn up for work.

'I'll be fine. And yes, thanks, a shower would be good. A strategy for dealing with this, so all will become clear.'

She smiled ruefully at her aunt. 'I might bash my head against the wall a few times, so ignore strange sounds.'

Just before two-thirty that afternoon Faith walked through the glass doors of the Lighthouse Bay Mothers and Babies Wing of the tiny hospital and slipped her bag into the cupboard underneath the desk.

When the world was going crazy thank goodness there was work.

The ward seemed quiet and nobody sat at the desk. She let a small sigh of relief escape her. It would be nice to settle into the shift before the ward focused on an impending birth but she knew what to do regardless when she was here. Unlike in her social life at the moment. She could hear a baby crying so at least they had inpatients. She didn't want it so quiet she needed to work elsewhere in the hospital, which they sometimes did between rushes of babies. She didn't have the head space for that today.

Today there had been too many upheavals in her peaceful private world and the question marks for the future unsettled her in a way she hadn't felt for many years.

Raimondo had the knack of that.

'Hey there, Faith.'

Ellie appeared from one of the side rooms on the ward with a grizzling baby tucked under her arm. The manager of the ward, and sometimes the whole hospital, Ellie preferred when she could work as a hands-on midwife, like today.

'Hi, Ellie.' Her boss looked so happy. 'How's your day been?' Not like hers, that was for sure.

'Excellent. Apart from this baby, who seems to have

missed the rules on settling after a feed—but I have the technology—new nappy.'

She looked calm and content carrying the little football baby under her arm, the baby's neck securely supported by her cupped hand. She smiled a warm welcome.

Faith tried to smile back but a sudden unexpected fear that she'd never be like Ellie, with a man who worshipped her and a proper family, assailed her. A fear she'd never had before, and shouldn't have now, made her realise how much Raimondo had punctured her serene balloon of existence she'd floated in until now.

Her boss was very, very happily married to an obstetrician. Sam consulted at their regional referral centre and not Lighthouse Bay, but he did emergency calls when needed here. Having Sam in the wings was one of the reasons their birth rate had risen so much.

Faith's mouth opened. 'Chloe's dad turned up this morning at the caves.' She slapped a hand over her mouth. She had not meant to blurt that out. What was wrong with her?

Except for a slight pucker of her forehead, Ellie's demeanour didn't change. 'I have supreme confidence in your good sense, Faith. Come into the nursery while I change this poo-bottomed boy. Then I'll give you a handover of our one patient and you can tell me all about "him".'

Faith followed her into the nursery, a space with wide sun-filled windows, a soft chair for breastfeeding mothers and tall benches for dressing and bathing babies. Ellie flipped out a fresh bunny rug and gently eased the little boy down until his head was resting on a folded cloth and began to unwrap him. Faith reached for the cleaning wipes to help and then, noting the disaster uncovered, instead wet a cloth nappy and handed it to Ellie, who laughed.

'Yep. I think we need the big guns to fix this mess.'

She smiled down at the baby as she swiftly righted the world. 'So, this is Jonathon, born this morning at seven-thirty to Maurine McKay.'

Faith felt the smile as it stretched her face. 'Little Maurine?' Maurine barely topped a metre and half tall, though her body was all curves and perfectly proportioned. 'How cool.' Faith shared her midwifery case load with Ellie so she knew Maurine well. 'And was it as easy for her as her last one? She was worried.'

'He flew out,' Ellie said. 'She was here about an hour, not saying much, then she did that thing she did with you last time. You know. The stare. And lay down and had him. The woman is a marvel.'

Faith shook her head in awe. 'Some mums are just designed to have babies. Probably helps that her husband is not much bigger than she is.'

'That too, maybe. Maurine's well, no damage, no extra blood loss, and this young man weighed three thousand grams so a nice size for her.'

Faith calculated quickly. 'About six pound six? Her biggest yet, then. Can't wait to congratulate her.' Faith could feel the tensions of the day falling away from her. This was the world she loved and she felt the calming of her lost equilibrium as it settled over her.

'She's looking forward to seeing you.' Ellie rewrapped the now clean baby. 'So. He's fed twice already, his temperature and respirations are normal and he's going to settle for a good sleep now.' This last was said firmly to the baby, who lay quietly with big dark blue eyes gazing steadily at Ellie.

Ellie picked him up. 'I'll take him back to mum and you pop the kettle on. Then you can tell me about your interesting day.'

By the time Ellie had left the ward and Faith had settled Jonathon again with his boisterous siblings and parents in Maurine's room, she was feeling like herself.

Okay. It had been unexpected—she snorted at that and the memory of her first greeting to Raimondo—and decided there was nothing she could do so she would take the benefits provided.

Mentally she ticked them off.

At least her daughter would remember a man called Raimondo when she was asked about her father.

Chloe would have some rapport to build on if she went to meet him one day in Italy when she was grown.

Raimondo could write to Chloe and possibly, though she was still thinking about this, contribute to Chloe's senior school or university in later life if he wished—because education was the best gift to give anyone.

She had to admit Raimondo still seemed the lovely man she'd become briefly infatuated with and, yes, she did feel she could trust him with contact with Chloe from the little she'd seen today. But that didn't mean she would.

She wasn't so sure she could trust herself, so she would be vigilant in guarding her good sense and her heart.

They'd do Christmas cards and maybe phone calls on birthdays—surely he could manage that, though she wasn't sure, and in this initial visit he'd be here for Chloe's birthday at least. Faith would put out the albums of Chloe's childhood for him to see.

She sat back. Yes. All ordered in her head nicely.

Chloe would probably enjoy showing Raimondo her photos over and over again. Faith wasn't so sure she was okay with some of the birth ones but, then again, he had seen her naked before.

Oh, my goodness. Quickly she picked up a pen and began to write out the diet list.

The sound of a car arriving in the driveway outside the ward had her out of her seat. Someone in labour?

Then she saw the sleek black Mustang. What the heck…?

Raimondo's big form climbed out and strode to the passenger seat and now Faith could see the shape of another person through the darkly tinted windows. She proved to be a woman and heavily pregnant. Where had Raimondo found a pregnant woman?

Faith grasped the handles of the wheelchair they left tucked handily behind the corner to the birthing rooms and pushed it towards the now opening door. The woman limped in on an obviously tender right leg and held her stomach.

Yep. In labour. Raimondo had brought her to the right place. His words carried. 'Traffic accident.'

What traffic? Faith thought, but she hurried over. The woman leaned on the door as she waited for Faith to park the chair next to her.

'Can you sit down?' Faith held the chair and Raimondo helped her settle into the chair. 'I'm Faith, the midwife on duty.'

'Cynthia Day. My husband is hurt and going in the ambulance. This man said he was a doctor and thought I should come here. Just until the ambulance is ready to leave and can take me too.' She glanced at Raimondo ruefully. 'I've had a few labour pains.'

'I saw the accident and called the ambulance,' Raimondo said. 'Her husband is stable but there may be a delay before they extricate him and are ready to leave. It seemed better to bring Cynthia to be checked before transfer.'

She looked at him. 'Yes. Good thinking. There's at least an hour's road trip in the ambulance so very sensible.' Then to the woman, 'When is your baby due?'

'Four weeks tomorrow.'

Technically premature, Faith thought, but not perilous. 'We'll check you both out and have the ambulance call here to pick you up. I'll pop you through into the assessment room, which is where we have our babies here. Is that okay?'

'Of course.'

Faith turned the chair and began to push it the other way towards the birthing rooms. Raimondo followed and Faith allowed him for the moment. It wasn't as if he was a stranger to hospitals and she'd keep an extra pair of hands until she could get help.

'Have you been here before?' She spoke from behind the woman as her brain sorted priorities.

She didn't recognise the woman and thought she knew all the ladies booked in to give birth at Lighthouse Bay. So medical or obstetric history might not be available.

'No. We're having the baby in Sydney.'

'That's fine. We can get your notes from there.' She'd have them emailed through once Cynthia had signed the release of information form. Or the supervisor could arrange all that because Faith would be busy on her own.

Cynthia sighed. 'We were going home after visiting relatives when my husband took a funny turn at the wheel. I grabbed the steering wheel but it was too late. We ran into a low wall and the front of the car crumpled in, making it difficult to get him out.'

Unlucky. And scary as a risk for possible hidden pregnancy-related trauma. Risk even from the sudden stop. 'Did you hit your stomach?'

'No. The seat belt jerked me when we hit, but that's all.'

Faith nodded to herself. She would have to watch baby for any signs of distress which could be a shearing bleed from the placenta. 'Was the car going fast when you hit?'

'No. I think John must have known something because he hit the brake just before he went unconscious.' She swivelled her head and looked at Raimondo. 'I'm so worried about him. When can you ring and find out how he is?'

'Dr Salvanelli will be able to do that soon.' She knew there was a good reason she'd subconsciously wanted Raimondo to stay. He'd been helpful already.

'Of course,' he said.

Raimondo and Faith stood on each side of Cynthia, supporting her until she was comfortably sitting upright on the bed, the back raised and one pillow supporting her head.

Faith turned to Raimondo as he stepped back. 'Thank you. I'll make a call and a nurse should be here soon. Will you stay by the desk in case I need you before anyone else arrives?'

'Of course.'

'Thank you. It's a good place to find out about Cynthia's husband. The ambulance control number is in red above the desk. They should be able to give you some information if you explain to them or they'll call you back. Tell them we have Cynthia here and expect her to be transferred as well.'

'Sì.'

Faith crossed to the phone in the room and quickly dialled the hospital supervisor. She tucked the phone into her neck to free her hands and twitched the cover off the baby resuscitation trolley, then reached to turn the heater to warm just in case. She'd only checked the equipment half an hour ago, an early in the shift task everyone completed, so she knew everything was ready if they needed it.

'Yes?' the supervisor answered.

'Hi, it's Faith in Maternity. We have an admission, a lady in a car accident. She's stable but contracting and could be in early labour. Can you send over a nurse as my second, please, and phone for Dr Southwell senior? There's an out-of-town doctor here at the moment, so tell the nurse that's who's at the desk when she arrives. Too busy to explain just now.'

She paused. Listened. Said 'Thanks' and put down the phone. 'Right then, Cynthia. Let's have a gentle feel of your tummy and listen to your baby. Raimondo will tell us as soon as he hears any news of your husband.'

Cynthia nodded, her face shining pale against the white pillow, her dark eyes concerned as she held her stomach. 'There's another contraction.'

Faith knitted her forehead. She needed obstetric history soon but the nurse could follow that up when she arrived. Faith crossed to the sink and washed her hands then went back to the bed, drying her fingers on the paper towel. She lowered the bed until Cynthia was lying flat with just the pillow under her head. Palpating a uterus in the upright position wouldn't give the clear picture she needed from an unknown woman.

'Is this your first baby?' They'd have more time if it was, she thought; the contraction had finished as she lifted the pretty blue maternity shirt and gently began to palpate the woman's stomach. Not her first baby, judging by the older silver stretch marks. She laid her fingers each side of the bulge and palpated in Leopold's manoeuvre. 'Nothing painful when I do this?'

'No.'

Good. Less chance of a quiet bleed from the accident then. The height of the uterus was consistent with thirty-six weeks, though the baby didn't shift under her hands, which was a concerning indication of vigour.

'She's not my first baby. This is my fourth. Four in five years.'

'Oh, my. Congratulations.' Faith's brows rose as she looked at the woman again. 'You look too young for four young kids. I have one and look much more careworn.'

Cynthia smiled wanly. 'John and I have just been on a week's holiday together. We were feeling relaxed.' She clutched her stomach again. 'I think this baby is wanting out.'

Faith narrowed her eyes and glanced at the clock. Only two minutes since the last contraction. 'Were there any complications in your previous births? Like a Caesarean or forceps. Or bleeding after the birth?'

'No. Apparently I'm made to have babies.'

Faith smiled. 'Pleased to hear it.' She listened to the clop of the baby's heart rate, which made the mother's mouth tilt up in relief at the comforting sound. Then Cynthia gasped, 'Oops. I think I just had a show or my waters broke a little. Something feels wet.'

By the time Faith had confirmed that there had been a small loss of blood and they'd sorted that development, Cynthia was returned to the sitting position. 'Um.' She fluttered her hands and her eyes darted around the room. 'I need John. I think I want to push.' Cynthia's voice sounded tremulous, alarmed at the speed of change, and Faith frowned and looked at the phone across the room just as the nurse poked her head into the room.

Faith blew out her breath in relief. 'Perfect timing. Can I have a delivery set-up ASAP? And get the supervisor to find out how far away Dr Southwell is. We need him now.' Faith didn't often call the doctor but this was a post-accident baby and it could be born compromised.

There was still that concern about abruption of the placenta from the sudden stop. 'Can you also ask Dr Salvanelli to stand outside the door in case I need to call him in, please, until the doctor arrives?'

The nurse nodded and hurried off after pulling the resus trolley closer to Faith.

Cynthia sighed heavily on the bed and Faith pulled back the sheet she'd lain over her. 'How about we just ditch the whole idea of underwear and check what's going on so we know for sure?'

By the time they'd done that Faith didn't need to check anything more because there was an unmistakable bulge of baby's crown inching into the world.

'I need to move,' Cynthia gasped. Already she was rolling onto her knees. Faith hurriedly stacked pillows so Cynthia could lean over a support. Things were progressing very quickly and the email of pre-birth papers would be moot until after baby's arrival now.

Faith leaned forward and pressed the call bell for the nurse to return. For now she needed an injection for after the birth so they didn't have a haemorrhage. Fourth baby made the risk increased. They could find out the medical history later.

Because the bag of waters was still intact, a large odd-shaped bag of fluid encased in membranes formed in front of the baby's head and through that a dark-haired skull could be seen descending. 'Looks like this baby wants to be born without breaking your waters first.'

'One of my others did that,' Cynthia panted. 'Won't drown, they said.'

Faith did love old wives' tales about midwifery, and even more she loved uncomplicated women like Cynthia who just went ahead and had their babies without any help from anyone.

'Come on, you,' Cynthia muttered as she bore down, because after progressing rapidly, with the birth of more of the head, now the speed of descent seemed to have stopped.

Faith glanced towards the door; it was good knowing she did have backup help if needed, but she refrained from calling in Raimondo.

The nurse came back in carrying an injection tray. Faith smiled at her. 'Brownie points for you.' She nodded at the injection. 'Did you get onto Dr Southwell?' Faith's eyes returned to Cynthia, who had become more distressed.

'They had to find him but he's coming.'

Without looking at the nurse, Faith nodded. 'Great. Thanks.'

'It feels stuck. I need to move.' Faith wasn't surprised. But with a sore ankle, squatting would be hard.

'Would it be okay if I ask Dr Salvanelli to come in? He

could take some of your weight as you try to get comfortable while the nurse sets up the rest of the equipment.'

'Do it.' Cynthia didn't have words to waste.

Faith raised her voice. 'Raimondo?'

Within seconds Raimondo stood beside her and between them they lowered the bed closer to the floor, helped Cynthia shift sideways on her knees until she was at the edge of the bed, and waited for the next contraction to ease before they moved further.

A minute later she stretched her left leg down towards the floor, then moaned and they all froze.

Cynthia sucked in a breath. 'That shifted a little. Let's go for a squat, which is how all my other babies were born.' Except this time her right leg wouldn't bear her weight.

Faith and Raimondo's eyes met across the woman's head. 'I always listen to the mother,' Faith said quietly and Raimondo nodded.

'I have you.' Raimondo's hands were under Cynthia's armpits. 'Stand and then you can release the weight.'

Cynthia shuffled sideways with Raimondo taking her full weight, not something Faith or the nurse could have done, and the woman sagged against him and bent her knees. She sighed with relief. 'Better. Much better.'

Faith took the warmed towel the nurse had handed her and wondered philosophically what would happen to Raimondo when the waters broke.

A sudden whoosh delivered the answer as the membranes overextended their elasticity and a wave of amniotic fluid hit the floor and bounced backwards, covering his shoes behind the mother in a hot wave of sticky fluid. Faith bit her lip to stop the smile, safe behind the towel and concentrating on what she hoped would happen next.

As expected, the baby's impacted shoulder that had held up the birth suddenly freed with the extra room in the pelvis from the squatting position, and baby slid into the warm towel Faith caught her with. A slithery cord-wrapped bundle who lay still.

'A girl,' Faith murmured.

The nurse, standing to the side of all the drama, reached over and clicked on the timer to begin recording time passed since birth.

Cynthia swayed and her face paled. 'I need to lie down.' Almost before she'd finished the words Raimondo had scooped her up and put her back against the pillows. The nurse stepped forward with a warm blanket to cover her and Faith juggled the still attached baby onto the edge of the mattress and dried the infant, waiting for the mewling to start.

At the end of the pulsating cord the silent baby didn't cry. Or move.

'Right then,' Faith said quietly as she clamped and cut the cord. 'I'm just going to take her to the trolley and check your baby out, Cynthia. I think she's stunned by the quick trip through the birth canal.'

The nurse took Faith's place beside the bed and patted Cynthia's shoulder. 'I'll take over here. We'll ask if I need any help. Here's a warm blanket as we wait for the afterbirth and your baby to come back. Let's get you comfortable while we wait.'

Raimondo followed Faith as she lifted the little towel-wrapped bundle onto the wheeled resuscitation bench and removed the damp cloth. She began to rub the baby with the new towel waiting under the overhead heater and Raimondo took the stethoscope that hung there and put it in his ears to listen to the baby's chest as soon as Faith finished.

With the lack of response she glanced at the ticking clock and reached for the little mask. 'Positive pressure ventilation at thirty seconds after birth.'

'Heart rate one-ten.' Raimondo stepped back as Faith slid the tiny clear breathing mask over the baby's mouth and nose. They watched the rise of the little chest as she began to puff small breaths of pressured air every second. Raimondo unwound the tiny pulse oximeter lead and strapped the sensor onto the pale baby hand. 'I'll get this running so we can tell how her oxygen levels are.'

'Good. Still think she's just stunned.' Faith turned her head towards the bed. 'Heart rate is good, Cynthia. She's just figuring out this breathing game.'

The nurse called out, 'And we've finished third stage over here and no bleeding after the placenta.'

That was a blessing. 'Thanks, Nurse.'

After thirty seconds of further inflations the tiny limbs began to move. Raimondo had calibrated the pulse oximeter and now the constant read-out of heart rate confirmed baby's heart was chugging along as it should but baby's breathing was still gasping and ineffectual, though Faith's maintenance of air entry stopped deterioration.

'I'll do another thirty seconds of air.' But Faith wasn't happy. Baby should have recovered by now. 'Can you have a look with a laryngoscope? Might be something that blocked the airway.'

Raimondo nodded and the tension in her shoulders increased as he took over the hand-held intermittent positive pressure ventilation for the baby while she assembled the equipment needed. Her hands collected the necessary equipment swiftly as her mind searched for reasons. Simple obstruction was the most likely cause for baby not breathing when the heart rate was so good but she was getting worried.

They didn't have sick babies often but this baby had been in an accident and was slightly premature.

Having Raimondo here beside her while she waited for the other doctor was surreal, wonderful in the circumstances, but probably not legal. Where was their backup?

She took the ventilation mask off Raimondo and he took the laryngoscope gently—angling the curved beak with a light at the end and peering down the baby's throat into the airways. She noted how skilfully he inserted the steel blade and narrowed his eyes at the now open and visible airway. 'A small blood clot obscuring the trachea—it must flop back when you stop forcing the air in.' He held out his hand, still focused on the airway. 'Sucker?'

Faith had the thin clear tubing ready and handed it to him to slide down the curve of the laryngoscope. His finger occluded the mechanism, they heard the gurgling sound of suction, then a dark clot slid up the tube and flashed past towards the vacuum bottle.

Raimondo removed the tube and the laryngoscope from the baby's throat in one smooth movement and Faith felt relief expand inside her. That skill was one she didn't have.

He smoothed the baby's forehead. 'Is this better?' he asked her.

The baby gasped and cried and Faith sagged a little with the rush of success and knew everything would be fine. Her eyes met Raimondo's in a moment of pure relief and satisfaction. 'Thank you,' she mouthed, and when he smiled at her the connection between them flooded all the way down to her toes.

CHAPTER SEVEN

RAIMONDO FELT THE link between them as if it were a physical bond drawing them closer. How was this so? He watched as Faith, after a last glance at him, turned away and carried the now wriggling baby across to the mother, and knew that his life would always hold this so precious memory of working with Faith.

A moment in time.

The beginning of a child's life.

A moment such as this he had missed at his own child's birth.

He jerked himself back to the present. It had been a simple thing to find the airway obstruction, but Faith's adeptness was also a reason for much satisfaction. He'd known she would be efficient and kind in her work but her calmness and competence during the rapid birth and the subsequent neonatal resuscitation made him feel a strange emotion he wasn't familiar with.

Was it pride? Approval that the mother of his daughter was so admirable? He thought about that. No. It was simple pleasure at helping Faith, at sharing a moment of release of tension, of mutual satisfaction and appreciation for the goodness of others. He was glad and thankful to be here for her. That was the emotion he felt. Gratitude.

But standing here now was not needed and impacted on the privacy of the patient. 'Congratulations, Cynthia. I will go out and try the ambulance control again for an update. Would you like me to pass the news on to your husband?'

The woman looked up. 'Yes. Please. I want to know how he is.'

As Raimondo walked down the hallway an elderly gentleman with a stethoscope around his neck, and a decided limp, hobbled past him towards the birthing unit. The doctor had arrived.

Raimondo didn't slow him with introductions.

By the time he had contacted ambulance control and ascertained the transport for Cynthia would be here soon, the nurse had returned to find out the results of his call. He passed them on and decided he would leave Faith to the no doubt mountain of paperwork she would have after such a rushed birth.

He would see her tomorrow. Today he needed to find himself a base in Lighthouse Bay because already he could tell he would always want to spend time here.

The next morning, just before eight, Raimondo strode up the cliff path towards a small house that sat to the left of the three crofts perched over Lighthouse Bay. He glanced back behind him to the soaring white stone lighthouse silhouetted against the sapphire-blue sky. The white tower seemed to watch him with guarded eyes from the big hill behind the hospital. Willing him to do this right.

So much at stake.

Perhaps even his whole future at stake.

Not just for Chloe, the daughter he had not known he

was blessed with, but for Faith. For their future. His and Faith's future as parents together.

A week ago he had only a throwaway comment from a colleague to suggest he had a child.

Twenty-four hours ago he had not known that inside his chest lay a switch that would illuminate the dormant fascination and feelings he still held for Faith. This woman who had borne his child alone yet forgiven his absence so that Chloe would not be soured by a mother's bitterness.

How had he stumbled on this rainbow of hope that could change his life? How did he not destroy his chance here, as he had so many times by taking the wrong path?

Faith had to see he could be trusted and would take as much care not to hurt their daughter as she would.

A stone flew away from the side of his boot and he slowed. He could have driven to Faith's house up the steeply inclined hill from the hospital but he'd preferred to walk to loosen the excited apprehension that had made him toss and turn for most of the night.

He'd run over and over the episode at the hospital and marvelled at the opportunity to see Faith in her work. She'd been as wonderful as he'd expected and the privilege of sharing those moments stayed with him. Comforted him in his anxiety to do everything that was right by Faith.

He shook his head ruefully and smiled at the ancient front gate he approached. The new padlock.

There had been such a high from that shared medical emergency, and perhaps his soaring mood could have been partially responsible for his impulsive purchase of the building he was about to pass.

He turned his head and studied his new acquisition in the morning light: the run-down almost-mansion next door to Faith's home that he'd seen in the real estate window, walking home from the excitement at the hospital.

Still, the technicalities of purchasing something in a foreign country had taken his mind off his nervousness about meeting his daughter today. Perhaps if Chloe knew that her father had actually bought a house in her own town then she would feel more confident he was planning to be a part of her life. Faith would see this too. He hoped that was what she'd see.

But this morning the importance of this meeting with his new daughter had him edgy and unsettled. An unaccustomed apprehension that had not been helped even by rising at dawn and jogging down along the beach to freshen his mind. The cool white Australian sand under his bare feet had reminded him not at all of the hard pebbles of Amalfi beaches, his family holiday destination, and he felt the outsider even more despite his appreciation of the beauty surrounding him.

He'd jogged the sweeping inlet of Lighthouse Bay, the coarse sand curved like a new moon, and passed the rushing of the tide through the fish-filled creek back into the sea.

So few people passed him, strange for a man used to the crowds of Florence! So different to his homeland, but everything was different. His future was different because the occupants of this house he'd stopped outside now held his new world in their hands.

Now the moment had arrived his nerves were taut again and the day felt harshly warm against his skin already.

Or was he hot from nerves?

What if Faith had had a change of heart overnight

and decided to exclude him for some reason he could not fight?

What if his daughter cried when she saw him?

Would the father she had never met be a disappointment?

'Calm yourself, Raimondo,' he admonished out loud. His pocket held a small, traditionally dressed Italian doll, a whim he'd scooped up at the airport and had the clerk wrap in tissue paper for protection. The vivid red peasant apron and hat had caught his eye because the figurine had been exclaimed over by a passing young girl of around the same age as Chloe. Such a purchase might give the child he'd come to see a smile.

For that was what he wanted the most.

A smile from a little girl who could be such a shining light in his suddenly empty life—if she'd let him in.

If her mother let him. If he was invited into their world.

The door opened and Faith stood like a Renaissance vision of dark wavy hair and warm tanned skin, framed in the glow of sun that shone across from the windows overlooking the bay. He blinked and, incredibly, forgot for a moment his reason for being here. This woman, how she grabbed his chest and squeezed always.

'You look beautiful.' The words were soft and heartfelt and she stilled while her cheeks pinked.

'Thank you,' said politely like a schoolgirl, which reminded him abruptly about another girl. He had a daughter. *Madonna mia.* So much to take in.

While he still struggled she said, 'Thank you so much for yesterday.' Then she smiled. 'Both times.'

His mind flashed back to the old man and the new

infant and the drama that followed the birth. 'You are very welcome.'

'Sorry about your shoes.' They smiled at each other.

'Nothing a shower and clean couldn't fix,' he demurred.

'Come in. I've told Chloe I have a friend from Italy coming this morning.'

Her words sank in and reality slapped him as his fogged brain cleared. The irrational disappointment of not being introduced as Chloe's father redirected his mind from the mother but he schooled his disappointment behind his professional mask.

Of course she would think this was better for the child, less pressure.

Later, he reassured himself, later they could change his title when all went well.

They would. Yes. A definite, not an 'if'.

But his heart sank as he was reminded that his position was precarious still and it wasn't this woman's fault he was the outsider.

His eyes roamed the room as he entered but he couldn't see Chloe.

A tall woman in her forties with Faith's dark hair in a blunt bob stood to one side, a calm expression in her green eyes as she watched him enter. He glimpsed a quickly suppressed smile and his nerves settled a little. No hostility here either, though he wasn't sure he deserved such generosity from the woman he assumed was Faith's aunt.

Faith gestured with her hand. 'Izzy? This is Raimondo. Raimondo, my aunt Isabel.'

'It's a pleasure to meet you, Raimondo.' She stepped forward and took his hand in both of hers. When she squeezed his fingers he felt the friendliness and lack of reserve her niece had projected from the first moment he'd met her.

An amazing family—and one he had let down so badly.

'And you. Thank you for your kindness, Isabel.' Instead of shaking her hand, he leaned forward and gently kissed both soft cheeks.

Then Faith moved from where she'd been blocking his view of Chloe, and finally he could see the child in the room.

His daughter.

There she was.

He could never mistake her for any but his own, though she had Faith's eyes.

'Mia cara bambina...'

The words were low and heartfelt. Except for the green eyes of her mother, she was his own dear *mamma*, a beauty as a young girl, judging from the photo he had in his home.

My darling child. Words failed him and inside his chest it felt as though someone squeezed his heart in warm hands. His Chloe was taller than he'd expected and more curious than he had hoped for as her little face tilted sideways and she examined him with interest.

He looked back at his daughter. She held out her hand as if she were a five-year-old queen. *'Buongiorno,'* she said with an Australian accent and he laughed.

'Buongiorno, piccolo.' He glanced at Faith and for an instant he saw what she had hidden behind her apparent serenity. The clenched hands of trepidation that he would hurt her child, the chewed lip of hope that he would be a

good father for Chloe, and the bowed head of having to share her baby with another parent after all these years.

In a second he saw that and vowed he would protect the mother as well as the child from hurt.

Then Faith smiled, shaking her head at her daughter despite the worry in her eyes. He needed to remember this was so hard for her.

Faith nodded towards her daughter. 'Our one Italian word she practised for you.'

'Spoken perfectly,' he said gravely to Chloe with sincere hope he hadn't embarrassed her by laughing. 'You took me by surprise and I am very impressed. Thank you for learning the greeting.' His heart felt as if it were bursting. She was glorious and intelligent and had humour. And she looked like her beautiful mother. And somehow his. How had he been so blessed?

This was all due to his Faith.

'You're welcome,' she said primly and looked at her mother then back at him. 'Mummy says you're staying for breakfast and then we're going to the beach. We've made coffee in the coffee machine for you. I helped put the froth on top of the cup.'

'This is wonderful. Thank you.' Again his eyes were drawn to Faith, who seemed so remarkably calm, while his heart was pounding and his mouth was dry with excitement. He had a daughter.

He wondered at Faith's serenity then noted the repetitive reach for her necklace when she thought he wasn't looking. Perhaps not so calm.

He owed her so much for this meeting.

Inside he was wanting to shout with unexpected pride and joy and already the idea of leaving in less than a week caused pain that he would have to address and make plans for. Plans that meant his return. But that was for later. Today he would spend time with the daughter he had just found and try to mend bridges with the woman he had so badly disappointed.

Faith's aunt stepped forward. 'Would you like a pastry for breakfast?' She pointed to the dish of steaming croissants curled on the dish. 'There's butter and jam to go with it. We're having cereal and you can join us as well if you'd prefer.' She glanced around at the girls. 'Then we'll have a croissant to finish with too.'

'Grazie.'

'Before she came to live with us, Izzy travelled a fair bit,' Faith said. 'She says this is the only time of the day to drink cappuccino in Italy without being teased. Is that true?'

Raimondo smiled again. 'True. Milk is for morning *caffè*, and too heavy for the afternoon. And your croissants are perfect, Izzy. Thank you.'

They all stood there for an uncomfortable few seconds until Faith motioned them all to the table.

Again, she had taken control, Raimondo noted. This assertive woman was not how he remembered her, but then years had passed. She intrigued him even more, but then he too had aged. Matured.

He wondered if she noted that. Wondered if she thought of him like that at all. But this was not to be his concern. His concern was the young girl hopping from foot to foot as she tried to understand what was going on. This was about how he could become a part of Chloe's life to her benefit.

'Sit down, everyone. We'll eat then we'll go down to the beach for the morning.' Faith looked at her aunt. 'Have you decided if you're coming to the beach, Izzy?'

'I'll go up and see Myra. She's upset by her husband's fall yesterday.'

Faith turned to Raimondo. 'You would have seen Dr Southwell yesterday, as he came into the hospital limping?'

Raimondo nodded.

'He fell on the path on the way down to our emergency yesterday. He's okay but Myra is upset and worried. It's his second fall. She wants him to retire. They live in one of the crofts up higher.'

'Ah. I'm sorry to hear of his accident. I have seen those crofts. The view must be as good as from here.'

They all glanced towards the windows overlooking the road and the sea. All except his daughter, whose eyes he could feel on him.

'Even better. The ocean seems to go on for ever out of the windows.' He listened to Faith's answer though a part of him remained focused on his daughter. He turned and smiled at the child.

Chloe watched him as the conversation continued and finally she said diffidently, 'Excuse me. Would you like to try your coffee?' Obediently he lifted his cup. Her gaze followed the mug, watching him for his expression, her tiny pink mouth compressed in concentration.

He sipped and, though weak, the flavour tasted very pleasant. *'Perfetto,'* he said.

Her brows creased as she thought about that. 'Perfect?'

Pride expanded in him with an unfamiliar exuberance. 'See. You are a natural.'

CHAPTER EIGHT

A NATURAL? A natural what? A natural linguist?

Her daughter wasn't Italian.

Her daughter was a little Aussie through and through, Faith reassured herself as she remembered the stillness on his face and the blossoming wonder when he first saw Chloe.

And before that the moment when she'd said she'd introduce him as her friend not Chloe's dad. He'd looked gutted and for a moment she wished she could change that and erase his pain. Tell Chloe this man was her father and let Raimondo bask in the moment.

No. It was far too early to trust him not to illuminate their lives and then plunge them back into darkness.

Her brain whirled with each new direction the day was taking. Was it only yesterday Raimondo had reappeared? Her life lay scattered in unexpected directions like the sand down at the beach, covered after a storm with new treasures and new sadness. But they would sort it out. She would sort it out.

She guessed at some stage Chloe would travel to see the land her father came from. Whether or not Faith went along as well would depend on how old her daughter was when this hypothetical trip happened.

Stop. Faith drew a deep breath and sipped her coffee too fast and had to furtively wipe away the moustache that coated her lip. Cappuccino and croissants for breakfast. Good grief. These logistical issues were all Raimondo's problems, not hers.

She had her own many things to think about and the nebulous future was not as important as today would be.

Raimondo turned his head to answer a question from Izzy. Faith watched her daughter as Chloe gazed at the big Italian, her eyes wide and her attention settled squarely on this stranger at their table. True, it was an unusual sight to see a man in their feminine household. And true, Raimondo was difficult to tear your eyes away from.

Faith had thought that the first time she'd seen him at Sydney Airport—the young excited midwife returning to her little rural hospital after an exciting weekend birthing conference and then tangling gazes with the big handsome Italian man. The overhead announcement of flight delays drawing them together in mutual acceptance of the fickleness of fate.

Then, later, when he'd insisted on buying her dinner when their flights were rescheduled again to an even later flight. The instant, compelling attraction that had leapt between them growing bigger and brighter like a flame the more time they'd spent together. A flame that had taken over all good sense on both sides so that when the flights had been put back again until the next day they'd ended up in her hotel room provided by the airline instead of each to their own room later that night.

The next morning, with stars in their eyes, instead of going their separate ways, he'd followed her home to see this place she loved so much and they'd spent every minute together until the fateful phone call that had torn them apart.

That moment when the magical, marvellous moments had ended abruptly.

With an almost brutal finality.

Raimondo turned back and caught her haunted expression. Yes, I'm shell-shocked, she thought, and wished she could say it out loud. Just like I was years ago, and I don't know why I was destined to meet you like this twice in my lifetime. Not fair, really.

But she would have to deal with the moment and trust that he was trying to right a wrong and not cause more trouble.

What did he expect of her? Of Chloe? And what was the best way to keep her and Chloe safe from falling under his spell again and being hurt? That was what she needed to know. The order of her world seemed to have been snatched from beneath her feet yesterday, but hopefully it would return to how it had been.

Almost six years since she'd been swept along on a wild ride that culminated with the birth of this pretty, dark-haired child who brightened her life with such joy. What would it mean to share her with Raimondo—for that was what she could see coming? Maybe it would be for the best as Chloe did miss having a dad she could at least picture in her mind.

What was not for the best was to risk her own heart falling for the same attraction that had skittled her life last time.

Mentally she checked her defences and they were in place. She would see how the day panned out and make sure she too stayed safe.

* * *

An hour later the three of them walked down the hill to the beach.

Chloe was dressed head to foot in a delightful blue-striped rash shirt, frilled tights and matching soft peaked sunhat. The only parts of her that could be burnt were her face, hands and feet and Faith had sunscreened them. They spent so much time at the beach the covering swimwear was easier than catching Chloe for the trauma of sunscreen, which she hated.

For herself she wore a long sleeve cotton shirt and took it off to swim only. It was disquietingly odd to be going on a 'family' outing with Raimondo and her daughter, even if Chloe didn't know that was what it was.

The path swung in narrowly beside the road and Faith chose to follow behind the other two as it gave her time to think, and she could catch snatches of conversation as they floated back. Though, walking behind him, it did draw her eyes to the taut definition of his muscular arm as he swung the basket and the shift of thick muscles on his shoulders through his thin white shirt.

She'd loaded Raimondo with the two folding chairs and the not-feather-light food basket and he'd very happily accepted them. *His arms will have grown by the time he gets there*, she thought with an amused acknowledgement—it was easy to picnic when he carried most of the stuff. Faith carried the umbrella, towels and a blanket and Chloe swung her bucket and spade.

Chloe was saying, 'The beach has a low and a high tide and you have to be careful when you walk on the rocks when the tide's coming in.'

Her daughter definitely wasn't fazed, talking to this big Italian her mother said was a friend.

'Thank you for the warning. I will be careful,' Raimondo assured her.

A small arm pointed to the opposite cliff. 'That lighthouse is so the ships know that the land is there. Especially in a storm. Aunty Trina's house has big windows and in the storm the wind howls.'

A sage nod from Raimondo. 'That must be very exciting in a storm.'

'I don't like storms,' Chloe said severely, and Faith had to smile as Raimondo backtracked adroitly.

'Neither do I.'

Chloe looked at him under her brows as if assessing his truthfulness and Faith suppressed a laugh.

As if reassured, Chloe went on. 'Mummy works at the hospital on the hill and I'll be going to big school next year, which is just down the road from the hospital.' Her daughter could talk.

Faith could also be amused by how mystified Raimondo looked by Chloe's running commentary because he kept turning back to Faith and smiling in pleased bemusement and she suspected he hadn't had much to do with children.

Well, Faith had had a lot to do with children. Especially this one. Twenty-four hours a day and seven days a week for almost five years and still Chloe could stump her.

He had no chance of nailing it on one brief weeklong visit.

Chloe had always been included in the conversations between Faith and Izzy and, while a very polite little girl, she was happy to share her views on the small world she inhabited.

No doubt, soon Chloe would ask Raimondo about his town and his life so that he could share things with them—things that she had no knowledge of. Her daughter was thirsty for knowledge of new things. New places. There were certainly opportunities coming up for her there. For Faith too.

Crossing her fingers, Faith hoped her daughter could wait for those questions until they reached the beach so she could hear the answers too.

'The book Mummy is reading me at the moment is called *Chicken Little*. Have you read it?'

Faith smiled to herself at Raimondo's answer. 'No. What is this story about?'

Chloe turned her head to look at him. Faith suspected her daughter rolled her eyes at that point. 'A silly chicken thinks the sky is falling and tells all the animals they have to leave. To run. It's very funny.'

'I am glad that it is funny.' Raimondo turned slightly to look at Faith for an instant. 'Perhaps your mummy could read that story to you again, and I could listen?'

Chloe stopped and turned back to Faith. 'Mummy? Could you read the *Chicken Little* story when Mr Salvanelli comes to visit?'

Faith shooed her on. 'We'll see.'

'So is Italy bigger than Lighthouse Bay?' Chloe's question came as his daughter settled down again on the sand. They were on the beach and had made a small area their own with their things.

Raimondo liked that there was nobody else here. So

strange when it was such a picturesque spot, but perhaps more families would come later.

The chairs Faith had given him to bring were set up and the umbrella she'd carried angled over them all. His daughter played at their feet with a small bucket and spade in the sand and he felt like pinching himself to be sure he wasn't dreaming this moment in time.

He was with his family.

Every now and then his daughter would run on sturdy legs to the water's edge and fill her bucket with water and bring it back to pour over sand so she could plaster the walls of the mound she said was a castle.

It began to take shape. He'd never made a sandcastle as a boy but could see the attraction. Perhaps he could try? To help her. Chloe began to stick shells on the walls. He glanced at Faith but she was staring out over the sea, deep in thought.

'May I join you?' he asked Chloe.

Chloe nodded vigorously. 'We can make it taller.'

So, awkwardly, for he had no skills with children, he crouched down on the sand beside his daughter and began to scoop out the sand in a narrow line to build a moat, putting the sand he removed on the top of her mound. The sand was cool and damp and coarse and felt strangely comforting as he ran his fingers across its salty cleanness to smooth the new walls of the castle.

'I see you build good castles. I am a man. We build forts. So, with your permission, I will dig a moat and build a wall to keep our castle safe from those who might attack while you make it pretty.' Was he being too stereotypical?

She laughed. 'The water will attack it.'

'I will build a diversion for the water.'

Each time she patted on another handful of sand it was as if she had also found a question. He had to smile at her fertile and free-flowing mind.

He had hundreds of questions and couldn't seem to ask any.

So instead he thought how to describe his home when she asked about it. 'I live on the outskirts of the city of Florence. It is much bigger than Lighthouse Bay.' He thought about his beautiful Florence and the thousands of people who lived there and the hundreds who visited every day. Unlike this tiny place. 'Our house is part of a very old villa belonging to a nobleman many years ago but purchased by my grandfather and restored. It has several buildings and many rooms and a garden that grows olives and looks over Florence and the Arno Valley.'

He saw Faith look up at that. She raised her brows at him with shock in her eyes but he pretended not to see. They had not spoken of Italy much in the time they'd spent together.

'How many rooms?' His daughter remained persistent.

'There are four other dwellings but the main house has ten bedrooms.' He shrugged. 'My brother's house has nine bedrooms. Mine has six.'

'That sounds big.' Here she looked at her mother. 'That's big, isn't it, Mummy?'

Faith looked at her daughter. 'Sounds a bit like the size of the hospital, really,' she said, her voice dry. 'You know how it has some separate buildings with other wards in them. Instead of looking over the ocean, his house looks over a city and a valley.'

His daughter nodded and looked much struck. 'You must have a big family.'

He spread his hands. 'And this is our sadness.' He shrugged. 'No. My twin lost his wife and son and I am not married any more. We are the last of our family.'

Chloe lowered her brows and shook her head, her little face serious. 'You should get married and have a family.'

'Yes, I should.' He glanced ruefully at Faith. 'My brother and I both should marry but his love died and mine wasn't meant to be.'

He saw Faith turn away to hide her expression, or to look at something he could not see. He wished she had not turned her face. Then she turned back and there was something in her face that made him pause in his explanation.

Faith said quietly, 'It's not polite for little girls to tell adults what they should do, Chloe.'

'Oh?' She glanced at her mother and sighed. 'Okay. Sorry, Mr Salvanelli.'

Just like that. No angst from either, just a correction. Different to his upbringing, where the emotion always ran high and even the wrath of God was often introduced. So different. He searched for a way to reassure both. 'I am not offended but thank you for your apology. I have a question. Do you always make sandcastles or do you make other things in the sand?'

The change of topic was gratefully accepted by all parties.

'I make sandcastles, though they're not really castles. I've never seen a castle except in books about princesses. I love princesses.'

She could certainly hold a conversation. He was glad English was his second language and he didn't have to translate in his thoughts. She was adorable and he couldn't help considering how his family home was very much like a castle.

He would show her one day, hopefully not too far away in time, and with luck she would be enchanted. But that possibility remained with her mother, who was watching him with an inscrutable expression on her beautiful face. Inside himself he knew that he would also like to show Faith his world, but at the moment that look on her face warned him to be careful.

'Mummy said you are a doctor?'

His eyes returned to his daughter. 'Yes, I work in a part of Florence that is poor and the people come to our clinic because it is free. Sometimes I work in other countries if there is a disaster.' Though he couldn't get away as much as he liked since his brother's wife had died.

'Mummy is a midwife.'

'I know. I saw her at her work yesterday.'

'Do you catch babies too?'

This he didn't understand. 'Catch babies?' He looked at Faith. 'Babies who fall?'

When Faith laughed her mouth curved with amusement, her eyes crinkled and the already ridiculously bright day seemed to grow sunnier to him.

She explained, 'In the past it was said that the doctor "delivered" the baby. Of course, it is the mother who does all the work so here we say we are only there to ensure the safe gathering of the mother's work. So to "catch a baby" as it is born. Chloe has heard me say it many times.'

He smiled at his daughter. 'Yes. Rarely I catch babies but mostly I help those who are sick. Little girls and boys your age. Old ladies and men who are frail. I have come to know many families from the outskirts and it is something I am proud of.'

Chloe was so interested in him. Thirsty for knowledge he could share. He was having a wonderful conversation with his daughter!

For a moment he so deeply regretted the lost time. Maria had a lot to answer for by keeping this news from him... He could feel his mood slipping and Faith's calmness seemed to wrap around him as he considered who really had suffered.

That was not all Maria's doing and bitterness would taint this new promise of a family. He would not do that. No. This was his doing and he would be the one to repair any damage. He had been the one who had flown from Australia into his family's turmoil, into deathbed promises to a man he owed everything, and into funerals. He had been distracted but had not once paused to check, to confirm the safety or check for unexpected complications from his incredible but reckless Australian liaison.

It did not matter that he'd had a marriage to arrange. Then a funeral.

Years he had wasted.

But at the time he'd thought they hadn't been reckless. He had used protection and she also. The thought of this accident of birth occurring sixteen thousand kilometres away had never occurred to him.

It should have occurred to confirm Faith's wellbeing though.

And after Maria had left? Why had he accepted that Faith was in his past and would be settled happily without him? Why had he assumed their amazing connection had meant so little to her when its magic had settled in a space in his heart that it would never leave?

He'd been determined to fill his life with work when he should have returned at least once to Australia to confirm she was happily settled and his own thoughts were the only ones wistful for what had ended. He still didn't know the answer to that question but had yet to be convinced there wasn't hope.

The time after divorcing Maria he hadn't wasted, because he'd given it to others. It had been healing to draw strength from those in poverty wearing quiet fortitude so that he could not feel sorry for himself. Both locally and abroad in disaster zones.

Helping others after the dissolution of his marriage, and the tragic loss of his brother's family, he'd found peace from unobtrusively being present in their need.

But he'd wasted his chance of happiness.

Wasted Faith's chance of happiness.

Wasted time he could have spent with Chloe.

But now he would work towards the challenge of proving himself worthy of Faith and Chloe. This was his new goal for a future that stretched ahead. He stared out over the white sand, over the tumbling shallows, over the rolling waves to the place where the ocean met the sky and prayed that he could be worthy to become a part of their lives.

CHAPTER NINE

FAITH COULDN'T HELP responding to the depth in Raimondo's voice when he told Chloe about his practice in Florence and his aid work, though she knew his simple version was watered down for young ears.

Somewhere inside her a warm gladness expanded that he'd found a vocation he'd been lacking before. None of this passion had been there when he'd spoken of the business side of the pharmaceutical company. It had all been her enthusiasm for her work.

So now she was glad for him. Glad he'd found a purpose in life, even if he hadn't found a happy marriage.

But that didn't change anything. He hadn't looked back to what they'd had in those magical few days. If she let him into their lives now, and she couldn't see how she had a choice about that, it was going to be hard to trust him not to fly in like a comet until Chloe was starry-eyed and then zoom away again.

Certainly she would guard her own heart from him this time.

Looking back, she could see so clearly, his tilted head, his warm eyes as she'd raved about why she loved her job in maternity. He'd watched her as if she'd been the most beautiful, interesting woman he'd ever seen and she, young that she'd been, had been flattered and eager to expound her beliefs.

She even remembered that next day, taking him through the cave, raving about the way water seeped through limestone and dissolved the rocks to form caves. How wonderful it was.

He'd surely known that but she'd been too besotted not to spout all the things that inspired her in her cave tours and dragging him down to the ancient riverbed had seemed the best gift she could give him for the gift he'd given her—a whole new world of wonderful love, sensuality and awareness.

Which, sadly, had ended when he flew away for good.

The warmth in her belly abruptly changed to a chill.

Yes.

Be careful.

And be careful of Chloe falling in love too.

She glanced at her waterproof watch and recognised the sudden need to cool down. She struggled inelegantly out of her beach chair. 'Enough time has passed since breakfast. I think I'll go for a swim. Would you like to come and splash with me, Chloe?'

Her daughter jumped up immediately. 'Are you coming, Mr Salvanelli?'

Faith noted Raimondo's grimace at Chloe's formal address and, yes, she could see this was hard for him. But some of the softening she'd been unaware of had already caught her out.

She needed to stay vigilant and firm on boundaries between him and Chloe until she knew what he hoped for.

He might become the perfect dad.

Or not.

But she wasn't creating storybook fantasies of what daddies were like and wouldn't risk breaking Chloe's heart until she was sure the devotion would be reciprocated. For all she knew, he could be called away again tomorrow and off he'd go to answer a summons without a backward glance at them.

He had the right to leave any time.

She had the responsibility to protect her daughter in case he did.

'*Sí*, I will come.' He rose, a smooth uncoiling of muscles, and she dragged her eyes away from the leashed power of him. Darn him. How could getting out of a folding chair seem sexy? She turned away.

Then he said, 'Are you sure you do not need help with suncream on your back, Faith?'

The body part in question was directed to him so he couldn't see her eyes close as she imagined that. Big hands. Powerful fingers with slow movements. Sigh. Sensible was so darn sucky. 'No, I'm fine, thanks, I'll only be in and out of the water.'

She pushed herself forward through the sand, Chloe hopping beside her, as she headed for the sea. She needed to be clear on the boundaries for herself too.

They stayed at the beach for the morning, picking through the basket for food and drinks, choosing topics that sat easily as well, while the solitude of the beach slowly disappeared. Two surfers arrived and ran out into the waves. A lone fisherman walked the beach edge further along the bay.

Soon more families arrived, just as they were packing up. Ellie and her husband and daughter. The new arrivals dumped their chairs and towels beside them to greet them.

'Hello, people. Nice to see you.' Faith had relaxed enough for this to be almost true. Though she did wonder if Ellie had told Sam that Raimondo was Chloe's father. And what they all thought about Raimondo helping in maternity. At least she'd told Ellie about Raimondo.

It was actually neat that she could introduce him to the Southwells after the years of them knowing he'd been briefly in her past. 'This is Dr Raimondo Salvanelli from Florence. Raimondo, this is Ellie, my boss, and her husband, Dr Sam Southwell, and their daughter Emily.'

'Good to meet you, Raimondo,' Ellie said. 'I'm more the paper pusher than Faith's boss. We're self-directed here. Heard you two have been busy already.'

Faith thought of the birth yesterday, and then remembered the man who had collapsed. She needed to phone and find out how he was, but he'd been swept from her mind by Raimondo. How awful.

Raimondo must have read her thoughts. 'He was improving this morning when I rang.' Thank you, she thought silently.

Ellie had carried on. 'Congratulations on the successful resuscitation. Both of them. Faith was lucky you were there.'

Raimondo nodded a friendly greeting. 'Your midwife had it under control. Very nice to meet you both. Faith has mentioned you, Ellie. All good things,' Raimondo said, smiling, and his ease of manner made Faith's jangled nerves settle as he held out his hand to meet Sam's.

'Welcome to Lighthouse Bay,' Sam said. 'This your first time here?'

Raimondo smiled blandly. 'Second. I couldn't believe

how deserted the beach was this morning. It is very different to Italy.'

Another family group hailed them. Catrina, another of the midwives and only recently on maternity leave, a month before her baby was due, waddled a little with the weight of her pregnancy. Her husband Finn arrived with his daughter Piper, who'd not long ago turned three, and two chairs. The little girls whooped and ran in circles, excited to see each other, and all the mothers smiled.

Introductions continued as Finn and Raimondo shook hands.

'You should join us for dinner tonight,' Ellie said. 'It's Sam's dad's birthday, and we're having a barbecue. Chloe would be excited to see the girls as well.'

'Who's working?' Trina asked as she shook hands with Raimondo.

'Broni. It's her last shift before holidays and then we have Stacey back from the base hospital.'

Faith, Raimondo and Chloe left the beach a few minutes later, having agreed to meet everyone for the barbecue, and wandered back up the hill with chairs, umbrella, a much lighter basket and a tired little girl with a bucket and spade bringing up the rear.

Faith struggled with herself on whether to invite Raimondo in as they neared the house. Did he need some time to himself? She guessed it had been a pretty big twenty-four hours.

The thought made her almost laugh out loud.

Here she was being a coward at the thought of inviting him in. Scared to be alone with him because Chloe would probably go to sleep for an hour, something she'd been doing lately in the afternoon, and she did need to find out what Raimondo's plans were.

Perhaps better to search for answers, even if he was not ready for more time with her.

She looked across at him. 'Would you like to spend the afternoon with us, though Chloe will probably have a rest now, or are you jet-lagged and want to come back later before the barbecue?'

'Thank you, Faith.' He shook his head. 'Again, you surprise me with your kindness. And yes, please. I would like to talk with you this afternoon.'

She looked at this tall, handsome, serious man outside her door and tried again to think of this from his point of view. 'I don't think I'm being kind. Just practical.' She lowered her voice. 'We need to discuss things.'

She opened the gate, walked to the door and pushed it open.

When she looked back to invite him in his face had paled. 'You do not lock your door?'

She glanced back at the wooden door she'd pushed open off the latch. 'Only if we go away. And that's more to stop it blowing open.' She watched Chloe put her sand bucket down wearily outside the door and kick off her sandy flip-flops. Faith brushed her daughter's dark hair with her hand as the little girl passed in front of them. 'Straight through into the bathroom, Missy.'

She turned back to watch Raimondo remove his beach shoes, trying to ignore the way his broad back rippled and his dark hair curled on his strong neck. Shook her head at herself. 'Come in when you're ready. I'll just get Chloe showered and she'll have a lie down and rest.'

She followed her daughter in but a subtle, sensitive part of her was very aware of the man following. 'There's an album on the table of Chloe's baby photos if you'd like to look at that while I sort Chloe out.'

His face lit when he saw the album she'd discreetly placed this morning before they left.

'Thank you.' Then a quirked brow in her direction and a slight smile. 'And after Chloe will you sort me out?'

She met his eyes. 'That's my plan.'

CHAPTER TEN

WHEN RAIMONDO LOOKED at his watch only fifteen minutes had passed since Faith had left him. Yet his daughter's whole life had passed before his eyes.

His chin felt raw where he'd continually rubbed in deep emotion with his chest tight and painful as he'd slowly turned the pages of his daughter's, and the beautiful Faith's, world.

A life he'd known nothing of while he'd passed his time on the other side of the planet, missing it all completely.

In his mind that first album page still haunted him and he could have wept for the loss for himself and for his Australian family. Could have wept for what might have been if he had known of Faith's pregnancy and Chloe's impending arrival.

Faith had done this alone.

Though no, not alone, for her aunt had been there. He and his family owed an enormous debt to Faith's aunt Isabel.

But he should have been the one to support the mother of his child.

He turned the pages back to the start, not for the first time, and gazed again. A rosy-skinned and radiantly exultant Faith, so young and so smiling up at the camera from a large circular bath, water lapping the swell of her breasts, and a little higher on her chest lay his brand-new owl-eyed baby daughter, staring into her mother's eyes, her tiny body slightly blue, patches of white vernix from the pregnancy still covering her plump baby creases as another woman leaned across to lay a towel over them both.

Dios. His heart actually felt as if it grew and expanded inside him and would explode out of his ribs, tearing his chest apart.

He turned forward the pages to the photos of his daughter's last birthday. The starfish cake, four candles, her baby face maturing into a bigger little girl, her mother's loving smile as she leaned across towards her daughter and helped blow out the candles. Such a moment, captured with love from the photographer. *Sì*, he owed Izzy a great debt. So many wonderful moments to be shared with him even as a future observer.

He heard Faith close the door gently to his daughter's room and then cross the lounge area towards him. Her bare feet whispered on the rugs that covered the wooden floors in circles of bright colour.

Her home radiated the same welcoming charm the woman did.

He looked down at the album and then towards her. Words failed him.

She brushed his shoulder in a fleeting touch of sympathy as she passed to sit opposite. 'You look…upset.' She was giving comfort to him when it should have been the other way around.

'Regretful.' He moistened his tight throat. 'The photographs are very beautiful.' Thankfully his voice remained steady. He pushed the album towards her chair when in fact he wanted to tuck it under his arm and run with it. 'Thank you for showing me.'

She straightened the big album on the table without opening the cover. 'Chloe looks at the photographs a lot.'

He laughed and even he could hear the exasperation. 'As would I. The photographer is gifted.'

'Izzy, of course. She's been good with everything.'

'I can see that I let you down.' Then he leaned forward. The silence stretched between them as he tried to form the words he needed. 'I don't understand. I never dreamed… How did this happen?

'Bah.' He waved his hand at the past, at his ludicrous statement. 'We know how…' And for a brief moment their eyes met and humour danced between them. Then it was gone.

'How do I ask this?' He ran his hand through his hair, anxious not to place blame because that would do neither of them good. 'I am sure we were exuberant, young and excited for this thing that sprang so powerfully between us…' he looked at her and the faint blush on her cheeks only made her more painfully beautiful '…but I thought we were careful?'

'It's a fair question…' she smiled ruefully '…and one I continually asked myself when that pregnancy stick proved positive.' She shrugged. 'We were careful.' Yet he could see she was embarrassed.

Her, embarrassed? A joke. Nothing she could do was anywhere near the moral catastrophe he had achieved and left her to deal with.

'I missed two pills during the conference before we met, though took them when we were together. So must have been susceptible to ovulate.' Her voice lowered.

'Apparently, we had needed that second defence. But by the time I found out it was too late as I was pregnant.'

He thought about that.

Thought about the lovely young woman he'd fallen for in the airport, fresh and vibrant. Almost innocent. So full of life and passion and enthusiasm for her work— and he had left her pregnant and with the heartbreak he'd caused her.

He could have destroyed her with his carelessness if she hadn't been so resilient. He thought about what he'd done to her ordered life and then he'd flown away without a backward glance. No. Even that hadn't been true.

He'd glanced back a lot. But those few days he had shared with Faith had been dreamlike. A mirage. Something he didn't deserve.

As if she'd read his mind she said softly, 'Maybe it's different for men. I'd like to know how you felt as you flew away.'

He owed her that.

Though he wondered if he could be as honest as she was. Regardless, he needed to be. Such a small price to pay. 'What you gave me in those few days was a gift and I cherished the memories in the months and years ahead. Yet it was strange how little I felt I deserved such happiness. Perhaps that is why I did not make it back. Wedding Marie was a return to the time of my grandfather. Without joy. But my duty. You were the dream I didn't deserve.'

He shrugged. 'Melodramatic, perhaps. You have to understand my family to understand my actions. But, even for my family, I would never have left you to face that alone. I never thought I would leave you pregnant.'

* * *

Faith recognised the sincerity. She hadn't imagined a child either or she would have asked for a morning after pill when she'd recovered from Raimondo's departure.

Thank goodness she hadn't or she wouldn't have her darling Chloe.

But Chloe was now a part of Raimondo's family and she'd better at least try to understand the Salvanellis to help her daughter when her time came to meet them.

'Tell me about your family.'

He looked struck by the suggestion. Then he said softly with wry humour as he held her gaze, 'Chloe's other family?'

'So it seems,' she said and tried to ignore the fission of fear that raised the hairs on her arms.

'One day.' No. She wouldn't lose her daughter to them as she had lost Raimondo when his family demanded his return. Nobody could demand Chloe did anything. 'But I do want to know why you didn't feel as if you deserved the happiness we so briefly found together.' They hadn't spoken of his family much at all back then.

'It is fair that you know of my family. Where to begin? Dominico, my brother, is ten minutes older, and with me was sent to live with our grandfather after the loss of our parents. That loss left nothing to soften the already stern man who was my *nonno*. Like our father before us, we studied medicine, despite a lack of enthusiasm from our grandfather, because neither of us had a passion for the business he loved. My brother took over the running of the business when my grandfather became ill. I am grateful to him for that.'

There was a lot there he wasn't saying but she got the

general idea. Not the ideal childhood but she'd had loss in her life too, even though it had been later. 'No grandmother on the scene?'

'Gone at my father's birth. Our grandfather's estate was a loveless home, despite the beauty of Florence. Though that altered when Dominico found Teresa.'

She watched his face transform and had a sudden wish that she could have met this Teresa.

'Teresa brought joy,' Raimondo went on, but there was sadness in his voice. 'Soon their son arrived to liven their villa. Finally, my grandfather could relax, my brother was happy, I could stop feeling guilty that I was still furthering my career in medicine and not marrying. Now the family business was secure with two generations of sons to pass it down to.'

'Your brother and his wife were happy?'

'Indeed. Too brief happiness. Again, tragedy struck. We are not blessed with luck.' He stopped for a moment and she saw the shadow of that time as it passed through his mind.

'Not long before I came to Australia for business meetings, and met you, Teresa and my brother's son were killed in a hot-air balloon ride. Broken, my brother withdrew from everyone. I had to travel for the business—the Sydney trip already had been arranged—and suddenly it was back to me to ensure the line when my grandfather became terminally ill. But first I needed to complete the trip to Australia my brother wanted to cancel.'

'And you met me.'

'*Sì.*' His voice dropped and she almost missed the words as he spoke them more to himself. 'My Australian wildflower.'

She remembered he'd called her that. Faith felt the

sting behind her eyes, the tightness in her throat, and chewed the inside of her top lip as she struggled to push it all back. This was too important to lose in an emotional blowout. One she'd dealt with years ago and locked securely behind iron gates inside her soul.

Hopefully he missed her struggle as he looked within himself to the painful past. 'You must understand my grandfather's whole world was centred on the pharmaceutical company he'd built. That it must stay in the Salvanelli family. Now, suddenly, my grandfather had days to live. My brother struggled with his demands and called me to come at once—so I went.'

She remembered his sudden departure. The first available flight arranged. The rush.

He looked up and sighed. 'The marriage between Maria and I had been spoken of for a long time and I had resisted. Both my promised wife and I had opposed the match. But my grandfather had so little time, and her father agreed, and it was either I wed the woman he wished or my brother could be persuaded into wedding Maria, and there was no marriage he could face, still grieving for his wife and son. I could feel his pain and would not ask it of him.'

Tough love. She could see his dilemma. And even why he hadn't explained the whole of it when he'd left.

But that was almost six years ago and he'd been free for a while. If she'd been his Australian wildflower, why hadn't he come back to see if what they'd had been real when he had the chance?

She quashed that bitterness. Needed to remember she had let it go a long while past.

But she couldn't help wondering what would happen if his brother called again. She wouldn't be stupid enough to expect him not to go instantly if he needed him, but what if Chloe was the one left heartbroken—what then?

'You didn't think to come back when the marriage was annulled?'

His heavy sigh lowered his shoulders until he straightened and faced her. 'Who was I to ruin your life again? I had no doubt you would have moved on without me. What we had was a few days on the other side of the world and you were young and not bitter with life like I had become.'

That was true. She had moved on. And she hadn't become bitter. Just thankful for her daughter and occasionally nostalgic for a man who could have been a big part of her life but had told her he would never be back.

She'd made the break he'd told her was permanent.

Raimondo went on. 'I believed you were better without me. Vibrant and passionate about your work. You gave me that. After Maria left I found an area in my work that brought me great satisfaction.' He met her gaze and held it. 'Until someone spoke of you, and your Lighthouse Bay...' a pause '...and your daughter—and suddenly there was nothing that was more important than coming here to see.'

At least the mention of the Bay had jogged him at last. He'd remembered them. 'And here you are.' There was no mistaking the hint of dryness in her tone.

'*Sì*. Here I am.'

Yes. Here stood the major concern. He was very capable of wreaking more havoc. She'd only have to remember the response her body made when he was near. Let alone if he turned the full force of his Italian gallantry and accomplishments her way. Plus, she suspected he had a depth of purpose and strong will he wasn't showing her.

Well, she had that too.

She lifted her head. 'Did you come with plans, Raimondo?'

She watched him blink at her direct question. 'If you are here for Chloe's birthday, are you leaving, never to come back again after this week?'

She shrugged as if unable to know what to believe, but all the time her eyes remained on his. 'No evasion, please. Is she to look for Christmas and birthday cards? Or are you hoping for more?'

He stared at her.

Well he might, but she was deadly serious.

Black widow serious.

She would protect her daughter from his charm if necessary. To the death. Nothing in his explanation said he wouldn't leave them suddenly if called.

Now, while Chloe was asleep, they needed to get this sorted and labelled for what it was.

'I understand your concern. You have become a strong woman, Faith.'

Pointless flattery. 'I've needed to be.'

'I have never lied to you.'

Bully for him. 'I've never lied either.' She raised one brow. 'So don't lie now.'

His turn to lift his chin and she saw the narrowing of his eyes, the implacable set to his chin, and now she could see the man he'd become. Perhaps he wouldn't run to do his family's bidding quite so quickly this time, but she wasn't sorry she'd pulled the tiger's tail.

Hopefully she hadn't set in motion the whole attack mode response but he needed to know she was on her guard.

He leaned forward and it was as if he'd flipped a

switch because in his eyes shone the force of his personality she'd suspected might be shaded.

Whoa.

Where had he been concealing this man?

His dark eyes glittered and his sensual mouth flattened into a straight line. 'Yes, I have plans. I did not come with them but after seeing you at the cave yesterday, hearing your story, I lay awake and dreamed of the future. Of what could be. Of the possibilities before all of us.

'Not just showing my daughter her Italian family and the world she needs to be now aware of.' His voice was deep. Clipped. Belying the fierce emotion in his eyes. 'I will do what needs to be done to achieve that dream. And other dreams.'

A little more of the strong guy than she needed. But she'd dealt with stressed dads before in the labour ward and she knew where she was going with this. Her end goal. 'Without pain to Chloe?'

He looked at her and then, miraculously, his eyes softened. Even held a glint of admiration. 'Correct. I agree. She is the most important part of the equation.'

'Thank you. More important than you. More important than me.' She sat back and he followed suit. 'That was the point I was trying to make.'

He measured her with an assessing look. 'I can see that now. I will not underestimate you again.'

Well, that wasn't quite what she'd been hoping for but she might as well get the answers she needed.

'And your immediate plans?'

He blew out his breath but in his eyes there was a definite admiration for her. The glint of a smile. The hint of a challenge. 'Three things. I would like to be here for Chloe's birthday. Be a part of her celebration.'

She nodded. That was easy. She'd already agreed.

'I would like to be allowed to buy her a gift.'

Again, Faith nodded. Chloe would be happy with that. And she was only five so he couldn't spend too much on her. 'As long as you don't buy her a house, the gift is fine.'

To her surprise he laughed out loud. 'That house has bolted.'

She blinked. 'It's "That horse has bolted".' The second time Raimondo had mistaken his metaphors. He didn't appear any less amused when she corrected him. Suspicion and disbelief raised the hairs on her arms. 'What do you mean?'

'In this case, I have bought a house, and the gate is bolted.' He grinned a wicked flash of white teeth at her. 'We are off topic and Chloe will wake soon, I imagine.'

Faith glanced at her watch but her head still spun at the assertive man she had definitely underestimated.

No. He did not just say that. 'Bull. When did you have time to do something that complicated?'

Dark brows arched at her. 'It is not complicated if others do the paperwork. Did you not spend eight hours at your place of work yesterday?' He spread his hands in a very Italian gesture. 'I am a rich man. I saw something I liked and it is done. But I can wait to put it in Chloe's name if you prefer.'

That was scary. He had done it. Bought a house for a five-year-old.

Or for himself to have access to Chloe. On his first day back and before meeting her daughter. His actions defied sense.

'What house did you buy?' She guessed that meant he wasn't planning on never seeing Chloe again. She'd wanted that reassurance, hadn't she? But with this new broadside she didn't feel as confident she had everything under control.

He settled back and studied her. 'Which house do you think I would buy? Which house would be useful to me?'

She could feel her own temper slipping and knowing that he was goading her because she'd goaded him didn't help. 'Well, you can't buy mine because I own it.'

He waved the comment away. 'The one beside you. It is nothing. Me dealing with inactivity.'

Next door? Which house was for sale? Only one. The old Sea Captain's house. With the turrets. It was a wreck. She shook off the wild thoughts and concentrated. He had her off balance. That wasn't good. He'd just bought the house next door! That was huge. And had huge implications for him being around more. Her turn to blow out a breath.

How he spent his money could not affect her. She wouldn't let it, or she could try not to let it. But holy heck.

And there was more. What was his third request? What more could he want? 'And the last?'

He paused. 'I would like Chloe to know I am her father before I leave to return to Italy. In fact, I would like her to know now, but...' Another shrug. 'I agree to wait until you decide the time is right, as long as it is before I leave.'

And there it was.

The endgame. She could understand that. And he obviously had real plans to return to see his daughter in the future—he'd started proceedings to become a property owner—she had no valid reason not to confirm his relationship to her daughter. But the thought sat, terrifying her like a black hole of unknown depth just the same.

What if he let Chloe down?

What if Chloe began to want something she couldn't have?

Even more terrifying. What if Faith did?

'I have no control over your second condition except it would have been more sensible to buy her an expensive doll's house, not a real one. Your third request I will consider and let you know tonight. I can understand you wanting her to know.'

'Thank you.' He stood. 'I have given you much to think about.'

Yes. He had given her a lot to think about. And did she want him to arrive with them as a part of their party at the barbecue later? No real choice. He was in their life. Now. Probably for ever.

He looked a little uncertain and, even in their short acquaintance, she could see it sat oddly on him. 'Do you still wish me to join you tonight, at your friend's dinner?'

'Of course.' She looked at him with a resigned expression. Shook her head. He was reading her mind again. 'I'll have to get used to you popping up out of the woodwork.'

'You will.' His eyes crinkled. 'And I will too. Pop up, as you say. Reappear with regularity. Regularity, that I promise.' His brows raised. 'I hope you grow to welcome my arrival.'

Welcome his arrival? Would she? A transference of awareness settled over her, as if from his aura to hers, a melding of their senses while not touching, as he captured her gaze with his. 'Let us see where this leads us, Faith. I will not let you down again.'

Her barriers quivered under the strain but held. 'As you say. We'll see.'

She watched his eyes narrow at her less than trusting response.

He held out his palm and reluctantly she took his strong fingers in hers and his warmth seeped into her like it had from the first moment they'd met years ago—until their hands separated, slowly.

She tucked her fingers behind her back. 'We'll leave here by six. It won't be a late night. Chloe gets tired.'

Instead of stepping away, he stepped closer, his bulk blocking out the light from the open door. His male scent coated with the salt of the sea. His strong jaw coming closer as he leaned in and she turned her head until he kissed her cheek. His breath was warm on her face, his mouth even warmer, and despite herself her body softened even with that light touch. His hand came up and caressed the other side of her cheek, cupping her face with more warmth and such tenderness that slowly she turned her head towards him. Towards his full, sensuous mouth, until their lips were a breath apart. Inhaling the life force between them as they hovered on the brink of the kiss they shouldn't have.

Yet it was she who leaned forward and offered her mouth, her first sign of trust, her first forgiveness.

But it was he who propelled them slowly but surely into a kiss that buckled her knees and sent her hands up between them to clutch his shirt. His arms came around her with a certainty and possession that jammed them together until her breasts were hard against his rock-like chest. She wanted to be lost like this so much.

She pushed him away.

He stilled at once. Nodded, turned and left before she

could make her feet move. Her breath eased out. She sagged against the door she moved to shut.

Phew.

She glanced down at the table and a small package lay there.

Her brow furrowed as she opened the door again and called out to him softly, 'You left something.'

He turned and his smile lit his dark, handsome face and made her knees weaken again. 'It is a small gift for Chloe when she wakes.'

She held the package but almost forgot it in her hands as she watched him walk away. That kiss. They could have ended up in bed if she'd let that go on.

A kiss that had shattered her reserves. Thank goodness she'd managed to cling onto the extremely tattered remains of her protective coat by a few wispy threads. See. This was the problem with the man. Once he touched she became lost on the ocean of his expertise.

She hated that. She'd been like seafoam in his hands until the thought had crashed in that this had happened before. That he couldn't be trusted, despite her body telling her he could. But why did she lean into the kiss knowing this?

She should regret that kiss but in her heart she knew she didn't. And even more worrying was the fact she didn't care that she held no regrets.

She wrapped her arms around her middle and stared at the closed door as if it were the man who had just left. How did this change things for her, for Chloe, for them as a family?

If she didn't know the answer to that, then thank goodness she'd pushed him away.

CHAPTER ELEVEN

WHEN CHLOE WOKE an hour later she wandered out of her room, rubbing her pale face with small fists. Faith saw the moment she realised only her mother was there and their visitor had departed while she'd slept.

'Has Mr Salvanelli gone?'

The sudden droop to her daughter's mouth gave Faith a pang in her stomach.

'Yes, darling. But he'll be back tonight.' She suppressed a worried sigh. Already he was charming her daughter too.

'Oh. Okay. He's nice.' Chloe's gaze landed on the small parcel Raimondo had left. 'What's that?'

'Mr Salvanelli said it was for you. A present he thought you might like.'

'For me?' She hopped up and down and then hurried towards it, just as Izzy came in through the front door. 'Aunt Izzy, I have a present!'

Chloe caressed the tissue-wrapped gift carefully. 'Can I open it?' This to Faith.

'Yes. Open it.'

Faith's eyes met those of her aunt. 'Hello, Izzy. Raimondo left Chloe a present while she was sleeping.'

'Nice of him.' They both watched Chloe burrow

through the tissue paper carefully. Luckily there was only one piece of tape so it didn't take too long.

While they waited Faith asked, 'How's Myra?'

'Good. Looking forward to tonight. I hear we're all going up to Reg's impromptu party.

'Raimondo is coming.'

Izzy's brows rose.

'Oh, she's beautiful!' Chloe's reverent voice interrupted them. She spun to show her mother and aunt the gaily dressed Italian peasant doll. 'Look at her apron. And her scarf and hat.' The red touches did make the little figure glow with colour.

'Lovely, darling,' Faith said and suppressed another exhalation. This was just the beginning.

'She must be from Italy.' Her aunt was watching her. Faith avoided her aunt's eye and looked at her daughter. Forced a gay smile.

'She needs a name and she should meet all your other little dolls.'

Chloe nodded seriously. 'She doesn't have blonde hair but I'm going to call her Elsa. Like in *Frozen*.' Chloe clutched the doll to her chest.

'Elsa is a lovely name,' Faith said. 'Why don't you take her into your room and show her to your other dolls?'

Chloe flashed a brilliant smile at them both and dashed off.

Izzy tilted her head at Faith. 'You look like you need a cup of tea.'

'I think I need two.' She lowered her voice to a whisper. 'He's put a deposit on a house here. Next door.'

Izzy's startled eyes flew to Faith's from the hot water jug she'd been plugging in. 'The Captain's house?

Right next door?' Saw the confirmation in Faith's face. 'Good grief!'

Faith nodded heavily. 'Apparently for Chloe. In trust.'

'Did you tell him a doll's house would have been more sensible?'

Faith felt the burden of her worry lighten. She had to laugh. She loved her aunt. 'I did, actually.'

'Well.' Izzy finished plugging in the appliance and came across to hold out her hands for Faith to take. Izzy's warm squeeze of her fingers settled her thumping heart. 'He seems a good man. You wouldn't have been attracted to him if he hadn't been. Perhaps just see where this leads? I guess this means he's planning on sticking around.' Izzy dropped her hands and patted her shoulder.

'I don't see that. He'll return to Italy, leaving us all unsettled again. Including Chloe now. I'm worried this means he's planning on popping in and out of our lives like a jack-in-the-box.'

They both looked towards Chloe's room, where the sound of animated one-sided conversation carried on. Quietly Izzy pointed out, 'She does need a father.'

'And he wants me to tell Chloe before he leaves.'

Izzy nodded. As Faith knew she would. 'I think that's fair. Now that we all know he's invested, literally, but also I believe emotionally in finding his daughter.'

Faith closed her eyes for a second to centre herself. To calm, and be sensible, like she normally was. But again that man had thrown her life into turmoil. She could see where Izzy's usual sense was leading. 'I believe he cares for her already too. And you're right. I know that. I just don't know how to tell her.'

Her aunt laughed. 'Darling. She's five. She'll take to

the news as easily as she took to the doll. It's adults who complicate things.'

Izzy was probably right. In fact Faith knew she was. 'How did I get such a wise aunt?'

'Just lucky, I guess.' They hugged and stepped apart. 'Right. Tea.'

'Hold that thought. I should do it now.'

'May as well. Keep it simple.'

'Chloe?'

Chloe's head popped out of the room and then her whole body appeared. She had a doll in each hand. 'Susan and Elsa said they are going to be best friends.'

'That's lovely. Friends are very special. And I've got a secret to tell you.'

Chloe scooted right up to her mother. 'A secret?'

'Well, after I tell you it won't be a secret but it is true. Come sit with me.' She drew her daughter across to the settee and then onto her lap as they sat. She couldn't help a last glance at her aunt, who waved her on. Her heart thumped in her chest as she smoothed her daughter's hair. Inhaled the scent of her baby beside her.

'Do you remember me telling you that before you were born your daddy had to go away and wasn't ever able to come back here? That we wrote to him when you were born but he still couldn't come.'

Chloe's little brow furrowed and her big eyes blinked as she concentrated on her mother's serious tone. 'Yes.'

'Good.' A quick glance to Izzy and another deep breath. 'Well, he still lives away, but it seems that sometimes he *will* be able to visit us.' And she'd better add one of those big forced smiles here. She actually felt like crying as she watched her daughter process the information. Then the little face beside her jerked up as the penny dropped.

'My daddy? My real daddy? Like Piper has a daddy and Emily has a daddy?'

Oh, good grief, Faith thought, and her heart cracked. 'Yes. Though he won't be living with us like that. But you will be able to write to him. And maybe talk to him on the phone sometimes.'

'And he'll visit. And I'll be able to see him?'

'Sometimes.' Faith thought her heart would break for her little girl, who'd missed out on a daddy like Piper and Emily but liked the idea of a part-time parent zooming in and out of their lives because she knew no better. Izzy must have sensed that because she came and sat down beside them both.

Izzy said brightly, 'I think a daddy who can come sometimes is still better than a daddy who is never here. What do you think, Chloe?'

Chloe glanced at Izzy. 'Yes.' Though Faith thought her daughter didn't sound too sure.

Izzy waved Faith on. 'Simple,' she mouthed.

'Anyway. The secret is…' in a rush '… Mr Salvanelli is your father and he's very excited to finally meet you and know you are his daughter.' The words were out, never to be taken back, and Chloe stared at her.

'Really?' Her daughter frowned, searched her mother's face as if sensing Faith's mixed feelings.

'Yes. Really.'

'That's exciting. It must be why he gave me the doll.' Her hand slipped into her mother's and small fingers tightened around hers. Chloe's big green eyes searched Faith's face. 'But you're still going to be my mummy, aren't you?'

Faith hugged Chloe to her, the soft floating hair surrounded her, the tiny body wiggled in closer. 'Yes, my darling baby.' She smoothed Chloe's silken hair again, the strands so precious under her fingers. 'I will always be your mummy and I will always be here for you.'

Chloe slipped her arms around Faith and squeezed her back and then wriggled away. 'I'll have a daddy here for my birthday. That's lovely. Can I go play with my dolls again now?'

Faith's eyes met Izzy's and she blinked away the emotion that clouded her vision. Her daughter's world was secure. She wished her own world was as simple.

'Yes. Off you go.'

Two hours later, as he strode uphill towards Faith's house, Raimondo knew his life was about to change in ways he'd only ever imagined in weak moments. He was a father. A real family with warmth and joy and he was a part of it.

His axis had already shifted, meeting Faith again and being forcibly reminded by her beauty and calm how much they had connected so briefly so long ago. And earlier today.

That kiss.

Dios, that kiss.

He must not be distracted.

Because now, knowing of his daughter, he was already growing to love the child. She was such a beautiful young girl and he only hoped Chloe would come to love him when she knew him.

For his daughter was easy to love, like the mother had been almost six years ago, though he hadn't known at the time the indelible imprint Faith Fetherstone would have on his soul.

And on his life. On his future. He should have been here earlier.

His daughter. He crossed his fingers behind his back. Now he was being childish, but perhaps Faith had already told his daughter since he'd seen them this afternoon and Chloe would call him *papà*.

Though he couldn't help but wonder if he deserved such kindness.

He stopped outside the house with the sold sign. Barely saw the neglected gardens and peeling paint on the old weatherboards. *Pah*, it would fix with money. He glanced up at the turret that looked over the top of Faith's house and out to the sea. Remembered his daughter's words and the synchronicity of his purchase before he had even heard them.

A castle for his princess. He imagined his daughter looking though the polished brass telescope he would buy her, perhaps standing on a set of wheeled steps until she grew of a height, but excited and pointing at a passing ship. Yes. He could see that.

And that wasn't all he could see—though this part was more fanciful. He saw her beautiful mother watching fondly, imagined all the things in the wide world he could show them both. The Italy he could show them. The life they could share. If they'd let him. Patience. Already he was bursting with impatience.

It was still difficult to comprehend he had left Faith pregnant, that Maria had hidden the letters Faith sent; that his wife had kept such a secret from him was too petty to comprehend. Too cruel.

He could not imagine the hardships his child's mother,

his Faith, had to endure, the judgements he'd exposed her to with his carelessness, but he would not sour this coming evening with bitter thoughts. His daughter waited.

He started walking again and his stride lengthened until he turned into the gate of Faith's house.

As he reached up to knock his fingers on the white wooden door, it opened. His miracle of a daughter stood there, her excited face tilted sideways, her dark hair pulled back and tied with a yellow ribbon, her tiny pink mouth pursed as she studied him. Then she smiled.

'What a pretty ribbon,' he said, more to see her smile widen than anything else.

'Yellow is my favourite colour.' Then, without pause, 'Thank you for my doll. Mummy said you're my daddy. Is that right?'

His heart jumped in his chest and he wanted to lift her and swing her up, hug her to his chest, but instead he was careful not to expect too much and said, '*Sì*. That is right. I am your *papà*, and I am very glad to have found you.'

'So? Can I tell my friend, Piper?'

'Of course. If your mother is fine with that.' He looked past his daughter to Faith as she hovered protectively, as any mother would when an almost-stranger wanted to claim half her child. She was incredible, this woman. Brave. Honest. His heart swelled.

'Thank you,' he said quietly, and she nodded and gestured him in.

'Excuse me,' Chloe's voice piped up. 'Do I have any brothers or sisters or cousins? Or grandparents? Piper has cousins and grandparents.'

'I'm afraid not, Chloe. You do have an Uncle Dominico in Italy. But he has no family.' He caught Faith's eye and shook his head slightly. He didn't want Chloe to become sad with the history of loss in his family.

'So my Uncle Dominico won't be here for my birthday?'

He smiled. 'No. I am sorry.'

An intense stare. 'But you will be?'

This he could say. 'Yes.'

She nodded once then looked back at him. 'Promise?'

His daughter's head was tilted and she looked suddenly like her mother. He moistened his lips to say yes, and then considered his first ever promise to his daughter. The magnitude of that. 'Unless the sky falls in.'

She nodded and he saw that she understood. Instead she said, 'Is my Uncle Dominico bigger than you?'

'No. We are the same size. But he is older. By ten minutes. He is my twin. Though sometimes he seems much older.'

Isabel stood against the window watching them, a small welcoming smile flashing briefly his way before she turned to give them privacy.

An odd fleeting thought crossed his mind. His brother would appreciate Isabel, if only he could get him here. How incongruous that this place across the world made him think of Dominico and his painful past.

'We're almost ready to leave.' Faith's voice brought him back to the present moment. 'It's just up the hill at the far croft.'

'I am ready. Today I will see one of the little houses on the edge of the cliffs—they intrigue me.'

She narrowed her eyes at him and said very softly, 'They are not for sale.' His purchase had obviously unsettled her. Then she went on, 'The views are spectacular, yes, and they're built from the same stone blocks as the lighthouse.'

He thought of the imposing structure on the far sky-line across the bay. 'Your lighthouse is most picturesque.'

Faith smiled. Her tense posture eased a little and he was glad. 'I love it. The first time I saw it I felt like it stood benignly over a place I wanted to live. I came here for the work and found my world.'

He had thought that the first time he'd met her—how much she suited this little bay. Which was a problem in itself, but an issue for later. 'Then you are lucky. To feel at home is a special thing. As I walked here I was think-ing that a telescope in the Captain's house would give a fine view as well.'

'I haven't been inside.' She turned to her aunt. 'Have you seen next door, Izzy?'

'Yes. Once.' Isabel gave him an assessing look. As if she too had thought his purchase too impulsive. 'Beneath the wear and tear there's lots of beautiful woodwork and the stairs are lovely. The view of the ocean from the tur-ret is indeed impressive.'

Faith glanced at her watch. 'I'm sorry. Time's march-ing on.' She picked up a small white-paper-wrapped par-cel with a child's drawing covering it and shooed Chloe towards the door. 'Shall we go? We made some Rocky Road chocolate for Dr Southwell. He loves Rocky Road, doesn't he, Chloe?'

'He always has some in a jar.' His new daughter nod-ded enthusiastically and Raimondo had to smile. 'He says I make the best Rocky Road.'

She looked so pleased with herself and her mother smiled indulgently. He imagined the preparation of the sweets would be a shared task. 'I'm sure you do, little one.'

Raimondo's phone vibrated discreetly and he pulled the instrument from his pocket, frowning at the interruption. Dominico. He glanced at Faith. 'Excuse me, I must take this.' He turned to the doorway and stepped outside into the street.

'*Ciao*, Dominico.'

'Brother. Bad news. The factory has been destroyed. It lies in ruin.'

Raimondo sucked in a breath. His grandfather's legacy, which neither of them had wanted but both felt obliged to continue.

His brother answered the question before he could ask. 'Fire. I'm sorry. There are questions I cannot answer and I need you to return.'

No. He couldn't. Not yet. He glanced towards the family who were filing from the house towards him. He'd promised. 'This is difficult.' He lowered his voice. 'I gave my word to stay until Chloe's birthday tomorrow. It is only an extra twenty-four hours.'

Dominico's sigh sounded despairing. 'I'm sorry. The police wish to talk to us both.'

Pah. 'How can they expect me to travel so far for their whim? I will be back in two days.'

Another sigh. 'Then don't. It is just my need. This wearies me. Too much.'

Raimondo could hear the despair in his brother's voice. He was not the decisive and upbeat Dominico of old. He knew how hard it had been for his brother to climb back from his heartbreak, how he had buried his grief in becoming like his grandfather, lost in the business. Raimondo felt the tearing of himself in two as he wished to be in both places.

Was this the last straw? Dominico had worried him lately.

Yet he needed to stay for Chloe's birthday.

He needed to be there for his brother, who had always been there for him. He could feel his twin's pain across the distance between them. A hint of instability. A risk he could not take.

'If I come, will you travel with me to Australia when I return? A change of scenery may lighten your weariness and I have a young lady who wishes to meet her uncle.'

'I think not.'

'I think so. Or I will not come.'

'You must come.'

'Then we will discuss it soon. Arrange for a friend to stay with you until I arrive. You must promise this.'

'As you wish.' A weary agreement, not a happy one.

'Done. Have Rosa arrange the flights. I will leave in a few hours to make the midnight flight from Brisbane tonight, use Singapore.'

'*Sì.*' A pause. 'Thank you.'

'Look after yourself until I arrive. Yes?'

'Yes.'

'*Ciao.* Now to tell my daughter I must break my promise I have only just made.' He ended the call.

It was the mother who would be angry on her daughter's behalf, and he didn't blame her. He just hoped the rapport they had begun to enjoy would not be damaged, but he knew it would.

Knew he had done damage to the fledgling trust she had offered him today and he cursed fate and fires and the lack of free will.

CHAPTER TWELVE

FAITH LOOKED UP from straightening Chloe's hair to the man waiting at the gate. There was something in his face that said all was not well. Deep inside she knew she wasn't going to like this and her heart began to pound. 'Everything all right, I hope?'

He looked at her and the worry and frustration in his eyes forewarned her. Her stomach sank. 'A fire. The company headquarters have been destroyed in Florence. My brother asks that I return immediately.'

And so it begins.

Of course he would go. She'd known that. 'When?'

'Tonight. Later.' Faith sucked in her breath as he finished with, 'I will fly at midnight.'

Hot words wanted to pour out but she wouldn't let them. She'd expected this, hadn't she? She looked at her daughter, who had skipped ahead with Izzy. Instead of berating him, she said calmly, 'Before Chloe's birthday?'

'*Si.* My apologies.'

'I expected nothing from you.' Her tone said she was unsurprised. She raised her brows and as her heart iced over she shot him a cold look. 'And it is not me you need to apologise to. Perhaps you'd better tell her before she tells all and sundry you'll be at her party.'

Raimondo winced and glanced at his daughter, a few large strides ahead, chatting to her aunt.

Faith seethed. As well he should consider Chloe. Broken promise number one. That hadn't taken long. She felt like stamping her foot and asking if one more day would make such a difference. But of course he would go.

'Chloe?' Faith called and Chloe skipped back down to them. 'Your father has something to tell you. You walk with him here and I'll talk to Aunty Izzy about something she needs to know.' Because if she didn't move away she was going to say something she regretted and Chloe was the important one. She was the one who had told him that.

She turned and walked a little too quickly back to where Izzy was admiring a rose bush in the next-door garden but Raimondo and Chloe's voices carried on the still air. She'd known his priorities so why was she surprised?

'He has to leave for a family emergency.' She could hear the tartness and was glad she'd spoken softly to Izzy. They both turned to see how Chloe took it.

She heard him say, 'Chloe, I am so sorry that I must break my first promise to you. Something has happened in my home town and I have to leave and go back to Italy before your birthday.'

Chloe's face fell and then she furrowed her brows. 'You said you would be here. Did the sky fall in? Like *Chicken Little*?'

He stopped and crouched down to her level. '*Sì*, little one. You are very clever. The sky has fallen in on our factory because of a bad fire and I must help my brother sort the mess.'

Chloe's face creased. 'In the story the sky didn't really

fall.' Faith heard the forlorn note in her daughter's words and her eyes narrowed at Raimondo. She hoped she'd done the right thing agreeing to his request of access but she didn't see how she could have done any different.

Raimondo nodded solemnly. 'But in Italy this has really happened. Though when I have finished the sorting I will return as fast as I can. And perhaps bring your Uncle Dominico as well. But I am very sad that I cannot be here for your birthday tomorrow, little one. I broke a promise, which is not good.'

Chloe sighed and shrugged her shoulders with resignation. 'It's not broken if the sky fell in.'

Faith felt tears prickle behind her eyes as her young daughter behaved so very kindly. Watched Chloe tuck her hand in his. 'But you are coming tonight to the party and I can tell Piper you are my daddy. And you said you will be back.'

Faith heard it all. Tried to be as philosophical as her five-year-old daughter and struggled.

Izzy squeezed her hand and made her walk forward up the hill. 'Come on. Let's go ahead or we'll be late.'

The party was in full swing when they arrived. Reg and Myra met them at the door, and it seemed half of the Lighthouse Bay hospital was in attendance inside. The other half must be working, Faith thought with a forced smile at another of her colleagues.

She couldn't help notice the curious glances Raimondo drew. A stranger and a darkly attractive one at that. Plus he'd actually been present for a birth and two resuscitations as well. He'd been busy in the short time he'd been here. He'd been busy with her too, and even more she regretted that kiss. She sighed.

Of course the first thing Chloe did was drag Piper across to Raimondo and announce in a loud voice, 'He's my real dad. He's from Italy so I call him *Papà*, not Daddy. He has to go home tonight but he's coming back soon.'

And that pretty well sums it up, Faith thought as she felt the heat push past her chest, up her neck and into her cheeks. Piper's mouth fell open, along with the half a dozen people in earshot.

Izzy laughed.

Trina, Faith's friend and fellow midwife, and Piper's stepmother, held her pregnant belly and laughed as well. Then she sent a quizzical look Faith's way. 'Gotta love kids.' She put out her hand and Raimondo took her fingers and shook. 'So, you're Chloe's dad, not just a friend. That explains a lot.'

'It does?'

'It will,' she said cryptically and Faith knew she was in for a grilling. 'Welcome, Raimondo, even though we already met at the beach this morning,' Trina said with a laugh. 'I'm sure Faith will fill us in on the details.' Then she clapped her hands. 'Everyone! Please meet Raimondo Salvanelli, a GP from Florence and a friend of the Fetherstones.'

She turned to the tall man who had come up at the commotion. 'Finn, darling. It seems Raimondo is Chloe's surprise daddy, all the way from Italy.'

Finn glanced at Faith of the red cheeks. Then he met Raimondo's eyes and nodded. 'Kids. I'm the local paediatrician so I understand them a little. I see your daughter has taken my daughter's hand after causing a stir and blithely run off to play dolls.'

'As children do,' Raimondo said with a smiling glance

in his Chloe's direction. Then he looked towards her. 'Her mother is equally charming.'

Faith rolled her eyes. Not that easy, buddy, she thought, and was touched when Finn championed her.

'Faith is well appreciated here.' There was no force in the statement but Raimondo nodded at the gentle warning.

'Unfortunately, I must leave tonight, but I will return soon to better acquaint myself with Chloe and renew my acquaintance with Faith.'

Good lord, that almost sounded like a statement of claim and Faith resisted the urge to call him on it. She was the calm one. She was the one in control here. He was the blow-in.

'We look forward to knowing you better.' Finn shook his hand. 'Another doctor in town is always good. And my dad said you did well. We don't have emergencies often here but handy to know when there's extra help in the bay.'

'I'll make sure I'm accredited with your government for such times. The Electronic Portfolio of International Credentials have my CV for the aid work I do, so it should be possible.'

'Excellent. Come, and I'll introduce you.'

Raimondo followed Finn and Faith sagged a little now all announcements of Chloe's paternity were out of her hands. There was no going back from here.

'You've had a wild couple of days. And then he leaves?' Trina linked her arm. 'Come on, I'll get you a nice glass of Sav Blanc even though I can't join you. Ellie said Raimondo popped up at one of your cave tours. Must have been a shock.'

Faith looked at her friend. Saw no judgement, just

sympathy. 'Understatement. Apparently, the letters I sent didn't make it to him. It was Sam's sister's Italian guests from your wedding who started the chain reaction. I could say this is all your fault.'

Trina held up her hands and laughed. 'Francesca? My bad. But he is a bit of a dish. I can see how he must have been tempting if he turned all that charm on you. What were you? Twenty?'

'First year out of uni.' Faith took the crystal glass Trina handed her with a nod of thanks. 'He has charm. But the gloves are off if he disappoints Chloe.'

'I'm sure he knows that. Though Chloe is tough like her mother. And her aunt. You've laid good groundwork there for your daughter's coping ability.'

Faith looked at her friend and felt a swell of emotion. For the last twenty-four hours her feelings had been like the waves outside the window. Rolling in one after another. No wonder she was feeling buffeted by Raimondo's arrival. But Trina's belief in her daughter felt reassuring. And similar to Izzy's confidence. 'Thank you. I hope so.'

'Let him do all the work, Faith. You've done your bit. Just enjoy the ride.'

She almost choked. 'The ride? Good lord. I feel like I'm learning to surf and a big wave is going to knock me off the board and pummel me to bits.'

'Not you. You have great balance. Besides, you have plenty of friends to help keep you afloat.'

'Okay. Let's go see what new challenge has appeared with Raimondo loose in the room and my daughter telling all and sundry.'

'You've got this. There's only friends here,' Trina replied as she linked arms again.

* * *

Raimondo shook hands and responded to the kindness as he was introduced to many and moved through the room and out into the sunny backyard where tables and chairs were scattered. He had a beer in his hand bestowed by Finn, children played on a swing set in the corner and the ocean stretched away like a tufted blue carpet.

This was so different to the formality of his world in Florence.

The salt air made him breathe deeply, as did the sight of Faith coming towards him with Finn's wife. He knew now he could have done this better with some warning to her and certainly it would have been better not to rush away tonight. He stamped down the frustration his impending journey caused. The sooner he left, the sooner he could come back.

He watched her approach, this woman from the past whom he wanted in his future. So beautiful, and he could see she tried hard to be light and calm when he had certainly complicated her serene world.

'Here you are,' she said quietly. 'How have you survived the gauntlet of Lighthouse Bay medical community?'

'I have been made most welcome.'

Someone called out to Finn and Trina. Trina said, 'See you soon,' and the couple waved and moved away.

Raimondo kept his eyes on Faith. 'Thank you for allowing me to meet your friends.'

Faith spread her hands. 'There was a gathering. We do it a lot and you were here.'

'I have made this very confronting for you, have I not?'

'Yes.' She half laughed when she really wanted to cry.

'Our past relationship is certainly out there for public consumption. But Chloe did need to know her dad existed so I guess I had hoped this would happen at some time.'

'I am truly sorry I leave tonight.'

Her green eyes studied him as if to seek the truth of his words. But she didn't say anything. What could she say?

He was a fool to leave but he would ensure it didn't happen again. The more he saw her, the more he needed to know more. He needed to be with her longer to understand the woman Faith had become and rearrange his priorities. But he'd needed to reassure Dominico that he would be there soon. A frisson of fear reminded him he could not delay this trip—he needed to see his brother for himself. And ensure something had been put in place that would keep Dominico safe until he arrived.

Chloe appeared beside them and snuggled into her mother and yawned. Softly, Faith patted her head. 'You're tired, sweetheart.'

Raimondo shot a glance at his new daughter. Saw her paleness. She had already slept today. 'Always tired?'

Why tired?

Faith met his questioning look. 'Chloe had a nasty cold two weeks ago and she's been easily worn out since then. She's taking vitamins and getting sunshine, and she's been good about resting.'

He heard the tiny thread of worry under the light description of illness. Felt his own concern stir. Grow suddenly huge. Had a sudden memory of his brother's devastation at the loss of his son. No. This would not happen when he had just found them. 'Has she had blood tests for this?'

Faith looked down at her daughter. 'Yesterday morning before preschool. We have an appointment with Uncle Finn on Monday for the results, don't we, Chloe, before I go to work.'

Chloe nodded and yawned again. Faith turned the child away from him towards the door. He said very quietly, 'This is the first you tell me of this?'

Faith raised her brows at him. 'Yes. Thank you for your concern. Chloe and I will say our goodbyes inside. You don't need to come with us. Have a comfortable flight tonight.'

He bit back an instinctive command it would have been very foolish to issue. Yes, he'd erred in that question, been undiplomatic, but he felt the slap of not having rights and knew it was his own fault. 'I will come with you now.'

Faith paused and turned back to him. 'And if I don't want you to?'

He shrugged. 'I will follow anyway.'

So he shadowed them and nodded his goodbyes along with Faith and Chloe. Isabel, Raimondo noted, was observant of his presence beside them and chose to leave them to continue their departure unaccompanied.

No doubt she would have left with her niece if Faith had been alone.

He truly appreciated her understanding.

While Raimondo waited in the open lounge Faith had ushered Chloe straight to bed.

As he paced the room for her to come back he considered all that had happened over the last two days, the enormous change to his life and his future plans. That shock of seeing Faith again and her effect on him, the way the world had suddenly opened up in the most marvellous and unexpected way with the confirmation of his being a father.

But now the bombshell of Chloe's strange lethargy. All this and he was leaving!

He needed to plan his return, assess his options for gaining further information on his daughter while he was away. Especially as he'd almost alienated Faith with his stupid accusation of her withholding Chloe's illness from him.

So how to approach this new turn sensibly?

He stared at the photo album lying on the table. The urgency of responsibilities he wanted to share ate at him.

Firstly, Faith needed to be able to contact him in any emergency. *Dios*, imagine if something happened to Chloe, something he could help with, and she couldn't access him. It didn't bear thinking about.

Twitching with suppressed urgency, he pulled a business card and a small pen from his wallet and crossed to the table to lean on the surface.

Faith needed his personal mobile number, though that would help little on the flight. Then he wrote his home number as well on the back of the card. The business number was on the front and Dominico would have set up a temporary phone office at least. He thought again and wrote Dominico's details down as well.

Now the numbers he needed. He produced a new card and wrote Faith, Isabel, Finn. He needed the paediatrician's last name as a contact. By the time he'd made his list Faith had returned.

'She's asleep.'

What if his daughter was truly unwell? A surge of panic, a premonition swamped him suddenly, perhaps because he'd seen so much loss and this could not go that way. Unease twisted in his stomach and made his tone more forceful than it should have been. 'Asleep already?'

Faith's brows went up at his doubting tone. 'As I said. I'm not lying.'

He pulled himself back. 'This is not what I mean. I do not doubt you. But her lethargy. What are your thoughts?'

He watched the lowering of her stiff shoulders as she passed a hand across her brow and sighed and now another emotion swamped him. This was not easy and everything had happened very fast for her—he'd had time to consider the impending reconnection.

Suddenly he wanted to take her in his arms and console her. Tell her all would be well, as any father would console a mother, but he didn't have that right. And they didn't know that.

'Faith, I'm sorry.' He stepped closer. 'For everything.' He put one hand on her arm. 'You have done everything right and I'm not saying this well.'

She interrupted him. 'I'm sure she's fine.' She said what they both prayed. 'We will have the results on Monday and make sure.'

Yes. Monday. Two days' time. When he would be over the ocean and thousands of miles away—though he could email from the aircraft if needed. Even telephone if the conditions were right.

'How will I get the results?' He needed Finn's number. He reached across and placed the business card in her hand. 'These contact details allow you to find me any time.' He handed her the other card.

'Please may I have yours and Finn's numbers? And

perhaps Isabel if I cannot contact you?' Had that come out too abruptly?

She looked at him. Cocked her head at his insistent tone. 'I will give you the house telephone number, and my mobile,' she said slowly. 'But I would prefer to share Chloe's results with you myself rather than have you contact Finn.'

More delay. 'That is not acceptable to me.'

Her hand brushed her face again. 'Let me think.'

He lifted his chin. 'Fine. There is no need. I will find out for myself. It is no secret where we are and who the paediatrician in this town is.' He regretted the words as soon as they left his lips.

She narrowed her eyes at him. 'So. Is this the real Raimondo Salvanelli? Are you trying to intimidate me? In my own home?'

'That is not my intention.' Impatience was still in his tone and he tried to rein it back. He could not lose Chloe now.

'Isn't it? Then why are you ordering me around? Laying down laws? You have no say over me.'

He lifted his chin at her. 'My daughter may be unwell and I will not be told at your convenience.'

Her eyes widened. 'Chloe is my daughter and I will let you know the result of the test when I get it.' Her voice held warning and again he saw she was not the diffident girl he'd met nearly six years ago.

'Though—' here a flash of unusual anger in her eyes '—of course you can go behind my back and source them from Finn.'

'Stop.' He held up his hand. How had it come to this? His fault. Doing this wrong. 'You are right.' He ran his hands through his hair, almost pulling it free from its roots. 'My fault. We are friends. Were once more. Your kindness has astounded me and I repay you with this impatience. My apologies.' He touched her arm. 'Forgive me.'

When she looked at him he could see the shimmer of distress, and possibly fear for her daughter, in her eyes and it pierced him with an arrow of protective instinct that surged from his very soul.

Of course she was terrified that Chloe was unwell.

Of course he wasn't helping by being demanding.

Unable to stop himself, he reached out and very slowly, very surely, he drew her against his chest into what he hoped was a comforting embrace. He needed to reassure her he cared.

'I want to be here for you and Chloe.'

'What if when you leave you become caught up in your other life again?' Her voice was so uncertain it stabbed him. 'What if I have to tell Chloe you've forgotten her, like you forgot me?'

It stabbed him again. 'I never forgot you. You have always been a part of a shining star which went home with me nearly six years ago and I tucked that star into my heart and never forgot you.'

She shook her head against him. 'I find that hard to believe.' Her voice was very soft.

'I'm not surprised.' He stroked her hair. 'But it is true.'

His fingers continued to stroke her silky head as she laid her cheek against him, not pulling back as he'd feared she would, and he remembered the feel of her against him from so long ago. The kiss of earlier. The feel of her skin under his fingers triggering memories and transporting him. Her scent was so sweet, her smooth flesh so right in his arms. Perfect.

Too perfect not to act on. His grip tightened with one arm and with the other hand, so slowly, he tilted her chin upwards.

'What if I said when I come back I will never leave you and our daughter again?'

Now he could look down into her face. He waited for her answer as he lost himself in the green pools of her siren's eyes. Could not resist the stretch of his thumb to so gently trace the soft, trembling curve of her pink lips. So beautiful.

'No answer?'

A shake of her head. 'How can I believe that?'

'When I come back I will convince you. For now I must do this task for my brother and tie up some ends that need to be complete. For the moment, begin to trust. At least try.'

'I'll try.'

As her body softened against his he too loosened the bands of the restraint that had been crushing him and lowered his head. Their breath mingled and their mouths touched and finally, after so long being lost, he found the one place for him that was home.

CHAPTER THIRTEEN

RAIMONDO'S MOUTH AGAINST hers felt like a homecoming. Her arms wrapped around him. How had she spent so long without this in her life? How had she spent so long without this man in her life?

That scent of Raimondo against her, something she remembered from the last time they'd kissed, the warmth of his whisper on her cheek as he brushed her face with light kisses before returning to her mouth. The heat in his lips as he gently nudged his tongue against hers and she opened her mouth to him.

Her knees wobbled as he drew her into him and all Faith could do was close her eyes and hang on.

It was just a kiss. Again.

And another kiss. So, with each gentle probe or tender stroke, she forgot more of the world outside his embrace. Took comfort from the craziness of the last few days of turmoil in the last place she'd expected to find shelter from the fear in her heart.

Her hands left his waist to splay against his solid upper body and then curled into his shirt, straining him closer. Her breasts pushed almost painfully into his chest and through their clothes the heat between their skin built into a slow cauldron of need that swirled in on itself, creating a whirlpool of desire drawing her deeper. It had been so long since she'd felt a strong man's arms about her. So long since Raimondo had taught her the secrets of this place. Too long if she responded like this.

From just a kiss.

Faith dragged her mouth reluctantly from his and searched his face. His beautiful eyes. Saw the aroused darkness of desire and promise to transport them both to a place she'd almost forgotten existed. A wisp of fear curled around her. She wasn't sure she could survive from revisiting the magic if he walked away afterwards and never came back.

'Should we do this?'

'Should we not?' His voice as bemused as hers.

'What is this between us?'

'Destiny. Tonight I will be gone, but I will be back.'

A cold tendril of foreboding touched her with a chill.

Abruptly it hit her that accidents happened, aeroplanes crashed, moments were to be grasped. Fleeting opportunities to be loved by someone were like clouds that you reached for in the sky and suddenly she didn't want this ray of hope for the future to pass without grasping the possibilities. If something happened to Raimondo now, how would she survive if she knew she could have had this?

'Make love to me before you go.'

Raimondo's eyes darkened even more and bored into hers. 'My most burning desire.'

'Please.' The word floated from her mouth in a whisper, barely heard, barely believable, and yet brazenly sure. She needed to feel his arms around her one more time before he left because inside she still wasn't sure

Raimondo would ever be back and, regardless of the pain to come, she wanted this from him.

The ground disappeared from beneath her feet as he swept her up, carried her tenderly, and she rested her cheek against his chest, listening to the strong beat of his heart to drown out the voices clamouring in her head.

With infinite care he lowered her to the bed and joined her.

CHAPTER FOURTEEN

ON SUNDAY MORNING, twelve hours after he'd left, Faith lay on the same crumpled bed where she had made love with Raimondo and stared at the fluffy clouds passing in the small gap in the curtains, not seeing them. What she saw was a glorious, tumultuous storm of reconnection, the gentle whispers, the tender caresses—all the reasons they had both been crazy before—the memories now returned to heat her cheeks and make her draw her arms to cradle her stomach as she mourned the loss of Raimondo beside her.

Put simply, wrapped together they made magic.

So she couldn't regret the pure joy of it or the risk to her heart in the making. But where would it end? She had given herself to him before he'd left, their mutual need overcoming their reserve, perhaps each seeking the reassurance holding the other would give. But it had been more. It had been everything they'd found before, with greater poignancy because of the past mistakes he'd made. Their combined worry for Chloe, the risk to the family that was so close to being possible. She saw that it had been hard for him to tear himself away, hard for him to look one last brief time at his sleeping daughter, and she didn't doubt that it would be hard to drive from Lighthouse Bay and catch a plane.

It had been a few days of craziness again.

The upheaval to her life that ridiculously gorgeous Italian man could create in forty-eight action-packed hours. He'd better come back. At least she was sure she was covered for contraception this time.

But he would be back. He'd promised. Chloe would have a dad. And Faith? What would she have?

She shifted to sit up. *That way madness lies...* She couldn't imagine yet.

Now, it was the morning of Chloe's birthday and the sun crept fingers of soft yellow up the wall of her bedroom so she should rise and try to ease the new memories Raimondo had created back into her secret place for later. It was going to be a beautiful November day for a children's party.

How fast those five years had flown since her baby had been born—and hadn't their lives been blessed with the joy of Chloe.

She wondered what the next five years would bring. Which drew her thoughts back to Raimondo.

To their kiss. And the progression from there.

Of course he stayed on her mind.

He would still be over the ocean on his flight, barely halfway to Italy, soon to land in Singapore. So no call had come yet for Chloe on her birthday. She would not think he had already relegated them to the back of his businessman's brain as the drama in Italy came closer. And was it so bad if he did; he'd said he needed to tie ends, sort out his many commitments before he could come back. He'd said he would be back—it was a shame a part of her didn't believe him. But that was for later.

She didn't care if he came back without his possessions. Wealth and assets did not have the same importance in her own life.

Though, she supposed, now she would have to be more vigilant for Chloe to appreciate both sides of the financial coin if her father persisted in spoiling her with extravagant gifts.

Her daughter would not be spoiled by a rich man's whims. A little voice whispered that perhaps she was being harsh. She didn't want to listen. She'd been so darned unsettled since he'd arrived and even more unsettled since he'd left. Not surprising. Making love with Raimondo before he'd left had been an incredibly stupid, and incredibly wonderful, thing to do. It wasn't fair.

Chloe would wake soon, though, the way she had been sleeping in lately, one never knew.

Surely the lure of the enormous parcel that had arrived yesterday—on a Saturday; who knew how he had arranged that before he'd even known he would fly out?—would have her daughter up early. Obviously from Raimondo, and goodness knew what it would be in all its largeness and expensive express courier, but Chloe had been remarkably patient to wait until today to open it.

Like Christmas, she'd said.

Her little friends were arriving this morning at ten a.m. Faith had decided an early party would be more fun for Chloe than waiting around for the afternoon when she could be weary.

Dear Myra, a pastry chef and cake decorator in a past life before Lighthouse Bay, had made the 'Elsa from *Frozen*' cake and would bring the no doubt magnificent creation down at ten. Because it was Sunday, the adults would come for brunch after the children had been here an hour and done their party games, then they were having a sausage sizzle in the backyard which Finn had offered to cook for young and old.

It would be a typical extended family and friends day, held to celebrate one of theirs. All those coming who genuinely cared…

Raimondo should have been here to see his daughter's pleasure in being the star for the day.

But he wasn't. She shouldn't be surprised.

She shouldn't be disappointed.

Not at all. Really. But she was and not only for Chloe.

Faith pushed away the recently familiar flustered feeling in her stomach and opened the blinds properly to see the day.

Just as she thought. Glorious. She pushed open the window and the salt-laden air wafted into the room, forcing her to appreciate the good things. Forcing her to smile.

She loved living here. This was her home. Regardless of the ups and downs of the last few days, she was so very fortunate. And here came the footsteps of her precious daughter.

'Mummy, Mummy! It's my birthday!' A pink-pyjamaed missile fired through Faith's bedroom door and into her arms.

Faith hugged the warm tousled body into her and inhaled the tear-free shampoo scent of Chloe's soft hair. Her baby. Her life. 'Good morning, darling Birthday Girl. How exciting. Today you are how old…?' Faith pretended to scratch her chin.

'I'm five! I'm five!' Chloe bounced back off the bed

and onto the balls of her feet and grinned at her mother. 'You're tricking.'

'Five? My goodness. So big. Off to school next year. But first—we have a party!'

Chloe's eyes rounded. 'I know! My first party. Piper said she has a present for me.'

'Well, that's very nice. You must remember to thank all the people for coming and also for presents and cards.'

'I will.'

Such a solemn vow, Faith thought with amusement and stroked her daughter's soft cheek. Then she frowned at the small bruise on Chloe's neck.

'Did you bump yourself here?'

'Maybe.' Chloe was peering towards the kitchen and Faith let it go, though unease slid under her skin. 'Let's go and have breakfast and maybe you could open a present from me too. And one from Aunty Izzy.'

'And one from Mr Salvanelli. I mean *Papà*.' The little girl crinkled her forehead. '*Papà* is a funny word.'

'Maybe we can find a different word that works as well. But let's go see what we can find for your birthday breakfast.'

By eleven o'clock, when the adults were due to arrive, the presents had all been unwrapped and the children had begun to settle from the frenzy of pass the parcel. Everyone had a prize and the mood had calmed to staring with admiration at Chloe's wonderful cake and her wonderful doll's house.

Gift-wise, it seemed that Elsa and the *Frozen* story had won the day as well, with a set of *Frozen* dolls, a set of bed sheets, a *Frozen* duvet cover and even a cushion with Elsa's blonde head gazing out from it. It culminated with Raimondo's outrageously expensive *Frozen* castle doll's house, which impressed all the little girls mightily.

Faith remembered she'd suggested a doll's house, more fool her.

She thought of the three-storey, furnished, fantastical fairy tale extravaganza, and wondered how on earth he'd managed to order that and have it delivered in the space of a Saturday afternoon. It had proved well over-the-top but Chloe, of course, was ecstatic. Faith decided she'd need to talk to him about restraint with gifts—and she hadn't told her friends who had bought the Captain's house next door.

Soon enough when Raimondo took ownership, because then everyone would know.

She sighed. The man was turning into a headache of mammoth proportions. And heart-hugging secrets.

Trina and Finn were the parents who arrived last and Piper squealed and ran towards them with Chloe following. Until she slowed.

As if in slow motion, Chloe faltered, stopped and then silently she toppled sideways in a dead faint onto a discarded Elsa cushion, and Faith's heart missed a beat.

Faith reached out but she missed and by the time she knelt beside her daughter Finn was there too, easing her back. Faith didn't understand as her heart seemed to slowly gather momentum in her chest. What had happened?

His voice reached her shocked brain. Calm. Soothing. Like at work when that voice was directed at a patient, not at her. 'She's breathing, Faith. Fainted. Could just be excitement. I'll take her,' he said gently, 'to her bed. We'll look at her there.'

Then he lifted Chloe into his arms and carried Faith's baby away and she couldn't see her daughter's face as she hurried behind.

Once in the bedroom with the door closed, Finn examined Chloe and they found more bruises like the one Faith had seen that morning. Two on her belly and a dozen on her back and both lymph glands under her thin arms were suspiciously swollen.

When Chloe stirred from the faint, only a minute after she'd been put on her bed, she woke slowly, still groggy and vague.

Sadly, there would be no more birthday celebrations for Chloe.

Faith could hear Izzy in the distance as she ushered the guests out with a gentle, 'No, Chloe will be fine,' quietly dispersing the party behind the door as she took control. Her 'Thank you for coming' seemed surreal in the distance to Faith as she watched Finn examine Chloe with growing alarm that she tried to hide. Her anxiety ramped up to real terror as Finn took out his mobile phone and arranged emergency admission to the regional hospital for tests, but she smiled at Chloe and said, 'Uncle Finn knows best.'

But she was thinking, *My daughter is too sick for Lighthouse Bay Hospital.*

The ambulance ride took them to the base hospital and more blood tests were conducted.

Test results that proved serious enough to transfer her from the country to the city, and thankfully Faith was allowed in the aircraft too. So they both travelled by the rescue helicopter down to the Children's Hospital in Sydney.

As soon as they arrived, around three p.m., Faith slipped outside the hospital to leave another message for Raimondo, this time at his place of work, and she jammed her phone up against her ear to try to block the noise of the traffic. She drew a deep breath as finally the long-distance call connected, and a woman's rolling accent answered at the other end.

'Salvanelli Compagnia Farmaceutica.'

Faith prayed the receptionist at his brother's temporary office could speak English. She had no Italian. 'I wish to speak to Dominico Salvanelli, please.'

'Signor Salvanelli is not available. I do not know when he will be back. I am sorry.' The accent was thick but the English perfect. Not that it helped.

That was it then. Raimondo's mobile phone and home number had only accepted voice messages as he would still be flying. She enunciated as clearly as she could, 'This is Faith Fetherstone from Australia. Please try to pass on a message to Dominico to contact his brother. Raimondo must phone me back as soon as possible. It is very urgent.'

So she'd done what she could about informing Raimondo and the forlorn hope that he would immediately begin his return to support her and Chloe through this terrifying ordeal had failed, as she should have expected. She would be alone.

No. That wasn't fair. Isabel would drive down as soon as she'd shaken her slight cold and the unacceptable risk of her infecting Chloe now she was so very susceptible.

Hours later, as visiting hours closed, the sounds of the Children's Hospital in Sydney made resting difficult on the chair beside Chloe's bed. Crying babies, toys being tossed or banged on the side of cots, the beeping of high-tech medical machines that whirred and trilled and the constant swish of nurses checking on her daughter.

At least no more fruitless time had been wasted on unsuccessful phone calls because now her phone was dead without her charger. She would concentrate on her daughter, as she should have been the last few days instead of being sidetracked by a man from her past.

Nine torrid hours after Chloe's collapse, on the longest day of Faith's life, Faith felt like a zombie as she paced the room. It was true that finally, after the terrifying provisional diagnosis, when acute myeloid leukaemia had been suggested at the regional hospital, and Faith had felt as if her body had turned to a lump of ice, things were tentatively looking up. Frozen-faced, she'd nodded, outwardly calm, and clutched Chloe's hand and they had to wait for more test results.

Now, after the bone marrow biopsy in Sydney, some hope for a different diagnosis seemed possible.

An hour ago Finn had phoned Faith on the ward phone with the results.

'The news is better than expected, Faith.'

She'd sagged against the wall, the ward phone clamped to her ear.

Finn went on. 'The latest tests and overall diagnostic pictures have pointed more towards a severe secondary bacterial infection on top of the recent viral infection. That combination mimicked the leukaemia symptoms.'

'Oh, my.' Faith had sagged further down the wall.

She'd almost missed the rest of Finn's news. 'The repeat blood tests still show Chloe's red cells are down and her white cells sky-high. That's why she's spiked that raging temperature.'

'The paediatrician here knows that?' She was trying to understand what this meant for Chloe.

'He rang me. He's been called to the operating theatre until later tonight. Sorry he couldn't tell you himself. We're cautiously hopeful that with the antibiotics Chloe will make a full recovery.'

Faith swallowed again the lump that had seemed lodged in her throat for hours. She hadn't been able to answer Izzy's questions when other calls had been brought to her, her mouth unable to form words as her throat closed. So Trina and Izzy had left messages.

'You need to rest, Faith. Try to sleep so you have reserves for tomorrow.'

She'd nodded and then realised he couldn't see her. 'Yes. I'll try.'

'What of Raimondo?'

'I left messages. He's still flying. Won't land until one a.m. tonight.'

'Hang in there. He'll be back.'

'It will take another two days at least. Thank you for ringing, Finn.'

'Get some rest.'

'Yes.' Then she'd hung up.

Raimondo would be very close to Florence, but that wouldn't help her. He was twenty-six hours' flight in the wrong direction.

But he could have rung the hospital at one of the stops. Despite the fact there was no wife to hijack her messages, he still hadn't answered.

She shouldn't be surprised he was not there for her. *Out of sight, out of mind.*

She should have expected that.

The deep disappointment of Raimondo's absence sat in her chest like a stone. Didn't he know she needed strong arms and a chest to cry on at this moment as she watched their daughter sleeping with horror of her childish mortality so fresh in her mind?

Had that two days of upheaval he'd caused in her and Chloe's life meant nothing to him?

Faith stared at her daughter, weary tears she didn't have the energy to wipe as they dripped damply down her cheeks. Chloe's small fingers were tucked under her so pale chin and the other arm lay by her side strapped to the IV line with a bandage and a board to keep her arm straight. Her daughter shone ethereally white against the pillows, and all her mother could do was sit alone, watching, powerless to help her.

Two separate antibiotics were running through the drip she was connected to now the blood transfusion she'd needed was finished.

Still, the news was so much better than it could have been and now that she had allowed the hope to filter in, after the horrific dread that had filled her before, not unexpectedly, exhaustion swamped Faith. She put her head in her hands and closed her eyes.

They would beat this.

She and Chloe. They had to.

The door opened. It would be another nurse to check Chloe and she couldn't summon the energy to open her eyes.

'Faith.' A voice she knew.

Raimondo, looking slightly harried and slightly crumpled, very unlike himself, stood there, his hair mussed, his beautiful warm, reassuring eyes searching hers as he crossed the room towards her, his long strides eating up the distance between them.

Faith struggled to her feet. 'You're here?' Then she sagged and he crossed the last gap to catch her in his warm embrace.

CHAPTER FIFTEEN

RAIMONDO CROSSED THE room in a rush and pulled her into his arms and she sobbed against him. His strong hands held her as he pulled her against the chest she'd needed so much. Hugged her tighter to him until almost she couldn't breathe but it was so worth it as she felt the warmth of his body warming the chill that had soaked all the way into her bones.

His voice rumbled in her hair. 'I should never have left. I will not leave again unless I take you both with me.'

Faith didn't have the headspace to compute that. Her brain had shut down. She could only deal with this moment. 'She's been so sick.' Her voice sounded thick with tears, and relief, and exhaustion, but it felt so overwhelming that he'd come back. She'd hoped for a call and wasn't sure how he could have arrived but this was so much better than she'd hoped for.

'My poor Faith. The things I do to you without the intention to hurt you. I should never have left.'

'No, I wish you hadn't.' She looked up into his face. 'How are you back so quickly?'

He ran his hand through his hair at the memory. 'I flew back from Singapore. Your message appeared as we taxied in. I sent a doctor friend to sit with Dominico. That is another story. There was some dilemma as I retrieved my bags but it was arranged that instead of flying on I could change planes and fly back.'

'You must be exhausted.' The shadows under his eyes attested to that.

'Not like you. Not like Chloe. I should never have left,' he said again. They turned to stare at their daughter and his mouth compressed as he held back his emotion.

Faith touched his arm. 'You're here now.'

They crossed to the bed and Raimondo sat carefully on the edge and stroked Chloe's free hand at the end of the strapping of IV line. She stirred, mumbled, 'Mummy?' without opening her eyes, and resettled.

Raimondo closed his eyes. Then opened them to stare up at Faith. 'And you have been alone through this.'

Faith nodded.

'She looks so pale.' He compressed his lips and gave her a rueful smile. 'I spoke to Finn. Your phone? He said it was dead, which was better than me thinking you had banned me from talking to you.'

She'd so wanted to talk to him. 'I wouldn't do that.'

He shrugged and squeezed her for a moment. 'How can I know that when I have wronged you again?'

'You did what you had to. And I had no charger. We left so quickly. One of the nurses is bringing me one from home tomorrow.'

'Of course.' He touched her hand. 'But I could not sit in the back of the taxi as I was being driven here from the airport and not find out what was happening. So I found Finn.' He shrugged apologetically.

She had to smile, though it felt so long since she had smiled her face felt stiff. 'I forgive you.'

'You will not need a phone to contact me for I will be here.'

'You're staying?'

'I have said I would never leave again.' His face was intense. 'Believe me.'

And looking at his strong, tired face, his warm eyes that searched to see if she was able to believe him, she did. 'Then I will. Now. With all my heart.'

He squeezed her to him. Then, even with that brief hug, she could feel the recharge of energy she'd stolen from him and straightened her shoulders. There was hope everywhere.

CHAPTER SIXTEEN

Isabel

ONE MONTH LATER, and two days before the wedding, Dominico Salvanelli, the groom's twin brother, stood by Isabel's side in the church as everyone practised for the wedding.

Isabel's hand rested on his admittedly very powerful forearm as they walked together back up the aisle, and she tried not to inhale the particularly divine aftershave he wore. Or glance across at his impressive chest that rose beside her so that she felt tiny.

Seriously, he was there every time she turned around, not saying anything. As if he was trying to understand something. Watching her. Which was ridiculous.

She wasn't one for toy boys and the man was seven years her junior. Though, behind his eyes, she had the feeling he was decades older than her. These Salvanellis certainly knew how to do dark and mysterious.

Look at her niece's man. Though when she did, all she could see was joy. Which made Isabel smile.

Dominico leaned in to say something but paused as another instruction came from the priest. They turned and Dominico reluctantly let her go to return to the altar to stand beside his brother. They did it all again one more time.

'I think he likes you.' Faith was grinning at her as she did her stately bridal walk past, a particularly unfazed, calm bride. How come she, Isabel, the maid of honour, had all the nerves since Dominico had arrived?

Isabel whispered as she and Faith stood together to enter, 'He's too young. And he's got issues.'

Faith rolled her eyes at her. 'Issues are right up your alley.'

'You're being silly.' But she couldn't stop the heat creeping up her cheeks.

'I've never seen you blush before, Izzy,' Faith teased. 'Even when that locum doctor asked you out.'

The next few minutes were blessedly question-free until she was back down the aisle with Dominico's corded muscles beneath her arm again.

'It should be you who brings Chloe over to our villa while the honeymooners tour Italy and France.' Dominico's voice was low.

Isabel raised her brows. 'They will only be away two weeks.'

Dominico inclined his head. 'They could then stay longer.' He shrugged. 'For my new sister-in-law's peace of mind when her daughter is in Europe while she is away from Australian shores, of course.'

Isabel glanced sideways with mild amusement at him. 'And what would Chloe and I do while waiting in Florence?'

'There is much to see.' He lifted his head and smiled. Slowly and with a definitely wicked slant. Quite shocking after all the serious faces she'd seen from him earlier. 'I would show you both around, of course.'

Isabel laughed. 'Thank you for the invitation. We'll see what Faith wants to do.'

'Not what you wish?'

'I always do what I wish.'

Two days later

Raimondo's heart thumped with slow, vast joy at the front of the white church on the hill above the waves. He lifted his face to the light and with infinite patience, indeed he owed his bride that, and with his brother Dominico's shoulders level with his, they faced the round stained-glass depiction of Christ together and waited for Faith and her party to arrive.

To those seated on the pews, waiting with them for the ceremony to begin, they must look like two dark men in this place of light.

Beside him, Dominico's face seemed hewn like the painted granite of the church, inscrutable as he stared ahead in his matching black suit. Raimondo had no doubt his brother was remembering his own tragic marriage and the loss of his family.

He would not have gloom today. 'Brother?' Dominico turned to look at him and thankfully Raimondo noted the strain ease away. 'Today is for rejoicing, yes?'

'Indeed.' Dominico's mouth kinked upwards. 'I rejoice. You managed to wait a whole month before you married her.'

Raimondo laughed quietly. 'It was not possible for more speed or it certainly would have been sooner. Thank you for being here.' It had been difficult to extricate his brother from the many technicalities of an incinerated business, and a lethargy steeped in despair, but even Dominico had known he would have to come if Raimondo married in Australia.

Raimondo smiled internally to himself as he stood, basking in the early afternoon sunshine through the round window, and waited with an eager heart for his beautiful bride. How much time he, Raimondo, had wasted without Faith by his side.

Faith and Chloe. How could a man be so fortunate? He would ensure that he earned it in his care of his wife and daughter for the rest of his life. Perhaps they would be blessed by more family as well.

He had to sympathise with his brother on the irresistible attraction of the Fetherstone women.

At the wedding rehearsal his brother had been unusually taken with the maid of honour, but Isabel had brushed off Dominico's attention as if she were the older, wiser woman fussed over by a boy. It had been amusing to Raimondo when she was only seven years the elder and Dominico... Well, his brother had been markedly ruffled by her dismissal.

His smile kicked at the thought but he knew better than to say anything.

Dominico had reluctantly left Florence with every intention of hurrying home as soon as the nuptials were completed. Though, to Raimondo's delight, it had taken just one evening in the company of Isabel Fetherstone for Dominico to mention to his brother that he might stay 'perhaps a little longer'.

After the honeymoon, he and Faith would return here to live, where the sea breeze blew salty whispers through the open windows of the houses along with the sound of crashing waves and circling gulls.

This bay, this place, held magic the like of which he

had never seen before and watching his brother had made him pray for the healing of his sibling's heart as well.

He glanced over his shoulder to see in the congregation Faith's friends and colleagues who would be his associates when he began work here. Yes, he could live here very happily for the rest of his life. There would be many times when he flew home but never again would he leave his new family behind.

But that did not dim the expectation of showing Faith and Chloe his world. The delight of that was for the future.

A car pulled up. He heard the doors open and his heart rate picked up. Soon. Soon he would see the woman he would spend the rest of his life with.

The music started and a rustling at the door and shift of light drew all eyes to the entrance.

Raimondo strained to see his bride.

Ah. The little flower girls. His daughter, his Chloe like a daffodil in her sunshine-yellow dress, the lilac sash so pretty, her dark hair plaited around her sweet, serious face as she solemnly sprinkled yellow rose petals down the aisle for the bride. Little Piper followed her, her own basket of dewy softness on her arm as she copied her friend. They looked like fairies as their glowing faces spread joy like petals among the congregation.

Isabel stepped into view, head up, large eyes excited, yet her face serene, her mouth curved in the happiness of the moment, and Raimondo felt his brother tense beside him. *Sì*, she was a vision. But not Raimondo's vision.

There Faith's aunt waited, the maid of honour who'd refused to be a bridesmaid, the pale lilac dress highlighting the dark auburn of her hair, the silk that slid and slithered over the slim body modestly but with that hint of allure he found abundantly in Faith. Isabel stepped sideways and the music lifted to a climax and there she was.

His bride. Standing in the doorway. Her inner light bathing him with love from fifty feet away as she caught and captured his gaze. His angel. His love. His Faith.

Dios. So beautiful. Glorious. In that moment he swore he would never fall short of her needs again as he stood drinking in the sight of her as she paused in her walk towards him. His swelling heart overflowed with gratitude for this woman, so beautiful inside and out, and the love she offered him made his heart swell.

Faith stopped at the entrance to the church as she reached out and rested her hand lightly on Isabel's arm. Isabel, her aunt, her friend, her rock, was the one to give her away for safekeeping into the arms of the man she loved, as she should be.

She'd never thought this time would come, her at the front of a church, Raimondo waiting at the end of the aisle with such a powerful love shining her way she almost lifted off the ground with it, so it was with surprise she realised her fingers didn't shake. That there was no caution as she threw herself and Chloe into this headlong rush of marriage.

No doubts since the hospital, no doubts since Raimondo had promised his inclusion fully in their future. No doubts since he'd returned to stay by her side.

Now she could imagine nothing else.

The time was here.

She looked ahead to where her husband-to-be seemed to fill the end of the aisle in his black tuxedo and white silk shirt, a yellow rose in his lapel, his eyes on her. Yes, his brother stood beside him but she had eyes only for Raimondo.

Their eyes held and now her belly twitched and came alive. Her heart rate sped up and her breathing increased.

Yes, Raimondo. I'm coming. She lifted her head and stepped forward, Isabel by her side, and closed the distance between herself and the man she would always love.

* * * * *

MILLS & BOON

Coming next month

CINDERELLA AND THE SURGEON
Scarlet Wilson

'You're the midwife?'

The deep voice was practically at her ear and she jumped, stumbling over her own feet.

Esther spun around. Mr Imposing was standing in her personal space, his arms folded across his chest, looking her up and down in a disapproving manner. Okay, so the NICU probably wasn't big enough for all these people, which could explain the space thing. And, the massive splatter of coffee all over her scrub trousers probably wasn't helping her appearance.

But right now she could smell his clean aftershave and see into those toffee-coloured eyes.

'Weren't you the nurse who was sleeping in the canteen?'

She could feel the blood rush to her face and all the hairs on her body prickle in indignation. Who did this guy think he was, sweeping in here with his giant entourage?

Nope. No way.

'I'm sure you know that we limit visitors to NICU. Maybe other NICUs relax rules for you and your entourage, but Queen Victoria's doesn't.'

She started to count in her head just how many people were in his little gang. She'd reached twelve when his deep voice sounded right in front of her again.

'Isn't this a teaching hospital? Famous the world over

for its training programmes?' There was a mocking tone in his voice.

Esther had been around long enough to recognise an arrogant doctor. As a nurse, and a midwife, she'd met more than her fair share—both male and female.

She hated anyone being dismissive with her. And she didn't stand for it. More than once she'd used her Scottish accent to the best of her ability to give someone short shrift.

There was something about her accent that generally made people take a step back—particularly when she was angry. If this guy didn't watch out, he'd soon find out exactly who Esther McDonald was. She'd barely had a chance to look this guy up. All she knew was he was one of a few specialist surgeons who could do the procedure that Billy needed.

She mirrored his stance and folded her arms, tilting her chin towards him as she put a fake smile on her face. 'Maybe you'd like to introduce yourself and let me know why you think your needs are more important than the needs of the very special babies we have in here?'

She could do sarcasm too.

He inhaled deeply, almost like he wanted to show her just how broad his chest was. But Esther had never been easily intimidated by anyone. 'I'm Harry Beaumont. I'm here to do the surgery on your patient.'

Continue reading
CINDERELLA AND THE SURGEON
Scarlet Wilson

Available next month
www.millsandboon.co.uk

COMING SOON!

We really hope you enjoyed reading this book. If you're looking for more romance, be sure to head to the shops when new books are available on

Thursday 23rd January

To see which titles are coming soon, please visit

millsandboon.co.uk/nextmonth

JOIN US ON SOCIAL MEDIA!

Stay up to date with our latest releases, author news and gossip, special offers and discounts, and all the behind-the-scenes action from Mills & Boon...

 millsandboon

 millsandboonuk

 millsandboon

It might just be true love...

MILLS & BOON

THE HEART OF ROMANCE

A ROMANCE FOR EVERY KIND OF READER

MODERN

Prepare to be swept off your feet by sophisticated, sexy and seductive heroes, in some of the world's most glamourous and romantic locations, where power and passion collide.
8 stories per month.

HISTORICAL

Escape with historical heroes from time gone by. Whether your passion is for wicked Regency Rakes, muscled Vikings or rugged Highlanders, awaken the romance of the past.
6 stories per month.

MEDICAL

Set your pulse racing with dedicated, delectable doctors in the high-pressure world of medicine, where emotions run high and passion, comfort and love are the best medicine.
6 stories per month.

Celebrate true love with tender stories of heartfelt romance, from the rush of falling in love to the joy a new baby can bring, and a focus on the emotional heart of a relationship.
8 stories per month.

Indulge in secrets and scandal, intense drama and plenty of sizzlin hot action with powerful and passionate heroes who have it all: wealth, status, good looks...everything but the right woman.
6 stories per month.

HEROES

Experience all the excitement of a gripping thriller, with an intens romance at its heart. Resourceful, true-to-life women and strong, fearless men face danger and desire - a killer combination!
8 stories per month.

DARE

Sensual love stories featuring smart, sassy heroines you'd want as a best friend, and compelling intense heroes who are worthy of ther
4 stories per month.

To see which titles are coming soon, please visit

millsandboon.co.uk/nextmonth